MARINA WARNER

INDIGO

OR

Mapping the Waters

SIMON & SCHUSTER

New York   London   Toronto   Sydney   Tokyo   Singapore

SIMON & SCHUSTER
Simon & Schuster Building
Rockefeller Center
1230 Avenue of the Americas
New York, New York 10020

Designed by Caroline Cunningham

Manufactured in the United States of America

1   3   5   7   9   10   8   6   4   2

Library of Congress Cataloging-in-Publication Data
Warner, Marina, date.
Indigo, or Mapping the waters / Marina Warner.
p.   cm.
"Originally published in Great Britain by Chatto & Windus Ltd"—
T. p. verso.
I. Title.   II. Title: Indigo.   III. Title: Mapping the waters.
PR6073.A7274I5   1992
823'.914—dc20   92-13968
CIP

ISBN: 0-671-70156-8

Acknowledgments

The author would like to offer much gratitude to: Peter Hulme, whose book *Colonial Encounters: Europe and the Native Caribbean 1492–1797* (London, 1986) provided inspiring insights; and to Peter Dronke and Roy Foster, who generously commented on an earlier draft and gave invaluable responses. She also wishes to thank Faber & Faber Ltd, London, and Farrar Straus & Giroux, Inc., New York, for permission to quote from "Child's Song" from *For The Union Dead* (1965) by Robert Lowell, and from *Omeros* (1990) by Derek Walcott; Faber & Faber Ltd for permission to quote from "Four Cabaret Songs for Miss Hedli Anderson" (No 2 "Tell Me The Truth About Love") from *Another Time* by W. H. Auden; S. Fischer Verlag and Persea Books for Michael Hamburger's translation of Paul Celan's "Psalm" from *Die Niemandsrose*, in *Paul Celan: Poems* (New York, 1980); Little, Brown and Co., Boston for "Poem # 546" from *The Complete Poems of Emily Dickinson* edited by Thomas H. Johnson (Copyright 1929 by Martha Dickinson Bianchi, Copyright © renewed 1957 by Mary L. Hampson); McGraw-Hill, Inc., New York, for the lines from *Soul on Ice* (1964) by Eldridge Cleaver; Sterling Lord Literistic, New York, for the lines from "Black Dada Nihilismus" from *The Dead Lecturer* (© 1964) by LeRoi Jones (A. Baraka).

For Ann and Ian
and
In Memoriam E. P. W.

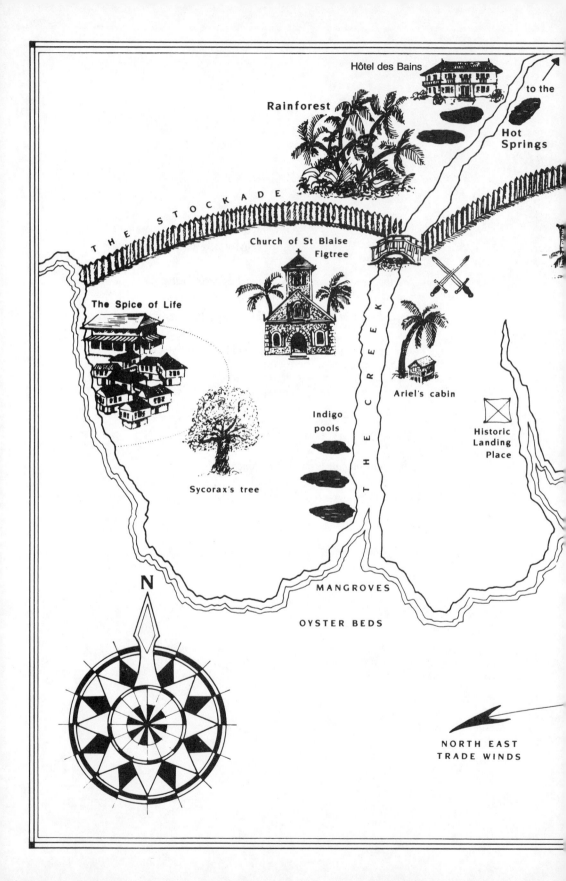

Hôtel des Bains

to the

Rainforest

Hot
Springs

THE STOCKADE

Church of St Blaise
Figtree

The Spice of Life

THE CREEK

Ariel's cabin

Indigo
pools

Historic
Landing
Place

Sycorax's tree

N

MANGROVES

OYSTER BEDS

NORTH EAST
TRADE WINDS

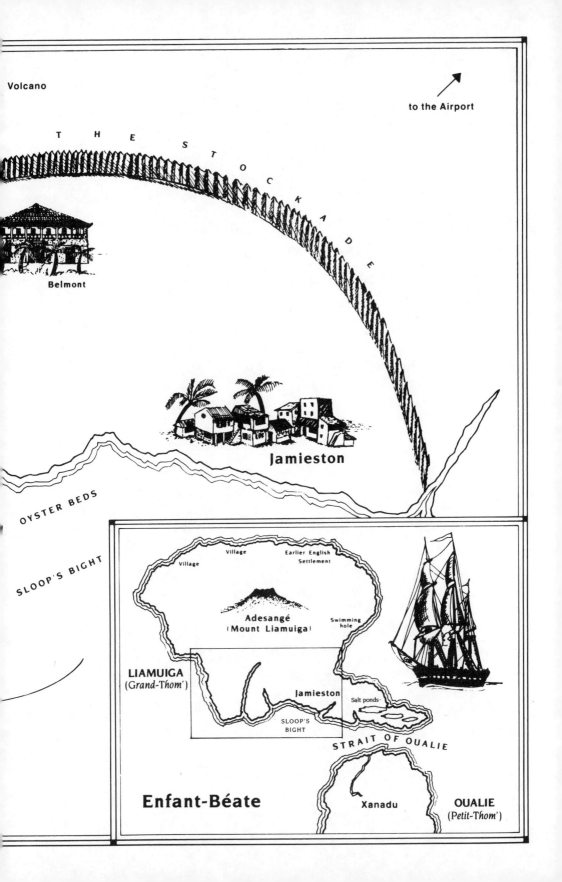

Volcano

to the Airport

T H E S T O C K A D E

Belmont

Jamieston

OYSTER BEDS

SLOOP'S BIGHT

Village

Village

Earlier English
Settlement

Adesangé
(Mount Liamuiga)

Swimming
hole

LIAMUIGA
(Grand-Thom')

Jamieston

Salt ponds

SLOOP'S
BIGHT

STRAIT OF OUALIE

Enfant-Béate

Xanadu

OUALIE
(Petit-Thom')

Principal Characters

NOW

Sir Anthony Everard "ANT" (b. 1897)

m. 1. (1919) Estelle Desjours (d. 1934)   2. (1939) GILLIAN (b. 1915)

| |

KIT Everard (b. 1920) m. ASTRID (b. 1918)

| |

MIRANDA (b. 1942)   XANTHE (b. 1948)

SERAFINE Killebree (b. c. 1892)

THEN

By Christian reckoning (C.E.)

SYCORAX (b. 1560)

DULÉ (b. 1600)

ARIEL (b. 1604)

Christopher Everard "KIT" (b. 1595)

❦ SERAFINE I ❦

1

—WHEN HE WAKES up, the fat man finds he's been tied hand and foot, and something powerful's smelling all around him.

The ladies who keep him company, they like to wear strong perfume—cinnamon and coriander and mace, pounded with a little musk oil and a little essence of jasmine too, maybe—but this smell is different—

Serafine dabbed behind her ears and wriggled her long neck on her shoulders, closing her eyes in mock abandon; she had soft, full lids and high eyebrows, so even shut her eyes expressed a certain rueful humor. Serafine used to tell Miranda alarming stories and Miranda would remember this one, later: she'd remember how they were sitting in the garden of the square where her grandfather lived, before Xanthe was born, when Miranda was still the only little Everard.

—Heavy perfume was necessary, sweetheart, 'cause they were smelly, yes, on account of their partying lasting day in, day out, night in, night out, not a moment to draw breath, jumping till the sweat poured down. Washing would have spoiled their fun—tsst, don't you get ideas, now—

Miranda was picking daisies, and trying to slit their stalks without breaking them. Some had plump hairy stems, others drooped their heads, though the pads of leaves they sprang from looked sturdy enough and the plants stuck fast in the ground, as Miranda knew because she tried to pull them up; she liked the flowers' resistance, their taproot clinging.

The gate in the privet hedge was kept locked; only tenants had a key, and Sir Anthony Everard gave Serafine his. There was nobody else with them that morning as the damp grass dried in the weak spring sunshine and the daisies' faces grew wide. Miranda was sitting on a rug Serafine had spread near the bench she usually chose, beside the huge marble log that lay athwart the lawn like a shipwrecked spar. It was so old the wood had turned into stone, its veins and sinews in perfect porphyry-colored impression like a very big boiled sweet; it was much older than Serafine, who was herself even older than Miranda's grandfather, though she did not seem it to the child.

Miranda fancied that Serafine had something to do with the change that had overtaken the tree's nature and turned it into a rock; in her stories everything risked changing shape.

Her daisy chain had grown two links, she was poking out her tongue in concentration. Serafine did not stop talking, but with her nail, which was the brown-mauve color of a wild fowl's egg, she showed the little girl how to push more gently into the end of the stem to make an eye in it. Miranda watched her hands, which she had every reason to love, for these were the hands which washed her in the bath and patted her dry and spooned food into her breakfast bowl and beat up the milk powder till the lumps were gone and spread jam on her bread, specially saved from her grandpa's rations, with more confidence and ease than her own mother's. (Miranda's mother was young, and she liked to sleep in of a morning, because frequently she'd been out the night before.) Serafine's palms were mapped with darker lines, as if she had steeped them in ink to bring out the pattern; the lines crisscrossed and wandered, and Miranda would have liked to be able to puzzle out the script, for she was beginning to read. Feeny's palms were dry and hard like the paper in a storybook, and when they handled Miranda she felt safe.

—You change partners, and your new girl's smell goes straight up your nose and it explodes there—like stardust, behind your eyes. Aaah. (Put that tongue away, little sweetheart, it's not nice to stick it out like that.) But the stink the fat man smells now is different, as I say, it recalls his mother to him, and that time long ago when she used to bend over him to give him a kiss. Sixty years have gone by since that fat old man's been a baby, but now he can feel her like rosewater by his side, so soft he starts to go drowsing off again, with a little smile playing in the dimples of his plump chin and pink cheeks. (The pinkness looked like a healthy glow—from a distance, you know. Close up, cracked veins—don't you get a liking for wine, Miss Miranda, white skin show all its footprints—though you're kind of a high yellow, that's what we call it, ha!) The fat man's life is one long, roaring feast: food, drink, music, boys, girls, jumping and dancing, joking, singing, talk, crik-crak, one big long carnival, 'cause he followed a beautiful wild young master, who does just as he pleases and makes everyone around him do so too. The fat man hadn't ever been beautiful—but his laughter is so. He's a funnyman, he likes to make people laugh. People laugh at him, too, and so he exaggerates his big sprawling shape like a hippopotamus and he lurches on purpose when others jig and jive round him—

Miranda handed Feeny a wilted string of daisies, stood up, arranged it on the nurse's hair, a crooked garland resting lightly on her stiff, brushed-down mat. Serafine touched it, left it there, then carried on:

—Now this fat man finds he's pricked all over and here and there— Serafine wriggled, as if itching, she stabbed her nails, gently, though, into the little girl's ribs and made her giggle. —Even he—and he's padded—can't go on ignoring the little shooting pains in his wrists and ankles and even under his right hip, the one pressed to the ground. He tries to roll himself over to lie flat on his back. But those pricks get worse. He lifts his hands but they're tied, and he can't draw out the trouble, it's like sleeping under a pincushion, when nobody knows you're there. He chuckles, you know, just the same, 'cause when he squeezes his face to push open his eyes he sees that he's tied up in nothing but roses. So the fat man just lolls. He knows someone'll come along and rescue him. He's stayed sweet-tempered through worse trouble than this bed of roses!

—The king orders the fat man's capture when he hears about the partying that's gone and reached his land. This king has a daughter— she's fifteen, an innocent, white as snow, pink as roses, gold hair like corn, and she's never seen anyone outside her father's palace. Her mother is dead, yes, just like in one of those fairy tales. It's so hard for a man all alone to know how to bring up a girl. He goes and scares himself all the time. (This is easy to do—like a young animal fooling with its own shadow.) He remembers the way he thought about girls

who looked like her when he was a young man–oh, I'll keep that for
when you're older. No, don't prick me, there's nothing to tell, nothing
of interest to you—

Miranda was poking grass-blades into Feeny's cheek and nose, but
she brushed her off.

—All right, I'll tell you: knowing men like himself, he'd rather men
were different. (This is why I tell you to keep your knees together
when you're sitting down, and not sprawl like you're some intoxicated
sailorman.)

—So the king, all of a sudden, feels this raging curiosity get ahold
of him, what exactly do the young people get up to? I really ought to
know, he tells himself, so I can protect my daughter–ha! So he has
champagne poured into the stream in the palace rose garden, he sets
this trap for those party-goers. The fat man, he's the biggest drunkard
of the lot, he laps and laps like a big old hunting dog and he laughs
and laughs and then he collapses. When the king's men report they've
taken the fat man, but he's all alone, the king's disappointed. He wants
a girl or two as well, to be a friend to his daughter. But the young
ones have strong heads and healthy livers, and they're carrying on the
party.

—The officers get the fat man to his feet and bring him, all wound
up in roses, to the king. He stumbles forward and takes the king in
his arms and hugs him tight, his little eyes wet with loving feelings.
"My dear fellow," he keeps murmuring. "Wonderful to see you again,
old boy. What jolly times we had, eh?" You see, they used to know
each other in the old days, when the king was young—

Serafine was puffing out her chest and her cheeks and swaggering
a little, doing the fat man, and Miranda giggled. She recognized the
type, certain friends of her grandfather, though they wore beards and
mustaches, umbrellas and hats, not roses.

—The fat man sighs over the wines poured for him, and picks from
the dishes set down on the table—many, many dishes—and oysters all
shiny on a big dish of ice. Oh, the king twitches and narrows his
shoulders, and refuses the oyster the fat man pushes at him, sitting on
the soft cushion of his fat white hand. He likes oysters, oh yes, but
he's mean, he's scared that if he eat some too, his guest'll make him
go call for more. He stares at the fat man, who's carefully sprinkling
each oyster with a little cayenne and squeezing a little lemon juice out
till the oysters squirm like tickled toes. And all the time words keep

coming on. The fat man knows how to eat and talk at the same time (something ladies should never do, you better remember that).

—Gradually, the people in the palace are coming in closer to listen. The servants, the ministers, and . . . the king's daughter. She's now in the room, she sees her father but he doesn't see her. The fat man's speaking of an island—he and all the gang have been there all together once and never forgotten it, how could they? It's called Enfant-Béate, Blessed Child (you know this, sweetheart), the fat man is telling them, and it lies to the west, down the path of the setting sun, curving in the sea. Like the spine of a sea dragon, we say. They sailed there in a big ship with white sails and came in to land in little boats. They rowed ashore from the deep-water harbor where two rivers flow together from the red mountain at the center. This is where I was born, right there, in that village, that's called Belmont. Where your granddaddy was born, and your father too.

—The king's daughter is creeping closer, still no one pays her attention. "The people there are fine people, generous, and brave," says the fat man to the king, and he's no fool, though he likes his liquor like most men do now—

And Serafine laughed, stretching her fingertips upward to send her laugh soaring.

—Never mind—she added—Your father too, he's like all the rest.

—The princess wants to hear about my people, living out there, far beyond the palace. The fat man's telling how they used to live in houses like baskets. Hanging up from the branches of high trees. How they had fourteen words for the way a crocodile moves his head— (Serafine was poking her neck out and snapping her teeth now)—and ten words for the sound of the wind in the palms along the shore. And bushes that turn everything blue and berries that turn everything red, and sweet-smelling fruits and flowers and carapate oil to smooth your hair before you braid it; I wish I had some here, now—(She touched the daisy chain again, perched on the stiff thatch of her London hairdo.)—And creatures like my name, Killebree—the tiniest bird in the Lord's creation—ah, the list can go till night come down if I start on that.

—Then the fat man leans over to slap the king on the thigh. "Wouldn't you like to be there, dear boy? What?" You see when people hear about such things, they always want to have them for themselves. Human beings can't leave well alone, they go leave dirty marks on everything. Like you messing those poor daisies. The king nods, he wants to go there and take it for himself. To the fat man he says, "You're always exaggerating." "By no means," he answers him.

—The king's dreaming of being king there as well, and, by his side, his daughter's got a dream too—a new world, a new life. You know that people often dream of being different. Never content with what we are. No, no. She longs—(And Serafine tapped her chest.)—In here, the princess feels a hole she wants to fill all up with something, she don't yet know what it might be. She'll find out, in time. But that's a long story and'll have to keep.

—Then, at that moment, the fat man's young master roars through the door, a gang of young boys and girls all about him. A girl on each arm, a boy tugging at the paw of a wild animal skin he has tossed across his shoulders. Others, they're blowing whistles and banging tambourines and shaking bells, hooting and shouting and kissing and squealing and jumping. With them a cloud of stale jasmine and coriander, musk and cinnamon, sweat and liquor—a powerful rich stink! The fat man beams from ear to ear to see them again. "Darling boy," he murmurs. "Found you! At long last!" the young man his master says, and throws himself down beside his fat friend and leans over to drink from the same glass. "I was beginning to think we'd lost you forever. And I didn't like it." He pouts—(Serafine pouted, Miranda giggled)— and he puts his curly brown head on the fat man's half-naked shoulder. "I never go missing for long," the fat man replies, and he pats the curly handsome boy. "No, you shan't get rid of me that easily."

—The boy tucks himself up against the body of the fat man—he goes and lies on him like he's a big sofa. The king meanwhile's in a fluster, he tells the servants to bring more food, more wine, in spite of the agony the cost gives him. (Never be mean, it'll make you suffer— cast your bread upon the waters and it'll come back, sweetheart, you'll see.) "So," says the young master to his host, "make a wish—as your reward for looking after my fat friend! I'll grant you anything!" "Oh, no," says the king. "It was nothing—the least I could do." "Come, come, make a wish, do what I tell you. That's the law when I'm around. Isn't it? And I don't like being contradicted, neither." He's a real young master, you see, the fat man's leader. He tosses his head—you mustn't do like him, never. And says, crossly—(Serafine sounded now like one of the young men who came to visit Miranda's grandfather for tea and conversation)—"There must be some reward you'd like, some treasure, some delightful little thing."

—Then he catches sight of the princess, at the same time as the king himself realizes that she's been standing there all along. "For your daughter's sake, he says."

—The princess starts, "Where have you come from?" She's never seen anyone like him, so polished and smooth, like a cob-nut shell all over and with shining black eyes like licorish. Her father sees her looking like that, and he feels a pain inside, he gets to feel scared he'll be bound to lose her.

—The master laughs, reaches out a hand, he's about to make her sit beside him, and whisper to her, her father can·tell, so he cuts in quickly instead and says, "Her mother . . . I . . . I have always wanted nothing but her happiness . . . " He's afraid, he's stammering. The young master frowns, the fat man giggles. "I want her safe . . . You see, she's the most precious thing I have." "My word, so serious! What about some fun? What about her fun?" He throws back the cloak of fur he wears off his shoulders, he holds out his hand to the girl once more. But her father puts his arm around her. The youth shrugs, he turns to the fat man. "God, I don't know how you hung around here so long, my old friend. It's been five days you've been gone, you know." "He's not so bad," the fat man replies. "It's your fault, dear boy. You're . . . overwhelming." He laughs, and he turns to the king, who's forcing a smile of agreement. His daughter stands quietly by, wishing, wishing—for something, she wishes she knew what.

—"Well, I suppose I could do with some improvement in my financial arrangements," the king starts again—(Serafine was blowing out her cheeks, huffing and puffing grampus-like.)—"That would help her future. I mean, then she could have a good settlement . . . " He sees the young master looking cross. "I mean a good party . . . a huge dance . . . a wedding feast . . . you know." He's thinking to himself, and this is where he made his big mistake, listen to this part, because it's so easy to take the wrong path—listen, child—sweetheart, listen—and want the wrong things in life. He's thinking, wouldn't it be lovely if I was really rich, if everything I had was as precious to me as my lovely daughter.

—"So, some money, is it," the young god says. "Not very imaginative, is he?"

—"Not just a lump sum, you know. How about making sure everything I have is really worth something? Making everything I've got worth its weight in gold? How about that? That would be good fun, wouldn't it?"

—"If you say so," says the bad young master, rolling his eyes. Then he's tugging at his fat friend, he wants to go, he's prodding him to his feet.

—"So be it." He gives the word.

—"Bye-bye, dear boy," calls out the fat man, as he's swept away in a big hullabaloo by the pack of them. "Take care of yourself! Thanks awfully—marvelous oysters!"

—The king's standing in the room, facing the door, and he sighs a big sigh of relief. Silence spreads out again from wall to wall. But his daughter can still hear the laughter, it's ringing in her head and she's so full up with longing for something to change her life. Her father turns back to the table. There's a mess of food and drink scattered all over it, and he slumps down in a chair. He reaches out for the remains of a bread roll. His mouth closes on gold. He picks up a glass. The drink in it turns solid, the glass too. He begins to laugh. He touches an oyster shell. Gold, again. A half-eaten bowl of this, gold, another of that, gold again, a candle, even the flame turns gold. He begins to panic, he falls forward on the table, choking on the gold bread. The king's daughter tries to calm him by calling out to him softly, then, when he don't stop, he can't bear it and she kneels down by his side, and she reaches out to soothe him, to tell him they were a mob of no-good snobs, useless trash and so on, and she'd never really wanted to spend another moment with them, when he lifts himself from the table and clutches at her. Then she too, her hair, her skin, her clothes, her hands, her eyebrows and her eyelashes, all of her, changes to gold—

And Miranda, when she heard this story, gasped and forgot about the daisies and came closer to Serafine to look at her mouth while she was speaking, as if by watching her lips move she might understand the story better.

—The king cries out, "Oh my sweetheart, my treasure, my daughter! Oh, what have I done?" His breath mists on her cold and shining cheeks. He rubs at it. She's all hard and smooth and chilly to touch. Then he do swear to himself the most solemn promise he's ever made that he'll give his whole life to undoing the curse he's gone and brought down on them both. If she comes back to life, he'll take such care of her, nobody'd ever do her harm again.

—His tears are still falling down on her gold face when she finds her voice again, and stutters, "Where am I? What happened?"

—Now he's crying from happiness. Inside her gold shell, his daughter's still alive! She even puts her gold hand in his. "My precious girl," he whispers in her ear. "You're here, at home, with me. Everything'll be all right, you'll see. Your life is only just beginning."—

Miranda's eyes had grown huge with listening. "And then, oh Feeny, and then?"

"You'll see. But not today." Serafine stood up, smoothed her coat; she bent to look at Miranda; the child's own daisy garland had come to pieces, a broken end was trailing over her brow, so Serafine plucked it from Miranda's head and let it fall into her palm. She closed her hand over it and laughed, a deep low gurgle, then pinched Miranda's cheek softly, between her finger and thumb. "Don't you let anyone know what you are, or notice you too much. Always be a secret princess, sweetheart."

Then Serafine let them out of the garden with her key, dropping the daisy wreath behind her.

P A R T   I

Lilac/Pink

La lengua no tiene dientes y más que ellos muerde.
(The tongue has no teeth, but a deeper bite.)

—SPANISH PROVERB

2

As Miranda was slipping her fingers into her father's warm gloved hand and was following him out of the door, she heard a cry from the kitchen; her mother was dragging out the kitchen drawers one by one and banging them in again, till she jerked at one so hard it fell out of the dresser altogether and the cooking utensils inside crashed onto the worn lino in a twisted heap: knives and ladles and pierced spoons and potato mashers and meat-mincing disks of different gauges. Astrid Everard abandoned it with a flailing gesture of the hand, flung herself onto a chair at the kitchen table, and grasping a double whisk and a mixing bowl, set to sobbing. "That jumped-up creature with her little crimson mouth and her prissy curls—you think I'm going anywhere near her or her rotten baby?"

Kit Everard left the hall and returned down the corridor of the flat to the kitchen at the bottom and stood by the door, looking in at his wife; Astrid's black hair flew about and striped the pale formica of the table, where she now banged her head. Bundled in his winter coat and scarf and hat, he seemed too bulky and stiff to pass back through the door and bend to succor her, to lift her face gently by the chin and smooth away the shiny dark strands of her dishevelment. She could be wild, as Miranda knew, and there were many tools scattered within her reach. So Kit made no move to assuage her, but instead coaxed,

his voice melting soft and rich as malt into the breach between them;
it still carried the trace of his island youth.

But he did not always wish to keep the peace; Miranda was to know
times when Kit refused to ease her mother, and instead retaliated so
ferociously that Miranda, lying in bed, shook as the bedhead rattled
against the wall that separated her room from theirs.

On this occasion, however, Kit stood, anxious to leave for the church
where the new baby was being christened, turning his deep black fedora
in his hands and letting the ash fall from his cigarette onto his coat.

"Astrid, Astrid, sweetheart," he called out. "Don't take on so."

Sometimes, when Miranda heard their quarreling, she'd lie in bed,
saying over and over with joined hands, "Please make them stop, dear
Lord, please make them stop. Please, Lord, if they stop, I swear I'll
never . . . " And then would follow her part of the bargain: she'd
renounce jam roll for a whole term (it was the best sweet at school,
which made the children give a cheer when it appeared on the kitchen
trolley at the end of the dining hall). Or she'd wear newspaper in the
toes of her shoes to make her toes hurt and bear the pain in exchange;
or promise to try really hard to vault the horse in gym and turn a neat
somersault on the scratchy coir mat instead of pretending she had
cramps; or swear she'd become a nun, and go to Africa, to care for
babies and the sick who were suffering from swamp fever or yellow
fever or the plague. She was her parents' protector, their guide, and
it was her duty to help them to be happy, hard as it seemed for them.
By her mere presence, if she could only summon up the courage to
materialize in their bedroom when they were fighting, she could make
them be still. "Pas devant," they'd say, recalling her existence. She
tried to count on it, to stop them.

Miranda was six and a half when the new baby, Xanthe, was born.

Xanthe was not technically her sister, though Miranda always
thought of her as such, but her father's half-sister, which made her
Miranda's aunt. But the small age gap between them closed the gen-
erations, and from the start they were brought up to be sisters, in a
manner of speaking.

"Come here," Astrid Everard raised her head and beckoned Miranda
over. "Even if I haven't got anything to wear, at least you could look
decent."

She plumped the bow on the side of the child's head, and ran her
fingers through her hair, fluffing it as much as she could. Miranda's

grew in a pigeon's nest; she'd inherited neither her mother's black and tendrilly waves, nor her father's springy curls, so there wasn't much Astrid could do with it. She undid her daughter's coat and spun her and tweaked out the hem of the nylon organza frock she had made for her so that it stood out. Miranda liked the feel of her mother's hands, working, smoothing, pinching, lifting, for it was seldom that she touched her. Occasionally, she cut her hair, and then the firm sweep of the comb and her deft fingertips on her head, and her need to trust in her mother's scissors as they snip-snipped against her neck made the infrequent nighttime ceremony one of the steadiest moments they shared together.

"How could I come to that house, with everyone dressed up to the nines, when you can't even get your daughter a proper pair of shoes?"

The child quickly rubbed one toe against the back of her leg and then the other, while her father was saying slowly, keeping a hold on himself, "Astrid, nobody is going to pay a single bit of attention to what Miranda's wearing on her feet." Her father's eyelids closed, stayed closed, he was still counting to ten. Her mother snatched up the packet of egg powder and savagely tore it and shook it into the bowl in front of her, and then began beating water into it, flying at him again with her mouth. His shut face said, "You cross me at every turn. You never give me peace."

"You'd be surprised," she was crying out, "What people notice. You may miss it. But I know I don't." She pulled the mixing bowl closer, beating the mixture till it frothed. "I haven't had a new coat since before the war. And it was no great shakes then."

Kit began advancing on his wife, with the stub of his cigarette in his hand. He put it out in front of Astrid with a sizzle in a slick of egg flown from the bowl into the ashtray on the table, and then leaned over and sibilated into her face, "One day, Astrid, you'll get so cross you'll just burst into tiny little pieces."

Miranda was still beside her mother, and as her father spoke so close, she could smell the bay rum in his hair, mingled with the burning tobacco in his hand. (When she got into their bed to be with them and keep them quiet by her presence, his side prickled her nose with these scents, while her mother's exuded a delicate trace of almonds from the steam rub she sometimes gave her hair.)

Miranda found herself between them now, standing and looking up at them, and saw her father's mouth and nose from underneath, crumpled, as if underwater, and he was saying into his wife's face, but still screwing down on the butt, "You are too proud, Astrid."

To their daughter later, it seemed that she had always seen them like this, the breath of their mouths twisting, so closely were their heads together, while she stood, often inadvertently, between them. She could never know if her interventions weakened the savagery of their clashes.

During the war, they'd all three been intermittently separated—Kit fighting, in Burma, Egypt, Italy; Miranda evacuated. When the family was reunited, Miranda became the third who was always there, but behind, between, to one side; never with; the early child whose existence becomes a slash parting the halves of a couple, not a hyphen that links them together. So, when Xanthe was born, Miranda's hope began that she could attach herself to her grandparents instead. She would play the elder sister as well as she could, she would cast herself as Xanthe's indispensable shadow; above all, she longed to retain access to Serafine.

"As for you," Astrid returned, level, just holding her head back on her thin neck so that she could look at Kit without going cross-eyed, "you have no pride. You're not a man. You're a dog, their little dog. When they call, you run. They throw the stick and you leap right after it. Pity it never turns out a carrot."

"He's my father, Astrid." Kit Everard straightened, held his hand out to his daughter, and she took it.

When Miranda was much older and began to exchange experiences with friends, she learned that fathers and mothers do not forever do violence to one another as hers did. Xanthe's parents were always even-tempered, for instance; Miranda's grandpa was a mild and reticent man, who never raised his voice in a rebuke, let alone a rage. But Miranda was brought up with anger close at hand and constant, and she came to know its heat so well she developed fakir's flesh, and in consequence could meet and handle rage in others almost fearlessly. But she was not cauterized against some of the other deadly sins: envy, for instance, which made her mother suffer so much as well, later caused her great grief; and lust, too. The rest of the sisterhood left her pretty much alone, though gluttony would catch hold of her one day, a late-blooming appetite. She did not hold the tempests of her childhood against her parents; her father could be grand, a fierce and savage man at times, with an eloquence that her mother's fits could never defeat, her maneuvers never match. But Astrid was sharp-eared and sharp-tongued in her bile, and Miranda learned to listen to her well. Together, her parents tempered her; she saw their anger some-times as a fiery angel, helping her defend the walled garden of her privacy.

They were late arriving at the church; they saw the cars outside and the chauffeurs in a group, stamping their feet in the damp leaves on the pavement, for the season had turned cold. It was darker inside, the mid-morning grayness deepened to steel wool in the shadows of the stone columns of the nave, and though her father trod softly—under his heavy winter clothes, Kit Everard was slight in build—his steps threw back echoes off the stark walls as they approached the font, which stood by the barred west door. She held on tight to her father's hand; tongues of shadow leapt at the columns beside the font. The guests were murmuring bits in English after the priest, and it sounded to her like an unfamiliar language—when she went to church, which wasn't often, it was to Latin mass with her mother.

As they drew near, Sir Anthony Everard turned his head and gave his son and granddaughter a quick nod, not a smile, for at a service a smile would not be appropriate, and Sir Anthony's strong point, it was widely held, was his impeccable decorum. It went with his "unerr-ing instinct for fair play," which was acknowledged even by adversaries who had suffered defeat at his hands, either on playing fields in the old days, or across the boardroom table in present times.

Miranda couldn't see the new baby, only the coats of the other guests and their hands, studded with rings. A man, at her eye level as she passed, wore a gold signet ring on his little finger. Her father pushed her forward; her frock was squashed as she squeezed through, to join three women and two men in the front row who were making the responses at the invitation of the vicar. One was the baby's mother, Gillian, who wasn't holding her, but the prayer book from which she was following the service.

The character of Granny fitted pert Gillian Everard so ill that Miranda never thought of her as her grandmother at all, and certainly never called her so, after the time when her mother took her to tea there and kept up such a stream of "Say thank you to your granny, darling," and "Now wipe the jam off your mouth, otherwise what'll your granny think of you?" until "Granny" Gillian, barely thirty (though she kept her date of birth a secret), gave a cold peal of laughter and, her neat shoulders presented to Astrid, told Miranda to call her Auntie.

"Go on, Miranda dear," she cooed. "Say, 'Yes, Auntie Gillian.' "

She had a tiny face of surprising roundness; it looked the same shape from any angle, and her shingle fitted it neatly as a cap; her neck was spindle-like, and her neatly molded body was invariably turned out in tailored suits and cashmere twin sets or satin cocktail dresses, smooth and close, as if they had been gently steam-pressed onto her. Astrid would recognize the *marques* Gillian wore and schooled Miranda in the lore of fashion from an early age.

"If I had the money that woman has, my God, if I could afford Schiaparelli and Chanel, I wouldn't look a frump like her. She manages to put a twin set to a skirt by Patou—it's beyond belief. She looks as dull as ditchwater, with clothes that would make a tramp look like a film star."

Miranda didn't agree, and when she grew up, began to wear Gillian's hand-downs—if she could get into them—with glee. Xanthe wouldn't touch her mother's clothes, so she had first pick. She loved the interior handiwork above all, the satin linings hemmed over silk grosgrain stiffeners, the firm interlinings basted down underneath, the buttons sewn onto narrow ribbons so as not to pull at the fabric, the over-stitched hooks and eyes, and the embroidered labels saying Maison de Worth, Chanel, whatever.

"Dost thou, in the name of this child, renounce the Devil and all his works, the vain pomp and glory of the world, with all covetous desires of the same, and the carnal desires of the flesh, so that thou wilt not follow, nor be led by them?"

Miranda was trying to see the baby; she could not make out her face, or really which end of the bundle was which. In the clinic where Xanthe was born, visiting with her father—Astrid had also refused that earlier act of family piety—Miranda had glimpsed a nose and mouth and a blotchy head in one of the cots downstairs, lined up alongside look-alikes, in identical cots, all of them pink, all of them beribboned. She asked then how they managed to stop babies from getting mixed up. Wouldn't Xanthe be taken home by someone else by mistake, and Auntie Gillian and her grandfather would find them-selves with another child, switched for their own daughter? The anxiety came back now and then—or was it a wish?—that somewhere out there was her true sister, the twin of her soul, wandering, unknown; that Xanthe was a changeling.

The baby made no sound or movement in the church. White lace wrapped her in a scalloped veil sprinkled with raised rosettes, as she was clasped in the arms of the godmother who now answered, in the deep and crackly voice of the very old and often pickled, "I renounce them all."

Gillian smiled, reached out, tucked a stray portion of lace around her infant daughter's shoulders. Miranda was lifting one foot after another to bring back sensation, for the cold was seeping through her soles and numbing her legs, until her grandfather signaled to her to keep still with a finger to his lips. The prayers continued; she grew colder. Her father's voice behind her seemed to boom more loudly than the others'. He was joining in for everyone to hear, and no mistake, though his energetic enthusiasm betrayed his unease.

For over twenty years Kit had been his father's only child, his son and heir apparent. Everything was changed by the advent of Xanthe. "He's the very spit of you," friends would say to Sir Anthony about his son, though it was clearly not the case, as the boy's mother was born Estelle Desjours on Enfant-Béate, so that Kit Everard had "a touch of the tar brush" from his mother's Creole blood. Or so everyone murmured.

Never in front of Sir Anthony himself, of course.

Not that the tar showed, not unless you knew. Once you did know, however, Kit's hairline, so neat and densely planted with dark curls, looked telltale proof.

"Ant" Everard, his father, was small and light-boned, with a narrow head like a vane; his gray-blue eyes were set close together, his binocular vision aligned as accurately as the single closed eye of a sharpshooter; at Flinders, the game that had made him a national hero, he'd given the impression he could survey the four quarters of the field all at once.

The vicar now beckoned to the godmother, who held the baby in her arms. In an astrakhan beret wound in lilac-spotted tulle, the old woman stepped forward carefully, Gillian following close, taking her by the elbow for support. The gesture of assistance made the handbag looped over Gillian's arm swing and knock against her hip and she gave a small gasp, for she thought she had dropped it. The godmother exclaimed, in a low crackle like dry wood catching, "What is it now? I haven't let the creature fall, at least not yet, I haven't."

A titter rustled through the group of guests; she was a character, a famous princess, much observed, often quoted, widely indulged.

"It's nothing, Ma'am, nothing. Do proceed."

The ancient princess at last handed over the tiny lace papoose in her swathe of dazzling white, and the minister bowed unctuously, and mumbled. The infant Xanthe's principal godmother—there were other, lesser, sponsors there—was the eldest survivor of a royal generation born in the previous century, the only living granddaughter of the Queen then on the throne, by a daughter's marriage into the Empire that the Great War had broken up. Her violet-gray astrakhan coat, hanging to midcalf, weighed down her fleshless bones, but the beret pitched to one side revealed a thick fringe of hair, bluish-violet under the matching froth of dotted veiling.

Gillian leaned toward her, whispered, "We appreciate it so much, Ma'am."

At the moment of transferral from the Princess to the priest, the baby was held upright like a host at the elevation, and Miranda saw Xanthe full-face for the first time. A small fist reached for her lips, which opened, like a nestling feeding, and gnawed at her bunched hand. Her head bobbed with surprise at finding no sweetness or nourishment, and her eyes flew open for an instant and appeared to swirl. It seemed to Miranda that Xanthe had cat eyes even then, the pupils dilated to a wider aperture than the light around required, as if a camera lay inside, loaded with slow film.

"Name this child," said the vicar.

"Xanthe," came a mismatched chorus of voices.

He held her across his chest again and maneuvered her head over the edge of the stone basin; Gillian sprang forward and slipped off Xanthe's white frilled christening bonnet and untied its satin ribbons, and the minister took a scoop of water and dribbled it over the hairless crown of the baby's head. She twitched and both fists worked their way out of her cocoon and her tiny body flexed with startling force in his hands until he nearly dropped her in.

The words of the service came to Miranda, incomprehensible and threatening. The sponsors were promising that they would make sure the child would grow up—

". . . mortifying all our evil and corrupt affections . . ."

Suddenly afraid her turn would come next, Miranda pushed through the legs and furs of the guests to her father at the back, the sound of her crying burst against the stone walls and grew louder.

"Tst, tst, child," someone muttered as she passed, "surely you're too big to cry?"

Her father swung her up into his arms, where he added his shushing to the others', but kindly. "What's this, my little lady? My brave girl, this isn't like you!"

She rubbed the tears from her eyes, and turned to watch the final stages of the baptism her father was attending to so alertly. They would bring the baby up, the assembly promised.

". . . daily proceeding in all virtue and godliness of living . . ."

"Will I be done too?" she asked.

"Darling girl! You have been, when you were born. In another church."

All our evil and corrupt affections.

Elsewhere, the promises had been made for her. She could not understand. She took fright and cried, and then cried louder when the resonance in the church's recesses startled her and intensified the disapproval of the grown-ups she'd disturbed. She could not ask herself then, in so many words: Could this be so, that affections might be evil, corrupt? She denied it, her heart beat against it; she rebelled with that first fright at the christening, and she would continue to do so. She did not want to be defended against affections; she wanted to live by faith in their strong armor. But later, when the love that Xanthe inspired in so many people around her from the moment she was born— in herself, her father Kit, and, especially, in Xanthe's own father, Anthony—had changed all their lives so profoundly, Miranda would have to accept doubt and answer, Why yes, all our evil and corrupt affections.

3

Outside the church after the christening, mist draped in veils the cedars' hanging branches, and the cries of the guests, escaping upward in small puffs, were gathered into it:

"What temperament that child shows—already!" Sir Anthony exclaimed to his wife. Xanthe felt like his firstborn, he was so proud of her. "She's my late sprog," he was saying. "The last blossom of my life."

"So good of you to come. I know what it's like trying to get here without a car . . . ": Gillian, to Kit and Miranda; she meant it too, for Gillian had a generous streak and wanted everyone to enjoy the comforts she had inherited.

"Isn't she absolutely splendid? Looks sixty-five at the most. A wonderful lady, a remarkable lady": Sir Anthony, of the Princess. She was in fact over eighty; they enjoyed a coquettish relation ever since she had presented him with a trophy one milky June, when he was captain of Flinders at school and she had been invited to give the prizes.

"You must have a secret of immortal life, Ma'am": a guest, abased and gallant, to the Princess.

"I do," she answered. "And I'm not telling it to you." Her pointed nose quivered for an instant, and her eyes, still mischievously alight in spite of the pouchy sockets old age had wrought, flashed at him an invitation to learn more.

The guests were murmuring more words of wonder in the cold churchyard, and stamping their feet. One or two were wearing galoshes over their good shoes. A photographer invited by the family made them keep still, and with a small explosion, took their picture. It would be sent to an illustrated weekly subscribed by all the best households. He began to distribute his card. "Tuck & Tuck—Portraits, Weddings, All Festive Occasions." The other Tuck was his wife, but she concentrated on printing and presentation, and did not do the festive occasions, as Mr. Tuck worried that a "Mrs." would not inspire confidence in quality revelers. A group from the popular press was also assembled, and they too popped a few bulbs in the baby's honor. "A big smile, Sir Ant!" The former Flinders champion was a favorite with the newspapermen, always ready with a word for them, communicating a sense they were his colleagues, his equals. "And another! Cheese, everyone, cheese."

Miranda watched the Princess strike a practiced pose, the features composed, eyes wide, mouth full as she faced the photographers. Her father, holding her by the shoulders, greeted Serafine, who was standing back from the crowd, making sure she was not in the camera's view. Kit squeezed his daughter to show her that he, too, was affectionately aware of the servant's presence.

A guest was mewing, "Those little fists, my word—I just see them with a ball—she'll take after you, just you wait and see."

"Lovely plain service, Vicar," said another to the minister, whose face was ruddy from the winter's bite. "None of this newfangled High Church nonsense."

"And not too long, either."

Civilized laughter rang out.

"Yes, I can picture her on the field, with a devilish fast spin. I can just see it coming . . ."

"Such an exquisite robe! And such a pretty child!"

"Darling little thing, isn't she?"

Then Anthony turned to Kit. "No Astrid, then? I'm sorry, she's a special girl. Give her my special love, now, don't forget."

In the prints they were shown later, Miranda was blurred: she was shifting when the photograph was taken; in the low light, she would have had to keep stock-still to come out clearly.

"Astrid's got a touch of flu," Kit told his father. "In this weather, one does well not to venture forth. You'll agree, I know."

•   •   •

Astrid Everard was, however, at that moment preparing to go out. One by one she had picked up the cooking utensils from the floor, and with each one, as she aligned it in its place in the drawer, she cursed—her husband, her husband's father, his wife—that ghastly Gillian with her silly little-girl airs and graces—and, above all, with special spite, Gillian and Anthony's daughter, the new Everard baby, Xanthe. Astrid would have no more children; when she bore Miranda, so much had gone wrong the doctors had suggested taking out her tubes and most of the rest as well, but she had managed to keep some of her insides, while thoroughly terrorized into swearing she'd take every precaution not to conceive again. She was twenty-three at the time (Kit was twenty-one); he was understanding about it, didn't mind making love in safe ways, was rather good at it, truth to tell, enjoyed licking and sucking her with patience and at length till all her restraints were loosed and she flowed for him.

Astrid's curses were now powered by remembered humiliations. (Indeed she had only imagined that she had not been asked to the christening: Gillian, lying in among the flowers and chocolates at the clinic, had not written her guests' names on the engraved card, and only inscribed "Kit" on the envelope.) Astrid's curses envisaged very mundane plagues for her victims; she had insight into the triviality of the worst psychic hurts, the pinches of envy, the smarts of disgrace, the stab wound of exclusion. They produced the kind of pain she felt most acutely herself.

The christening group moved towards the streets where some cars waited, passing under the tall black cedars that draped the railed graveyard in shadow. Xanthe was back in Gillian's arms, making unseeing cross-eyes at admirers; Serafine now hovered to take her, but Gillian did not hand her over. Some cars had drivers, who started up the engines to warm them; the cars began to steam like horses. The day had turned light-mustard in color, the streets lamps were already lit, and in the winter gloom their yellow plumes reflected back from the fog closing in on the terraced houses in the street. The trunks of the lime trees rising from the pavement looked inked in: a dark and early dusk lay gathering strength already in their branches.

"Time for a snifter, what?" proposed a guest, producing a hip flask and offering it to his companion. "See you all chez Everard in a jiffy," he called out, as he handed her into the passenger seat and banged the door.

As one by one the cars began to leave, Miranda sensed that her father was uncertain how they were to travel to the party; Sir Anthony's car would be full, with Gillian and Anthony themselves, plus the vicar, Serafine, Xanthe and all her tackle.

Then Kit saw the Princess waving a man out of the driver's seat of a cream-and-coffee-colored saloon to take it herself. "Climb on board, come along, Maud." As Kit Everard approached, she was gesturing impatiently to her lady-in-waiting, who was smoothing a plaid around her mistress's knees. The Princess was celebrated for her motoring, indeed, had even flown in the First World War—hospital planes, from the combat zone to behind the lines.

Gillian put out a hand warningly. "No, no, Miranda dear, you ride with us." But Miranda was gone to be with her father, and soon settled beside the Princess's lady-in-waiting in the back, with Kit opposite them on the low dickey seat of pleated leather the chauffeur had folded down for him before getting into the passenger seat in the front, beside the Princess.

Kit was smiling at the look on Gillian's face as they glided past, and he pressed his daughter's hand.

"Now we're all shipshape," he said. "Thanks to the Princess." Then, turning to address her, he added, "Please excuse my giving you my back, Ma'am. It's the arrangement in the car."

"I do see," said the Princess. "Why don't you change places with the child?"

"She's a lady, Ma'am, and should ride like one," replied Kit.

They passed a slower motor with a swinging movement, and the old princess hooted as she reentered the line of traffic; as a pilot, she had always regretted that in an airplane there was no horn.

They reached a set of lights. Taking a lipstick in a golden tube from her highly polished crocodile handbag and turning down the sun flap, where a round mirror had been embedded on the driver's side at her request, she began to paint in the paired brackets of her lips. Her cheeks were dusted with a pinkish-violet powder, and there emanated from her a light fragrance that Miranda recognized had hung around the font and in the air outside the church as well. The car was steeped in it, a smell of pressed lilac and violets, stuffy and ancient, like the interior intimacy of a drawer that encloses keepsakes, old photographs, letters.

When she was done, and the lights had changed, she started up again, and turning her head, gave Kit a look. The lady-in-waiting beside Miranda gripped the strap more tightly.

"I am the Princess Alicia, you know. And you? I forget."

Her lips were covered with a fine net of lines, like the veins of a leaf, and the crimson seeped into them, setting off the startling pallor of her skin; she could have been a member of a tribe who whiten and daub their ancient chiefs before they lead the ritual. Miranda's father told her his name. This royal survivor was famous for her romantic life. She had never married, though; her first scandal arose when someone who fell in love with her was caught by a keen palace guard, in the corridor on the way to—or was it from?—her room. (Or so the rumor, not quite thoroughly suppressed, maintained.) He had been smoking a cigarette: the scent of the tobacco alerted the guard to an intruder's presence. It had become embarrassing; he was a commoner.

Hearing her parents talk about the episode, Miranda had tried to match the word with other "occupations" in her *Encyclopedia of World History*, beside the fowler, the archer, the hawker, the huntsman, and the monk, who appeared illustrated in its pages. When she could not identify such a man in the book, she imagined him on a common, among gorse bushes and bracken and jumping hares, striding.

The car pounced through the misty streets in darts and sorties, like a mouser enjoying herself with her prey, the Princess smoking the while. She was no longer in line for the succession, the Palace had declared. (She had only been thirty-sixth, but no matter, the statement still counted as disgrace.) But she had kept on the apartments in the Palace that her family had been given when the revolution in their original realm had toppled them. The commoner remained one and later married someone else, abroad, and whenever Italian photo magazines captured the Princess with her face screwed up, they made it look as if she were weeping, and published a photograph alongside her of his children and their children, large happy families next to her solitude.

It was stranger still, it seemed to Miranda, that a princess could not do exactly as she pleased in the end. Even if at first she's thwarted by a spell, and the ashes conceal her radiance or the briars tangle her as she sleeps or the apple lodges in her throat and makes her look as if she's dead.

They rolled on through the sulfur city, the lady-in-waiting jerking with the Princess's fitful control of her car. Watching her, Miranda let slip a giggle, then covered her mouth. The old woman waved a papery hand, threaded with gold and ringed with amethyst, and asked, "If you were that baby, child, what would you like to be given?"

Miranda was brought up to know that it was bad manners to ask for anything, no matter how much you wanted it. "I want shan't get," her mother said. At table, she was told to offer food to others as a way of saying that she herself would like some more. Hearing her parents talk about the daughter of a friend of theirs, and how she was so pretty and so good, she once interrupted, "And me? What about me?" and was scolded. "When others are being praised, you're not automatically left out, you know," her mother said. "You must learn to wait your turn. Me-too, that's what I'll call you from now on. Miss Me-too."

So she did not answer the Princess straightaway, until the thin old hand crooked a finger and summoned a reply.

"Come, now, as her godmother, what should I give her?"

That way round should be all right, she thought, making a like-list in her head. To give away wouldn't be the same as saying she wanted it for herself.

She told the Princess:

"One doll with eyes that open and close, and real blond hair, rooted. One treasure box with lock and key. And I shouldn't really say, but here goes: long yellow hair, with bouncy curls. For me. No, for her, I mean.

"I don't know any more after that," Miranda concluded. There were plenty of other things, but she mustn't seem greedy. "I'm stuck."

"I dare say that's enough for a start."

The Princess then twisted the rear mirror round so that she could see Miranda reflected in it and nodded. "I was considering a handsome Bible, perhaps, or a string of pearls. A pipe of port's traditional, you know. For boys. Though I may say I can't see why. I like a little port myself. It's an excellent nightcap, sends me straight off to Nod."

"I know!" Miranda blurted out. "Not a Bible! No, I know a really good wish: a pot of porridge that goes on and on and never gets empty. It means enough money for the housekeeping, all the time—that's what Mummy says."

"Ah yes," the Princess replied. There was a pause, while Kit gave a cough. Then she went on, "A pot of porridge that never fails? Indeed, that would be nice on a cold winter day, like today."

Kit Everard tried to demur, and the Princess addressed him now, with some archness, "And you, Mr. Everard, what would you give the baby, if you were her baptismal sponsor, rather than her brother?"

He laughed, as if the idea were preposterous, and turned from contemplation of the dankness outside to face his daughter.

"She has everything," he said. "She'll be the apple of her father's eye. 'The last blossom of my life.' The youngest and most dear. I can't imagine what you might give her, Ma'am."

"How do you know? Have you second sight? Come now, don't look on the dark side. You must have some idea."

"If you insist." He took a breath, and then declared, "I'd give her goodness of heart, a loving nature, all the female things—pity and gentleness, you know. A voice that's gentle, soft and low, as the Bard says." He thought awhile, the Princess was silent too, thinking with him, it seemed. Then he plunged on, determined not to appear a dreamer, a man out of step with his time. "And a good sense of fun. You can't survive without a sense of humor, not these days. Yes, she'd have to be a good sport too. I'd give her that." He stopped, and took off his glasses to wipe them clear—the heat inside the car was clouding them, or was the pressure of his feelings the cause? Miranda thought of her mother, and could not grasp his drift, but all of a sudden felt a different air in the glassed-in back compartment of the car, as if some sound had been struck at such high frequency, it could not be heard consciously, but only sensed.

"I like a dash of gallantry myself," the Princess said. "In young women too, by the bye."

Kit Everard was a young man of sentiment, and he found proof of his belief in its power and truth even when Astrid was in her fury, for in the well of the night he could always dissolve her bitterness. Sir Anthony, on the other hand, was rarely moved; even apotheosis left him dry-eyed. Raised shoulder-high by his team after a triumphant match, he used to wave with his usual controlled grace at the ecstatic crowds as they roared and raced around him and extended arms to touch him; Kit had run along beside with them in the past, transported too by his father's victory, and had felt uncomfortable that the champion did not seem to care for the acclaim, and even seemed to spurn his followers, so steady and restrained was his response.

Sir Anthony's maxim was "Keep a straight stick and a modest heart," and unlike most, he had managed to live by it. He had never known the abandon he himself could so often excite, and this nervelessness was part of the secret of his skill on the field as well as his aura off it. Possessed by purpose, he seemed to have no inner demons to draw him from the task in hand, soften his concentration or snap the tension of his energy. The honeyed commentators on the air would caress him with metaphors learned from studying the Persian and the Trojan wars in squalid classrooms at the best schools: Ant Everard was an arrow loosed from the bow of a master archer, undeflected, fast and clear, as it flies true to the target.

By comparison, Kit was at cross-purposes with life; from early youth he had felt more like an arrow that falls to the ground from the string at the moment of launching. His game, which he could play well too (a little volatility did no hurt) was poker or bridge or backgammon, or, sometimes, chess (where his temperament did interfere), a contest where the human factor mattered more than physical powers of eye and hand, where the aim was money, and luck a factor; they had this in common, father and son, their lucky touch. "How wise the Greeks were," Ant Everard would say. "They cultivated a sense of order and the civilized virtues, but they understood the importance of luck as well. They picked their leaders, like Alcibiades, because he'd proved himself lucky. It wasn't his fault they lost faith in him—his own touch didn't falter. Their trust in him weakened, and that can prove fatal, you know, in any team effort. It cost them Sicily—more fools they."

But Anthony Everard was disappointed that his son did not play his game too; that he claimed a childhood injury to his foot prevented him from following in his father's steps in the Flinders stockades.

As the entrance with the carriage lamps of Severn Court came into view, Kit exclaimed, "We've arrived! At last! It's so dark already, it feels as if we've been on board for hours!"

"Remember, my dear Maud, I'd like a cigarette now and then when we're inside," the Princess said to her lady-in-waiting as the latter helped her down and took the plaid from her legs before the old woman stumbled in its heavy folds.

"Very well, Ma'am."

The chauffeur prepared to take the driving seat, as the Princess turned to give a final word to Kit. "I think I'll wish for common sense for the child. Nobody else will watch out for her in that regard, I think."

"Oh no—" he began, but she waved him to be quiet.

"She'll need it if all you say is correct, and I dare say it is. As for innocence, that doesn't mix with common sense. Believe me. I was innocent once. Now I know better. But it's far too late."

Kit helped escort her into the hall, tipping the chauffeur a shilling as he passed.

If Astrid had seen her husband show off like that, pretending he was a man of means, she would have given him bitter words. But she was still on her way, sitting in the underground, the bedroom she had left behind heaped with clothes that had been tried on and stripped off in mounting anger until, at last, Astrid had hit upon a combination to her liking. In the tunnel, when the window opposite her seat was black against the soot-furred bricks speeding past outside, she rocked to the train's rhythm and appraised her silhouette, allowing herself a small snort of anticipation.

4

SIR ANTHONY AND Gillian Everard lived in a large flat on the
top floor of a mansion block; on one side, they had a view of
the exclusive enclosed garden in the square below, where pink
wintersweet flowered in January, and in May white cherry blossom
bespattered the plaque in memory of a fossil expert—he had be-
queathed to his neighbors the petrified log like swirled sugar near
Serafine's preferred bench. Inside the flat, servants' stairs laid with
spongy brown lino led from the kitchen up one flight to the attic story,
which gave a clearer vantage over the mock Tudor chimneys and
castellated Dutch gables, the fancy plasterwork and dainty pargeting
of the prewar luxury flats that made up Severn Court. There Serafine
lived, and her hair brushed the plaster of the ceiling, for she was a
tall woman who stooped her shoulders and poked her neck forward;
she had wanted to look more compact, less rangy, ever since she had
suddenly shot up in her twelfth year.

The mansion block was kept unusually heated inside from the huge
boilers in the basement, which the hall porter tended and fueled and
which gave a whiff of oil smoke to the linked corridors above. He also
took in the post and deliveries and brought them up to the residents,
laying the packets bound by flat rubber bands outside each varnished
walnut door with its substantial polished number; the stain of metal

cleaning fluid created halos around the brasses that belonged to the most assiduous cleaners. The Everards' was not one of these house-proud front doors; its furniture was mottled, on account of Serafine's lack of interest in it. The porter had a gammy leg, so the early delivery hour was marked by the syncopation of his gait. It had spared him service in the recent war. In the summer, he ran a book for the greatest national races, but otherwise allowed himself so little fraternization that one day Sir Anthony had crossed him on the approach to the stockade at Doggett's Fields before a game and had not recognized the cheerful young man who greeted him respectfully, for he wasn't wearing his customary serge uniform and was accompanied by a woman who appeared to be his mother. Anthony Everard prided himself on a royal ability never to forget a face, but he had not noticed the porter sufficiently to see that he was indeed a young man, young enough to have a mother living; this lapse of courtesy to an inferior gave him a moment's shame.

On the other side of the mansion flats and their private gardens, at the intersection of three busy streets, stood an underground station, smartly moderne in glazed burgundy luster tiles; the arcade was visible from the flat's windows when the trees weren't in leaf. Under the ornamental canopy of wrought-iron, a pet shop—Our Best Friends—displayed its living goods under a warming naked light bulb in the window: canaries, white mice and the odd litter of spaniel puppies asleep in straw bedding. A famous neighborhood Scotch terrier met his owner off the train every day at rush hour; from the mansard of her room, Serafine could see the pepper-and-salt drugget of his back as he bustled up to the corner of the arcade and took up his post by the newspaper vendor's box where great events were chalked in black: "Butter's Back!" "London Airport Opens."

"Dogs are so filled with love," Serafine would say. "They lay down their own cleverness to serve us."

One or two restaurants from countries of the fading empire opened in the rotunda of shops that backed onto the arcade; new shops from the war's diaspora, too, gradually brought goods and foods never seen before in the victors' country: Polish dumplings and cherry cheesecake under plastic dish covers; hot peppers and spices from India and the islands—which Serafine sniffed to identify and knew how to use—dyed food unexpectedly scarlet and yellow and orange; through the glass-ceiling area vents and basement gratings the scents of distant bazaars rose and pierced the city's home brew of car exhausts and tea-urns and industrial smoke and printer's ink, so that landowners up in town to do a spot of shopping were taken by surprise, as when the cinnabar of dogwood's stems flares in the hedge of a stone-cold winter field; passersby wrinkled their noses suspiciously, thought darkly of the way even half-civilized people like the French ate horses and frogs and snails, and wondered about dogs, dolphins, goats and sharks, and birds' nests.

From China there also came syrupy mangoes and sticky vermilion pork pieces, as well as ivory pagodas and lacy balls carved within lacy balls, and lychees of mother-of-pearl-veined flesh so delicate it would defeat even their nimble carvers' skills at counterfeiting; painted silk lanterns with scarlet fringes showing dragons bringing rain, and porcelain bowls with rice baked translucent into the clay, lacquered chopsticks tarty as nail varnish, and dolls in palace robes with nodding heads and drop earrings.

The first time Miranda was taken out to lunch by Gillian (her own parents couldn't afford restaurants, neither then, nor indeed later), Gillian noticed her gazing at a set of nine white china horses under the glass counter by the till. One was prancing, one at full stretch in the gallop, the others were rearing and bucking and trotting and walking, recumbent and grazing. Not one of them was in harness, and so they seemed quite different from the big dray geldings, heavily clopping down the streets, which she had seen in the city, or the sleek and quivering police mounts in the park where Serafine took her for a walk on Wednesday afternoons, before Xanthe was born. Behind the wing case of a blinker, she'd once glimpsed one liquid eye, revolving and dewy, while the animal's velvet lips had mashed the bit between its teeth until foam flecked the corners. But Miranda sensed a different quality of wildness—not the restlessness of discontent, but the exhilaration of refusal—in the snow-white, unbroken Chinese herd. Even at only an inch high, she could envisage them flying like seed on the wind; they answered to no riders and yet they kept one another company in the herd.

In Miranda's dreams, she'd put out her hand to a living creature, and it would not take fright. But she hardly knew any animals for real; she hadn't visited the zoo (it was evacuated, as she had been, during the war), and in her picture books and the nursery frieze above her bed at home, the shyest and wildest creatures were domestic, wore aprons and bonnets, and carried shopping bags.

When Gillian bought the set of horses and pushed the box toward her across the table, Miranda's own mother felt a stab of annoyance, the child's face shone so bright; for nothing could ever bring Astrid so much evident joy any longer, neither the offer of such a gift, nor the giving of it.

In the early years, Miranda's mother had trusted Gillian's spontaneous and regular kindnesses. But she gradually began to resent the woman's capacity to give; it begun to strike her as a mere unthinking demonstration of Gillian's power to spend. Gillian had family money of her own from her father's paper mill. Sir Anthony still had tenants on the old plantation land back in Enfant-Béate, Belmont, now part of Jamieston, the main town on the island; but they yielded a pittance compared to Gillian's income. Prestige, not wealth, was the marriage lot Gillian had desired, and she had been glad to exchange her fortune for social standing.

Soon after Xanthe was born, Astrid told Gillian that presents were ruled out, except at Christmas and birthdays, and then must be modest, as she did not want her daughter spoiled. (She also wanted to forestall her own sense of injury, should Gillian overlook Miranda now that she had a little girl of her own.)

Sir Anthony Everard's bachelor flat was beneath them, in the opinion of his young wife, in spite of the exclusive use of the garden and the desirable address. "Does everyone here have to eat cabbage?" she'd wail as she came in from shopping to the fust in the hall. They were to move as soon as she had found something more suitable. But Gillian worried about balancing decorum with comfort, discretion with luxury, which was delaying the choice, while the area was circumscribed by Anthony's needs: Doggett's Fields had to be within walking distance. He loved to swing out in the summer light with his hat and cane and make for the pavilion, where he ruled as an unofficial monarch, to watch games unfolding in the green velvet conch of the stockade. From Ant Everard's point of view, his flat, his widower's portion, was perfectly situated.

Gillian was happy about the arrangements she had made for the christening, in spite of postwar shortages—angel cake and a good Sauterne (Château Rieussec, '37), which a friend of Anthony's in the wine trade had bought at a sale from the cellar of one of the great houses that was packing up in the aftermath of the war. There was tea for those who preferred it (she'd saved enough sugar to go round) and punch, too, cherry brandy and orange squash, heated up, so she could display without too much ostentation Anthony's great silver-gilt bowl, which he'd been presented on his fiftieth birthday by all his colleagues in the Game of Flinders. *Ars ludendi gratiaque celeritatis victor ludorum sempiternus* . . . The motto of the game was chased into the bowl, with a list of names, of scores, dates, and famous games in distant places in which he'd excelled; and for the knop on the lid, a small figure of a player with his equipment, all in miniature, down to the seams on the ball.

The Princess made her way to the lighted glass-paneled revolving doors of the hall, where a large majolica umbrella stand and a mahogany board gilded with tenants' names provided useful decoration. There lingered the stuffy odors of other people's Sunday dinners, of boiling vegetables in aluminum pans, of the smell of London water in the hot-water pipes, faintly carbolic and also overcooked, at which Gillian twitched, as she precipitated herself forward to greet the Princess and hand her into the lift. The porter in his uniform stood in the corner, and after a bow, began hauling hand-over-hand on the thick rope in the corner to make the ascent.

"Not far to go now!" exclaimed Gillian. "It's a clanking old trap, I'm afraid. I'm just longing to move, but it's so hard to find anywhere suitable, you know."

"My dear! I was born down the corridor, in my mama's bedroom, only a few yards from my present quarters, and I rather regret, do you know, moving that far." They arrived. The porter adjusted the floor levels to match with a last tug on the rope and then pushed open the double flaps of the outside doors of the lift. Anthony was facing them, his hands, which were famous for their strength, yet oddly slight and small for a catcher like him, extended in greeting.

The guests from the church had been joined by one or two others: a singer of a certain fame had come with a composer who had starved until a film producer, making *Macbeth* in the light of the recent fighting, had commissioned a score. She was a mezzo and she was wearing a fetching hat of chocolate velours with a long cock-pheasant feather dashingly stabbed through it, and the sight of her—and it—made Gillian chirrup. They had been at school together. Another school friend was there, a widow; her husband had died in Burma in the very last year of the struggle in the East. One or two other players of the game, Anthony Everard's successors, were also of the company, including the present captain, a man with thick hair and browned skin and a full strong trunk.

Flinders did not make men's fortunes, only their reputation—in such

men's eyes, the greater reward. The singer and the composer glowed
to be admitted to this invisibly marked-out company, for Flinders was
paramount among sports; its players were the fighter pilots of the
ground. Some physical arts, like swimming, also made heroes of their
champions, but heroes around whom hung a whiff of something suspiciously self-serving. Swimmers weren't social heroes, like the athletes
at Flinders, because swimmers competed as individuals against individuals, setting themselves ordeals—crossing waters at fiercely low
temperatures, holding their breath over longer and longer distances—
whereas at Flinders, teams pitted themselves against teams and the
heroic gesture was made on behalf of others, as well as bringing glory
on oneself. The game mirrored the nation's ideals, its athletes were
patriots. There was a move to appoint the most proven players, like
Everard, to the second chamber to sit behind the bishops and give
that upper house the benefit of the patient wisdom they had learned
on Doggett's Fields and other stockades all over the empire where the
game was played. It was still a possibility: the suggestion was popular
both in the palace (as might be expected) and in the street.

When Sir Anthony married Gillian, there was a certain public sad-
ness: his widowed solitude had filled his admirers with fantasies. Some
people were made edgy by Lady Everard's raw need to please; others,
like her schoolfriend the singer, were amused and comforted by Gillian's
bubbling, and such stalwarts as the new captain ribbed old Ant for his
giddy bride. People liked to stand by while she gave of herself; they'd
stay imperturbable or even faintly derisive, yet attracted all the same,
agnostics in the face of her belief, yet glad that someone could have
faith at all. Like the spectators at Flinders, Gillian could be overexcited,
and though someone might make a gesture to calm her, her agitation
was at the same time due tribute, and to some extent expected. A true
hero could not show any desire for acclamation, but acclamation was
still the measure of his exploits. His stature was dependent upon it.

Followers of the game had a name for the quality they most acclaimed
in a hero—they called it "sangay," and Anthony Everard was credited
with possessing it as fully as any human being can have sangay.

The Princess was settled in a high-backed Welsh armchair by the
heaped coal fire; Anthony drew up a cushioned stool beside her.

"Lady Everard was telling me, Anthony"—the composer, an eager
guest, sought to interest the Princess—"how your grandfather once
saw Admiral Nelson—my goodness!"

"Yes, he was born before Trafalgar—remarkable." Ant laughed. "He played with the great man's dog, we are led to believe, while Himself was busy getting married."

The composer broke off a piece of angel cake and ate it carefully with plump mitteny hands, to avoid making crumbs.

"So he would have been born not in the last century, but the one before, if you please!" He batted his eyelids.

"He was a young lad at the time. We're long-lived, we Everards, and we marry late, and have our offspring late too."

Anthony did not add that the women were not so fortunate: the family tombs in the graveyard of Saint Blaise Figtree on the big island had often been reopened to bury a husband, usually some good while after his wife or wives had been interred. Like his own Estelle Desjours, his mother had died long before her husband, of an abcess of the breast, in the way women did.

"My father was sixty when I was born—in 1897, as you know, I made a half century last year—" (There was a round of soft, knowing laughter.) "And his father before him was even older when he became a father—this was the time of honest cannonballs, swords, and pistols—before airplanes and doodlebugs and blitzkrieg. Oh, Nelson was passing through Enfant-Béate—my old home, as you know—fighting the French, I dare say, and he stopped and carried off a local beauty, married her then and there. My grandfather played with the dog—it was a terrier of some kind—under a cotton-silk tree in the Governor's garden, waiting for the happy pair to come out. Splendid natural confetti, don't you know."

Gillian joined them and put in, "The Governor was his uncle! Ant'll never say it, but his family ran the place. Come on, Ant, old bean, don't be bashful. Own up!"

There was a pause, while the reverie of colonial sunniness passed over them and Serafine in black uniform with white bib filled their glasses from the bottle she carried on a silver tray, and came back to pour for the tea drinkers.

"Quite something, to see you two together, and realize that you, Ma'am, knew . . ."

"Tstt," said the Princess. "I may be old, but I've had enough of auld lang syne, I can tell you." She had been furious that the medical corps had refused to let her fly casualties in this recent war. She smiled now, like a small animal baring its teeth, and Miranda, watching and listening from a corner of the sitting room, by the sleeping baby in her pram, took her expression as a grimace.

So much contradiction can twist a smile, she was to learn in the confusion of her growing up. A hand wave can mean hello and good-bye, laughter can sympathize or mock alike; when someone lays a hand squeezingly on another's arm, it doesn't always reassure—it some-times coerces. A child will wail when an adult smiles at her, showing teeth in friendship; or, as unpredictably, squirm with pleasure when another growls and snaps his jaws as if to eat her up. The signals are treacherous, saboteurs have turned them back to front; the signs of affection can often betray.

When she could not understand what older people were saying, she scanned their faces and then she would see them as a deaf person sees, their contractions and spasms, the caressing hand contradicted by the screwed-up face, the frank smile canceled by the shadow in the eyes. Miranda sensed then how unhappy the Princess was, for though she had passed the age when people become proud to be old, she did not enjoy attention being drawn to it in front of Ant Everard. She still exchanged billets-doux with him, often barbed in tone to disguise her hunger for his attentions. ("You are becoming dull, my dear, with contentment. Marriage suits no one. When we next meet, please have something of consequence to relate. I shan't receive you unless you guarantee to make me laugh at least twice.")

"Have you had any cake, darling?" Gillian asked her husband. He was a light eater, and had to be coaxed. In the flat, cups still full of tea or coffee, grown quite cold, lay abandoned by him with their uneaten biscuits in the saucer. "He lives on air," Gillian would exclaim, chiding, but proud.

The Princess Alicia dropped cake crumbs into her mouth as if into a beak. Now that she had taken off her fur, her tiny body could be seen sheathed in a ruched lilac dress with clinging sleeves cut long over her sticklike wrists; with her veil caught up on top of her hat now, she looked like a small crested bird, a kind of tropical finch, a fancied species that sometimes comes caged, but can be seen more often stuffed and perched on a jeweled tree.

The quality of Anthony Everard's attentiveness was never rude, like the staring that Serafine admonished Miranda to stop and stop im-mediately. But it was intense, and it conveyed strong admiration to the recipient, so the Princess did not flinch as she opened her mouth and saw him looking at her. With his light and supple build, he seemed to adapt himself to a companion as a fruit tree grows to a southern wall in a garden. Nobody feared that he might cling too hard: his independence was well-known, and the aloofness that remained at the deep center of his easy and obliging manner continued to inspire both trust in his integrity and desire to enter into greater, hard-won familiarity.

Anthony Everard is still a household name, in certain circles where Flinders is remembered in all its details and its annals are treasured. He had been one of the great players in the twenties and early thirties, and since his retirement from Doggett's itself, had become Flinders's chief ambassador and strategist, as well as its chronicler, in numerous articles in such volumes as *Playing the Game*, and in nearly a dozen books (*Flinders For Ever; On Doggett's Fields Again; How We Played; Gratia et Celeritas!*). He dictated them to disciples, from memory, without notes or reference to earlier records, never needing to change a word.

The Princess Alicia liked to rib him to show their intimacy and her sway: "You'd like to know what I think of Flinders? It's the one reason I was glad to be born a woman, that I never had to learn the rules." Anthony Everard could communicate complicity even with opponents, and begin the process of disarming them. "Rules are for men to make; women to break," he sallied back, and she smiled. The game is a form of pitch and toss, bat and ball, like others in which nations measure themselves against an adversary and in doing so establish their identity and status; in some ways, it resembles baseball, and cricket, in others scenes of civic struggle like the savage horse races of Italian hill towns. The defending striker in the "target" position on the creek, in the center of the game's playing area—the Stockade—flails at the projectiles that come whirling past him, thick and fast, lobbed by three marksmen at the other end of the creek while men of his side run to points marked along the Chase around the perimeter of the Stockade, gaining possession of areas with special designations. A combination of these gains creates the score. This basic structure contains a twist, however, that makes Flinders distinctive—superior—to other games of its kind played all over the world. Winning, for instance, does not necessarily involve an outright struggle until the opposing players are chased out—eliminated—or retired with wounds. The model for Flinders isn't a series of duels to the death—*à outrance*—but a sequence of finesses; judgment and stealth and nerve rather than feats of rude strength are required from a player.

Anthony Everard's particular skill was prediction; his *sangay* tuned him so perfectly he could calculate the outcome as if it were a mere column of figures, not a complex sequence of unknowable factors. The Game moves through a series of phases called Houses; access to the next House depends on reaching an exact combination of figures scored by a certain number of players for a certain number of balls thrown and positions gained. These patterns seem bristling with complication to outsiders, and even among seasoned players can lead to protracted and bitter discussion; but there is a book of tables and precedents to which disputants must refer. A good memory is part of a hero's *sangay*, as spectators do not appreciate long intervals of no play while a string of figures is verified. A captain must decide beforehand which House his team is aiming to enter and possess, for, as in some gambling games, there are high claims or bids as well as low ones, but the latter carry far less glory, and earn smaller scores, though they too can lead to victory. The Houses have different names, which recall places in the islands of Enfant-Béate, for it was there that the Game was first established as the Empire's sport: Grand-Thom' and Petit-Thom', Figtree and Mangrove, Creek and Jamieston, Sloop's Bight, Rebecca, Belmont.

Some of these once named great plantations, where sugar and tobacco, spices and dyes grew, as in the Everards' own lands at Belmont; others recalled events in the islands' history. Sloop's Bight, for instance, was the name of the bay on Grand-Thom' where a historic raid took place in 1620, when a British man-o'-war, the *Rebecca*, riding at anchor there, came under a daring nighttime assault from the natives. The uprising was summarily crushed, so inaugurating the prosperity of the island. That decisive engagement took place in the early years of the archipelago's settlement, just before the first Everard knight, Sir Kit, was appointed Governor by England's king.

Under Anthony Everard's captaincy, the national team had once gained, in 1923, a doubled Sloop's Bight in a single afternoon against the reigning champions, and Anthony had taken the gamble as captain, and then, standing in the Target, had scored the necessary hits in less than an hour—an achievement unique and unforgotten in the fervently chronicled history of the game.

At Flinders, a captain who wins consistently by making up the easier patterns and obtaining entry to the lesser Houses will not be loved by the crowd or by his players. Ant Everard had been a hard hitter (a straight stick) as well as a deadly pitcher in his time, who could sling

a ball high over the Chase and bring it skimming on steel wings into
the most undefended portion of the target area. But he was also quick
at choosing that particular game's goals, and aiming high. When the
flag was raised, proclaiming the House his side aimed to occupy, a
sigh of pleasure frequently rose in the crowd in the Stockade; they
would reach for their own versions of the flag, or the hawkers in the
grounds would start selling them to supporters. These flags were made
of silks that took the slightest breeze, lifting harmoniously in heraldic
colors, barred and quartered, checkered and crossed. (The bid for
Sloop's Bight featured a ship on a field azure with a sea monster *couchant*,
barred *or*.)

"There's poker play as well as fair play in the game," Ant Everard
would say, and he was observant of all numbers that occurred in his
life, knowing each one to have its own properties and function in
relation to others. He enjoyed the game's absorption of the history of
the islands; he liked to recall that Figtree had been the seat of the
Ingledew family, the Everards' principal rivals for authority in Enfant-
Béate. "That was in our heyday—when the islands didn't pay much
heed to the mother country's imperial edicts. They went their own
way, commanding fortunes! Oh, the reigning planter families in those
days used to shoe their horses with silver! Smashed crystalware, don't
you know, imported for the purpose from Ireland, in honor of the
king's birthday! Like the old potlatch chieftains I met on tour in Canada
one time—didn't spare the wastefulness a thought—pure extravagance
for the sake of it—can you beat it?"

On another occasion, he'd wonder at the planters' unruliness as well,
for he was a mild man, and orderly. "Their obedience to any outside
authority existed merely on paper. To the powers-that-be back home,
they showed a mind of their own, I can tell you. Westminster could
get into quite a lather about the islands—in the latter part of the wars
with Napoleon, they resumed friendly exchanges with the French, of
all people—the French! Who have never played Flinders, of course,
for the simple reason they haven't a chance of grasping the spirit of
the Game, not an earthly. Really. That's why the islands have these
Frog names, like Enfant-Béate, because on and off, they—we, I have
to admit—shared control . . . It's a long story . . . " He'd pause, apol-
ogetically, then resume the tale. "And when it came to slavery—a
shameful episode, of course—the islands fought long and hard against
abolition. They put up a ferocious resistance. Even a process called

'amelioration' got their blood up. It was some theory that slavery should continue, but the slaves be better treated. They were quick to heat—hotspurs one and all. Lord, how they petitioned Westminster for their own interests in the matter! For their trade to flourish, they needed men, they insisted—and cheaply."

In the drawing room at Severn Court, there was a portrait of the first Kit Everard, who went to Enfant-Béate before the French gave it that name, and claimed it on behalf of his nation and his King, calling it Everhope. Anthony Everard has told the story in between accounts of splendid play at Flinders in one of his books: how his ancestor was rewarded, after his long struggles planting and settling in those parts, with a charter granting him sole governorship of the big island, known to the natives as Liamuiga, as well as its smaller sister, Oualie, to the east, how he was dubbed a knight at the palace by the king, just two years before the same king had his head cut off; how, under the Protector, Sir Christopher "Kit" Everard was stripped of his rank and title—and authority over the islands—as a penalty for his loyalty to the dead monarch; so he was forced to give them up to the French and they renamed them after the latest craze at court in Versailles, the cult of the Christ Child. And this was the name which stuck, Enfant-Béate. How Sir Kit came to an agreement with the French and enjoyed his estates once more under his old enemy, Admiral Hypérion D'Estouteville. "Cargo ships brought him and his lady and their offspring stockings from Lyons, salted herrings from Amsterdam and lavender toothpaste from Grasse—there were no luxuries the first planters did without . . . " Whitehall later turned a blind eye to Sir Kit Everard's accommodations in the interval between royal reigns, and he was reinstated to full honors.

Miranda liked the first Kit Everard in his picture, plunged into the sea naked to the waist, with a pearly tint to his hairless skin, and one hand raised to haul, like Gulliver and the Lilliputian fleet, a galleon with puffed sails; while the other reached to grasp a volcano-tipped island with sea creatures cresting the shallows, and figures in feathered skirts and headdresses digging and planting the land beyond the sandy shore. The waves were crisp and scalloped, and one of the animals had a curly horn for a nose; in one corner, on the escutcheon of the island's coat of arms, there appeared a painted rose-pink beach, where an Indian brave, also in a feather skirt, and armed with a bow and arrow, was sitting astride another sea creature of a similarly fantastic species.

The painting was a copy, which didn't spoil it for Miranda at all. The original was lost, though some thought it might be with a younger branch of the family in America.

"Light-fingered rascals," her grandfather once commented to her. "We'll get it back from them one day, and make a present of it to the nation."

5

WHEN SERAFINE RETURNED to the kitchen with the empty cake tazza, Miranda followed; she'd had enough of watching and listening to the guests, so she settled herself instead on a stool in the kitchen by the chute, where now and then the sound of another family's rubbish came tumbling down on its flight to the basement and the big bin below—wet sounds of vegetable peelings and fumes of must or mold, dry clatterings of boxes, shufflings of papers. Serafine had decorated the entrance to the chute with labels from jars of pickles and preserves and tins of rice and beans and vegetables; she showed the children, first Miranda, then Xanthe, later on, how to soak them off in lukewarm water if they were stuck down with glue, and then pat them dry on a tea towel.

In the park, Miranda copied the boy chasing the bird with a handful of salt who'd been cut out from the round box kept on the shelf by the gas cooker, and tried to catch the pigeons who idled about, waggling and flat-footed, but they got away from her anyway with a lazy flap of their wings just as she was almost on top of them. There was a little black Sambo from the jam that was her grandfather's favorite (he could be persuaded to spread a little on a small triangle of toast at breakfast) whom Serafine had pasted up repeating under her breath, "Golliwog, golliwog." What did it mean? Miranda wondered. Was

Feeny a golliwog? Or couldn't a woman be one? She wasn't round-faced and red-lipped and she never stood with her legs apart like him, but she was a wog, for Miranda had heard her grandfather say that she must never be called this, and his tone was so serious that Miranda understood there must be some dangerous truth in it.

Serafine hadn't just stuck down the cuttings side by side but arranged them in the shape of a tree bearing bright patches of colors and shapes like fruits and flowers, branching over the dark green hatch of the chute. "My struggle against the darkness down below," she'd say, laughing. "My tree of life. What goes down must come up. One way or the other, Miranda, no thing on this earth ever do die. Nor goes to waste, neither."

Serafine quickly put down the empty plates and turned back to the corridor. "I'm fetching the child in here, she's about due to wake up now." She did things fast, but without hurrying, which itself was *sangay*, and had communicated itself to Anthony when he was a boy. Though only five years older than he, she had drifted into becoming his nursery maid at first, and then, after he married, she'd attended his first wife. When Ant Everard left Enfant-Béate immediately after Estelle's death, he took Serafine with him; Kit was thirteen, and they were going "home" to the Old Country, where Kit was going to school, unlike Ant himself, who was leaving Enfant-Béate for the first time in his life. So was Serafine, and they both suffered and, wordlessly, shared their suffering.

In the holidays, Ant Everard sometimes took them both along with him to a game, and set the boy down to watch from the pavilion, while Serafine remained outside to wait. In the informal photographs of the team which hung in the corridor in the flat at Severn Court, Miranda could pick out her father, a frowning schoolboy, hanging about on the team's fringes, not quite belonging, yet with nowhere else to go.

Serafine Killebree loved Anthony Everard, Kit's father, even more than she loved Kit, and could find nothing to reproach him with, not even her own long exile in the cold maze of the Old Country. Before Xanthe was born, she was often lent to Miranda for the night; when Kit and Astrid were going out, they'd bring their daughter round to the flat and leave her with Serafine, who'd put her to bed in the room next to hers and tell stories, staying with her, the clasp of her dry, worn hand giving Miranda comfort so she could let herself fall into sleep. Or sometimes, if she was in the mood, Serafine would sit the child on her knees and Miranda would loll against her so that she could feel her voice vibrate in her breast, like a cat purring, as she talked.

For Serafine could still conjure Enfant-Béate when she wanted, even for those who had never been there, like Miranda.

"You carry this, now, Miranda, you see if you can!" Serafine gave the child a clean ashtray to convey to the drawing room to replace the filled ones. "Find your pappy and give it him. Nicely, now."

Gillian was giving her husband a peep at a blue velveteen box: "Isn't that sweet?" she cried.

"Delightful," he assented, touching the brooch inside with two fingers as if blessing it, and casting a look of acknowledgment at the giver, his successor in the captaincy.

"Will it do?" he answered. "Deuced difficult to know what to present a baby girl." It was a gold Flinders stick, with a pearl ball.

Miranda was tickling Xanthe on the tummy and making fan shapes with her hands for her to follow with her boss-eyed infant look as she sucked on her bottle, when Gillian flapped into the kitchen, whooping, "There she is, my pretty lambkin, I couldn't think what had happened to her!" She snatched up her baby from Serafine's arms and held her in mid-air, aghast. "What's happened to her robe? Where is it?"

"The baby was feeding, Miss Gillian," Serafine said, wiping Xanthe's bewildered face gently in an effort to prevent her howling at the abrupt disappearance of her feed. "Here, let her have her bottle, or she'll start up squawking." She shook her head.

Gillian held out her child like a picture she was considering whether to buy, and when the baby began to turn her head and gnaw her fist and cry, begged her, "Don't start that, please don't." She rocked her, as she'd seen nurses do, but had no heart for the task, with so many guests waiting for entertainment, and handed her back to Serafine, saying, "Change her back. I want her in her robe. I want to show her to the guests. Before everyone leaves. The Princess is about to go. I want her to see Baby properly to say good-bye."

"I can put it on again, sure. I just don't like it to spoil; the child throws up this bottle feed."

Miranda, watching, chanted to herself, "I want never gets, I want never gets."

Gillian breathed in and met Serafine's reproach with an attempt at flippancy: "I wish you could have had her instead of me, and fed her, it was such a pain! But she's my baby, worse luck. I know you know best, you're an absolute treasure, but I do get vexed, Feeny old thing, when you go your own way with Baby without asking me."

"I don't need to ask you, Miss Gillian, ma'am," Serafine answered slowly, sliding the teat across the baby's cheek until her howling mouth sought it and closed to suck with desperate strength. "I've cared for more than you've ever seen." Serafine looked up now the baby was quiet, and blazed, "Since when is the blind man going to teach the sighted what they see?"

Gillian drew her breath in so sharply, Miranda thought something had hit her; her small round face reddened, then split, and she began to cry—dry, high sobs rather like her own baby's when Xanthe had wind after feeding, as she took in the comfortable alliance of the black maidservant and the child and burst from the room.

"Mummy was crying too," said Miranda in a small voice from the corner by the stove where she'd shrunk back from the quarrel. "When we were leaving to come here. Everyone's upset today." She paused, then imitated grown-ups she'd heard use a phrase she liked, though she didn't understand it. "I suppose you could say we're all at sixes and sevens." She imagined her mother at the table, slumped, like a figure six she had learned to draw, and Auntie Gillian, precipitating herself forward out of the kitchen, like a seven. "All at sixes and sevens," she repeated.

"I'm not sorry I made that one cry, no." Serafine put Xanthe against her shoulder and stood up, rubbing the baby's back with smooth, long strokes to help her digest.

Serafine looked anxious just the same.

Nobody ever fought over Miranda as they did from the start over Xanthe, Miranda was to realize, when she remembered the day of the baby's christening. Her own parents were wrapped up in each other; however savage and continual their fighting, they were never very interested in anyone else. When Miranda came into the room, they could go right on talking or kissing, or—unless she created one of her special diversions on purpose—yelling at each other; but where Xanthe went, there followed the gaze of all who surrounded her. She was the conduit through which Anthony and Gillian's love flowed, the proud proof of their union, rather than an adventitious by-product, for which no proper place or use had yet been found. Was Miranda indulging herself in self-pity when she perceived her parents' relation to herself in such a loveless light? For Miranda needed to portray the contrast between herself and Xanthe, as between a tin penny whistle and a precious, golden-haired doll in the same family toy trunk; it gave her pleasure to be lesser, to love and serve and admire Xanthe, while they were growing up, and afterward.

The tussles were not of Xanthe's own making; when she was a baby, it was hardly her fault that Astrid loathed the idea of her very existence, or that Serafine doted. Later, perhaps, it was another matter; later, Xanthe may have been responsible for her seductions.

Gillian had waited for a moment in the bathroom for her flushed face to fade a little before she returned to the drawing room with her lips determinedly turned up in imitation of a smile, but grief still in her eyes. Nobody would notice, she hoped, and she was right, though she did not realize the reason, that not even Ant her husband would realize her distress because she had so successfully imprinted herself in the minds of all as an unstoppable force of good cheer, too goose-brained to feel anything stir at any depths. But Gillian suffered: somehow she could not gain full possession of her child. As a connection with Anthony and his love, the baby made sense to her, but in herself alone, Xanthe eluded her mother. Or rather, the mother love Gillian had expected to well up, as everyone said it would, to engulf her and guide her, sprang only weakly. Her principal feeling when she was near Xanthe was fear. The baby's crying baffled her; from the moment she had seen the green-and-black wormlike stool that had been formed in the womb and been born with her, Gillian found her physical processes repulsive, her nappies made her gag. So Serafine had taken over changing the baby. Then Gillian's nipples became so sore, and the right one cracked across the top and burned with pain, and Anthony, without reminding her overtly of his mother's death from puerperal fever (or of other Everard women's deaths) encouraged her to bottle-feed.

"It's much the more modern way," he said consolingly.

Gillian used a paregoric Serafine had brewed for her from peppermint and ordinary tea leaves and the crack healed quickly and she never ran a fever, but by then she had very little milk and Xanthe was still waking four times a night and crying lustily for food. So Ant was pleased when she agreed to stop trying to nurse, and Gillian glad to sleep through while Serafine prepared the night feeds. Yet she was wretched that she could not display her child as trophy when she wanted to and gather the hosannahs, as she dandled and hushed her all by herself, naturally, and she at least knew English nursery rhymes; she knew "Hush-a-bye Baby" and "Lavender's blue, dilly dilly, Lavender's green" better than that ignorant woman from those benighted islands whom her husband insisted on indulging almost as if she were one of the family.

Gillian's sense of failure helped toward the spoiling of Xanthe later; Miranda was to comfort herself with the thought that a mother who was always compensating for her lack of commitment was much more dangerous than a mother like Astrid who never fussed or noticed that she didn't care. Gillian was forever making up to Xanthe the maternal inadequacy she had discovered in herself, to her shame, from the time her baby was born, and Serafine's comfortable and assured expertise only sharpened her anxieties. Besides, she wished that the woman would call her "your Ladyship," as she should do, or "my Lady," or at least "Lady Everard," instead of that "Miss Gillian," which sounded so coarse and was anyway so incorrect, almost insulting. They really should get a proper English nanny. It was too bad of Anthony to land her with that old witch.

Thinking such thoughts brightened her, and she stepped in to the drawing room with refreshed spirits.

"There you are, darling girl!" her husband called out to her. "We were wondering where you had got to."

"I was in with Baby—just putting her down, you know how it is."

Gillian confided in Kit to one side, as Miranda, joining them to watch the outcome, lingered in the room as well, and began to glow with pleasure when she overheard: "She could go to you, couldn't she? Once I'd found a nice English girl?"

"If Pa would . . . yes, of course, we'd like to have her." He didn't complete his thought, because it seemed unmannerly to remind Gillian that she'd been . . . well, Serafine had been so young when she replaced Ant's dead mother that she hadn't stood in loco parentis, exactly, but—what would be the word?—she'd been a kind of first wife, an island wife, a sort of concubine. Though of course nobody knew what exactly, if anything, had taken place between them; no one had any right to inquire.

"Oooh, do, that'd be such a relief. Honestly, she's a . . . savage, you know." Gillian gave a high laugh. "Not that I'm prejudiced. But I never know what she's getting up to, honestly!"

Kit smiled and raised an eyebrow, but did not gainsay his stepmother.

Inside Miranda as she listened, the warmth grew stronger, she hugged herself with glee; she'd have Feeny to herself, her voice, her words, her treats, her lap, her soft hair, her warm face, her hard dry palms, her toasty smell.

"Something's upset Gillian," Kit began, when he had managed to draw his father aside. "It's about Serafine."

"Too much excitement. Gillian's highly strung, you know." He exchanged a glance with the Princess, who had returned and was discussing the designs of war memorials. "She'll get used to Serafine. And besides, who would cope with Xanthe?"—he hit the name with a breathing wonder—"if Serafine goes?" He shook his head. "She's experienced, she's absolutely devoted to the family, she's indispensable."

Curious, thought Kit, how the moment before he had been certain the matter was settled, but a few words of his father's had dismissed all their wishes. Miranda, at her father's knee, bit her lip and hung on to his sleeve. Her grandfather noticed her, and, pulling out a handful of change from his pocket, picked out a sixpence and held it before her eyes between finger and thumb.

"Here's a silver sixpence for you, my dear. Did you like the christening? Splendid occasion, wasn't it?" He straightened and caught his son's gaze on him, and again pushed his hand into his pocket and this time found a sovereign and made to give it to him. Kit shrank back in dismay, and his father then changed the piece to a crown and pressed it on him.

"Go on, dear boy, I know how you enjoy a flutter." He eyed the remaining coins in his hand as Kit flinched from the offered money, then slowly returned it to the handful and put it back in his pocket. "Gillian will come round to Serafine, you'll see."

"Astrid would be glad of the help," Kit tried again, without much fire. He was so easily extinguished by his father's patronage.

"Oh, she can come to you and help, by all means."

The widow was confiding to the Princess, "They've moved poor Alan not just once, not just twice, but three times." She shook her head, she was near tears. "They say 'Rest in Peace,' then they come back and dig him up again. Why can't they let him alone?"

"Oh, my dear," said the Princess. "How hard on you. Why do they do it?"

"They want to create proper war cemeteries, they want to gather everyone together. The Burma Campaign here, North Africa there.

They dig them up, they dig them up, until there's almost nothing left. 'Only the leg bones, madam, only the leg bones.' That's what the officer told me, do you know, when I asked."

The Princess patted her hand. "It's too bad." She was making a move to depart, and after her, the other guests could do so too.

Her companion went on, "And the skull, too. They said they would send the skull. Like a pirate's flag, that's how my poor Alan's ending up."

"I thought so. A real pea souper coming down." Sir Anthony had stepped over to the window and lifted the curtain, and was looking out at the premature dark. "And the cold'll bite tonight, I expect." After over a decade in England, he was still unaccustomed to the weather. "It's best we call it a day." He began escorting the Princess to the door, where the lady-in-waiting stood with her fur.

"My gift will be delivered to you, my dear, tomorrow," she was telling Gillian. "Meanwhile, as I was saying to young Mr. Everard earlier, I wish the baby a good nose." Gillian couldn't help twitching, and the Princess smiled to reassure her. "Good, hard common sense, that's what a girl needs, these days."

She was in her coat and the door was about to be opened for her by Maud when the door bell rang, just above their heads, in the corner of the corridor ceiling where it was suspended. Like all unexpected rings, it struck unease into the company.

"Who could that be, at this time?" Gillian asked. Then her glance caught Kit's expression as he came through to the corridor from the drawing room.

Maud opened, and Astrid lurched in and cried out, "Thank God, at last! I thought I was going to expire out there, it's so bitter cold, and hellish night!" She was shaking out one of Kit's black hats over the carpet. It had not kept her hair dry, however, for she had not bothered to twist it up into the crown, and wet strands hung on her shoulders like kelp and dripped. She dropped the hat in Maud's hand and twisted her head to bunch her hair and wrung it.

"I'm sopping!" she cried out again. "And it's not even raining outside. It's just fog, fog like outer darkness. Like the ocean bottom. Like . . . " She flung her hair back onto her shoulders and patted it with a self-caressing movement of her fingers, pale between the knuckles with the cold; damp rose from her and her clothes, so that the company hung back from her and her mention of the ocean brought to mind a dark hybrid that lives on water, half mermaid, half stormy petrel, like the woman-faced feathered sirens of myth who blow about on the wind and plummet down to call the sailors to come their way.

She began unbuttoning her coat, and when she saw Gillian coming toward her, hands held out to greet her, she ducked her embrace and cried out, frantic, "I'm so late, I'm not here for the party, I've come for Kit. Kit, Kit! Darling! There you are!" Kit came forward, raised his hands on either side, and shook his head at her.

"My dear, it's a pleasure," Anthony intercepted his son, afraid of an exchange and, holding Astrid by the arm, propelled her forward. "We're all here, and we're very glad you've managed to come. Here, let me take your coat. And have a cup of tea. Nothing like tea on a cold night."

Even when her father-in-law courteously lifted her coat by the wet collar, Astrid did not repent her cursing. All the way in the tube she had cursed the Everards.

"I hate the aplomb of Sir Anthony," she'd repeated to herself, as she jolted through the tunnels. "May he lose everything he loves.

"I hate the fribbling prettiness of Gillian; may she find doors closed against her when she most wants them open.

"I hate Kit's vague and hopeless loyalty; I hate his forgivingness. May he burn and burn—for love and lust and fury at me. Hah!

"He won't look after himself, he won't look after us. He'll let them walk all over us, take everything that should be his.

"And that baby, that bloody baby. Xanthe. Oh yes, such a grand name, she'll get it all, what there is to get, and that's not saying much."

She had a glimpse in her mind's eye of a volcano and a sweep of beach, palm trees bending under the trade winds. But you never knew. Whatever there was should be Kit's by right. But now, with a new baby?

So she had cursed the baby with the most bitter curse she could dream up. It was a simple one, and she was confident that it wouldn't need much priming to work. It was easily visited on the golden girls, she knew. That Xanthe would never find a way to enjoy what she was given, that she would never believe that she was loved, that she would never trust her friends but always turn on them; that nothing, not all the abundance and heap of riches, friends, loves and gifts of body and mind, of clothes, would ever be enough.

Astrid had made up the sequence of imprecations as carefully as an inventory and had gone over them in her mind, checking each one was firmly uttered and could be performed; then she'd chuckled to herself and crossed her legs and settled to enjoy her advent at the Everards'.

If the Princess hadn't laughed when she saw Astrid in nothing but her underwear, Gillian would have fallen in a fit. It was a black slip she had on, a black silk petticoat, cut in a double inverted V over her breasts and on the bias for the skirt so that it clung to her hips and thighs, the kind of black thing a French whore would wear, satiny on her body and lacy round the edges, with bits of ribbon tied here and there.

Miranda came into the hall beside her father and saw him rush at her mother and grab the coat she had taken off and wrap her up in it again. "It's my best outfit—it's from Madame Jeanne—it's beautiful. You gave it me. After you had a win at Le Touquet that time." He was pushing her along the corridor towards the kitchen, and she was leaning on him, impeding him but nevertheless complying, as she went on babbling, "You don't have to shove me, I'm coming. But I'm all wet, this coat's on the wrong way, ugh, can't you see I don't want it on. I look terrific, it makes a gorgeous dress. You gave it to me, darling, you like it, you know you do."

He wasn't to slap her, he mustn't slap her; Miranda, clutching at them from behind, was hoping they would remember there were other people present to see them and they must behave, and then Kit threw open the door to the room that had been his old childhood den and tossed his wife onto the bed, all legs and arms flailing as she still struggled to get free of the coat; he was shouting for Serafine to come. She did, and Kit pushed Astrid down by the shoulders and growled in her face. Miranda didn't know if he was going to bite her, then suddenly he stood and called again for Serafine, who was there, and made him leave, and sat on the bed beside Astrid, who was in a fit of giggles, gasping through them, "Oh, oh, oh, the look on Gillian's face; I'll die happy now."

But the Princess had laughed, with genuine laughter, and given Gillian a lilac-scented peck on her cheek, as Gillian dipped a curtsy; then she'd held out a hand to Anthony and said, as she surveyed the corridor and Astrid kicking in Kit's grasp, "Congratulations, my dear, on your new family."

"I'll come down with you," said Anthony, escorting her to the lift shaft and ringing for the porter.

"I can manage the stairs, I'm not that decrepit."

He held her gently by the elbow as they went down.

The Princess went on, "Your little granddaughter suggested golden curls—you know, even at her age, she overestimates the importance of appearance. But I do think Xanthe—it is a pretty name, well chosen, dear boy—will need a hard head." They reached the hall, and the man appeared and made to hold steady the revolving door of the block, but the Princess paused, and looked up at her old flame and stood close to him. "Mind, there's so much anger here. You must see that. You're a charmer, you always were, and charmers create trouble. I should know." Her eyes twinkled at him. "We know, don't we, all about that. No, I think, in the tangles and barbs of family rivalries and jealousies and hatreds—don't deny it, don't play the ostrich, no one, not even you, can carry off having lots of wives and lots of family without paying the price!"

"You're unjust, Alicia," he murmured. "I was years without a wife— years and years."

She put her head to one side, skeptical, but did not take up his theme, preferring to stick to her vision of the future. "I think I'll wish a special, vintage-label common sense on your daughter. She'll be needing it, I'm sure—a certain distance, a kind of imperviousness. No one would want to be like that poor Astrid—so out of control. So storm-tossed, poor creature. You can't be harmed if you don't feel much. It's having a heart that allows the hurt. I would wish Xanthe the heartlessness of a statue, utter heartlessness. Like Baldur the Beautiful, let her repel all comers! Sticks and stones, words and deeds, let nothing touch her! We'll have her dipped in the Styx, not forgetting to put her heel in too.

"That's the best I can do for her. And now, dear boy, good night."

6

THE REVOLVING DOOR of the mansion block yielded with a
shallow sigh and exhaled the warm stewed foist of the hall to
meet defeat at last in the raw cold of a November fog. Kit
Everard edged forward, holding on to his daughter with one hand,
his other arm around his wife, who half-slumped against him, half-
struggled to be free of his hold. They couldn't see farther than the
space into which they fumbled forward, while behind, the fog welled
up to fill in the gap immediately. Miranda looked down at her feet,
emerging below the sallow cloud that hung down to her knees. " 'And
keep in the squares,' " she repeated, and skipped. " 'So the masses of
bears"—(all thick and woolly and brownish-yellow, just like the fog)
—"Would go back to their lairs . . . ' " But her father didn't sing out
with her, as he usually did, "It's ever so 'portant how you walk." Instead
he gave her hand a squeeze, so that she sensed how he was worried.

The street lamps hung above, smudged puffs with no stem for support, and the traffic lights, changing for phantom vehicles, seemed
also to float. He was tugging at his daughter, and Astrid, moaning
with the seeping cold, now and then stumbled against his longer stride,
so that Miranda missed a square, and the masses of bears, who wait
at the corners all ready to eat the sillies who tread on the lines in the
street, pounced; the thick air clutched at the inside of her nose, hard

and sharp, more like a knife than steam. When she opened her mouth, it burned and she gasped. Her father unwound his scarf and wrapped it round her face, and coaxed her, "Breathe through it, it won't hurt then." He was trying to clear his throat behind the turned-up collar of his coat.

"It's not far to the tube," he was saying. "We'll soon be home."

Her mother still said nothing. She was clutching Kit's arm with both hands, pitching into him as if there were no strength in her legs, and coughing every now and then into his chest. The fog caught in his lungs too, and seemed to pummel him, as he dragged them through the darkness, forcing the pace as if just ahead lay light and air again. The banner of the underground's blue-and-white sign on the canopy of the arcade grew a little brighter. The occasional car loomed, like a clumsy beast with weeping yellow eyes, then veered off hooting, moving slowly.

Kit shook Astrid loose and picked Miranda up. His wife gave a little cry and plucked at his sleeve. He held his daughter as if she were still a baby, across his body. "They'll knock you down," he muttered, and stopped below the pulse of a crossing beacon to get his breath.

The way across from the mansion block to the station was only a short distance: two traffic islands, three zebra crossings. But in that fog, distance and time unwound like a felt mat pressed out long and slow and silent and featureless, and the blue glow of the canopy still seemed very far.

He set her down close to him and they stood on the pavement, the twin beacons of the third crossing winking before them. The lamps' silence had never struck Kit before, but now he wanted them to boom, like buoys at sea, as he hugged his wife and child to him.

The fog was thickening; Miranda could no longer see the lines or the squares in the pavement. It was a fog of soot and smoke, composed of the dust of tons of coal delivered, through manholes in the pavement, to every house in the city, tipped in sackfuls down the chutes into basement cellars, and burned up a thousand chimneys, clogging the city with deep black carbon fur. The fog scraped at her eyes so that she could feel their shape inside their sockets, and the rheum it squeezed out was drying her cold cheeks and making them sore. She was crying too and wanted to take her mother's hand and hear her voice; but Astrid's spirit was somewhere else, while her body made the motions of walking.

Kit had tied a handkerchief over his mouth and nose, as if they were playing bandits or Dick Turpin. In spite of her father's loan of his scarf, Miranda's face was getting chapped; and because her bare legs were now numbed all the way up (only grown women wore stockings), she could only hear them move when the inside edge of one knee chafed the other. She moaned as she stumbled, and her father realized, and bent down and took off his gloves to rub each limb between his hands; but with the return of feeling came the hard nips of the cold again.

They had reached the traffic island before the last crossing. She could only pick out the stripes by bending down to peer at her feet. Her father held her hand tightly, and thought, Planes passing through cloud bump about, obscurity isn't entirely insubstantial, like a ghost. You can't set a foot on a path of cirrus or climb a fleecy pile of cumulus as if it were a haystack, no, but fog exerts pressure, it chokes you and blinds you and baffles you. Then, when you put your hand out to it, nothing's there, only the wet and the cold.

He squeezed his daughter's hand in his, fighting the melancholy that threatened to swallow him with the fog. The thought then came to him that this was a kind of London storm, a choking, poisoned equivalent of a high wind rushing and flattening trees and dwellings in the islands where he was born, a tempest whipping up the sea into a frenzy of destruction and casting fish ashore to die in the branches of trees.

He was creeping forward now almost on all fours, he felt ridiculous, but the way back would be just as hard. Miranda lifted her head to look over her shoulder in the direction they had come. She couldn't understand why they didn't just retrace their steps, return to her grandpa's and Auntie Gillian's. She jerked on her father's arm and nodded over her shoulder to plead.

"We can't go back. Not now," he said. He was talking to himself. "It wouldn't be right. We're not expected back."

She tugged at him some more, she called out, "Mummy, you tell him."

Astrid gave a laugh, half a snort, half a snigger, and spoke for the first time since they had left the block of flats. "Miranda, we wouldn't be welcome, not for the time being. We're in disgrace. It's not far, anyway. We'll take the tube, five stops, one change, then three more, and we'll be home."

"I'm cold."

"I know, darling, I'm perishing. But it won't be long now."

"Can't we go back?"

"No," Kit snapped. Then, almost to himself, into the cotton mask over his face, "We'll never hear the end of it, if we go back begging now."

They reached the station. Fog wreathed the wrought-iron grille with its branching gilded letters announcing the lines that converged below; it filled the interior of the arcade too. A lady usually sat in the window of the cleaners on the corner, working at the machine that picked up runs in stockings, but she wasn't there; the light in the pet-shop window was out; fog swirled on the steps leading down to the ticket office and the District Line they wanted to take. A board propped against the booth was chalked with a message: "No trains running."

"Let me think a moment," her father said. His voice was tighter in his throat. "We can't be marooned. Not here, not in London."

"We're stuck," Miranda began to wail. Her mother rolled against the counter, and started to laugh and choke at the same time.

"Astrid, stop that." He put his arms around her and propped her up again. They turned back to climb the stairs to the arcade. Miranda was crying hard now with cold and fright; it seemed they were the only people adrift and the city bewitched.

Kit had hoped at the very least for shelter in Dino's sandwich bar; on one of the red leatherette diner booths of tubular steel worn shiny by customers' use, under the consoling escutcheons of Italian coastal cities of the south (where he'd enjoyed himself on leave at the end of the war in Europe), he could have cherished his family back to warmth and confidence again with a hot drink, some Horlicks with milk frothed in the new shiny monster machine from Italy Miranda loved to see hiss and steam.

He held his daughter by the hand as they stood for cover under the arcade, then picked her up again, to comfort her. He was still behaving as if Astrid weren't there, or only there as some sack of goods he had to shoulder and bear along with him. Exposure had soaked them to the bone, Kit could hear Miranda's teeth chattering, and feel her chin working with cold as she wept against his neck.

She no longer asked about going back to his father's house again. She accepted what grown-ups do as reasonable; she'd been read the story of Tom Thumb, and knew that some families breakfast on babies; she was only grateful that things weren't like that in her home.

Gradually as she grew up, Miranda began to understand how Kit could not turn in need to his father who thought him such a flop, his marriage such a disaster, could not face his well-mannered scorn: "What? Still here? You've been out there all this while?" Kit didn't know how to beard the giant he feared, how to put questions to him that might ease the tension between them, or perform deeds of valor that would tilt the balance of authority between them. And, of course, the more Astrid felt Kit's subservience and incapacity, the more she taunted both of them.

Miranda did not grasp then, only much later, that Kit could not risk flattering his father with the proof of his inadequacy. He was picturing Ant with Gillian and Xanthe on the big bed, with the feather quilt of paisley pattern lined with a peach-colored silk which made it slide to the floor at the sleeper's smallest shift in movement. (Miranda was to know it too, later, playing caravans with Xanthe, when they'd pitch it in their make-believe desert, slung across the furniture in the drawing room.) Kit had had a small one like it as a boy, and Serafine had sewn panels on each side to tuck in with the blankets and stop it falling off and waking him in the night. Kit could see his father on his knees, beside the bed, and Gillian, in a peignoir with swansdown at the neck and hem, lying beside their new baby, the pair of them tickling her, while his father clucked and gurgled, his eye playing over his young wife's throat, where the creamy vent of her gown opened. Their lot was harmony, his was strife.

Few people—and Kit least of all—considered Gillian beautiful, she was rather "that pretty little thing" that his father fondly eyed, no more. Yet Kit ached at the image of her in his mind's eye just the same, with hurt on his own account, and for his long-dead mother's sake.

But he had not felt his heart burst like this before, before the birth of Xanthe his new sister.

His mother died in Grand-Thom', the big island of Enfant-Béate, that same year he'd been brought "home" to be sent to school, three thousand miles away; in the engagement photograph which Ant Everard still kept in his dressing room, the young Estelle Desjours was wearing a small Leghorn hat trimmed with ribbon, and a white lace blouse with leg-of-mutton sleeves. Her small waist dipped steeply to a point, so she looked as if she could hardly turn to the side, let alone swim. But swim she did, every morning before breakfast off Belmont's southern shore, from a wild beach where freshwater lagoons lay behind sandbars, and a few heron fished among the water lilies. One day as usual she drove herself there in her mule cart, and disappeared.

When her father told Miranda about his mother's death, Estelle Desjours became mixed up with stories that she'd heard about mermen and mermaids and dolphins that could talk and other sea creatures, like the ones on the Everard coat of arms; Kit used to say she'd sat astride a dolphin and struck out too far. He showed Miranda the silver dressing-table set which Gillian had been given, and told her that his mother under the sea had a comb of polished oyster shell and a mirror of mother-of-pearl mounted on a coral branch. He did not tell her that in the churchyard on Grand-Thom', epitaphs announced the tragic early deaths of lauded wives and mothers. Sir Anthony Everard had rather departed from family custom when he left such an interval— five and a half years—between Estelle's death and his marriage to Gillian at the beginning of the war.

At school back "home" in England, after his mother's death, Kit was teased; his schoolmates nicknamed him "Nigger" Everard behind his back. To his face it might have been a kind of chaffing he could have accepted, with a shrug or a grin. But he knew his name only by hearsay, and could never claim it as something he didn't mind, or defend his mother from insinuations. Not that he wanted to deny she was a Creole. But it was hard to shout out against his fellow pupils, "And what of it, anyway, what's the matter with mixed blood?" The words he knew from the islands themselves he never would let on to them, for they could turn local gradations to their own ends: musty, métis, quadroon, octaroon. The slavers had used charts like stockbreeders and tabulated blood degrees to the thirty-second drop.

"I'm hungry." Miranda was twisting to get down. "When are we getting home?"

"So am I," her mother said. "And I didn't even have christening cake."

"Be quiet," her father said in a fierce tone. "I know what I'm doing. Trust me." For the first time Miranda was really scared. He peered into the grim deserted street, but there was nothing now, not even the occasional passing car to hail.

Then suddenly a rumble passed beneath their feet, and he began to whirl to find the direction of the sound. Then came the slap of a cable in a shaft, and a crash of metal, and Kit Everard ran, holding on to them both, and pulled them fast into the street, and there, in the broad-mouthed entrance to the lift from the tunnels of the other, deeper, line down below, the shadow of a guard materialized in the dimness. The interior of the lift he manned was aglow with light, though the fog had drifted in to fill it as well. Two passengers stepped out and hurried on, bent against the cold, collars up against their mouths; they took in the stranded family and shook their heads.

"No night for a body to be out-of-doors," said one.

"How did you come?" Kit called out. "Was there a train?"

"There was," said the second man.

The guard's hand was on the handle of the drum that controlled the lift's ascent and plunge, but when they reached close enough to see him clearly, Kit pulling his daughter by the arm; the guard was securing a padlock to the gates with a clank of metal on metal, his back to them.

"Was there a train down there?" Everard shouted.

"Last one tonight, sir." The guard did not turn round, he was rattling the gates to check they were secure. "There's fog all through the tunnels now."

"Why weren't you here? To take us down below?" Everard had let go his child and was shouting in the guard's face, gesticulating with his gloved hands. "We've been bloody well stranded here for hours. No one to help us. No staff, no tickets, no lifts. No one. I ask you, it's impossible! Why didn't you come up before and fetch us down? We could have caught that train."

"I didn't expect no train through tonight, sir." He was facing them now, a slight and middle-aged black man, skin dusty from his subterranean life out of the open air, with rounded eyes, the whites all disappeared in dismay at the vehemence of Kit Everard.

Abruptly, Everard seized the man by both arms and picked him off his feet and shook him hard, then pushed him from him with disgust.

"My child's cold and hungry. My wife here too, she's shivering with the cold. Her chest is weak, the fog's choking us to death like mustard gas, and you thought the last train had gone and left us here. Goddamn you for a fool." He seized him again by the coat. "Do you think we fought the war for this? What's your name? I'll take your name, you hear. I'll bloody well report you to your boss. I'll get you sacked, you mark my words, I know people, and they'll give you what for when they hear of this, your incompetence, you fool."

Miranda was so frightened now she forgot the cold, the fog, her hunger.

Her mother tugged at Kit's sleeve. "Darling, don't. Please. You're overwrought. It's hardly this man's fault. We'll be all right."

"I did my best, sir," said the guard. His bunch of keys was shaking in his hand. "What else to do? The fog's in all the tunnels. It's a miracle that train came through. Let me go."

"We'd be on it but for you. You fool. You big black fool."

There was a beat, as the guard's face changed from consternation to plain and hurt affront, and Everard, with the family madness on him, attacked again. Astrid covered her face and pulled Miranda away.

"You'll lose your job for this, I'm telling you. Your boss'll hear of this. I'll see to it, you've probably no business working here, by rights." And then, again, the yelling voice, "You bloody fool, you bloody big black fool."

The guard's mouth went slack, and his eyes turned to dark bruises of pain. Then the features tautened and he lifted his face and spoke quietly.

"I'm a Negro, sir. But British too. What happened to you's not my fault."

"You're from the islands, of course, now I see that!"

Kit Everard's mood changed all of a sudden, the foulness cleared, chased away by other memories, as Miranda learned could sometimes happen when the rage had taken possession of him. Unlike the fog that clung and curled in every crevice, and every pore, his fury would lift suddenly and blow away, leaving him only steaming faintly like springtime fields in the first sunshine after a heavy dew, heedless of the wound he'd struck in others with his words, his anger.

"I'm from the islands too, you know—my father . . . I only spoke in anger, you can see that." He gave his father's famous name and almost hugged the guard, and then whirled around and bent down to dab at Miranda, "Don't cry, little lady. It's nothing. Our friend here understands. I was angry for a moment. But all's well, we'll get home soon." He nodded hard at Astrid, and turned back to the man, who stood stiff, eyes averted from the Everards, and yet staying by, as if awaiting orders.

Their business together was not completed yet. Quarrels, Miranda would learn, can lead to sudden intimacy as well as feuds; as a child her father's anger filled her with a pure fear that she would never know again. The fog, the tempest, which stranded them in the tube station that night until the guard appeared from below, was only the first time of many that she could recall when her father placed them all in jeopardy. What her mother never understood, as she played and goaded, pushed him to extremes and then pulled him back, was how it damaged him as much as those he fought and shouted at; she did not want to understand. For her, love between men and women was always warfare. She was elated by a fight, and she could keep the temperature running high for longer than Kit; she even, in her bitter comic way, found funny their shipwreck that night in the fog.

"I see Sir Anthony Everard almost every day," the guard assented. "Comes to the station, buys a paper, reads it waiting for the train. A fine gentleman, sir. Quiet." He braved this reproach against the angry man who still held him fast by the arm, but amicably now, trying to establish goodwill.

"Yes, yes, not a sore bear like someone we know," Everard trumpeted. "Where were you born—not Enfant-Béate, like me? I left when I was still a boy. And came to school in England, the Old Country, what? You're a grand people. Handy, warm-hearted, good. I love Enfant-Béate—Grand-Thom' and Petit-Thom'. It was my home as well." He laid a hand again on the man's forearm, but slowly. "I spoke in panic just now. My family . . ."

He nodded in Miranda's direction and she felt shame hot on her cheeks, along with the salt and the fog and the cold.

"I understand, sir," replied the guard. His eyes were still scared and dark, but he shook out the bunch of keys and chose one from the ring. "I myself came over recently; in the *Windrush*—maybe you hear of it?—many of us, so many, leaving from home, recruited, again." He mentioned another island in the archipelago. Kit slapped his arm again, and sighed. The man went on, "I was in the army." He tapped his upper arm. "Batman—to Major Shore, sir. Now I work down here, I see service on the tube. You come with me, the three of you, together. This way. You stay in the warm until the fog lifts."

There was still something fearful that cramped his back as he led them to the side of the lift, where a door marked "London Transport Staff Only" stood between the entrance to the arcade and the lift shaft itself.

The heavy door opened with a clang, and he took them down a spiral stair, stained concrete steps turning round a paint-chipped metal

shaft, which rang to their footsteps like a steel drum. Then he conducted them along a platform where the mist curled out of the mouths
of the train tunnels, carried by the strange warm wind of the underground, which felt like balm to Miranda after the street above. They
came to a door again marked "Staff Only," in blue letters on white,
and "First Aid" in red letters, and beyond it, to a small room, an off-
duty den. There was a fug inside, and a smell of tobacco mingled with
paraffin from the standing portable stove he'd kept alight; a brass bucket
full of sand stood by the door, and a muddle of table, chairs, brooms,
pails, roadworkers' orange lanterns and newspapers crowded the tiny
space. In the light, the guard seemed an older man, with touches of
gray in his curls, whereas Kit Everard and his family shone with youth,
with red noses and flushed cheeks. Kit slapped his arms around his
chest to warm himself, then sat Miranda on his knee and unwound
the scarf and rubbed her legs to bring them back to life. Looking up
at Astrid, he pointed to the only armchair, a wooden frame with a
burst seat, covered with a square of blackout cotton. She took it, and
clutched her knees tight to her chest.

"What bliss to be out of that fog," she said. "Thank you."

The guard looked at her. "How's tea for you? A cup of hot, sweet
tea?"

"Don't use your rations on us, my man," said Everard.

"I'd just love a cup of tea," said Astrid. "Let him, if he wants."

"I think the child need something, you know, sir."

The guard lit a ring of blue flames and as they waited for the kettle
to boil, a sense of ease grew stronger in the tiny, stuffy cell. He spooned
sugar into the mugs, a level measure for each of them, while Kit waved
to restrain his kindness; the steam made the kettle sing and he tipped
in condensed milk as well before he poured. Miranda took a mouthful—
it was this saturated sweetness of her first cup of tea that came back
to her afterward when she remembered that night, and the comfort
the guard brought her, solid as a new baked loaf.

Kit Everard was smiling, and the color on his face had evened out.
"Not too bad, after all, is it?" he said.

"It's lovely, darling," said Astrid and, beckoning Miranda over, took
her brush out of her bag and nodded to her to bend her head and let
her tidy her hair. "We're quite safe now."

Kit Everard began to talk. The guard listened, drank, accepted the
Player's the young man offered him. Fragments about land and battles,

home farms and far plantations where tobacco and sugar grew, the exploits of Ant Everard in the Stockades of Flinders scattered like dust motes in the snug room, while sometimes their rescuer nodded and interjected, returning with strings of figures from famous scores and games, and offering Miranda's father new and different names, of other heroes and the Houses they'd gained, even giving a hoot of pleasure sometimes, all rage apparently forgotten. Now and then Astrid gave a little twisted smile, for she knew better than this romance.

Miranda began drifting off, while Kit and their underground rescuer moved on to talk about the cold in England and the island families beginning to come, and shivering to the marrow of their bones, even in summer. But how could they refuse the work and the money? Then Kit was telling the guard of his schoolboy visits to the legendary pitch at Doggett's Fields: the guard shook his head, he hadn't yet been, he hoped to one day, meanwhile he listened to the matches on the wireless.

"I'll see what I can do about that," Kit said lordly.

Astrid heard him from far away, like a voice booming in a dream; a skeptical *moue* played on her lips.

On a normal day, it would have been a poky hole-in-the-corner kind of place, the underground workman's lair, but that foggy night it was a stout refuge against the elements, and in the deepening warmth, sitting against her dreaming mother's legs, as the brush slowed in Astrid's hand, Miranda fell asleep.

P A R T   I I

Indigo/Blue

No one moulds us again out of earth and clay,
No one conjures our dust.
No one.

Praised be your name, no one.
For your sake
we shall flower
Towards
you.

A nothing
we were, are, shall
remain, flowering;
the nothing—, the
no one's rose.

—PAUL CELAN

7

LIAMUIGA, 1600—C.E.

THE ISLE IS full of noises, so they say, and Sycorax is the source of many. Recent sound effects—the chattering of loose halyards against the masts on the fancy yachts riding at anchor in the bays, the gush and swoosh of water in the oyster pool at the luxury hotel—are not of her making: Sycorax speaks in the noises that fall from the mouth of the wind. It's a way of holding on to what was once hers, to pour herself out through fissures in the rock, to exhale from the caked mud bed of the island's rivers in the dry season, and mutter in the leaves of the saman tree where they buried her, which now stands in the cemetery of the Anglican church, Saint Blaise Figtree, adjoining the spacious amenities of the same five-star hotel.

The warty trunk of her tree is studded with nails, some tin, some brass, some copper, which people push into the bark to make a wish. Visitors follow the islanders' example, they grin with pleasure at the foreign magic of it, squirm at their daring to play at savage rites. They also shiver to think that within the tree, Sycorax is still a force to reckon with. Needless to say, it doesn't feel like that to her.

To Sycorax it feels as if she began to die the day the corpses landed on Liamuiga. She's been dead now for some time, though the exact moment when she could say she ceased to be has become a blur. She thinks—and speaks—of her death as beginning when the children first spotted the bodies and brought the report back to the village. When she sighs or clicks in the shaking of the palms and breathes out with the rip of the surf, you can hear her despair that her death will never come to an end; she hasn't got much imagination.

There's a swimming hole under a promontory, where the waves have hollowed a deep cave, and a broad ledge in the rock twelve feet above the water provides a perch from which children like to take flying leaps into the sea. The prevailing wind has fretted the northeastern shore into inlets and gullies, and this is the only place where the rocks underneath aren't so toothed or so near the surface that only the most daring risk jumping in or diving. The sun was riding high above that day as the boys and girls hurled themselves into the water and the green black bruises in the sea some of them saw as they hurtled down could have been the shadows pooling between the long, slow, turquoise-green waves of a slumbering, hot day; but as the breeze swept these welling shadows nearer, one boy thought he saw an arm or maybe a leg break the surface, and when he rose himself in a fizz of surf and dashed the salty wet from his eyes to look again he could see nothing from that vantage, so he scrambled up onto the rocks again, and called up to the diver at the top, "Look out! There's something out there!" And the girl held her jump, surveying the waves, while another climbed onto the ledge with her and clutched her and they toppled over and fell in, shrieking, limbs whirling. But meanwhile the child behind was scanning the incoming waves, and he saw the nearest body. He thought it might be a tree; sometimes the winds snapped off big branches or even uprooted entire trunks on nearby islands and drove them ashore. But if it were a tree, it was one of a whole stand that must have been uprooted by a freak whirlwind, because now he could see, and so could others joining him on the rock, at first impatient that he was lingering and delaying their turn to leap, but then silenced, too, by the sight, that the sea was bringing in a human catch to break on the promontory.

On the beach to the north of the headland, some of the bodies escaped the attrition of the rocks in the children's favorite swimming hole; there they were cast ashore in the shoals, more gently, their open weals sprinkled with the fine black sand of the island as if with ritual cinder dust. When the older people, alerted by the children, ran to the beach to see for themselves the horror that was reported, they found about twenty men and women lying on the tideline like fish

stranded after a hurricane has suddenly swelled the sea and raised its
level and then retreated as abruptly. Some were almost whole, but
waterlogged, so that even a friend would have found it hard to identify
their poor carrion. Others had lost extremities, become shorn of nose
and trimmed of fingers by nibbling fish, others were missing heads,
arms and legs; one was a floating head on its own, with long curly
hair, like a human octopus. Bones poked through the ribbons of their
battered flesh; it was so torn that it might have been rags had they
been wearing any clothes.

On the shore, they soon began to stink from their exposed entrails,
in spite of the brine that had delivered them up and saturated their
carcasses. When the villagers, winding their mouths and noses in cloth,
approached the bodies and examined them, they found particular
gashes in them, around their necks and ankles, and the flesh puffed
up and festering in a manner drowning would never inflict, but only
earlier, direct hurts.

When the drowned had landed on their backs, their tongues pro-
truded, engorged and blackened. Unlike when tempests strike and fling
dead men and women on that archipelago, this crop of corpses were
stranded on their own, no other flotsam with them, no sea creatures
lay tangled with them, further victims of a storm; no driftwood followed
them, no body had been lashed to a spar in hope of survival.

"They couldn't have been been shipwrecked," one villager cried out.

"There's been no high wind," said Tiguary, the headman of one
village, and the brother of Sycorax. "Not that we have felt."

"Yes, this didn't happen far away," Sycorax took up, through a panel
of her dress over her face. "We would have heard—we would have
felt any storm that hit them."

"Where have they come from?"

"There'd be nothing left of them by now if it had been so far away
that we here didn't hear or feel it."

"Where were they going?"

These responses, in other circumstances merely perfunctory, presented themselves ominously to the group who stood together gazing
at the dead, while the children pointed and giggled nervously at the
theatrical twist of one drowned man's limbs, at the leer on another
ruined face. Silently, each islander heard the questions that filled everyone's mind: "Who are these people?" "How did they die?"

Presently, still hushed by the conjectures the sea's strange fruit stirred in them, they disbanded to fetch what was necessary. Young men negotiated the rocks with their canoes and loaded the battered pieces of the ten or so victims who had been driven ashore there; the married women like Sycorax fetched herbs to sprinkle on the corpses, staunching the open wounds with aloe, and placing spices in the gullets and the sockets of their damaged faces. Then the remains were gathered together and furled on hammocks lined with larger fronds stripped from the banana trees. Wrapped in this fashion, and disposed as they had once lain in the womb, the bodies were carried to a shallow pit which the men, the young, unmarried women and the children (they who above all should not come into contact with putrefaction) had quickly dug in the shade of coconut trees by the beach where the bodies had been swept in.

Strong branches were laid over them and stones to weight the branches, so no animals could come and scavenge there until the proper funeral, which would be held later. Then the questions raised by the coming of these dead would be considered, the cremation properly arranged and due rites performed to keep the pollution of the strangers' deaths from spreading through the island and harming the living.

Sycorax could not sleep that night. She held on to her husband's warm, smooth back and laid her head against the comforting slope of his shoulders and tried to merge her breathing with his and find some rest; but as she was slipping away the rise and fall of his breath became the heave of the sea, and she saw the bodies caught in the surf and flung onto the island again, and her eyes flew wide open, and her nose caught the sour must of her own fear. So she eased herself away from him gently and tipped herself out of the hammock and, taking a light, left him and walked out into their yard; she went to her kitchen and gathered a bag of certain berries, a bushy bunch of dried grasses and leaves—bay and sedum, mangrove and aloe, jumbie tobacco and tamarind, conchona bark and soursop, and went out into the black night again. There was a moon, in the first quarter, smudged in outline as if someone had breathed on its glassy greenishness, and giving hardly any light, but Sycorax had good night vision anyway. Her pet then (she had always kept a bevy of animals—companions, helpers) was a cavey which she'd taught to follow her and perform simple tasks beside her, and she clicked to her now to come.

She called her Paca, which was just another word for the kind of animal she was. She was a dappled doe cavey, looking like a cross between a badger and a hare; a fine plump creature, but far too valuable a breeder to cook (she'd borne several litters the family had eaten well on), a loyal companion quite as good as a dog, who would sit by, alert on her haunches, paws incurled and head perked up while Sycorax ground powders or brewed up mixtures in the course of her experiments. Sycorax now slipped the catch on the pen and beckoned Paca to keep her company. Short-legged, the creature could burrow as fast as any master of underground tunneling, yet her sight was keen too and her scent acute and she'd hunt like a small hound, her scut bouncing on top of her short legs as she raced in pursuit.

Sycorax bent to pat her now, and picked her up, glad of the comfort of her fur and warmth, and then set her down again. The animal bounded ahead, returning to make sure she was on the right path, as Sycorax left the cluster of dwellings where they all lived and turned for the shore. On her way to the burial place, she rebelled against the terror inside her, and it angered her too that she could not understand what had landed the dead on the island. She was thinking, as she approached, I'll stand vigil over them in their temporary graves, then I might see into the mystery and then, whatever I may find there, however ghastly, I will at least be able to face it for what it is.

It was the beginning of a new world for her and her people, the start of a new time, and as yet Sycorax did not know it.

She made a circle around her with the herbs and sat down on the ground with her back against a coconut tree, while the winds that had brought in the dead stirred its leaves above and eddied about her neck. The cavey stretched out beside her, nose in her paws, and Sycorax scratched the animal's dry and stubbly orange fur as she looked into the darkness.

Sometimes, the mind is like one of those dreams of a beloved place; it offers pictures in familiar outline of beloved people and of beloved objects, it imbues them with familiar feelings and gives the intense pleasure of recognition, quickly followed by a presentiment of loss. And then, all of a sudden, it pushes open a door that never existed in the familiar and beloved place, and there, beyond that door, there's a new space, offering exciting and unknown objects, furnishings, persons, full of promise. None of it can be recognized—it has never come to the dreamer before. And yet it feels as if all of it has been lost and must be regained; as if it were always known, but inexplicably forgotten.

On that night, the door gave in the mind of Sycorax, and light

struck the contours of a place where she had never been, and she saw
the dead men and women under the shallow layer of earth as if she
knew them and she could hear them as they lay, with their faces turned
to the earth and murmuring.

"The boat had the motion of a cradle," one said. "It rocked us,
rocked us."

"Yet it gave no comfort."

"No comfort, no."

"We could hear the wind, but there was not a breath of air to
breathe."

Another cried, "I could not see you, my darling, in the dark! Call
to me so that I may know where you are."

The reply came, if it was a reply, "The bed we lie in is a grave."

"Yes, the vessel that brought us became our hearse."

Then yet another's whisper came to her, and she saw the speaker
rise before her, and face her with closed eyes and moving lips, "The
sea never harmed us, gave us heavy nets of fish. Now it would make
us food for fishes . . . " She seemed to chuckle, then turn, and sleep
more deeply.

Another cried, "Grit for oysters—"

Then another, "Bonemeal for vines—"

And yet another, "We'll make rich loam—"

"From our carcasses, the melon and the gourd—"

"From our flesh, mermaid's purses, dolphin garlands—ha-ha!"

And another seemed to laugh too, and said, "Blood roses for the
coral, black dust for the sand."

Sycorax heard their voices in the dark, and all of a sudden, the new
space she had entered was lit up as if by lightning, and in the flash
she remembered something from the bodies she had laid out before
their burial, something she had not properly understood in the strain
of tending to their dismemberment and rottenness.

So she sprang to her feet, and clicked her tongue to her cavey doe
and walked to the pit. And when the animal would not obey her and
trot out over the burial ground but whimpered at the stench of decay,
she picked her up and flung her on the branches that covered it and
gave her the command: "Someone is sleeping there, I can see her! Find
her, go, find her. Now."

Paca whimpered, and her limbs shivered, but then she lowered her
nose to sniff among the branches and the stones, running this way and

that, as if picking up no particular scent from the prevailing reek of decomposition.

Sycorax urged her on, she was almost weeping now, the image in her mind was so certain, its outlines clearer every minute: the young woman with the gashed legs and neck, she had wrapped her gently in glossy leaves after crumbling conchona bark and other spices over her stomach, her stomach, yes, where she had thought then that like the others, she was ballooning out with swallowed seawater. The other men and women, all swollen in their abdomens—a counterfeit fertility; but in that young woman's case, Sycorax had not seen past her outer shape to the form inside.

The cavey turned on a spot in the square patch occupied by the pit and squealed. Her nose went up in the air, and with her hind legs she began to dig. Sycorax ran to her, tucking the protective herbs into the fold of her dress at the waist in order to ward off the infection of contact with the corpses. She moved the branches and the stones, and taking one that was shaped like a tile and might do for a tool, she began to shift the earth above the spot. It had not been packed down tight, so the work was easy. The smell of rotting became overwhelming; she gagged as she worked and put a berry from her bag in her mouth and bit down hard until its pungency on her tongue overcame the stench outside.

She reached the body, below, curled up like a child, and feared for an instant that she might not be able to bend the limbs straight again to reach her belly; but the sea water had prevented rigor mortis from setting in. Or the victim had not been dead very long, and they had buried her alive. Had they? Sycorax feared that they had indeed buried her alive. And how many others? If she had understood earlier, she might have been able to deliver the child and save the mother too; not any longer. When she unfolded the young woman inside the green leaves in which she was wrapped, she could feel the shape of the infant inside as she had seen in her waking dream, so she took the oyster-shell knife and she cut through the wall of the young woman's abdomen. When she put her hands through the rent to take the baby, she clenched her teeth and felt it slip warm and greasy between her hands.

As soon as she had brought him into the night's soft air she set him down in a nest of grasses beside the cavey, who licked him clean of the creamy vernix that had preserved his life in the water, and breathed on him and pawed his back until he drew breath where he lay on the ground beside the grave; Sycorax then packed all the leaves and grasses that were left into the wound she had made in his mother's abdomen and strewed her again with branches to keep her out of reach of carrion birds and other predators.

Sycorax had now gone down so deep into fear that she thought she might never be able to surface and draw breath again herself. So she began to run to the stream to wash herself clean of so much foulness, and there she slid in awkwardly down the bank and began to be sick with a thin, slimy vomit like bilge water. Between heaves, she screamed for others to come and help, until animals nearby were roused and started howling with her and, at last, two other women joined her in that place and went out to the grave.

It wasn't natural, some said. It was pure witchcraft. Sycorax had cast a spell and brought the dead to life. Nor should she have done it, even if the child were still alive. "He isn't one of us," some muttered. "He comes from a people who are strangers to us, outsiders, wild men." Others remembered the sea monster Manjiku, who swallows babies in his burning desire to be a woman: "Manjiku has spewed up the children he once stole, this blackened carrion is his vomit." Others feared that Sycorax had accomplished what no one ever had before: the taming of Manjiku, and he had made a gift to her of his victims. But not all agreed: the baby was only a baby, pale-browed and mottled purplish from his amniotic limbo, with the umbilical cord still twisting from his small and drumlike belly like a flayed snake; the placenta that had nourished him like a rich loaf carefully nipped by the cavey and guarded by her still to ward off flies.

The baby had come from far away; he was the first African to arrive in the islands, and he came to be known later, to the settlers from Europe, as Caliban.

But Sycorax gave him the name Dulé, meaning grief, after his birth as an orphan from the sea.

When she and her people first beheld the Africans on the beach, they had not yet seen bilboes for ankles or hooped shackles for necks. They themselves had knives made of honed oyster- and snail-shells and handy tools of wood, feather, rope and thorn, but no metal. So they could not imagine, let alone identify, how the drowned men and women had come by their wounds.

Soon, however, reports began to reach them of other men of Dulé's kind and place, and women too, like his mother, who had landed alive on other islands—survivors of shipwrecks, mutinies, other accidents. They conveyed their stories to others, who passed them on in turn, until the news traveled through the waterways by fishing boats and other craft and became known throughout the archipelago. The sea crop that first day of Sycorax's death did not consist of rebels who had been cast away to keep them out of mischief, as was to happen later. On that occasion, the weak ones, the sick ones, the less than perfect goods had been thrown overboard. For it would soon be common knowledge that the slavers tossed out any among their load who were failing; if one in three survived the journey, the trade still worked out as a cheap method of acquiring labor.

Many were also pleased to see the powers of Sycorax at work when Dulé was born. His delivery set Sycorax apart: her husband proclaimed her magical powers marked her out an official wisewoman. At the same time, he took the opportunity to announce his own remarriage. He referred to deep sorcery in Dulé's origin, and sent Sycorax and the baby boy back to her brother's village with the dowry she had brought with her at the beginning of their life together. He had only been waiting for an excuse.

Not every generation produces a Sycorax, and so some religious-minded people of her island valued her; Dulé's arrival seemed to them a mark of favor from the gods. Her brother, Tiguary, did not object to her repudiation, or make it the pretext for a feud between their villages; he announced that Sycorax was filled with *sangay*, preternatural insight and power, and her membership of their family a signal blessing.

Behind their hands, others were not convinced. They murmured that Sycorax had not delivered Dulé from the sea at all but that she had secretly borne the baby herself, and concealed him, until chance played into her hands and allowed her to make believe she'd saved a baby from far away, who had nothing to do with her and her witchcraft. She'd produced the child in her concoctions, some said, by taking the fetus-curled black pit of a certain fruit only she understood; or she'd mated with one of the animals she tamed and this was the progeny. Her people blurred distinctions between man and beast, domestic and wild, the furred and the feathered, the five-toed and the web-footed, and there were some among the people of Liamuiga who thrilled to the powers of Sycorax's enchantments, and saw the baby Dulé as not only strange, but holy—darker in color, with curlier hair and fuller lips and a domed skull that looked vulnerable, as if natural entry into the world down the birth passage of his mother would have crushed his eggshell bones. A power lay in him too, they whispered, and they cherished how different they found him. He was different, and though they were particular about differences—it was, after all, the traditional skill of a woman like Sycorax to find out what a dried mango leaf could do that a fresh one couldn't—it was to cause Dulé long and bitter pain that his difference was of some account even to his allies and his friends.

Many in her village found pleasure too in merely talking about her prodigious powers, in attributing fantastic faculties to her, in muttering that she'd gathered up a changeling child, and smuggled him into her family. Others, not so given to fancies of the supernatural, countered with practical gossip and declared the baby had found her out: Sycorax had always been a hot one; now she'd landed herself in the fire.

Placed in her arms later that first morning, when the women found her again, the baby was mewling feebly; they had rubbed his mouth with honey water, and he lay alive, but limp and glassy with his flesh baggy and pleated on his tiny bones like an empty sausage skin. But when she put a little finger in his mouth, he sucked with startling force, and did not cry when he found no nourishment there, just went on pulling so hard that she wondered if he could start her old milk again. So she tried and felt a tingling in her stomach as if it might begin to rise again, but the infant this time spat out her nipple and began to wail. Her milk was thin and whey-like, it needed the child's mouth to sweeten it. She cradled his weak whimpering head near her breast and stroked his lips on her nipple again and felt the tide of love for this puny thing flood her from the knees up, so that, when he took it between his blunt gums and began sucking again, she was able to nurse him as if she were truly his mother.

This too, some people found miraculous. Her whelp, they said, and she a monster's dam.

He grew slowly and had many problems: with gummy eyes and aching ears and feeble digestion. But he grew, and he made his needs and his hunger plain in ways that she knew meant he was a survivor. At one month, he beat on her chest with his small fist to urge on his feeds; at two months, he palpated her breasts with both hands to make the milk flow more thickly. She weaned him at a year, when he was already walking, on thin bandy legs that looked too frail to hold up the weight of his domed head. Like many infants, he had an ancient expression in his round black eyes, but in his case she knew the sorrow was a memory trace laid down in his every cell and would not fade with age. The look dismayed her, for it seemed a reproach: he was puzzled by her from the start, a child out of time and place, then a boy alone with an old woman (as a mother in the fifth decade of her life she was old by the standards of her people), who was known to all the islands in the surrounding sea as a great sorceress.

After a time, she knew she would have to leave her natal family's home, too, for though her brother and his family and followers respected rather than feared her, she could sense how uneasy she now made the young women, especially the mothers and the expectant mothers. She had changed in their eyes; become charged with their fears of death, though it was life she had brought to Dulé.

So she told her brother that she was leaving, and he did not protest. He would have had to propose an end to her stay himself eventually, for women with certain powers of enchantment were customarily required to live in seclusion, to practice their magic outside the nexus of the tribe, so that factions or individuals could not corrupt them easily and bend them to their own purposes. She thought of leaving Dulé with them, but it was agreed that he should stay with her until, according to custom, he should leave to learn men's ways.

So they set out with her creatures alongside, her tame long-legged agami bird, a shoat and a gilt to breed pigs from (these animals had appeared recently, abandoned, for no clear purpose, by passing sailing ships). Paca kept close by, of course, and together they followed the shore, until they rounded the westernmost point; then she carried on, with Dulé wound in a cloth, on her back, avoiding the other villages on the sea, until after several days she reached the creek on the southwestern tip of the island, with the volcano, Mount Liamuiga, rising up behind her to the north. There Adesangé, god of fire, seethed and spurted in view all day, as the sun played on the shapes of the mountain slopes and its emeralds and purples changed in pitch and depth of color.

It was a sentence on her to live apart with Dulé; but it proved a sentence to her liking.

8

FOR THE MAKING of indigo, Sycorax needed plenty of sweet water; the steeping of the light foliage gathered from the bushes, the seethings and distillations that followed needed an accessible and constant supply. Salt would do for the first rinsing of the cloths, but the second and third rinses required yet more fresh water, to bring out the liveliness and the shadows in the blues she was setting fast in the cotton, to make the moodiness in the color sing. So when she arrived with Dulé at her chosen site, she set up her dyeing works on the slope by one of the streams that ran from the volcano in the center of the island and dammed it into large pools on either side that could also be used as mirrors to look at the sky far, far away beneath.

The pools were hollowed out from the clay and limestone banks and hardened by exposure to the sun; later, she planted mango and banana palms to throw shade over them, for the dye sizzled too fast in direct sunlight. The spot she had picked lay close to the seashore, the lee shore of the island at that, because the indigo, when it was fermenting in the caldron, smelled foul and the prevailing offshore breeze would blow it away, out to sea. When the wind changed to southerly, her relatives in the village she had left would catch a whiff and hold their noses and laugh and say, "That stinking Sycorax at her stews again."

Over a decade of dyeing, the indigo stained Sycorax blue; she couldn't wash it from the palms of her hands anymore, nor from the cuticles and beds of her nails. A bluish bloom lay on her dark skin, blue-black as a damson when it's picked and fingers leave shiny marks on the maroon-purple skin underneath. Her tongue, too, was blue, from tasting the grain of the indigo after she had ground it, to make sure no roughness was left in it that would leave irregular, darker stains in the cloth. It was easy to mistake her gray eyes for blue as well, for the whites were the color of the noonday sky, especially when she twisted to look up from a cistern where she was busy steeping the new cloth, turning it, wringing it, rinsing it, to check on the gathering of the storm clouds and possible rain.

She could hear the sea from her compound, but not see it, at least not from the ground, where she worked, for the thickness of the trees and the shrubby indigo itself created a green and shady spot for her; she prepared food in an area where she placed stones in a semicircle, and there she would build a fire to grill a bird or a fish or bake a sweet potato in the ashes. When it was ready, she would dust it off with the broad dappled wing of an agami bird, one of the creatures from her large troop of assorted animals, edible and other. For her afternoon nap and her nighttime rest, she climbed up a tall thick saman tree and slept there, in a hammock slung across a cabin.

Age and heavy work had turned Sycorax into a sturdy woman, who threw out her arms and legs firmly when she walked, and liked to dance with bunched fists and heels slap to the ground. She'd enjoyed the work of building her house; the floor or platform was made from palm trunks split and lashed with tough nebees from the forest, and she and Dulé climbed up onto it using the burls and warts of the great saman for footholds. Ferns and orchids also grew on its trunk, stagsheads and maidenhair, and it was so thick that Sycorax and Dulé could not join hands around it.

The sides and roof of Sycorax's perch were woven from palm fronds in a herringbone pattern, with a window overlooking the green and bushy clouds of plants below, so she could keep watch over the sea. She'd placed her hammock beside this view; and would survey it in the morning when she worked the gaps widening between her teeth with a mintstick from her herb patch. The hammock where Dulé slept as a child hung at an angle to hers in the small space, by another aperture, overlooking the sea to the south.

There was nothing on the island that Sycorax feared; but more incomers were expected from the sea. The strangers were passing more frequently; some drifted in on the spars of burst vessels, others sailed by in whole ships. They were also plying the local waterways in greater numbers than before—and nowadays when they landed, they were more often alive than they had been in the past, at the time of Dulé's birth.

As soon as he was strong enough to hold a paddle, Dulé began to handle a canoe. But he was not content with it, and at the age of seven, he lashed a platform to a framework of spars and found that when he sculled with a long oar from the stern, he could skim the waves without labor. The sight of the foreign ships gave him inspiration: he improvised a sail from the broad tough leaves of a banana tree and pinned them together with thorns. Soon, he was making the crossing to the other island, to Oualie, regularly, and striking up friendships with the youths who lived over there. They had plans to sail on, to find other islands and meet their inhabitants and maybe set more traps for fish, discover rich crabbing and shrimping grounds, and bring their harvest back.

From her cabin in the saman's top, Sycorax could watch him set out; she had taught herself not to keep vigil for his return, as her solicitude—he took it as surveillance—made the boy sulky. There were practical reasons for her choice of a high vantage, though: it spared her the forest dew, which soaked the earth after the sudden nightfall, swelling the produce in her kitchen garden as well as watering the loose and feathery branches of the indigo, her staple and her work. She could also keep most of the island's predators at bay by sleeping high above: greedy tree rats, and chigoes that burrowed between the toes, and red ants that could munch a bale of hard-won velvety blue cloth in a single midnight feast. So she'd had a broad belt of lime painted round the tree's trunk (she'd rewarded her helpers with some bright beetles she'd caught, dried and dipped in gum to preserve them).

Ground level was safe for daylight work, but for thinking, Sycorax liked to lift her feet from the soil into which they sank too easily; the earth of her island was a rich red loam, the only kind of soil that would support the exacting indigo bush. Unlike her crop, she needed to lose connection with the island at times, and when she wanted a clear head to look back into the past and forward into the future, she needed to abandon the continual commitment to the task of survival that it demanded.

In her high bedroom, Sycorax still had to guard against flying creatures, of course. Limes and lemons rubbed on the skin warded off the
bites of the mosquitoes. Like all the islanders, Sycorax always smelled
lemony (indigo, like cooked beans, stopped stinking once the boiling
let off the gas, and the liquid was sluiced away into the sea). Over the
windows and the entrance and each hammock, she'd hung a fine mesh
a fisherwoman from the village had knotted for her, and in the branches
of the saman, she kept a swarm of bees that one day had alighted
there.

The bees knew her by her smell, her particular smell, under the
tang of lemon juice, and recognizing her, never stung her; they took
her for their mistress and stood guard over her. They learned to know
her family and her friends too. Dulé, of course, and others who came,
though few of her visitors entered her cabin in the tree, the bees'
special area of duty. An intruder, if one could ever climb as far as her
room, would disturb them in the hive and feel their fury.

From all over the island of Liamuiga, and sometimes from the nearby
islands too, petitioners came to ask her to interpret their dreams; to
make someone fall in love with them; to cure, even to raise from the
dead. Sycorax accepted gifts of fruit and fish, dried meat, lengths of
cloth, hulled and roasted ground nuts, and responded to the requests
as well as she could. She did not give away her knowledge of the
properties of stones, of grasses and seeds, the different uses of the
nimbril and the husk of the same berry when seethed with a certain
fluid, or describe the important timings necessary in her cures; it
amused her that she had diagnosed over a hundred varieties of indi-
gestion arising from the variable ailments of different organs and had
perfected remedies for nearly half of them.

It was working with indigo, however, that gave her most pleasure
and made her prosper; she developed a lively trade in bricks of the
dyestuff as well as in the cloths she took in from weavers and tinted
the desired depth of blue. As a result of her industry, her stores were
piled higgledy-piggledy in the shade around her shell-strewn compound, stacked up on stilts with rings of powder encircling them to
keep away insects, or in smooth clay jars stuck foot-first in the earth
to prevent sliding or climbing creatures from entering. These stores
were among the best-stocked in the island.

For nearly ten years she remained alone with Dulé, who gradually
changed from the weakling she had first taken into her care into a

strong, squat boy, with square shoulders and feet and hands hardened by his adventures in the countryside around their home. His eyes were weak, the principal mark of his near death in birth, and one of them swiveled outward more and more as he grew older. But he did not need sharp sight to range the island from end to end and explore the narrows between Liamuiga and Oualie, to learn the streams, their seasonal highs and lows, the watering places of every creature, and the nests of every bird; he learned to whistle and call in mimicry of a dozen kinds, and even greet individuals with a modified series of notes; he would scrape scamels from rocks under the sea and oysters from the mangrove swamps and bring them to Sycorax for her experiments. She knew that crushing the shell of a certain snail yielded a rare rich purple; she had seen it stain the mouth of one of her animals who had sampled it at her urging. Dulé gathered such snails for her from the sea. Their dye was much harder to obtain than indigo from the shrub, and therefore costly, so she reserved it only for special requests for luxury gifts, on the wedding of a chieftain's daughter, or at the birth of twins.

Even when Dulé acknowledged her skills by such assistance, Sycorax felt he was not entirely with her, that their way of life did not satisfy him. He was still displaced. She sensed, even in the boy's playing, his inner restlessness. He rarely sat still, or even lay down. The night and its cargo of sleep and dreams seemed to burden him; he crushed berries that she had once told him had wakeful properties, and continued to look out to sea in the starlight. He developed skills on the water and experimented with fish traps, with the knotting of nets suitable for certain small, delectable species, and he set rigs with spring-triggered baskets in the tidal wash at the mouth of the river to catch larger kinds.

By the age of nine, he was traveling farther and farther, either in his light canoe, or his skiff under sail. For her, their solitude on the island was an inspiration; for Dulé, it was an exile. Some people have their eyes turned inward, others are always scanning the horizon. Sycorax knew that she belonged to the first kind, Dulé to the other. And Sycorax could not mold him differently, though she tried.

He spoke to her of the past, too, and wanted to know. On his travels, he often encountered others, men and a few women, who resembled him in features and in coloring; they tried to communicate, using hand gestures and signs and drawings, what had happened to them to bring them to the archipelago.

Dulé developed an idea of the past that was foreign to the people among whom Sycorax had been born and raised; it was a lost country for him, which he wanted to rediscover, whereas for her, the past abided, rolling into the present, an ocean swelling and falling back, then returning again. But Dulé apprehended that he was born in a place that the ocean never brought back to lay at his feet, even in fragments, a shell here, a pebble there: something lay far, far beneath him, and he could not dive deep enough to retrieve it.

He began to teach himself a skill to reach it, in dream language, in a form of mimesis: he stripped boughs and lashed them together for a light ladder, stood it up on one end on the shore and balanced it with the tips of his fingers, then set foot on the bottom rung, then the next, and so on, until the ladder swayed and fell. He practiced, laughingly, in the cool hours, at daybreak or in the evening, until he could climb the ladder to the top, all twelve or fifteen rungs of it. He became so skilled that he could rise more than twice his own height off the ground (he never did grow tall) and hang in the air, as if the ladder were held upright by an invisible hand. It would sway like a palm trunk while he balanced with one outstretched arm, fingertips flickering, and the weight of his body calibrated to every tremor. His eyes flickered with the prowess of it, and when he leapt down onto the sand after he had had enough, the ladder would fall after him, the tensile spirit which Dulé had danced and caressed to life inside it departed, as snuffing a flame leaves only the drowned wick behind.

"I'll throw a ladder between . . ." Dulé paused, laughed. "You wouldn't understand."

She said, "Yes, I do." But it saddened her that he could not allow himself to belong wholly to her place, her present.

He went on, a slight mockery turning up the corners of his lips, "Between earth and sky, of course!"

She knew he had meant something different, some other link.

"Between the time now and the time I can't remember."

Then Ariel came to live with them.

When Sycorax took her in, Ariel was homeless, another strangers' child, who refused to work for food and shelter, but stood by gnawing at the skin around her nails until her fingers were raw, and reddening with the effort not to cry. Tiguary had arrived one day to visit his sequestered sister (as he did now and then), and had brought with him the five-year-old girl.

Sycorax had watched her brother paddling from the stern of the skiff as he rode on the surf, the small child in the prow looking far out to sea, one hand trailing in the water, her back to the land, as if she were indifferent to the new place. He then told his sister her story as they sat together side by side in the shade, while Dulé roamed the pools, teased the hens, played ducks and drakes in the water, inspected the pens of animals, poked here and there in the stores, took a fruit, threw the pit as far as he could, and the girl whose attention he was trying to attract roamed unmoved on the edge of his activity.

"She's never become used to us," her brother was saying. "We want you to try with her. She could do better with you. You'll have to become her foster mother too. It's for someone like you, not a family like ours, to take care of these odd children who belong to no one. We met to talk—this was the decision we came to . . ."

"Did you? You didn't ask me."

"You live here, Sycorax." He resumed, with a look at the child, now leaning over the edge of the pool. "She's a solitary, a dreamer, she doesn't fit in. She could make a companion for you. And a help." He nodded his head in the direction of her heaped work, the fruitful disorder around the vats, the sluices, the draining channels and the ponds. "You could do with another pair of hands. Woman's hands, to do this work."

Dyeing was women's work, so Dulé, though he helped her with the crop and the harvest, could not be apprenticed. She would like a helper, it was true. In time, she would find the wringing and the hanging of the sodden cloths heavy work.

The foundling child: Sycorax remembered the story, from when the tallow men came to the island and built a village to the north.

"But she's not one of them," she prompted her brother.

"No, but connected. She came with them, from the mainland. We helped them at first—you know that. We showed them this and that, no secrets, of course, but just enough to keep them from death's door. They gave us pigs, we taught them . . . the simplest things!" He laughed and took a draft of juice Sycorax offered him. It was fresh and foamy, pressed by his sister from the big warty soursop he'd brought with him as a gift.

He motioned to Dulé to come and have a drink of it too, and waved the little girl over to sit down beside them. She hung back, so Sycorax looked at her and winked, and went to one of her pools and came out with both hands behind her back and told the child, "Choose, go on."

The girl set her mouth, her eyes revolved in fright. She was undersized for five, with a skinny chest and crooked legs. Her look still had something of a newborn's bafflement and pain, and her brow, under a jagged basin crop, was barred with two frown lines like a much older woman's.

"Tst, tst, try, I'm not going to eat you." Sycorax jerked her head toward her left side to coax her to pick that hand. "Try, go on. Ariel."

At the sound of her name in Sycorax's slow deep voice, the fear faded a little from the girl's round black eyes, which were lightless like the lava on the summit of Mount Liamuiga above them. But still she did not make a move. So Sycorax brought out from behind her back in her blue hands a toad like a stone, which gulped the air and blinked.

"Would you like him for a pet? They make very good pets, didn't you know? As well as being delicious barbecued!" The girl hesitated, but looked as if she might step forward and at least examine the animal, when it took a leap and sprang down onto the ground and flew, legs trailing behind like the tail feathers of a bird, back into the pond, where it disappeared with a determined plop. The girl, watching it go, suddenly twisted round and ran after it.

"They only make friends if they like you, and they can tell," Sycorax called out, and turned to her brother to hear more. She held out her palm toward Dulé, where the toad had left a trace of pee in fright at being handled. "Dip your finger in it, go on. Then wipe it on your eyes. It'll strengthen your vision."

He did as she said, closing his eyes and wiping the finger across his lids, while Tiguary went on with his story. "They left, those strangers, after three summers. Or, rather, the few of them who remained sailed away. Many had died, of sickness, hunger, even."

"They usually do."

"Unless you, unless we, decide to help them."

"I change my mind about it all the time." She sighed. "Never see clearly what way we should take. We make our offerings, as usual. But the exchanges wither, then we begin to begrudge what we have given . . ." She paused. "They left the child?"

"She wasn't one of theirs, it's clear from the look of her. No, she's a mainlander, Arawak, from over there." He looked to the south, over the sea. "The tallow men came from further away—their lids are so thin and pale, their eyeballs burn in the sun even when they keep their eyes closed. You know the kind!"

"Ah, them. I remember that, ha. Kin to Manjiku. Are they a kind of shellfish? Heat turns them pink."

"They build very large boats and sail them in storms though they know that sinks them."

"Their boats are floating villages," muttered Dulé. "They can travel in them a long time, over great seas, huge distances."

"They have no women. It's a great misfortune."

"For them? For others who cross their path! But it depends." She laughed. "When I was young, I wondered about such things. No longer."

"They need watching. We watched. And they did not see us, watching."

The little girl was by the pool, face-to-face with a smaller toad that was now squatting in the sunshine on one of the round rocks used to build its containing walls. Tiguary looked toward her, and went on, "This time the tallow men brought with them a group of mainlanders, Arawak men and women, who know how to cultivate our island plants, as well as different fruits they wished to grow and introduce to our soil. Good things—cocoa beans—has anyone given you their paste to try? Next time, I'll bring some and you'll see, it makes a good sauce, for plaintains, or for any fowl. If you're thinking of a treat." He paused, picked up the thread. "These men had promised her people"—he gestured to the child—"that they would take them back once the crops were planted and established. Once they'd learned their methods, copied their tools and discovered how to set the seed of "—he waved a hand about—"melons and tobacco, soursop, mango, potatoes, plantain, tomatoes, okra, guava . . . you know. Indigo. And how to make chocolate, from those cocoa beans I told you of. They were so ignorant they couldn't tell one seedling from another. Well, I suppose they were sailors and fishermen, really, so it's not to be expected they understand farming too.

"But they have no idea of what it means to give your word, the shellfish people, they have double faces and double tongues and never keep their promises. This is why we have learned to watch them, not to listen, for they reveal their inner thoughts and plans by their deeds far more surely than by their speech.

"Their speech is valueless." He fell silent and reached out to touch his sister's hand. "And I fear their deeds too."

The girl Ariel had the toad in the palm of her hand and was gently stroking the blue-black knobs on its back. Sycorax looked over at her, stood up and said, as she started to walk toward her, "She's an Arawak girl, I see that now, of course."

"Is she going to live here?" Dulé tried to look as if the matter were of no consequence.

Sycorax said quickly, for she noted his pretense, "I don't know yet. Would you like a sister?"

"She came here to the island as a baby," the older man continued, "with her mother and her father when they were brought to work the new crops."

Dulé interrupted. "It's not up to me, and anyway I'll be gone soon. To the men's house, to the men's house." He half chanted the phrase; in a few years' time he would leave the care of women to live with the young men and learn their ways.

Sycorax overlooked his taunts. "And now, where are they now? Her parents?"

Her brother gestured a question in the air. "You could keep her with you here—until . . ." He shrugged. "The father died." He was beginning to sound irritable. "The mother . . . was taken by another man to be his woman. One of the tallow men. She was put on the boat with him when they left."

Sycorax nodded, and raised her hands in understanding. "She left her daughter here, rather than take her to be with them." She looked up at the trees, which were fanning their broad leaves in the steady warm breeze, and sighed; then, lowering her gaze, paused on the girl and said, almost to herself, "Yes, leave her here."

Ariel turned to the older woman hesitantly, with the unblinking animal on the palm of her hand. Sycorax stood up and went over to her, and held out a finger to the toad as she approached so that it would not jump away; then she squatted down beside the child to look at her and say, "I've had other daughters, Ariel, but now I'm old they've left me all by myself with only one young man for company." She laughed. "I'm considered a famous witch, you know." She growled in play, and showed her teeth. "I can do all sorts of things, and make friends with all manner of creatures. We'll give each other support, you'll see. You've been sent to me, as a gift. And what a gift! Do I deserve you, do you think? Here." She did not wait for an answer from the girl, but crooked a finger and beckoned her toward her tree house. "I'll show you where we're going to be safe. Bring your pet too—carefully now."

Sometimes, in the heat of the afternoon, with Ariel curled in the hammock where Dulé used to lie, Sycorax would look out to sea, now lifting into shining peaks under the breeze, now hard and shiny as a black rock after rain, and feel that its mirror concealed a menace she could not quite decipher. Lurking there were more ships, more men seeking harbors, fresh water, sustenance and equipment. Some sailors had been seen refreshing themselves in the sweet-water lagoons behind the dunes on the southeastern peninsula of the island. There were no villages on that stretch of shore, only fishing grounds, as the soil was poor for anything but coconuts; some strangers had also picked up salt from the salt ponds on the northern beach. Then, one day, the island settlers on Oualie, her son reported, claimed to have seen a boat recently sail past close-hauled to their windward shore, and carry on down the channel, as if seeking an anchorage, along the coast where Sycorax and Ariel lived. He himself had seen the same vessel, he thought, after it had passed.

The ocean currents and the speed of the prevailing wind had carried it on, past the island. It was all too easy to miss the moment of tacking in to land on that southwesterly shore, and have to sail on by, and make the circle of three islands to the north in the archipelago and bear down with the wind behind and start the approach once more, beating again, but from farther south.

This time, the strangers' boat had failed to make a landfall.

That year, 1618 by Christian reckoning, Kit Everard was on board the four-gun brigantine that sailed close in past Oualie and then past Liamuiga, which Dulé saw as he was fishing, checking a net he had set. He reported this new sighting to his companions on Oualie, and they confirmed his news; it was then he sailed across the strait to visit his mother and warn her.

Columbus had marked the twin volcanoes on his map when he first saw them side by side, one a smaller echo of the other. He called them after the Saint who doubted Christ, Thomas, because he also fancied he saw, in the fissures on their slopes, three gashes on one island and two on the other. They were the gaps in the rain-forest cover on the slopes made by cascades of hot springs from the craters, and he counted them as the five wounds of the Saviour.

Sycorax asked Dulé, "So it seemed they wanted to land nearby?"

"The wind was high, their boats are big, and their helmsmen don't know the force of the current or the position of the rocks." He paused. "But they'll be back. They've come back before, they'll come back again."

"What do they want?" It was not a question she expected him to answer.

"You're the one who sees hidden things—you tell me."

"They usually leave—in due course."

Dulé searched her face. "But will they always?"

"Leave?"

"I wouldn't give them presents, as your brother did," Dulé said, and came closer to her. "Curse them, Mother. Use your arts, change their condition with your skills, alter their shape, as only you know how. So that they learn to fear us and do not stay. They use our water and eat our substance, they're not welcome. Not on Liamuiga, nor on Oualie."

"You're too scared inside," she replied to him. "You're too young. You must have more belief in our capacities. Trust our strength, our wisdom. Strangers can't do us harm, not here, where we have our ways and they know nothing without our help."

"Me, scared?" The youth laughed hoarsely, and with that, he nodded to her, made the formal gesture of leave-taking, and ran his canoe back down the beach and tugged at the sheet till the sail filled.

Kit Everard saw the same shining whiteness over the twin volcanoes of the islands that Columbus had named on his map, and the Englishman cursed that he had overshot and could not turn to windward and sail back. He watched from the poop and tossed a few dry crumbs to the birds to see what kind they were, and as the boobies swooped to catch his offerings, he resolved he'd make good his monarch's claim to those islands, against all comers, against the Spanish and the Dutch, the French and the Portuguese, the pirates and the Indians or any other enemies of Albion marauding in those promising waters.

Kit was twenty years old in 1615 when his first patron, Roger Pole, had summoned him. He embarked with him at Woodbridge in Suffolk, and joined the English settlement in Surinam on the north coast of the South America mainland, Eldorado, where, with the backing of some royal favorites, Roger Pole was questing after the famed gold of the Indies. Kit worked with a will for the owners of the settlement, and though they failed to find gold, they had grown tobacco there successfully in the soft rich soil of the riverbanks.

They'd fought off the tribe who were famous cannibals and befriended the Indians who weren't, like the Arawaks, and put them to work. For, by God, some were good workers, all green fingers and thumbs, with a yeoman's knowledge of the properties of the ground, of weather and seed and drainage. There was a fortune to be made. The first ship to sail with a cargo of tobacco brought them a handsome profit, enough to provision two more ships to make the return journey, and Kit, who had no money in his native Suffolk, found himself notably rich in Surinam, though the living there wasn't easy. The colony was continually harassed, its fields damaged, its equipment sabotaged by enemies who materialized from the jungle upstream and vanished back into it.

Roger Pole told Kit, "An island, an island, that's where we should be. It's a natural fortress, Kit! You could take an island or maybe two or three, and hold them with a mere handful of men. But here, on the mainland, we cannot defend ourselves without a garrison."

Roger Pole had made an attempt ten years before at planting the larger of the two Thom's, the islanders' Liamuiga; but the colony he left there had failed through sickness and lack of provisions; they waited in vain for the ship that should have brought them the necessary goods to trade with the inhabitants—the scissors, candles, knives, mirrors, metal saucepans and bowls they could use for barter. At last, when their numbers had decreased to seven men from thirty-three, they abandoned their enterprise, the Arawaks whom they had imported to work for them (with the exception of one or two women they had taken as mistresses), and rejoined Roger Pole in Surinam.

When Kit Everard, who had remained in the colony on the mainland, heard their story, he resolved to return with Roger Pole and plant the island again with people of his own kind. They would gain renewed support for another American venture, from land-poor nobles who would lend their prestige, and from merchants who would lend their gold. But then Roger had died in Surinam, and so Kit returned to England to make his bid for favor on his own.

Providence had blessed him, it seemed, for he soon found an ambitious patron, a Suffolk man like himself, the Lord Clovelly, who had formed a merchants' company to back just such enterprises as Kit proposed. Kit Everard was among those men who were quick to realize that settling, not roving, could lead to great bounty, and he was determined to stake his claim, on behalf of England and the King and the Worshipful Company of the Hesperides. And there was enough of the buccaneer about him, enough of the dreamer, and enough of the gentleman to realize his ambition; Kit Everard was a pioneer among planters.

9

THE LOVE FOR Ariel that grew in Sycorax was greater than any she had felt for the children she had borne; it was sweeter than the passion for survival that had attached her to Dulé. When the boy she had saved appeared before her, returning from one of his forays on land or sea, her heartbeat still jumped under her ribs; but the pleasure was quickly past, dissolved in his furious need to place distance between himself and Sycorax.

She understood how much he wanted to feel in charge of himself; yet his defiance challenged her, his always knowing best heated her blood in spite of herself, in spite of seeing clearly that to the youth any consent to his mother's wishes signified weakness, any obedience or conciliation sapped his energy. Inwardly, she relished his pride, at the same time as she was wounded by his scorn. She chuckled to herself at his hauteur, in the very midst of snapping back at him. Had she been born male, she would have liked to resemble him, in his contrariness, his fierce and secretive training sessions, his imaginative struggle to remain apart.

"You can undo the most cunning poisons," he'd call to her. "You can charm shy creatures out of the deepest lairs. You can smell mushrooms from a hundred yards. But you can't make me do anything I won't!" And she would laugh, with genuine delight, as he took off, throwing over his shoulder to her, with a child's clumsiness, "And I can do some of those things too! And more!"

Then he was gone altogether, to learn the language of the men in her tribe and leave childhood behind him, and there was something about the solitude of this middle period of her life that made her respond to the strangers' girl with so much sharper a passion than she had felt for her own while they were growing up. In her attachment to Ariel, Sycorax became needy.

Sycorax held her in the sea to accustom her to water, and put her on her back and struck out, to make the quiet child give one of her rare peals of laughter, half pleasure, half fright at the thrill of riding on her old mother's back; she made her a poppet from ends of cloth, and threaded beads for the doll to wear as a toy dowry and set jumbie beans in her face for eyes. She would sit Ariel between her knees and rub carapate oil into her scalp and plait her hair, and the girl would hold still, keeping her neck and back steady to encourage the depth of Sycorax's massage, meeting her ministrations in silence, but with that spirit of hers coiled inside her. Deep inside, as though she were a flint in which fire is hidden, Sycorax thought as she kneaded the delicate scalp and listened to the song that Ariel sometimes began to improvise to the rhythm of her fingers.

Between them, they raised a menagerie of creatures, some eager, some resistant, an agami bird with long dawn-gray plumage that followed Ariel like a dog and trumpeted in greeting with surprising clangor from its narrow neck and small pointed beak. She trained it to keep silent when its mistress was stalking. Iguanas followed them high up in the trees and quietly caught bothersome insects for them, and a couple of barnacled dark toads hopped beside them up onto the tree trunks they used as tables. Sycorax agreed to the child's protests and stopped her habit of reaching into the pond for a half dozen of them to spit for supper, or bringing down, with a well-aimed dart, a game bird that had happily roosted unharmed in her garden for weeks. They always kept a kennel of tame caveys, of Paca's line, not that the kennel could keep them confined; only their own inclination could do that. Quick-witted hunters, they liked to track and burrow for Ariel on her forages.

The girl did not speak much; she liked to sing, and was more gifted than Sycorax at inventing charms and tunes spontaneously. Sycorax would sometimes lift and straighten herself after stirring the reeking

indigo and find Ariel playing shadows on the ground, humming to
herself as she mimed a long-legged bird, or a diving booby, or, spreading her fingers and wiggling them, a small palm in the wind. She sang,

"The red one, the curly one, came down to the sea;
My oyster shell, my piece of the sky,
Shone there below, far down below,
But his hand is melting, his head is bursting,
Too far down, too far, aïe!"

When Sycorax asked her what she meant, she looked at her gravely
and did not answer. Then, all of a sudden, she would run to her and
throw her arms around her and hold on tight, head buried at her waist,
hands gripping the cloth Sycorax wore wrapped around her. Her kisses
were hard and dry. Then, as quickly, almost before Sycorax had time
to stroke the child's silky head and soothe her, Ariel would dart away
and fling more lines at the older woman, again in her child's croak,

"The flash of the green star,
And the monkey's bite in the mango's rind,
Not yet ripe, not yet ripe, open
Your blue throat and spit it out!"

Her muteness in response or explanation did not betoken any dullness of mind; she was as quick to absorb as open-weave cotton. Sycorax
realized gradually that Ariel's presence as her pupil and her heir had
made her acknowledge those powers in herself which previously she
had thought her customers imagined, and when Ariel was about twelve
and was leaving childhood behind her, Sycorax began to teach her
more than the arts of making indigo.

She had done none of this for her own children. At that time, when
she was the young wife of the village headman, she was interested in
other matters—in men (in her husband, in fact, for a while, as well
as some others). But above all she was captivated and intrigued by
herself, by the motions of her inner being, by the extent of her powers,
by the leaps and forkings of her wishes and the unpredictability of her
pleasures and her skills. As a young woman, she was undiscovered
territory to herself; and her passions took her by surprise and delighted
her (as well as leading to grief sometimes). So her children were looked
after by other young women engaged for that purpose; as the wife of
a powerful man, the daughter of one chief, and the sister of another
in a neighboring village, Sycorax had had plenty of kin to call on and
plenty of dependents needing favors in return for favors. Also, her

own mother was still living then and liked to bring up Sycorax's brood, much more suitably, she'd declare, than her daughter would herself.

There were two aspects of mothering Sycorax had relished: experimenting with food, especially colored food, and adorning her children with those gatherings from the rocks and the forest that turned out, after trials with various animals, to be inedible or otherwise useless. She had some of her husband's followers build split-cane cages, in which she kept an assortment of the island's fauna: she'd started with a pair of green vervet monkeys with sooty faces and hands, a porcupine, and an agouti or two, as well as her stalwarts, the caveys. One of the monkeys had the runs after she stuffed the cavity of a mango with some purple seaweed she'd picked, but it survived, though afterward she had difficulty using the animals again as testers for her concoctions, as they no longer trusted her food.

In this manner, by experimenting, Sycorax managed to discover the properties of certain stuffs. Some of her ways with spices were quickly adapted: the islanders had stopped scraping oysters from the mangrove roots because they were so tiny and insipid, but with a sprinkling of ground pepper and chili bean, and a drop of lime juice, they tasted more savory. She dried them in strings in the sun by bushes of aromatics, too, for eating in the months when the shells were spawning and should not be disturbed. She tried out poisons on the tree rats she shook out of the cabbage palms where they had been growing fat, and when she had the lethal dose for an animal of that size, tried out its antidote; for the venomous milk that flowed from a gash in the side of the manchineel tree, she developed a salve that combined with it and soothed the victim's torments. She could induce gripes with one kind of tea, and lift them with another.

Other old women of her village had known how to gather bundles of grasses and sweet-smelling leaves; indeed, she had picked up her fundamental lore from them. But they never attained her degree of skill at the caldron and the mortar; nobody on Liamuiga had ever become such an expert sorceress.

With her husband, Sycorax had had three daughters, and as a mother, in the old days before Dulé, her trials with this berry, that gum, this oil, that leaf, this bone, that shell made her own family run to other, more dependable cooks who were not always experimenting. Ultimately, she proved less sound with food than with fabric and color: it suited her to work indigo as a trade.

Sycorax's insouciance as a mother in the early years of family life was so pronounced that she did not care to stand up to her own mother over her children's rearing and shout down her claims, as she did on almost every other matter. But her attention to her offspring grew keener when they became adult too; for then they marked for her the end of her own youth.

Her desire to deliver Dulé had also sprung from this new apprehension of her impending barrenness, when her first children were growing up and she had no more babies or toddlers of her own. She had felt passion for the firstborn, her eldest daughter, in her infancy, and when, at the age of nineteen, she died of a fever after the stillbirth of her own first baby, pain had torn through Sycorax at all she had left undone, at the love she had forgotten to give. There was no reason for a mother to survive her children, she would rather have died herself. Her daughter became a ghost limb that aches at night and sets the whole body burning with its absence.

No men ever feel such pain for their offspring, she thought, no matter how much they try to merge with their wives, even when they gash themselves in imitation of menarche, and pretend to struggle in the coils of labor alongside them during the birth, no matter how much they love the child. It originates in flesh, she told herself—not even imagination, which can brand the marks of madness and mutilation on the body, reaches the doubled oneness of a woman and her child.

Sycorax had longed to have another to replace the dead daughter; Dulé had been the exchange. Not that she regretted the manner of his birth, though he had provided an easy pretext for her husband to repudiate her in favor of a new girl for a wife, and send Sycorax back to her brother's. She hadn't minded; he probably would have done so anyway, even if she had not saved the baby. And he could not have been expected to take in as his only son the strange sea-born child of the ghost crowd on the shore that day. Indeed, a spark of her old self-love flickered in her again as she discovered how enchanted she was with her transformed life, with the novel tasks she set herself, to stretch her powers and turn them to some use.

Dulé remained split from her, though, and he could not ease the gap inside her. Even she had never ceased to find him a stranger. It was as if he put himself out of her reach, in the same way as he chalked a circle round the foot of the ladder on which he balanced high up in the air.

On Oualie, he was gathering other strangers around him, the likes of him, fugitives from the settlements, pirates from foreign ships run aground for careening who had decided to stay, and some people of her own tribe who responded to Dulé's anger and joined him in his fledgling society on Oualie. Dulé made even Sycorax stand back in wonder; she could not find herself in him.

With Ariel, by contrast, she remembered herself young; Ariel opened the way to having her life over again.

"I used to change men into beasts," she'd chuckle to herself, as she walked the rows of indigo seedlings and hoed the weeds that would choke their delicate low branches. "Now I can only turn them blue."

More than half a century had passed since she was born and one or two of her teeth had fallen out and her once unruly hair had thinned and become docile to the comb. The sheen on her that had started the animal from many a reticent lover's cover had been dusted with indigo, but she had discovered that she no longer even wanted, let alone needed, the kind of power she had wielded then. Memories of her exploits appalled her now; the times she went from one man to another and back to her husband, daring fate (or her own body smells and juices) to expose her, hugging to herself the secret of her mischief, and crowing inwardly at the glances of anguish, the self-important pleas her lovers cast at her in secret. How they would rootle, lap and snuffle at her! How they would stamp and whinny when she made them wait for her, and butt and clench to prolong her pleasure! Like a jaguar, one would steal over her and seize her at the moment she called for him to do so; like a snake another unwound his tongue deep inside her; like the determined cavey, another scrambled and dug in the warren of her body; and one would sometimes let out a raucous shriek, like a parrot in scarlet flight.

But she'd lost interest in all that now. It was surprising: once upon a time she could have swived all day and all night.

10

On the island, it was the custom for the young to swim in the sea; but for a woman of Sycorax's age, it was considered unseemly, so she kept to herself and to a pool she had dammed in her stream for washing. However, every other month at the time of the full moon, she would take Ariel and walk to the hot springs inland, halfway up the mountain, to meet with islanders from different villages, answer their requests and respond to their worries; meanwhile Ariel would soak in the tonic salts of the spring waters and scrub the indigo from her skin; it didn't matter to Sycorax that she was stained, but Ariel was too young to be branded by their dyer's trade.

By the age of twelve Ariel had already grown taller than her foster mother; she was more strongly built too, with a back as supple as a tamarisk wand, and lithe limbs, rounded and muscled and covered with scratches and scabs from her explorations of the terrain around them. She was russet in complexion, like the shell of a pecan, and her black hair hung straight, with the short fringe that emphasized the stern chevrons of her eyebrows; sometimes, Sycorax braided it so that it wound round her head like a garland. She wore an ornament in it made of oyster shell whittled to look like a bird in flight, with a piece of black stone for an eye and feathers stuck in it. The bridge of her nose was slender, and her nostrils winged as though she were always filling her lungs to their depths. She was rounder in figure than Sycorax had ever been, even at her ripest. But Ariel carried her weight so easily that she could steal up on a small animal at feed in the forest more quietly than the sound of the animal's own jaws working, and catch it in her hands. Sycorax had always been far too impatient to hunt, but Ariel could persist in pursuit of the shyest creatures and bring them down with a pellet from her sling; she preferred the weapon to her bow and arrows because she could stun her prey rather than kill it and bring a new creature home to their menagerie.

The spring of 1618, when Kit Everard overshot the island where he had planned to land, where he would eventually make his personal fortune and by the bye set the course of his country's imperial ambitions, Ariel was fully grown, yet not entirely woman, not in the way that Sycorax had been at her age. She was fastidious, too, preferring not to speak of her menses to her mother, and when Sycorax once noticed she was pale or in pain, replied hotly, "You don't have them, so you can't help."

Sycorax would have told the girl, "But I remember all about it. Besides, I'm the one who knows the properties of plants, don't you remember? Me, the witch Sycorax, your old mother?" But something in Ariel's obsidian eyes gave warning to let her be.

Ariel's mouth in repose was set firm, in a fierce muteness, and her brow showed another deep crease line over one eye where she closed it to take aim. The child and the woman did not look like mother and daughter, the age gap of nearly forty-five years was too great, and Sycorax was too small and sturdy and dusty with indigo, compared to the gold-mahogany glow of the young girl, but their gait was the same, for they lived so intensely side by side, moving to each other's rhythm. They put down their feet firmly, heels first, hitting a fast easy stride and rarely stumbling, though they did not seem to look down at the ground they covered; both of them understood the terrain, the conch-strewn beach, the root-tangled forest floor, without need for a close watch.

(When Kit Everard and one or two of the fourteen men returning with him caught a glimpse of them moving, they marveled at the easy manner of their progress up the uneven and tangled mountain slopes.)

Sycorax and her daughter stooped and lifted at work in the same way, too, bending squarely from the waist, and squatting to tip the larger caldrons, because Ariel had helped Sycorax at her dyeing ever since she had first joined her; they spoke with the same intonation, in familiar counterpoint, and they added words to the language they used together, which according to the customs of Sycorax's people, was reserved for women when they were alone. There were no solemn forms of address as between men together, or between men and women in mixed company, no equivalents of "your Excellency" or "your Honor" in this form of communication: together, they relied on the simple "you," whereas, Sycorax warned the girl, when men and women spoke to one another, they were required to control the danger of their exchanges with honorifics and periphrases that might keep the distance between them: a solecism in mixed company, the mistaken use of the colloquial "thou" could so provoke the person Ariel might be speaking to that a quarrel might break out between the respective clans; a feud could last years over such a lapse in public.

Consequently, Ariel would have to leave her soon, Sycorax knew, to go back to the village and learn the current forms of address and deportment, which she had not been able to absorb in the seclusion of the forest. Unless she inherited her foster mother's calling and became a solitary too, a magician and wisewoman to the tribe. At one time Sycorax told her, "You'll enjoy it, being with girls of your own age, normal young women with normal desires." At another, she felt the hurt as she anticipated their parting and praised Ariel for her aptitude at handling and taming animals, at collecting grasses and berries for medicines.

And Ariel knew what price Sycorax put on "normal" and curled her lip. Though she wasn't as talkative as her adoptive mother, she communicated with the same animation when she chose to, her eyebrows knotting and arching in the same exaggerated way as Sycorax's, as if the conversation were full of wild truths and wilder fancies rather than an ordinary exchange about the value of the ingots of first-grade light indigo they had made, of the lengths of cloth which were finished and waiting to be collected to be traded in the market. Ariel's face at rest recalled the shut impassivity of her appearance when she first came to live with Sycorax, and there were moments when the older woman, glancing over at the girl she loved so much, was chilled by the remoteness of her expression, her stranger's distance. But then Ariel, noticing the glance resting on her, would rouse herself, and banish the phantom engraved on her features, and sing with laughter in her voice:

"Oriole, let me pull some feathers from your tail—
And you, my swift, bring me a grass to bind them—
Cavey, dig me a stone with your sharp nails—
And I'll hone the tip till my arrow flies
Into your milky mouth, old moon!"

Sycorax imputed Ariel's reticence to her earliest losses, and wondered how much she remembered in her dreams. Ariel never made reference to her earliest youth; when she heard mention of the mainland, she did not respond like a mainlander, but as an islander. She had been allowed to think her parents had both died in an accident, and the subject had not come up again; she called Sycorax Mother, or Old Mother, or sometimes, Old Queen Bee in honor of their tame hive. She refused to discuss her difference from the people who had adopted her—her Arawak bearing and coloring, her height.

During the time when Dulé was still living with Ariel and Sycorax, before he left for the men's house, he treated the child gingerly, with experimental gallantry, and talked to her earnestly of his different origins on another mainland, toward the rising sun, and held his hand palm-upward to show her the delta inked there, a map of the country of his birth so he should not forget, though he had never known a word of his people's language, since he had been born of water, before speech. But he had pieced together a story from others like himself whom he had encountered; on nearby islands, Dulé had in certain cases befriended youths who resembled him in skin and build. They were sometimes able to describe to him the places where they had come from, where they had lived, before.

She had listened gravely, and had accepted that she stood on some kind of common ground where others belonged, to which he felt himself a stranger, even though he was not treated like one by her, or by many others. Yet the difference was marked on him, he argued; he already dreamed of a place for men like himself—and women, too:

"There are others like me, who will always be cut at the root—I know it, I hear rumors—on other islands, escaped slaves, maroons, and pirates who slipped the noose. I'll join them, a runaway myself!"

Another time, on one of his visits after he had left, he'd taken Ariel aside and spoken to her more fiercely, one hand round her upper arm, his eyes close to hers, "You will be beautiful, Ariel. And you know. You're no more my sister than she's my mother." He laughed. "How about it, little sister? Come with me, now. What do you think?"

Her eyes clouded, and she tugged at him, as he pulled her round and watched her face, the tiny muscles flinching round her mouth as he stared; then he pushed her away and said, "You should stop her holding you prisoner, in her tree, up there with her on guard over you. You should be out in the world, with the women and the women-to-be. Learning another way of life."

Ariel, with tears rising, twisted in his grip and bit down on his hand until he shook her off.

"Aïe," he cried, but his tone was chaffing, "you could come too—over there." He pointed beyond the shore, to the islands sleeping between the sea and the sky like windblown clouds. "I can show you the fountainhead of the springs near the hot mouth of the crater, and the nests of the heron in the freshwater lagoons that lie between the sea and the hills, and the baby heron hatching, so small and transparent you can see their bones through their skin."

She bit harder, tasting the salt in his skin, to make him take her seriously.

"Aïe!" he cried, but went on. "I could show you, Ariel, my sister, my dear one, the way we live over there, together; no separation of men and women like here."

She let go her grip on his flesh, and he rubbed the ring of toothmarks she had left.

"You really hurt me," he said. "You should leave off biting and fighting—come and learn to sail and row and dive and fish with me. I'll catch you octopus. I'll show you where the sea horses spawn! I'll swim with you out to the reefs where the oysters sluice the freshness of the tide, and we'll go hunting the moon. By land and water. I'm not afraid of the darkness, and I know what fear is. I look hard at what scares me and face it, whatever it is, however strong. As I'm facing you now, my sister.

"Though I was brought up here, an islander and remember nothing. I am still different. And you are too. We are both odd ones out, but we could make a pattern all the same: I've seen under the sea when I dive—and you know, I see well under the sea, the blurring in the light doesn't bother me, not down there—I've seen conches walking about on feet when soft-shell crabs have taken shelter inside them and small fish picking the teeth of bigger fish and swimming out unharmed, with full stomachs, and strange birds taking water lilies' fruits to help feed a neighbor's nestlings, yes, you and me, we could find a way to be. Not like-to-like but two odd numbers fitting together, Ariel!"

He hit his chest, then his stomach, and reached out for Ariel's hand and clamped it tight against his ribs. "You don't remember anything either about where you come from. Doesn't it matter to you? Maybe no. But when I was in the men's house I saw that I'm the egg that hatched a different chick. Nobody treated it differently, but the difference is there—inside, outside, you can always tell and I can always feel it."

Now Ariel was looking at him scared; he was using the language of women to her, the language of food and animals and colors; words that were forbidden to young men, she knew.

"You'd be no good, anyway, for a wife." He tried to jeer, and she was full-lipped in mockery of him. He was still rubbing the bite marks she'd left on his arm. "Living with nobody but that old woman—you won't ever know anything different." He was weary with the waste of it, and gestured at Ariel as she stood there with her sling at her belt, and her quiver full of arrows and the feather twisted into her braid. "Even Sycorax won't be able to save you, you'll be chosen and next thing you know, you'll be one of the village wives. Come with me, Ariel, to Oualie, I promise you . . ."

But Ariel shrugged; he was tiresome, with his peculiar tabooed talk and his unblinking eyes, which bulged slightly piscine and out of alignment, as if the violent dreams inside him were pressing out. Alone with Sycorax, Ariel judged her circumstances odd enough; Dulé's entreaty only made her realize how much she longed for an ordinary life.

But ordinariness had eluded Ariel, since she was born among the strangers when her parents were brought from the mainland by them to work on their behalf, since she had been orphaned and given to Sycorax. Yet she had no means of understanding the different yearnings she intimated inside her.

Sycorax would tell herself, One day I will face the truth, I will tell her what really happened, I will own up that her real mother may still be alive, somewhere, that she isn't really free to be mine. But she deferred the time, until there seemed no longer any reason to describe the manner of her mother's going, and tell her that they did not belong to one another except by chance. So she deceived herself, not realizing that Dulé had always told his sister the circumstances of her infancy. Sycorax could not imagine he would be so bold or so casual as to usurp her place as the source of knowledge and the shaper of the order by which they lived.

Ariel slept in the tree house, on the other side of the room from Sycorax, until one day, she came to her and said, frowning and kicking at the ground, "Will you come and look at something?"

Sycorax handed Ariel the paddle they used to beat the indigo at the second stage, until the purple-colored particles separated from the liquid and fell to the lees. "Here, it's your turn, do your stint."

Ariel regarded the paddle and persisted, "Later. I'd like you to see this. Now."

Sycorax looked at her in surprise. She had always been so compliant, even in the midst of her dreaminess, that Sycorax was used to summoning her and dismissing her at will. Nor would Ariel be rebelling against the task, for she wasn't overworked: Sycorax by temperament liked to be in control and then to complain afterward that everything fell to her charge. It was one of her failings, she knew.

She put down the paddle, and skimmed the greenish-yellow froth on the surface of the vat with a spoon to observe the color of the liquid underneath. "It's coming on nicely, so I suppose I could leave it. If what you have to show me is so important."

Ariel brightened, and started down the bank of the stream away from the sea.

"This way."

They walked down a beaten path, crossed the stream by stepping stones, and began to penetrate the wilder part of the vegetation beyond the boundaries of the garden Sycorax had made, leaving the track at a point where it turned down to the sea. There, upstream on the other bank, in a coconut grove, Ariel showed her mother the enclave she had built herself, with a spliced fence, a cabin of palm fronds, and a hammock slung from one trunk of a shade tree to another.

"I'd like to live here now," she said. "I'll be quite safe."

Sycorax began, "But what about . . . ?" She was going to list the hazards of forest life, the necessity of the precautions she had taken against insects and other creatures, the need to survey the surrounding scene, as she did from her tree. But Ariel's look of pride in her creation stopped her, for Sycorax cared for her too much to damage the pleasure her claim to independence was bringing the girl. A first feeling of loss stabbed her; she found she could not speak.

They were still together at some stage every day, but Sycorax did not visit her daughter in her cabin in the forest. Ariel had communicated that her new sleeping place was her own, part of the privacy that she had always kept intact inside herself. Gradually she took things away from their shared compound: a fan, a set of bowls, some bone spoons. The animals at first stayed with Sycorax, then, at intervals, the free-roaming ones made the move to be with Ariel, and one or two of the caged animals she had helped to rear escaped and joined her; the piglets remained with Sycorax, and the caveys, except for the youngest pair of the last litter, which Ariel took for her own. The guardian bees still hung from the older woman's lintel.

Sycorax made as if she were proud of Ariel's newfound autonomy, though it hurt her that the young woman seemed to impugn her caring for her as constraint and the time that they had lived so closely as a period of captivity. She began to tell her, on the occasions when they sat and ate together, about her life, in order to impress her, in a way she had never felt she needed to do before. She boasted of adventures she had enjoyed in her youth, the range of experiences she had had, the imposing woman she had been, so that she might hold on to the love and trust and even admiration of her last, and most cherished, daughter. So when Ariel agreed that full moon to come as usual with her to the springs, and even expressed enthusiasm for the idea, Sycorax became full of hope that the present tension between them would pass, and Ariel not forsake her.

11

DURING THE RAINY season, especially when the moon was full, Sycorax had to show patience in the manufacture of indigo; if she misread signs in the weather and didn't bring them in under cover in time, a sudden shower could fill her vats and spoil her measures, and soak the light bricks of the stuff as they were drying. When she had stowed the forms in which the dye had been poured, she was able to set off for the springs with Ariel.

Over the years, the track had been marked out, though the lianas threw down long withies and the undergrowth flourished in the shelter of the jungle canopy. The ciphers on the boundary trees had swollen in the bark with time, and risen up the trunks, sometimes to shoulder height, sometimes higher. These timehri had been made by scraping; they consisted of the dots and strokes that Sycorax also used in her divining for what lay ahead or behind, for promise and destiny. Neither straight downstrokes, like the stems of letters in Kit Everard's log, nor tipped and fledged like the arrows that plotted the course of the *Hopewell* on Kit's portolan, the marks reflected the concept of time and direction Sycorax shared with her people; for as yet, they did not know time as a straight line that can be interrupted, even broken, as the people did who were arriving in their archipelago, the slaves from Africa, the adventurers from Europe; they did not possess a past, for they did not see themselves poised on a journey toward triumph, perhaps, or extinction.

But Dulé knew that at the very moment of his emergence something inalienably his had been drowned alongside the body of his mother, and been irretrievably lost to him, and he had formed his vision of a ladder, spanning one isolated phenomenon of space-time to another. He sensed that he and his friends had forfeited a way of life, and so history presented itself to them as a linear continuum; but the indigenous islanders could conceive differently of the time and space they occupied, and see it as a churn or a bowl, in which substances and essences were tumbled and mixed, always returning, now emerging into personal form, now submerged into the mass in the continuous present tense of existence, as in one of the vats in which Sycorax brewed the indigo.

The flux did not swallow up individuals, or snatch their own stories away from them, as had happened to Dulé, but folded them deeper into the pleats and folds of the whole tribe's existence, like spices in a dough that flavors the entire batch of baking.

The markers—and Sycorax's script—were not legible as signs to the English strangers when they began to explore the rain forests; they merely looked like the teeth or claws of small animals sampling barks. The path wound to the springs under tall ferns with curved plumes like the wings of geese alighting and the fleshier glossy broad-brimmed mangoes and manchineel and guaiacum, gleaming after their daily baths in the rain, and came out on a ridge where the torrent fell in veils of steam. Then it returned into the green shade of the forest, but not before the bosun on Kit Everard's ship, Bossy Phelps, picked out the two figures where they strode together on the exposed ledge.

"Savages, sir," he called out, excited.

"Many?" asked Kit, taking the telescope and training it.

"It was just a glimpse. Can't tell. They was bunched together, a pack of 'em, I'd say."

"I've lost them." Kit shrugged. "It won't be the last time we catch sight of savages, I can promise you."

"Let's hope we see them before they see us, sir. They say they'll clap one eye on us and—dinnertime!"

The path led to the clearing in the trees, where fissures in the ground sighed and spat warm fumes that smelled pungent as birdlime, for they were approaching the big rock where the main hot springs bubbled from the magma below. High above them still, the cone of the volcano seemed to boil, sending white vapor, solid as the froth in a pan of cooking beans, into the dancing sky; these clouds weren't hot, in spite of the mountain's caldron look, but cool, rain-bearing and fugitive.

The following morning, Kit Everard rounded the northern headland of the island, where the waters of the Atlantic swept up against the Caribbean Sea and met in a race, crisscrossing the surface of the shoals with lines of surf. Hugging the shore, he managed to trim his sails tight enough to haul into the prevailing wind along the southern beach. He was looking for an anchorage; and for water, as his supply was running low. He wasn't in the least perturbed; he knew that fresh water was abundant in this season. Through his telescope he could see the gray pumice of the beaches scattered with the blunt horned shells of empty conches; he couldn't see anyone, though he knew that there was always some Indian there, looking back at you; you couldn't know it, not for certain, but you could feel their funny, watchful eyes.

When he saw the creek's waters flowing into the sea he gave the order to lower the mainsail and turned even closer to the wind on a single jib. He was scanning the prospect before him slowly; slowly, the inscrutable shrouds of creepers and bushes and trees began to yield information, and he could pick up signs of cultivation—a kind of clearing, and even water channels. He marked his chart with a question mark, two stickmen and a rough drawing of a hut to remind himself. Then, under the lee of the shore, he brought the boat slowly round the next headland until it would be out of view of anyone who lived in that village, if it was a village, and dropped anchor.

"Five fathoms and still no bottom," called the sailor from the prow as they glided into a narrow bay between two dark banks of mangrove trees standing on bony stilt roots in the shallows.

The stream that flowed here was less bountiful than the one he had passed half a league back, he reckoned, but the chances were it was a tributary and he could follow it to the fork and then approach the village—if village it was—down the course of the other stream. He signaled for the longboat to go ashore and sat facing the land from the stern as the sailors rowed him toward the island. They were seven in all: James Lariot and Tom Ingledew, his officers, Bossy Phelps the bosun, three hands and Kit himself.

The hot springs rose from a crack in the crust of lava from the last eruption of the volcano; the crack ran across a plateau of rock on the mountainside where the water collected in a haphazard series of pools that over the decades had grown deeper and wider as the flow worked its way into the rock. The nearer to the bubbling source, the hotter the pool; the temperature could sometimes rise too high to bear. A sediment of soft white clay, rich in nutrients and tonic salts, was carried by the stream and spread over the rocky ledge, gradually encrusting it with layers of silt like a terrestrial coral reef. It blanched the lava and dried in the heat to an ossuary brittleness and pallor. As the pools' lining of black lava changed over time to this clayey whiteness, the minerals in the spring began to show their colors against it: the flare of magnesium green, the tang of turquoise from the chrysocolla crystals deposited by the evaporating waters, the orpiment rim of the sulfur itself. An object lost in the springs became quickly coated with a sandy gritty skin, while within, the waters transformed its substance, vitrifying it through and through until you could scrape off the outer crust and find inside the original form of the lost object, perfectly cast and glazed with pearl, so light and flaky it would break at the touch.

Users of the springs had helped the natural process of erosion by molding this lunar ooze, while it was still liquid, into small dikes and runnels to conduct the water from one pool to another and in them, below the milky surface, making a shelf for the bathers to sit on while they soaked.

The baths were the most sociable place Sycorax conducted her surgery, her combined business of curing and augury and advice. She would sit soaking in the second-to-hottest basin, while petitioners slipped in beside her, or opposite her, and began to tell her the troubles in their soul and the ailments in their limbs. Ariel was given the pharmacopoeia to carry, in pouches slung on her back, for she had collected the plants and pounded and crushed and tied them into small bundles under Sycorax's direction, though she was becoming increasingly independent in her gathering and measuring of ingredients. Indeed, Ariel seemed to her to take their science more seriously than Sycorax, who still, having come to the art by practical trial and error, had a tendency to scoff at its magical reputation.

They carried dried hibiscus petals for soothing sore gums and annatto powder to turn pale cheeks and lips ruddy and brighten dull hair, oil-of-vetiver grass to rub into the skin and summon a reluctant lover's attention, strands of dulse and other seaweeds bound together for strengthening the blood and stimulating the feet, fresh mangrove leaves from the swamp for soothing stings or calming blisters, aloe milk for healing wounds, various aromatics for ear, nose and throat afflictions, crushed oyster shells for knitting broken bones; in a folded banana leaf, they kept a sea horse or two—effective, when swallowed, in promoting male fertility. They offered smartweeds and fiery peppers, to make men hot and "cross" with passion. They also had a selection of harmful charms: the sharp nail clippings of their caveys', rear paws for wishing internal pains on enemies, and a small gourd of manchineel sap for a more direct approach, for this poison caused blindness when applied to the eyes, and used on an arrow would bring about violent vomiting and—if not remedied—a horrible slow death.

"Come to me afterwards," Sycorax would tell a man who could not attract the woman he wanted. "And I will give you a surefire means to bind her to you." Helping Sycorax with her recipes taught Ariel in turn. Sycorax often mocked her patients, and made light of her prescriptions for them and her skills. ("People run to others with their troubles—baf! I would never come to someone like me if I needed help!" So she would cry, and follow it with a laugh.)

Ariel asked her, "Why do you always do what they ask? Why do you give a love philter to a man who wants someone who doesn't notice him? And if she comes, saying he's bothering her, and she wants something to turn him away—what about that? You'd do that too?"

Sycorax looked into her frowning eyes, and answered, "I don't control what happens, even if it seems that I do. Nobody does. Except perhaps the gods! We're tumbling in the churn, round and round, over and under one another, forever in between one moment and the next. The gods are in with us, too—there's no wall between their space and ours—it's only a question of stepping through, as I can do, sometimes."

Ariel was puzzled. "You have powers others don't have—yes, they could have them, but they don't, they come to you to help them. Why don't you sometimes refuse to do as they wish? You could change things, you could . . . rearrange the pattern, give out a different rhythm. Make them think. I wouldn't like to find the remedy so simple, not to be challenged."

There were a mother and her baby at the springs that morning; when the father, coming in with a game bag from the high woods, joined them in the tepid pool, he called out to Ariel to tell them her name. She turned on him her knitted brows and said, "Everyone knows me, you're just teasing me. Sycorax is my mother, everyone knows her." The man giggled, and whispered to the woman with him, who smirked in response.

Sycorax beckoned Ariel to join her and pay them no attention. "You'll always be noticed and teased as long as you're on your own." She sighed. "It's a nuisance when you're young, and then you miss it when you're old. I could flaunt myself in front of that silly cockerel and he'd look straight through me. Try and enjoy the stir you make, my darling."

It was disconcerting to Sycorax how she could not convince her; in Ariel's view, the man had ribbed her for her strangeness, her orphaned difference.

The divining powers that Sycorax possessed, which she let drift to fit the random demands of the island suppliants, grew in importance under Ariel's severe scrutiny. Ariel sensed, as Sycorax carried on about her youth and its seductiveness, that her mother was avoiding telling her some truth, in the same way as she could not be bothered to face the full character and power of her skills. In turn, Sycorax sensed the young woman's hostility to her evasions, but could not do otherwise. "You will come to understand, Ariel, darling, that as you get older you have to compromise. Youth is ardent and pure and hard—later, wiliness, indolence, neglectfulness come to look so much more attractive."

Ariel set her chin and did not answer. The couple with the baby were joined by another group, who slipped into the pool with them and began splashing and laughing. The sun played on the beads of water flying up and in the dewy shadows of the forest around, invisible birds screeched. The ammoniac pungency of the springs did not matter after a while, even became pleasant, creaturely, intimate, while the steam hung in pale drifts stirred into rising spirals by the occasional breeze; through it, the tangled border of foliage and high trees became a phantom forest as if dissolving back into the spirits of the earth and the air.

Sycorax had brought a picnic; but Ariel shook her head. She would eat later, after bathing. She laid aside her sling and her bow and quiver full of arrows, pointed the pair of caveys to sit on guard by them, undid her belt, pulled the ornament from her hair and shook it free, then stepped into the middle pool.

Sycorax looked at her. And looked away, moved.

She unwound her pagne and slipped into the pool opposite Ariel, who had tilted her head back as she lay in the water, breathing in and out, and drinking in the sky, where clouds spooled lazily.

After a while Ariel said, "It makes me feel I have no edges any longer. I join the air, the sky, the water, the heat. And then there are no more joins."

The other people in the tepid pool seemed farther away than the sky itself, and Sycorax smiled. She exhaled slowly too, feeling the soft sediment under her settle and caress her and the warmth of the water ease her limbs and soften her roughened skin. Once she had been like Ariel—in that part of the bowl of the universe where the sensations break the surface for the first time, and every experience brings new consciousness and new elation. Now she was thoroughly beaten in, and it was hard for her to feel intensely anymore; cynicism was one of the conditions of age, as irreversible as shrinking limbs and weakening eyesight. The baths soothed her, but did not give her the pleasure Ariel clearly felt in their embrace. Yet through the girl she had a glimmering again and so she smiled.

"You'll find sex will do the same, my darling, when you come to it and learn how to have it the way you like it." She was dreamy, she was remembering.

Suddenly, the tranquillity in the hot pool was broken and Ariel was sitting upright, tense, crying across to her.

"Can't you stop it? Can't you stop your endless talk about it?"

"What do you mean?"

"Oh, I know you had all these men and and all this pleasure you tell me about. But how am I to learn? Where? How? Who with?"

She scrambled out of the water and brushed the wet and the tears out of her eyes, and Sycorax clambered out behind her, and called out, after her, her name. But she had run off in a half-crouch, below the branches and over the roots into the thick of the forest, scooping up her weapons and followed by her hunting helpers, including the caveys.

Sycorax felt an unfamiliar pain clutch her chest. She quelled it and determined, "I'll cast a spell for you, to find you ease." She lowered herself into the pool again and closed her eyes.

She began to dream a man for Ariel. But she had trouble deciphering his shape and features in the confusion behind her eyes. There was a disturbance in her; and she came to realize that just as she was regretting how numbed she had become, she was facing a new pain. She must let the young woman leave, as Dulé had left, to join people of her own age, and she must use her art well and let Ariel use it too, on her own account.

It was Ariel who had the sharp eyes and sharper ears, but Sycorax was alone when she went back to the creek, for her daughter had not returned to her at the baths. So she did not notice the presence of the strangers. She had postponed her petitioners to another time, and traipsed home, her mind on many things, so that all too soon she had stumbled upon them and could not hide or run. She walked into her clearing and heard the bees' ferocious buzz as they wheeled above; she saw her stores disturbed, her cloths on the bushes pulled awry, some branches snapped and trailing. She cried out, "Ariel!"

Could the girl be so angry with her?

Then she began to take in more: some chickens and piglets were missing from their pens, and the gourds in which she kept her stores were tumbled and in some cases opened. She grasped, in rising fear, that it could not be Ariel who would have done so much damage. She stood, she did not rummage to see what was missing, what was spilled and broken, she would look later. Now she would leave the ground, and clear her head and look out to sea so that she could think. She would curse the perpetrators, and to do that, she needed the height of her tree. She turned and put a foot on the first burl in the trunk and began to climb.

The bees veered in the air, their wings left a whirlpool near her cheek as she climbed, then she heard a cry and saw that they were swarming in one corner of her enclave; a man in a white shirt with a straw hat on his head staggered howling into her view and fell flailing as the bees clustered on him. She let a laugh join their buzzing and continued to climb, and was nearly inside her cabin when another man with thin gold-red plumes of hair, such as she had not seen before on a man but only on a bird, rose from behind one of the indigo vats and cried out.

She heard the tone of command in his voice and turned to confront him. She cursed the tallow man then, and swung herself into her cabin, lifting herself through the open hole heavily; nothing happened, no blow pursued her. She was not hunted, she could push on the head of anyone who dared come up and shake them off her tree till they fell and broke their necks or split their heads or shattered their backs. So it was with the first sailor who with grunting calls came climbing up; she took both hands and squeezed her thumbs into the scared eyes of Bossy Phelps till he let go and fell.

When the bosun fell heavily to the ground and lay there groaning, another Englishman, at a nod from his leader, lobbed a rag which he had set alight into the tree house; they would wait for the fire to smoke out the enemy. They did not want to be killers, not exactly; they wanted to trade, for their reconnoitering had shown them the skills of these tree-dwellers: the careful stores in their wax-sealed gourds, the lightweight, adamantine ingots of indigo, the cloths of deep purply blue, the vegetable patch, the fruitful orchards. As newcomers, they'd welcome all the advice they could obtain.

Ariel heard the howls and caught the scent of burning, but nothing had been left cooking in Sycorax's pots, neither food, nor dye. Then she saw the dense white smoke rising; so she made her approach quietly, keeping the wind in her face, which meant circling rather than coming at the attackers directly, but she did not know her strategy was wasted: they could never have smelled her on their own, and had no animals with them to pick up the scent on their behalf.

By the time Ariel had the scene in view from below, from her vantage at the mouth of the stream, the group of intruders had come out of cover and were gazing up at the smoking branches of the tree. The fire might not catch, the trees were damp from the rains. She counted five men standing, took in the body on the ground, pitching back and forth holding his leg and another huddled, clutching his face. They were gesticulating and shouting; the sounds were raw to her ears, incoherent, unlike the cries of animals, signifying however neither offense nor defense that she could understand, but merely noisy. They were beating the trunk of the tree; the woven cabin was smoldering.

Ariel took her oyster blade from her belt and picked out the small gourd of manchineel sap from the bag and dipped an arrow into its baneful milk. She fitted it to her bow and let it fly; the wooden point struck the shoulder of one of the men as he stood up, testing his leg. He let out a shriek of fury (this time she understood the noise) and fell forward, as he tried to pull the shaft free and could not. The blood trickled, but the wound counted for less than the poison—in a matter of hours it would turn him black and blue, or blind him if he touched the wound and then rubbed his eyes.

She ran to another position, took another arrow, dipped it too, and chose another target, this time the red man, the plume-headed red man with the rosy face, and the arrow flew just as he moved to one side and raised his hands in imprecation and grazed his arm but did not lodge in his flesh. She heard him shout and point in the direction from which it had come, while he searched for the wound with his mouth to suck it but could not reach, unfortunately, she noted, as the poison would have killed him more quickly taken by mouth.

The men with him went down on one knee and encircled him and raised their weapons. She smiled to herself and let another arrow fly, but she did not see this one land, for the men's weapons exploded in her eyes and she raised her hands to clap them over her ears to prevent the din from entering her head and shattering it into pieces. Then she saw a huge fragment from the flaming cabin fall on the attackers. They scattered, brushing the burning splinters from them and trampling them into embers on the earth.

Ariel stood up with her hands still over her ears and saw Sycorax holding on to a branch of the saman tree with one hand and pointing down at her assailants with the other, her mouth a jagged hole and her eyes dark slits. The fire leapt around her, her edges went black in the firelight. Like a bat she flapped blackly in the burning tree.

Ariel was standing and her edges too fell away from her, but not as they had in the transcendence of water and sky in the hot pools; no, as she stood now and saw what was happening to Sycorax her mother, one being that was Ariel was consumed and dissolved in the fire with her, while the other flew upward to survey the scene in cold help-lessness. The revolving of the world came to an end, space and time collapsed into a point and the point was there, where the tatters of Sycorax's pagne adhered to her flesh and burned her. Ariel, watching, longed to lose consciousness too, to cease to be aware and become instead obliterated utterly, so that she could stop seeing what was unfolding before her eyes. There was a bird calling a warning, she heard on one side of her head. The wind in the crests of the trees was driving the fire before it like spray on the surf and the uppermost leaves were sizzling in the flames, sap bubbling in the branches and oozing. One of her animals was yelping weakly at her heels. The creatures remaining in the pens were yowling and squawking, and the free-roaming animals rushing headlong from the compound in terror toward her, where she stood with her back to the sea. The men were screaming too, and shaking the tree while her victims and the stung man slapped and fretted at their wounds. The huge tree would not be swayed and drop Sycorax to the ground.

Ariel was standing witness, joined to the horror by her eyes and ears and the beat of her blood. She felt then that she would never be able to move again, to separate from her mother who was burning. Sycorax was burning Ariel with her, and the young woman began to run toward the clearing, and just as she felt the roots and leaves underfoot give way to the clinkers of shell that formed the domestic floor, a bullet caught her in the thigh and gashed it open, and she fell with a gasp as the hot pain began to rise and streak through her to hit her heart.

She came together again at the shot's touch of ice, her borders all defined in tension, her limbs and frame her own, but breached; she was pulling herself up to run forward to Sycorax's tree, and the men were advancing on her, when another part of the cabin gave way, sparks showered into the clearing, and Sycorax fell with them out of the saman to the ground.

They threw a coat over her and put out the flames; she was half asphyxiated and could not speak even if they had been able to understand her.

When they peeled off her incinerated clothing, they were surprised to find that she was a woman, and an old woman at that.

"She went up that tree like a monkey—I'd have sworn no woman could climb like that."

"And this one, it's a female too." The sailor had Ariel by the wrists. She was putting up no protest now, except to pull away and fall to her knees by Sycorax and put her mouth to her ear. She did not weep. She ordered her, "Don't die, Old Mother, tell me what to do."

Sycorax smelled of barbecued meat and the blisters on her skin had burst where her clothes had been ripped away and her flesh showed red as raw tuna fish underneath.

"You know my art," she said quietly.

"No," Ariel cried aloud. "Not enough. Not yet."

"You'll learn as you go along. I did." Her eyes were open now, her face puffy and twisted, her lashes and eyebrows frizzled orange and stunted. She stared up at the sky, where a pillar of black oily smoke rose from the smoldering mango leaves. Her cabin was all aflame, though the tree itself was not burning brightly: the interior of the rain forest was moist and would not catch as easily as the partitions of her room, where the fronds were tinder-dry.

"No," Ariel cried again. "Don't leave me here alone. Not with them."

One of the men began to pull at her, but she jumped up, though her leg blazed with pain, and stood at the ready with her knife in one hand, an arrow in the other held like a javelin, stabbing at the air to show them how she would deal with any comer.

The nearest stranger turned in alarm for confirmation to the leader, the red plumy man in the loose white shirt with the pistols in both hands and the broad-brimmed straw hat. He was keeping an eye on them, his guns leveled at them, and every now and then he glanced upward at the smoke and crackle in the trees to watch the progress of the fire. It was slowing down, but the air was thick and scented.

Sycorax said, "My darling, you're hurt too." Slowly, her breath harsh, she listed aloud the ingredients for a compress on her burns, the maca-pine-tree needles for stitching her wound, the leaves and grasses to infuse for a balm for both of them, different ones for a sleeping draft (this was a recipe Ariel knew).

Her speech came in short rattling bursts, and then she cried out and, twisting, caught hold of Ariel's ankle, nearly bringing her down. "You'll have to stop fighting them, I'm sorry. If you want to heal—if you want me to live. Treat with them, Ariel. It's the only way."

Ariel looked the red-haired man in the eye and made a gesture with her weapons, as if to throw them down, and then nodded sternly, pointing to his. Once she had his attention, she signaled to her mother on the ground and then pointing to the bees' victim, the groaning target of her first poisoned arrow and to the wound in the red man's arm, she made the sounds of the swarm on the rampage, the singing of the arrows.

The red man's eyes narrowed. There was a hubbub around, the fire made the foliage hiss and sigh, and Bossy Phelps, lying on the ground, gasped and retched. The poison was jerking his limbs; groans rose from others in the company where they sprawled and crouched in fear.

At Ariel's feet, Sycorax was whispering, "Give them back their health, darling, in exchange for my life, your pain."

In the shadow of his hat, Ariel could see the leader's eyes flickering between their squeezed lids; they were amber-colored, like glass versions of the freckles that bespattered his rosy face and forearms; a bee-sting over one eye had swollen up one side of his face and, in the sharp smoke, was making him weep. In fact, all of him was pinky-red and blistered-looking and, most fascinating of all, covered in a gold-red fuzz, particularly the skin showing where his shirt was open at his neck. She got wind of him too, and the smell of him was odd, not musky fragrant like the scents of red fruits or red flowers, but brackish, more like the high-tide wrack after the sun has baked it brittle.

No wonder Sycorax mocked them, calling them seashell people: this red man was like a husk after the prawn has been cooked and eaten—pink and whiskery and briny.

He repeated her gesture to her, and she nodded again. His eyes swept round the four men left unharmed in the clearing and she could see him give the command that they were not to assault her. They cringed, keeping their eyes on her miserably, like mice batted about by a cat. They were scared, she could smell that, too.

Ariel held her arms wide, let her arrow and her knife fall to the ground. The leader did not drop his weapons reciprocally, but, with an intake of breath, stuck his pistols in his blue belt, one on each side, and with a smile, began walking toward her and Sycorax.

"Go, my Ariel, go now." The old woman pushed herself into a sitting position to confront Kit Everard, who gasped as Ariel made a rush at him and then dodged him, running away, dragging her wounded leg. She threw a look behind her, at the burned body of her mother, and her black eyes grew blacker with urgency under her frown. Whimpering though they themselves had escaped hurt, her animals followed, an agami bird squalling as it half-flew, half-loped, her caveys scrabbling to flee with her, the monkeys, the squealing pigs, the guardian swarm, and even the toads, following her into the forest.

"Fine bloody mess," said Kit Everard, kicking experimentally the leg of Tom Ingledew, who lay weak from the multiple stings he had received. He wrapped a cloth round his hand and then pulled at the arrow stuck in the bosun's shoulder. Bossy Phelps gave a high cry and fell into a different position.

"At least you're still with us, you can thank Providence for that," said Kit.

He walked over to Sycorax and looked the body up and down. She was lying on one side, and there were blistering burns on her thighs and shoulders and hands. The flesh was most raw in appearance on her back, however. He glanced up at the smoking fragments of her cabin—the fire had leapt free into another part of the forest, it was almost out in the trees around the clearing itself. When his shadow fell across her, she twitched and fastened a look on him and held out her hands palms down and spoke.

Kit Everard heard her and began to pray, "Dear Lord, protect me from this benighted creature and her foul magic. Forgive me, dear God, forgive me, for I did not mean to bring hurt on any woman, but thought that in the hunt I'd beaten a horde of savages from cover. My error, my grievous error." He was backing away from Sycorax, who, with closed eyes, was still murmuring.

"We fired in self-defense," Kit went on, praying. "In your all-seeing wisdom, you know that, my Lord. And if I've done wrong, I'll do penance for it, in full measure."

The old woman dropped her hands and her body slumped as if the spirit in her were drifting away; she was dying, he could see, bent in the position of an infant in the womb. Should he baptize her to save her soul? He called to one of the men, his friend and fellow pioneer, James Lariot.

"Do what you like, Kit, it makes no odds to me. Her soul's bound for hell, Christian or not." He rubbed a bee-sting ballooning on his arm. "But give the men orders to return to the ship—I beg you. That column of smoke is signaling trouble for miles around. We'll be ambushed, if we delay. Let's abandon this place—this accursed place." He spoke feverishly.

"What? Leave now? When we've just achieved this territory? My dear James . . . you're ailing. Besides, we've a duty to the wounded. These women aren't our enemies . . . they can help us. They may teach us the secrets of the isle—decipher its noises for us—guide us to its treasures . . . We come to bring peace, remember, not the sword."

"Swords aren't worth a penny candle beside the arrows of those savages." James spat and pointed to the two prone men. "Not enemies? We've two dead . . ."

"Not altogether dead. Don't meet the devil with mourning. That's his work, you know. Despair. When she returns—and return she will to succor the old woman—we'll catch her and make her tend to our men first. I'll be bound they have a kind of cunning with herbs that we know nothing of, herbs to counteract the strongest venoms."

Together Kit and his two chief officers made a plan, and sent a man to fetch a rope and reinforcements from the ship, ready to bind Ariel when she came.

They did not hear her approach; in spite of her dragging leg, she reached Sycorax's side all at once, and was crouching by her, a gourd filled with a luminous liquid on the ground beside her, and on her back, a basket of leaves for compresses, bandages and decoctions, which she swung down to her other side.

"Oh, my mother," she was muttering. "Oh, my dear mother." She was half-moaning through her teeth in sympathy, as she began to tamp down the open weals on Sycorax. Then she heard the tread of the men's boots; the noose went over her head and the rope drew tight around her neck. She leapt up and faced her captors. The red man seemed to be smiling at her, with a funny look in his eyes, as though the act of roping her had reminded him of something he had to do, and had forgotten before. Another man came at her with the end of the rope and slicked it in her face, across her nose, and then pointed to the men on the floor and to her baskets and her gourd and then started pulling her by the rough halter to their side.

"These men first—then you can deal with that dark withered thing."

Ariel understood; she knelt to pick up her tackle and medicine and felt the bite of the rope on her flesh where he tugged.

"Don't you pretend now, or you'll not see another day, neither you nor that foul hag, I swear." He was shouting, she heard the fear and the fury in him from her position at Sycorax's side, and she turned to put her lips to Sycorax's ear, still tamping with the compress of moss and leaves soaked in lotion.

"Let her be, James. She's asking her, she understands. Let the old woman talk."

James Lariot let a moment pass, as Sycorax's lips moved and something floated into the air and was gathered by Ariel. When she felt the burn of the rope at her neck again, she drew herself up and walked to the bosun she had shot, and selecting certain herbs from her basket, she began to peel his soaking clothes from the area of his shoulder where the arrow had entered.

"Let her have the knife back," said Kit.

The men who were keeping watch at the edge of the clearing were drawn now to watch the girl as she began to nurse their companions. The cotton of her first victim's tunic was stiff with sweat from his convulsions; the hole was edged with gray foam and the flesh for a radius of four inches all around was livid and putrefying already to the depth of a finger joint.

Ariel forced a leaf between his lips and mimed a chewing action, and put her hands over his eyes to indicate he should keep them shut; then she cut into Bossy Phelps, and taking two large leaves, used them as protective mitts to lift out the diseased flesh, as one of the spectators gagged and Kit himself turned away. She pointed to the stones where the fire was usually built for cooking.

"Hot water, of course; she needs hot water." Kit gave orders, the men recovered themselves, and in a flurry, found tinder and kindling and set up the tripod and the calabash that had been tipped over and collected water from one of the ponds. But Ariel did not need hot water; she first numbed the wound with cool herbs and then took a brand from the fire and seared the exposed flesh. He did not cry out, the drug in the leaf in his mouth had stopped the pain for a while.

One spectator sat down on the ground; he felt nauseous and dizzy at the sight of her quick work.

"You can let go of the rope now," said Kit.

James Lariot cast an eye at him, and took the rope end and tied it round his waist.

"Safer this way, I think."

Ariel worked on; she bathed the bee-stings with a fizzing lotion that drew some of their heat, and then was beckoned over by the other victim of her envenomed arrows, Kit Everard, the red man. He was propped up now against a tree, and he pointed to the graze on his other arm and rolled up his sleeve to show her how, superficial as it was, it was already festering. It needed lancing, which she did, while he bit down on another wad of intoxicating foliage which she had pushed into his mouth; then she salved the graze with a mixture of styptic herbs, working at speed, lifting her head twice to look over at Sycorax. She did not mind if she hurt him; somehow the lesser seriousness of his wound made her wish to inflict greater pain on him than on the dying man on whom she had performed the best surgery she could.

The red man's skin was dappled, rather like the scales of a river fish, only the fine coating of red hairs made him more like a kind of pale and hairy fruit. She wondered what he was like—below; she wondered if he was pink and golden-haired there too, and, incongruously, almost chuckled. Then, moving as fast as her hurt leg allowed, she returned to Sycorax's side.

"Help her," commanded Kit from where he sat, drowsy with the opiate in his mouth. "Bring her everything. And for God's sake, James, untie that rope."

James shrugged, and let the rope fall, but made no move to lift the halter from Ariel's neck, until Kit flashed at him a look that made him approach her and undo the knot. She paid no attention, continuing in increasing distress to scan the piteous body of Sycorax to see where she should begin.

The men hung back from handing Ariel her baskets and bowls.

"Imbeciles!" muttered Kit. "She won't eat you, you prize imbeciles."

"That's exactly what she would do," said Tom Ingledew weakly. "If
we let her. And you're doing your best to help her." He indicated to
the sentries to begin carrying the boatswain back to the boat.

"Be quiet," said Kit thickly. "You have no grasp of the matter. No
idea how to handle this."

James gave a dry cough of a laugh.

"It's you—the poison's touched you and you've lost your wits." He
paused. "Kit, think! We must abandon them. The old woman's dying,
and what's the use of either of them? It'll only mean trouble, their
men'll come after us—you know what'll ensue."

At that moment, as he was saying it, James understood what his
leader and his friend had in mind. He took in Kit as he lay back against
a tree dreamily watching the scene, he saw him gazing at Ariel bent
over Sycorax. The girl was twisting a quill through her long braid to
keep it out of the way as she bent to her task of relieving the old
woman's pain. With a pair of reed tweezers in one hand, a compress
of painkilling juices in the other, she was plucking out the fragments
of burned clothing and grasses and shells where Sycorax had fallen,
dabbing the soothing liquor into the flesh with the other. Now and
then she paused to wipe the face of Sycorax, who had turned livid
except for dark-blue hollows all round her shut eyes, and tipped water
to her lips. He saw how Kit listened to the brief utterances of the girl,
as though he could understand them, and how he looked almost happy
as he gazed.

"You will be all right, my mother, you will be all right." Sycorax
gave a moan now and then, when Ariel tweaked out a deeper shard,
but the girl was pleased to hear her make any kind of sound.

"I'll be damned," said James. "You want to stay. Here. Now. With
everything at risk."

"We'd have been attacked already, my dear James," answered Kit,
opening languid eyes in which the dark and dilated pupils had turned
a deeper color than his usual amber pallor, "if these two women had
anyone living here with them. Nobody will attack us now. We'll camp
here tonight." He waved at the forest. "Take the appropriate steps."
He ordered the men, speaking softly and carefully, as if he were not
quite sure of the next word until he managed to alight on it. "One
hand to go back to the boat—all right, two hands. If you must. Give
news of us to the others on board, and return with supplies. And
buckets. I want to resupply. Meanwhile, the rest, remain. No, the

wounded stay here too. Better off here." He smiled, "It's a pleasant billet, in spite of the disorder our little trouble caused."

He raised himself and began to walk over to Ariel, approaching her this time from the front, not from her rear, and in dumb show indicated the clearing, and made pillow gestures like a child. Then he pointed at her leg, solicitously, and bent closer to peer into the features of the old woman on the ground.

The cracks in the yellowish mask of her face were blue, as if they'd been tattooed; her brow and her mouth were puckered with pain, and the shadows in the puckers were grayish-blue too. She was as ugly as a lump of lead, he decided.

He wondered what relation she bore to the young girl dressing her wounds. It was striking how similar the words for "Mother" were in the languages he'd heard in the course of his travels: he thought he heard Ariel call the savage and deformed crone something that resembled babies' first babbling, something like, "Mamma."

And so he was glad that the old hag seemed to be still stirring under Ariel's hands, as he would not want to appear a murderer in the eyes of her daughter or her granddaughter. Rather, he had a mind to persuade her to consider him a well-intentioned friend who had been horribly mistaken for a brief, unfortunate episode; which together they might put behind them now.

PART III

Orange/Red

That does not keep me from having a terrible need of—
shall I say the word—religion. Then I go out at night
and paint the stars.
—VINCENT VAN GOGH

12

IN THE PAST, Sycorax had been afraid of her knowledge. Gradually, however, she had grown into her role as wisewoman and witch, and come to accept the powers others attributed to her, and agree that she might be the special source and cause. But now, fallen from her cabin, she was cut off from all understanding, and had no strength to kick against the darkness that had come down around her. Her pelvis was cracked on her right side and her back broken, though neither she nor Ariel knew this yet in their attention to the burns she had received. When Ariel gently lifted the old woman to move her to her own quarters up the path in the forest, Sycorax gave a huge cry; the folding of her body in Ariel's arms shot fiery rivers of pain through her that for a while swallowed up all the others she suffered from her burns. Ariel wept and nearly stumbled, for her own leg was sore too, but she kept on going, determined to take Sycorax away from the men who were camping in their compound, drawing water from the stream, building a fire on their hearthstones, and beginning to roast a spitted shoat to eat.

Sycorax fainted, and Ariel bent her cheek to the discolored cheek of the old woman and licked the salt that fell in her tears, and when she reached the cabin took her inside, where the rush screens would keep the flies off her wounds, and made her as comfortable as she could on the ground, with fresh dressings on her burns, a cool soaked cloth on her forehead. She was singing to her hoarsely, struggling through exhaustion and grief to find breath.

So Ariel kept vigil as the night came down on that day nearly four hundred years ago, when everything changed for them. Yet the night stole in with habitual, velvet gentleness, as she sang, low and hoarse:

> "The holes in my net are so fine
> They catch the moon in the water;
> There is always a quarry greater by far,
> A tenderer fruit, a softer fur,
> Can you find honey in the crack of a tree,
> Hear the song in the mouth of the shell?"

As Ariel's voice reached through the darkness that had walled up Sycorax in pain, she tried to recall some of the things she had once known; she murmured and found that when she did so Ariel stopped singing, so she tried not to remember out loud, but to save the retrieved pieces inside her so that the low, scraping voice of the girl she loved would not be interrupted. She remembered there had been fire in starbursts never seen before, and explosions of noise. Even the fires in the depths of the crater mouth had a kind of slow sly laughter in them that did not erupt and scream and tear at you as these fires did. People used to talk about a time when the volcano also spat flames and rocks into the sky, like the strangers' guns, when the black strand on the northern promontory of the island was formed by the mountain's spewing. She thought she would pray to the power in the mountain to stop the pain, and her lips moved to begin her entreaty; Ariel bent to her to catch what she said. There seemed to Sycorax a great need to placate the gods; within the winding sheet of her bodily agony, she could feel another grief, that she had neglected them, had scorned the gifts they had lavished on her, taken them as they came instead with gratitude due. And now, too late. She was punished, and with her, Ariel.

Ariel heard her and managed to decipher the words: "Adesangé, god of the mountain, do not abandon me!" She fastened swollen eyes on Ariel. "And you, don't forget him: Adesangé!"

The young woman shook her head and steeped the cloth on Sycorax's brow again, and bent closer, keeping her mind focused on her song, for she knew that someone was at her back, at the opening of her cabin, beyond the screen of rushes that stood there, and he was waiting for her.

She heard the undergrowth squeak under his feet every now and then, but she stuck to her song, making herself think of healing, though her thoughts were wayward. In her mind's eye, she flayed the red man of his sparse pelt and hung it up to dry over a pole in her garden and then used it—as roofing for her animals' hutch perhaps, or a tunic for herself. He'd be red then, as red as Sycorax's open weals.

"I won't forget him," she promised her mother. "Adesangé, yes," she reassured her.

Red was close to blue, Sycorax thought. When you looked up too long without blinking on a day when the sun was high and the blue saturated the sky evenly and deeply from the horizon to the zenith, and closed your eyes, what you saw then was fire, crisscrossed with rivulets of blood. These were the veins in your lids, she knew that, though now, in the darkness of her pain, she remembered that Adesangé, lord of the volcano, the power that leapt in the crater and had leapt to set her on fire, moved along fissures in the earth that forked like those veins in her eyes. The sky—the aether, the immaterial arch of blue above her—had led her to neglect material presence of anger in fire. The blue should have reminded her of his flaming, instead of entrancing her by its own beauty, the beauty which had seemed to be utter and complete in itself. Now, swept by red wave upon wave, she had to expiate her failure.

The blue I used to make, she thought to herself, was the culmination of a sequence. It marked the end of the long process of transformations—starting with the seething leaves of the plant, then the reeking green stage of the first steepings, and the sulfurous yellow stage of the liquor before it was exposed to the air, then, binding with the air, it gradually turned to blue.

The emptiness in which all things revolve is blue, she went on, in her half-waking state. Time is no other color but blue, since distances are blue and water too. But when you enter into them, she now saw in sorrow, the blueness evaporates. It has no more substance than a smell. Like me, like us, who are dissolving into the whirling water too.

Then she checked herself, realizing she was wandering in her mind. The pain wound itself tighter round her.

The people who are seizing and occupying the present time cannot belong in my color, they're like the bits that leap out of a spinning bowl, too heavy, too separate and distinct to be blended in with the other substances; red-hot stones, flung out and setting on fire the place where they land.

Her mind was drifting on the waves of her pain. We do not exercise power over explosions and crackling and snapping of fire like the strangers, we fall back into the waves—as Dulé's mother did, the young woman I dug up all those years ago, who had been drowned, who had returned to the deep blue.

When Sycorax seemed to be quieter, her lips still and her breathing more regular, Ariel drew to the side of the room and stretched out her sore leg and leaned against the wall and closed her eyes.

She heard the red man approach, she saw the screen swell as his motions stirred the air outside. She did not move, she was too heavy with all that had happened, she could not even lift her hands to cover her face. She would kill him later, she thought, when she was strong again. Meanwhile, she must sleep.

He held the screen aside, and said something, in his language, and she understood he was inquiring about Sycorax. Then he pointed to his bandaged arm. "It's tingling, that's a good sign. A sign of healing."

He was standing in the entrance, with the reed door hanging bunched in his good hand. The tree frogs whistled—three urgent calls on a rising scale, one to another, again and again. She knew there was nothing she could do to make him go away; and she smelled him, and the acrid want in him.

In spite of her bone-weariness, all of a sudden she was facing him squarely, for she was the same height, and if anything, more strongly built. He caught hold of her hand and pushed it between his legs and ground his mouth against hers. The dullness she had felt in her exhaustion became a kind of sickness now, as for the second time that day she once again flew from her own body and split into two. Two Ariels, one outside the other, each watching the other, curious, inert, from the other side of consciousness, in the country where the souls wander. She was curious, about the whey in his mouth and the shaft of his cock under her palm and the paired kernels of his balls; about the possibility of pleasure her mother Sycorax, who was dying now beside her, had talked of so often. She would kill him later, but for the present, she was thinking of Sycorax, who had instructed her in love, and wondering if it would please her that here she was, filling a man with desire just as Sycorax had always said she should.

He flung his head to one side and muttered something, his face was twisted up; he pushed himself away and fell out through the entrance and onto his knees and she sat down on the floor, for her legs felt weak and the wounded one was throbbing painfully, and she crawled over to Sycorax and lay down beside her and sobbed hot, dry grief until she at last fell asleep.

Outside, crouching, his weight resting on his good arm, Kit Everard was praying, " 'The Lord is my shepherd; I'll not want.' " I want, he thought, I want, I want her still, but I subdued my want. He turned over on the ground, and put his hand to his cock and squeezed himself. "Dear Lord God, help me, help me not become today a murderer and a ravisher. 'Yea, though I walk through the valley of the shadow of death, I shall fear no evil.' I shall do no evil, I shall not cast the shadow of death around me. I was not made for this, my Lord, my shepherd. 'For thou art with me; thy rod and staff shall comfort me.' " He was holding himself rhythmically now, pumping with long, smooth strokes. "By pastures green, he leadeth me, the quiet waters by. Give me your rod," he implored, "give me your strength." He groaned at his blasphemy, then heaved the words onto his lips, "Lord, be my shepherd. Lead me beside the still waters. Though I should walk in the valley of the shadow of death, save me from this place, from the magic in it." With a series of sharp spasms, he ceased, and lying back quietly now, with no words teeming in his head, he wiped his hand on the ground.

Then he curled up where he lay, at the entrance of the cabin Ariel had build, where Sycorax lay dying, and began to fall asleep. He had been truly godforsaken today, he was thinking as he sank; he had never before done so much violence to anyone. I shall found a garden in these western isles, he swore. I've struggled to the edge of the navigable world—in my *Argo*—to find the golden fruits of the setting sun—and now I've found them—and they're guarded by maidens. Or at least by one maiden, and she has given me battle.

The fruit was still not in his grasp, but he would reach it, he would tend the tree that bore it, he would plant more from its magical pits and seeds.

His last thoughts were that he would make amends for this day: he could baptize the maiden, they could be saved together, they could marry, he would love her, his heathen maiden, no, his heathen hoyden, he like the rhyming of that, heathen hoyden; he would cherish her beneath the fruit-laden tree. All would be healed. "The Lord is my shepherd, I'll not want. He maketh me down to lie. In pastures green, he leadeth me, by the Hesperides, by the western isles."

13

From *"How We Played: A Memoir"* by Sir "Ant" Everard

Kit Everard to Rebecca Clovelly

Everhope Island, Eighteenth of April, Year of Our Lord 1619

Dear Cousin,

How should I begin to describe to you the many enchantments of this isle? It has been nigh on a full month since we first made a landfall onto the north shore: we rode in the longboat on the crest of the shining surf and I set my foot withal on this fair land in the name of the King. How I have longed to have you in my arms to show you its marvellous bounty, its plentiful springs and well-watered pastures, its salt ponds and forest arbours where gay birds fly and the trees bear abundantly! Yet ere now we were not ready to supply a ship to return to our dear native shore and bring you news of our safe passage and happy issue of our venture. My expectations have been met in full measure, as I think you may ascertain for yourself from our well-beloved Tom Ingledew, who conveys to you this packet. God himself has blessed this land with fruitfulness and beauty. You cannot count the features of loveliness here, but I attach some pages from my notebook to discover to you the ingenious flora of this fair isle and their many productive and rich uses. That which I trust shall make me worthy of your high esteem.

The first is a cotton bush: Figure (*a*) describes the fruit in bud, like a green mitten. The Figure (*b*) reveals the fuit in ripeness, when the floss inside is ready to be plucked, as soft as the lock of hair I keep with me always from your dear golden head.

The second drawing I submit to your lively discernment is the indigo bush, from which a deep and lustrous shade of blue is obtained by a kind of alchemy. The natives who abide here practise this art most skilfully: at the Figure (*a*), a sprig, like a tamarind in the size of leaf; then, (*b*) a piece of indigo compact and ready for use. The natives are amenable, for all their savage state, and impart their wisdom to us in exchange for fribbling items; a mere hairpin will set them to an ecstasy of delight, for they are like to children and have no metals.

The third is the tobacco plant: (*a*), the flower; (*b*), the leaves plucked and drying. I know you know of it and have even assayed it in a pipe, as they did at court when Astraea ruled and she was inclined to taste it now and then.

Companion of my heart, I trust in God that all we venture here bear fruit and I count on your prayers too, for the Lord must incline his will when such a one as you petitions him. We are settled on the southern shore, called Belmont for the amenity of the situation, within a stout stockade I am causing to be built. Though these measures are not due to necessity, as the people here are glad to be of service to us and treat us with courtesy in which not a little deference is admixed, for as I say they count many simple things great wonders: my fine paste shoe buckles (the only part remaining after some native rats that are very large and like to be tame devoured the rest of the appurtenances) inspired much clicking of teeth and clucking of tongues till I thought I should have to part with them. But I restrained the impulse, for it is as well to eke out such tokens of our goodwill as we possess.

I desire you to ask your good father if he can procure me a joiner or two and one or two masons. They will be very serviceable, and needs must bring their tools with them insofar as these be scant indeed on the island. Their labours will meet reward, for such serv-ants are as gold in these parts. I desire he would send also a box of Castile soap, a chest of candles, four hats (the sun does not like my complexion), a small case of drinking glasses (the supply on board the *Hopewell* was dashed to pieces), and should the passage lie by the isle of Madeira, a pipe of that nectar, for I have exhausted my store. But let not these requests from a young planter discourage you, my dear cousin. He has planted himself and his small company betimes;

indeed apart from the few native people, as I say, there is no one here to give us hindrance in our enterprise. Our sojourn here will raise such a city as Cadmus when he sowed the Theban field.

May God continue to give us his blessing. I would have you smile too, fair cousin, as it is my hope and one that you are privy to that you may soon be more to me than cousin. In this we will meet the desires of your good father, who has been gracious enough to give permission for my suit and endow his future son with the means withal to be worthy of your hand.

Fly here to stand by my side, sweet lady, for we can further the walls of Christendom on the isle in goodly state. Then shall my happiness be complete.

I give thanks to the Lord that He has seen fit now to bless my long devotion to the wind.

Ever yours in hope, from the fair new-found land of Everhope . . .

14

DULÉ SKIMMED INTO shore silently, under cover of darkness, and threaded through the banana fronds and mango groves to Ariel's cabin; a leaf here, a twig there gave under him, but the English sailor posted to keep watch in the clearing was fast asleep and the others would not have woken from their stone weariness if Dulé had hallooed at them.

Some of his companions had reported smoke, but Dulé had thought little of it—Sycorax could have been stewing the indigo with special enthusiasm. Then the fear reached him that there had been an assault— a ship had been seen, moored, the men had been observed returning with limbs dressed for wounds. Dulé had been at sea all day beyond the outer reef, fishing for rose conches and the sweet eggwhite-smooth lambie inside; he returned to his paddle and plied it swiftly, making the crossing under the stars.

He had overcome the islanders' deep dislike of the sea by night, when shadows welled in the phosphorescence and the pale monster Manjiku reared his snout from the waves. He addressed the invisible monster in an undertone, swearing at him till he laughed out loud at his own inventions: "You'll choke for greed one of these days, Manjiku! You'll open those jaws of yours so wide, the hinges will snap at the corners."

Manjiku was the creature who wanted to be a woman; the beast that stole children for his own because he could not give birth to them himself.

The youth drew the pirogue up the gray sand and crept forward to the clearing, and stood trying to piece together the disorder that he could dimly pick out in the darkness. He could taste the charred wood, the burned sap, still in the air, sniff the sourness of the indigo where it had been trampled and soaked into the ground. He began to rake the shadows, furious he could not set a light; his eyes were keener underwater than in this dark, all shapes around him were phantoms edged in blue in the starlight, but he saw no bundle among the sleeping men that could be Sycorax, no body that was Ariel's. He thought of the cabin up the creek to which his sister had withdrawn at his urging, and he turned to find the track, willing himself to control his horror, to keep moving nimbly and stealthily as if he did not feel unstrung.

It did not come to his mind to murder any of them; it was not his way, or the way he had been raised, to take life in cold blood, without a formal challenge or warning, without the necessary ritual preparation for combat and maybe death. If someone had suggested he should have killed them then, where they lay, and avert all the trouble that was to come, Dulé would have been astonished that such a cowardly procedure could be proposed, let alone seriously entertained. To attack in self-defense, as Ariel had done, was a warrior's response, justified in the heat of the battle. But to dispatch a victim in the dark, while he was sleeping, was not a method of attack or survival understood by Dulé or the people among whom he had grown up.

(So much that was to come would have not happened on Liamuiga and Oualie, or would have happened later, perhaps not to him, and with a difference, if Dulé had followed another code.)

When he reached the hut Ariel had built, he found Kit Everard asleep on the threshold, curled up like a worm when a hoe has struck it in the earth, grimacing with his whole body as if in pain. One hand was on the stock of his gun, the other on his groin. Dulé looked, gauged the depths of his sleep, and lifted the gun from his loose hand. He studied the stranger for a moment; a trickle of something shapeless, cold, disturbed him deep inside, a connection he did not care to splice, not then. He closed his fist on the gun; he had heard of such weapons, though never had one within his reach before. Then, gripping it, he passed through the rustle of the reed jalousie hanging in the doorway into the small interior, where Sycorax lay on her side, collapsed on the beaten earth like a child's poppet made from plaited grass, with Ariel on her haunches beside her, head sunk on her knees, a fan fallen to the ground beside her. A sickly, clotted stench filled the space. He squatted to take his sister by the shoulder and rouse her; she was groggy, she could barely lift her eyelids to look at him, but when she saw who it was, she wrapped her arms around him and pressed her head to his chest.

She whispered, hoarse from weariness, "She is dying, Dulé. Even her art can't save her, not now."

Dulé leaned to look at the dark husk that was the old woman's body; shadows bound the close air inside the room and he could see her only as a lighter shape. He put out his hand to touch her face; it felt on fire, hot and dry with fever, as she turned to his hand mouthing, as if to take some sustenance from it. Ariel poured water from a gourd onto a cloth and pressed it to Sycorax's lips, and she sucked like an infant.

Grief clutched Dulé in the heart. Opposed, he could breathe fire; contradicted or challenged, he could put up his fists and fight. If his enemy held a stave he could cross weapons with him. But here, in this dark, with the broken figures of his mother, her enchantments undone, and his sister, her winged limbs hobbled, and the unfamiliar wormlike red man curled at the entrance of their dwelling, Dulé was emptied of all feeling except a scarring, stabbing pity.

"Let me carry her. You follow." He squatted to take hold of Sycorax.

"No!" Ariel cried out. "She can't be moved, not now." She gestured at her own body, sweeping a hand over her thighs, her stomach, her chest to indicate the range of Sycorax's burns. "We can't move her. Not now. Not yet."

Dulé was sweating, and the sweat was drying cold in his armpits and the small of his back.

"What shall I do?"

"Bring the others. As many as possible. And food, presents, tobacco." Ariel was dry-eyed, but a lump stood in her throat. "Some people to help me. To stay with me. As soon as Sycorax can be moved, then we must come back, to the village." She paused. Her voice continued, low, stammering. "I don't want to live here anymore. Dulé! You left . . . I want to go too." She was weeping now, and he knelt beside her, stiffly, and promised her with the touch of his hand on her shoulder that he would bring help.

"Soon, Ariel, soon! You'll be able to go, to go wherever you want,

I swear it. Like me. Another island, another place, my island; you can have land there for yourself, for us, it can be ours."

"I want to be with other people, Dulé. Not alone. Not anymore."

"You shan't be."

"Adesangé," whispered Ariel. "He rules over fire. She said to me, 'Do not forget him. Adesangé.' " Her eyes in the darkness found his and her dry hand clasped his leg, where he now stood beside her, preparing to leave. " 'And he will not forget you.' "

For the first time, Ariel felt the need to worship a higher power, a fate who might avenge her and protect her in answer to her entreaties.

For a month Sycorax lay feverish; her dreams were filled with violence. Ariel took care of her. She washed her carefully, passing over the thin, dry limbs with smooth, light strokes, her hand filled with moss she had soaked in balm; combing out the sparse hair with quills and twisting it back up again into a knot. Sycorax no longer leaked whatever liquids or foods she was able to consume, as she had during the worst of her fever, and Ariel could prop her up into a sitting position, and then, presenting her shoulders to her, go down on one knee to hoist her piggy-back and carry her to the privy in the forest a few minutes' walk away.

In these early weeks of her dying, Sycorax slept, and in her sleep, cried out. And sometimes laughed, uproariously.

That cackling witch, Kit thought, when will she die? The Englishmen longed for her death; Kit even found himself praying sometimes for it. Sycorax was lodged in his conscience and she lamed him, like a stone in a horse's hoof; yet he could not bring himself to have her murdered. On the one hand, he sensed the anger of the island and its hot spirits if the powerful enchantress died (for so he saw her); he attempted to exorcise this fear with prayer and readings from the Bible, sometimes aloud to the uncomprehending heathen girl who tended the hag as if she were a lover.

On the other hand, he grasped the high value of the old woman and her nurse as hostages.

The deputation which arrived soon after the unfortunate events that attended their arrival had made it quite clear that he should not surrender such precious captives. He met the island's emissaries under the huge saman tree where the old woman had lived in her tree house, for Kit had established his command from this forest clearing; he sensed he was usurping the mana of the great tree, and it invigorated him. He had also quickly grasped that the islanders would do nothing to endanger the safety of Sycorax. The waxed calabashes of oils and spices, the pouches of prepared tobacco, the bricks of indigo and necklaces of shells and seeds they offered Kit and his party betrayed how important a stake he had unwittingly obtained; it had been a remarkable experience, he had to admit, receiving the embassy.

Beating drums and sticks and piping, with dancers and tumblers leaping ahead of them, the grave band of three old men and four younger ones in cloaks of feathers and aprons of leaves had approached him and they had parleyed, as far as their inability to communicate in language allowed. They had walked the perimeter his men had already marked out in preparation for the stockade he planned around the new settlement; the deputies had taken this in, uttering cries among themselves at the tools his men handled. He presented them with an ax, and set up a log to split. They had liked that, he could see. Then one of the older men, a chieftain he must have been, beckoned a young man, small and lithe and darker-skinned, with flared nostrils and springy black hair rising from a high brow, and he came forward and offered himself, it became clear, as a hostage in exchange for the old woman and the girl. But Kit wasn't having some young blood replace his female prizes. He would require a twenty-four-hour watch, as Kit could hardly trust his word; the women were much easier to supervise and hold. So he refused to accept Dulé in exchange.

Kit ordered Ariel brought, so that the islanders could see she was as well as could be expected, and recovering from the wound to her thigh. He allowed her to speak, briefly, and the youth who offered himself as hostage for her replied, in a low, feline voice that gave Kit a shiver. He saw the girl's smooth face like a polished fruit pucker with pain.

Dulé was saying, "We will let them stay—for a while. Then we will see. We cannot achieve your release yet. Not till we have found a way to outwit or even match their guns. Enough said. Now we must see Sycorax."

Tiguary accompanied the chief and Dulé to the cabin. Ariel had laid down Sycorax at the cabin entrance, under the dappled broad shade of a mango tree. She had made her a cool and sweet-smelling bed of grasses inside a circle of powder to keep away ants and other insects. They stood, in silent vigil, at her side; Tiguary implored the chief to find a way of bringing her back with them, offered himself in exchange, but Ariel knew that Sycorax could still not be moved any distance without endangering her life. The chief allotted Sycorax and Ariel three women to attend them, and then turned to face Kit, and traced between them three circles in the dust with his staff. He pointed to the sky and then to the clearing, to the path that led to the cabin where Sycorax lay, and Kit understood that he had been granted permission to remain three cycles of the moon. He took his sword, still sheathed in its scabbard, and in turn struck lines in the dust: adding four more full moons.

In seven months, he could get the *Hopewell* back to Virginia, and thence to London, with a request for more men and supplies to plant this colony. In the meantime, he could raise a harvest of tobacco, indigo and cotton, to be ripe and ready, on the *Hopewell's* return, to ship back home to Lord Clovelly; a load of perhaps ten thousand pounds of goods to increase his fortune, reinforce his foothold.

The chief rubbed out the seventh mark in the earth; at the look on his set face, Kit did not press his demand. In six months, could both passages, there and back, be effected? If he was fortunate; if God blessed his enterprise. He would pray for a happy outcome for his plan, he would pray fervently.

The chief disposed his attendants in a circle, and sat down on a hide spread for him. Dulé took the center of the ring, a finger drum began to pitter-pat, a pair of flutes at different pitches to call and coo; at the click of a rattle, Dulé lifted the ten-foot ladder into a vertical position and balanced it at arm's length; facing it, he dropped his head as if to a partner in a dance, placed one foot on the bottom rung and made a feint at climbing, the ladder pitched away from him and he let it fall, to rising laughter from the audience around him.

Strange, how these savages celebrate calamity, Kit Everard reflected. And mortifying.

Dulé stalked the ladder again, and circled it, turning it with him as he paced; again he bowed to his adversary, again he placed a foot on the lowest rung as it stood up, held lightly by his right hand. The drum grew louder in the final roll, the flautists blew steadily, keying up anticipation, and the rattle fell silent as Dulé took one step with his other foot and left the ground, then, hand over hand into the air, shinned up the free-standing ladder till he alighted at the tenth rung and hung there like a heron on a breakwater at home, it seemed to

Kit, even as he asked himself in wonder, What unearthly magic's here? What infernal arts?

Ariel, watching, wished that she too could defy the bonds that tied her to the earth, and her blood leapt with Dulé's ascent.

He was poised in the air, both arms outstretched for a moment, before the ladder swayed and he jumped clear, onto his haunches on the ground, while the music picked up again. The company made way for the next entertainment the islanders offered to mark the treaty they had made, and Tiguary gave Dulé a drink and hugged him, sitting him down beside him to watch the dancers who now occupied the clearing.

Kit wondered why the old hag and her lovely amazon of a daughter had proved such trump cards in his strategy of settlement. Not of an inquiring cast of mind, however, but rather a pragmatist, who seized his opportunities with a sure touch, he did not wonder long. Yet the two females' apparent significance also made him uneasy: he did not relish the revenge these men might mete out to him and his fellows if Sycorax were to die, or Ariel come to further harm.

The men must be tightly controlled, he resolved; no one must touch them.

Soon after the embassy, he assembled the lads and told them: anyone who laid a finger on the girl would be keelhauled. Then, if he survived by any chance, he would be hanged. No quarter would be shown. Kit Everard kept a Christian ship.

The chief and his embassy sent the three women to help Ariel attend Sycorax. Kit assigned them all a changing guard. But the appointed attendants sniveled by day and snored by night, and understood nothing of the pharmacopoeia and its uses, until Ariel, strained taut by her predicament, became impatient with them. When they nagged her to let them go, she conveyed to Kit he should allow it.

Ariel soon began to pick up some English, especially from Jack Elsey, a nineteen-year-old from Southwark, who'd been the cook on the outward journey, and was prompt to learn from her the flavors of the island vegetables and herbs, the edible flowers and fruits he'd never imagined could possibly exist when he was growing up as one of twelve offspring of a Thames waterman. He was obliging, and liked to run errands for the girl and help her with the care of her old lady. With familiarity, he grew less afraid than his mates from the *Hopewell*. From him, Ariel learned to speak her English with the accent of the Thames river rat. At first, it would make Kit Everard roar with laughter; he would scold her and try to change her speech into proximate lady-likeness.

When her moments of lucidity grew longer, Sycorax began to issue orders to Ariel, as she had done before the fire; first, she felt an urgency, while her long death continued, to pass on what she knew. But she would not speak when the guard was near; she did not want to betray her knowledge to the strangers. She hissed at Ariel to make him leave, and Ariel would wave him to keep his distance; Jack did not mind. Guard duty over the two women was much lighter than tree-felling in the steamy forest or sawing up the timbers into six-foot lengths, then splitting them into staves for the stockade, the master's house, and the other habitations they were erecting in the settlement.

The enclave throbbed to the sound of the ax, and shook to the rhythm of the saw. Sunlight beat down on them, now the tall mahogany and fig trees were thinned around; the ferns shriveled in the shafts; animals that had wandered in and out of Sycorax's compound now watered in the creek farther upstream, and avoided the company of men. Ariel had kept her cabin sheltered, persuading the strangers' headman how Sycorax and she needed the shade of the jungle canopy overhead. Her animals remained with her, the toads, the pigs and fowls and other birds; after the fighting, the bees had swarmed and left Sycorax's tree. And with Ariel a prisoner, her young caveys seemed to forget how once they too had loved to hunt.

Kit Everard had his men raise him a sleeping pavilion on the eastern bank across the creek from the saman tree where he had established his strategic headquarters. He called his future domicile Belmont, for it stood on the high ground, with a view sweeping down through the coconut palms to the shore where he had first landed that night he took possession. The island wind would blow freshly through the wooden casements of his bedroom there, and a columned veranda, like in a Roman country villa, would keep out the heat of the sun at its zenith from the interior. He was using scented woods: white cedar, resinous palm.

Soon after the landing that spring, he sent one of his officers, his friend and right-hand man, Tom Ingledew, to England in the *Hopewell* to fetch needed reinforcements—men, ordnance, and even, if they were willing to join the nursling venture, some women too. He carried a letter to Rebecca, as well as others to the merchants of Spitalfields, the sponsors, who had loaned Kit the means to equip the *Hopewell* on the outward journey.

The Ingledew mansion was going up across the creek on the other side, above the grove where the saman stood, and facing west; Tom had sited his Great House farther up the slope, by a magnificent specimen of an Indian fig tree with aerial roots falling like stilts and snaking over the ground below, and had designed a belvedere in the roof to give views to the four quarters. (The estate and its future vast sugar plantations came to be known as Figtree.)

With the exception of one or two unusual specimens, like the saman tree, which the settlers spared for their curiosity value, the forest was cleared on the west-facing slope of the stream, within the boundaries of Kit's personal estate; tobacco was planted, and maize, and peanuts, and cotton. When Tom returned, he too would clear his land and start planting the same crops—to begin with. In less than fifteen years after their landing, Kit and his fellow colonists would be sailing farther and farther in search of wood to build their settlements and fuel their fires.

Kit had learned how to grow certain lucrative crops on the mainland, when he served with Roger Pole, and the local Indians had been drafted to instruct them; but he was cultivating indigo for the first time in Sycorax's former enclave, and he found the plant tricky and demanding and considered its production women's work. When Ariel saw how the incomers failed to meet indigo's exacting standards of care, she could not restrain herself from offering her expertise; she tended, restaked, pruned and watered the trampled shrubberies of Sycorax, teaching the English how to cultivate the precious dye.

Tiguary and his people kept an eye on the Englishmen's building work; they watched their planting and their forest clearance with mounting apprehension.

Dulé sent word from Oualie: "They intend to remain; let me steal Sycorax and Ariel away, and then attack them. What else should we do?"

But the chief replied, "Let's wait. Others have tried before to do what these strangers are doing. They've never succeeded; sickness, hunger, wanderlust, something drives them on. This time too. Besides, we gave our word—six months."

It seemed miraculous to Kit that the old woman did not die; that she could haul herself back to life by miracles of her own devising, or

by the medicine Ariel applied. On the whole the Englishmen he commanded feared her: because death lay on her, and because she repelled
it too. Both her mortality and her immortality scared them until they
kept their distance, and invented stories about her powers that made
them shiver in their bones. Her burns had left pale patches on her
body, like distemper on windfallen fruit, and her pelvis had mended
in a twisted shape, leaving one leg four inches shorter than the other,
and shooting pains through her back and shoulders when she moved.
Her back had knitted, but doubled over, for after the first weeks, when
she was laid on the ground for fear of hurting her raw flesh, she had
preferred to lie in a hammock, where she had lain curved for weeks
on end. She had not thought to have Ariel set her whole spine on a
splint, so when, after three months, Sycorax raised herself and found
her weak legs and took a few steps, her whole weight slung against
Ariel on one side and Jack Elsey on the other, she was bent like a hoop
and could only shuffle forward, raising her head like a turtle poking
out of its shell to address anyone who was not actually on the floor
below her. She was in continual pain, and took tinctures she mixed
herself to deaden it; some had a bracing effect on her, others made
her soporific.

Ariel began to long for the peace the latter drafts brought to her.
For Sycorax was filled with rage at her condition. Each day Ariel fed
Sycorax, mixing ingredients she was allowed to collect under guard,
from the fenced area of the compound's grounds. The supply was
diminishing daily, and Ariel hoped that soon she would be able to
persuade her captors she needed to gather farther afield. As prisoners,
they were left eggs and some fish, and sometimes a piece of cooked
meat from the men's fire. On the other side of the stockade, the pattern
of the vegetation was changing, the earth burning up as the sun reached
the ground unchecked, so many big trees had been cut down to erect
the Belmont stockade.

As Ariel prepared to leave for one of her foraging expeditions,
Sycorax would poke up at her and hiss, "Don't let them see what you
pick! Trick them by hiding the leaf you want in a bunch of something
useless, or even poisonous. No! Not even that! They must not know
what can be used against anyone, for it might be us." She'd jab a finger
into Ariel's side and clutch her. "You'll not betray us, will you, my
darling? You are so lovely, and so young, what are we to do?" Her
ruined face, where her eyes now stared from a distance, like a reflection

of a look in a pond, not the look itself, would wrinkle up even more tightly.

"Don't. What do you think I can do? There's nothing I can do." Ariel was bitter; in turns Sycorax's power stifled her, then the old woman's weakness dragged at her like a disease afflicting her as well. She would remonstrate with her. "You'll make yourself more ill brooding like this."

"I might as well die. You'd rather I died, I know." Sycorax would push away the young woman and click dryly in her mouth. "I've made your life a misery."

"No, Mother. They have. Now shush."

She would press on, till Ariel wanted to clap a hand to her mouth to stop her. "You'll betray me, I know. You'll let me die. You will take my dyes, my remedies, my secrets away from me and use them for others. My skill! There's no faithfulness in anyone, it's a thing dead and useless, as I should be. We were noble, my people, we carried our heads high. But now? What now?"

During those early months, Kit Everard tried every evening to retire to his new quarters at Belmont and go to sleep; he read the Bible by the light of an oil lamp floating in a coconut shell, for they had used the last of their candles. The supply ship should be on its way, it should be arriving within a month, if the news had reached London safely. But as he read, restlessness would overcome him, the whistling of the tree frogs ground on his nerves, and sleep stayed a stranger. Once, a bat whirred inside his chamber, invisible and apprehensible only from the eerie displacement of the air, the frenzy of wings on a high note. He fancied in his exhaustion that the devil had taken bodily form to keep close by him and seize his soul.

To reach Ariel and her mother, he had to cross the stream; he did so, night after night, using stepping stones over unearthly flashes of phosphorescence in the water, and stepping up onto the farther bank, still unwilling, still keeping his mind on Rebecca, and the love he had sworn to her, until once more he found himself at the entrance of Ariel's cabin, once more gave orders to the guard to leave him, and entered to speak to her, disturbing her rest, though she had come to expect his call; then, after their unsatisfactory exchanges, he would lift the fronds at the entrance and leave again, only to succumb once more, and toss himself off in rage and helplessness, before he skulked back to Belmont.

Only after weeks had passed with him ablaze like this did the hag stir on one occasion when he came to call and curse him—or he felt she did—with her eyes open and one hand raised and pointing.

One night, soon after Sycorax had imprecated against his entry into their cell, Ariel gestured out-of-doors and seemed to want to follow him. The old woman lay in her hammock, sleeping; it was a time when she had taken a heavy dose, and he was able to lead Ariel out and let her walk before him, now and then turning to make sure he was not about to do something to her, put a halter on her or hit her, and she made for the fence and pointed over it and asked him with her hands and eyes if she could go there, beyond the stockade, into the receding forest, where the bromeliads pushed out their stiff blades and the monkeys nibbled at mango fruits and threw them down, when unripe, with tiny rows of toothmarks like some sharp-fanged fairy child's; where the birds of many colors screeched. A deeper pink suffused his face, coloring the skin between the freckles of pale orange that the tropical sun had cast there, and he took her by the wrists and said in English, "Maybe, we'll see; maybe one day." Then he pulled her to him and kissed her, and this time stayed kissing her, and when she did not struggle he pressed on and went down to the ground with her, and months of longing for her flooded him almost instantly, so that he had no time to swing with her long, cool firmness, as he had dreamed of so often, but the instant release in contact with her swept away all his turbulence.

Then, only a beat later, it seemed to him, shame and anger raced back to take possession of him again, and so overcome by these conflicting feelings was he that he had no consciousness of her in all this, until he became aware, to his surprise, that she was shaking him out of his stupor, bringing him to her again with her mouth and her hands. He fell forward on his knees and tried to implore his God to save him.

In this encounter and during many others following, as it turned out, his God proved more willing to try him than to catch him up to safety; and in this trial of his will, Kit Everard failed.

Ariel tasted a certain triumph in his weakness; she found cruelty a reward, now that she was penned in, her customary lightness fettered, her speed reined. With the once cool moist forest falling, the maidenhair ferns that had arched on fine black stems in the shade blistered, the bromeliads' sword points discolored by direct light and the monkeys and the birds of many colors in retreat, she wanted punishment, hers and others'.

She began to regard herself as she had not done before, and what she saw she no longer understood at all. Her confinement with Sycorax stretched back and back and she stood within it, a speck, a smudge. The man's trembling want of her made her feel that speck grow into a force; she began to enjoy denying him, then permitting him again, she used her strength to grip and pin him and squeeze him in parts that made him cry out, to gouge and scratch his pale, thin flesh; she fortified him with tisanes that make men what was called in her language "cross," and gave him leaves to chew to stay his excitement so she could explore the crustacean pinkness of his flesh and turn her curiosity and its tinge of disgust to a form of power over him which gave her pleasure. She liked the way he shuddered and groaned, docile as the pets that once had surrounded her and Sycorax, and who would have submitted likewise if she had chosen to maltreat them. She never liked the killing of them, though, whereas now she looked forward to the moment when she would finally take advantage of his surrender. When they were together, she felt in charge; and the feeling made her forget all that had brought her to this. But as it faded when they stopped, she wanted to repeat their coupling again, and drown again in the sweet rush of forgetfulness, until the time when she would bring it all to an end, or so she promised herself she would.

She nursed his ailments too, and with a needle from a certain yucca picked out the chigoes from his feet, neatly, so as not to burst the sac in which the nits were hatching and release them into his flesh; the insects between his pink-and-white toes were just like a shrimp's roe. She told him he should not squeeze his toes in borrowed shoes, but go barefoot and strengthen his feet; but he felt he would thereby dishonor his monarch and disparage the image of the Christian gentleman. He sent a lad along who was limping badly from the ulcers between his toes caused by an infestation of the chigoes; Ariel tended him. She could hardly send him away, though Sycorax from the hammock where she lay, surveying the scene, clicked her dry tongue impatiently and tossed about.

Ariel began to communicate with the strangers in English; she told Kit about the hot springs up the mountain, hoping he would let her go there. She described their properties of healing, of invigoration. Kit sometimes roared good-humoredly at the effect of her pronunciation, and sometimes sneered and tried to straighten out her vowels. At other times he'd smile, and teach her tricks to amuse him, unfitting words on the lips of a young woman that thrilled him to hear. She did not understand that he was mocking her or that he would take such a revenge on her for the pleasure he found in her.

The third month of their captivity passed, and Sycorax could now hobble farther, when the opiates for a moment eased her from her rack of pain. Sometimes, she fixed Ariel with her eyes, where albumen seemed to have congealed and dimmed to a blind blue, and wished her and any offspring she might bear all the evils she could call down upon them. When she did this, Ariel hugged her knees and rocked on the ground beside her, singing to herself charms against the spells of Sycorax: her antidote to the old woman's venom, her hopes for a different life far away from the ferocious spirit of her crooked mother.

She was able to roam farther afield now, for Kit Everard felt he could gamble on her honor (he hoped she was becoming attached to him too), and allowed her to walk on the beach by herself, and swim out to sea, even though he realized it meant she could slip out of the compound, for the sections of the stockade that he had left till last would enclose the shore. Besides, she could swim round the headland too, and vanish. But it would mean abandoning Sycorax, and Kit Everard conjectured, rightly, that she would not do that.

Some days Ariel carried the hooped Sycorax on her back (she would not ride on anyone else) down to the shore and into the water, and held her up under the arms so that she could let her contorted frame float free; small currents spun in the water as if to ease her, and the sky's blue height seemed to catch them up into its soft vastness and give them fins and wings to fly and swoop, so that they both felt airier and brighter than they had since the day that their freedom had come to an end, and the memory of their former peace returned for a space. Sometimes, the old woman's rage ebbed, and she was again the spirited and loving force Ariel had known when she was a child.

In these intervals of comparative serenity, she would instruct Ariel urgently in her lore; but these moments were brief, and soon she'd fly into a fury of pain again.

One afternoon after they had been for a swim together, Sycorax said, as Ariel took her on her back again, grunting, for the old woman had grown so much heavier, it seemed, since her immersion, "You are having the red man's child." The arch of the sky bore down on her like a chain, and the sounds of the camp returned, the shouts and jokes of the Englishmen, the ceaseless crash of the ax for wood and more wood to build. "I'll abort it for you, I can do it still with herbs. But if you wait, it will be hard, for my hands are not what they were."

Ariel did not falter but moved carefully on, up the hot sand of the shore following the creek, with the four-square house Kit Everard had erected far on her right, the huts and half-built dwellings of the men nearer, on her left.

"What do you say?" Sycorax squeezed her fingers into Ariel's arms where she held on. "You don't answer."

"I wasn't sure," she said. "I haven't been eating much. I thought that might be why my last bleed didn't come."

"Well, what do you say?"

Ariel kept on walking, and did not respond until she had lowered Sycorax from her back into her hammock and was sponging her limbs to rinse them free of salt. Then she said carefully, "He's a different man, you know, when he's alone with me. He—"

But the scorn of Sycorax stopped her there.

"You're a fool. I thought differently of you, but you're nothing but a fool, a lovesick fool, like every other idiot girl I've known. They come to me, whining and wheedling, 'Old Mother this, make him fall in love with me,' 'Old Mother, that, he's a good man, I love him, but he beats me and goes with other women.'" She would have spat if she had the spit to spare in her dry carcass.

Ariel made an effort. "I don't know what else . . ."

"No? I tell you now, Ariel, that you shan't have your way, not with him, nor with me. As soon as I saw what you were heading for, that you and he were hot at it, I cursed the baby you might have." She tugged at the sides of the hammock and hooked her head forward as she whispered to Ariel, who was standing away from her, the moss she had been using dripping water onto the dust.

"The child in your belly isn't a human child. I've changed him—your son, I know it is a son. For it will be a whelp you carry, a small, red-furred beast with sharp teeth and sharper claws that will grow up a bear, a fox, who knows? Some kind of savage creature. Like its father, and he will mangle you.

"You've lost your wits, my girl. And that will be your punishment."

15

Ariel's baby was born in the early spring, normal at around seven pounds, and healthy. She called him Roukoubé, which means Red Bear Cub: by accepting the curse Sycorax had laid on him, she meant to deflect it. Kit Everard sent for a midwife from the islanders to come and help her; two did so, and strained coffee roots in tisanes to strengthen her as she labored. They left soon after the birth, and Ariel could tell they were glad to. Sycorax was there when the baby was born, but she crumpled up when the infant was put in her arms by Ariel. A wild bearcub, he looked to her, before the full long shag has grown, with scanty red hairs on his head, pinkish creases in his flesh, at thigh and neck and elbow, the larval roundness, the white smell of milk—she pushed him away and pursed her lips to spit.

Kit Everard would not own to the baby either; and Ariel's changed body, the milk that rounded her breasts and the infant's leaky, necessitous presence filled Kit with a deeper fear of his transgressions. Sycorax saw that in this regard she had achieved her curse: for Kit too, Roukoubé was a mongrel whelp, the reminder of his weakness and Ariel's strangeness. He prayed to build on his aversion and include Ariel herself in his disgust; it was not as difficult as before to force himself to keep his distance, because he was angry at the child's existence, the visible emblem and consequence of their unlawful coupling, and he wanted to punish Ariel for not using her clever arts to prevent the baby coming. By the time Rebecca arrived, he would be free and pure again.

To Ariel, Roukoubé was the creamy color of a peanut kernel, as if she, in her cinnamon tawniness, had been shucked to reveal him inside her—and inside him, the pulse of his life, beating in the soft place of his head where the plates of his skull had not yet met. The baby was voluble: he snuffled and sighed and grunted and bawled. Noise had become Ariel's lot. She, who had lifted her feet and put them down again so quietly on the slopes that birds did not stir at her passing, was used to hearing a single song in her head at any one time. Otherwise she had lived in privacy, which was a kind of speaking silence. But since her captivity, a babel seethed around her constantly; the cries and demands of Sycorax, the commands of the men on guard over her, the hammering and planing of the pales for the stockade and for the settlers' other plans; the shouts of the men from the boat-building on the beach, the barking of orders to bondsmen brought from England on the ship that had returned, the yells of slaves whom they had loaded in Dahomey or Yoruba on the journey back and roped and chained and put to work under the whip, and the bellowing laughter now and then of the overseer, a tall African who had been taken out of chains himself to hold the lash over his fellows. And now, the calling of her infant.

Ariel herself made almost no sound; she choked on speech, for nobody could return an answer. Sycorax would not reply except to rasp her curses. Kit's language was bitter in her mouth. She sometimes pulled herself into a corner of the cabin with Roukoubé across her knees on his stomach and patted out a tune softly as she rubbed his back after feeding him, but she no longer made up words; she had no more words, indeed it seemed to her she no longer owned a voice, but only a hollow drum for a head on which others beat their summons. And it had been so since the day that she had turned to leave Sycorax at the hot springs.

Kit Everard continued to avoid her; but until he gave contrary orders, she and the child and the old woman were still supervised, their material needs met. The surveillance was assiduous, but not brutal. Sometimes, in the morning, there was even an offering on the threshold. As her own people had done before their captivity, the newcomers laid petitions at the sorceress's door, clandestinely, while by day the same Englishmen, from a safe distance, mocked and mimicked the bent hag and laughed loudly to show they were not afraid of her.

They had brought tales with them from England of witchcraft and the King's concern; an Essex man who had come with the *Hopewell* on the return voyage recalled how, when he was a child, a pricker was calling on all the households of the nearby villages to discover the sources of a murrain on the flocks. His family had feared that they too would be discovered to harbor some devil's servant.

The description of Sycorax's magic circulated and of course grew in the telling; scarred by fire, she now played with the element, burning circles of flame round creatures she had demanded Ariel procure for her; she watched their panic, as they spun in their prison of flames. She chuckled, then might pick up the animal by the scruff (a cavey or a bird) and dash it to death on the ground and spill the guts to read them for herself, then sprinkle blood inside the circle and on her cheeks and brow. She moaned to herself, and Ariel felt her scalp prick and her palms damp, and was frightened for her child. Adesangé, god of the volcano, was the lord of Sycorax's rites, and Ariel, even in her mutism, was startled by the fervor of the woman who had once been so skeptical of others' belief in her powers, who used to insist that all mysteries lay in the processes of nature and need only be observed and analyzed and understood.

One night Kit stumbled by, when Ariel was sitting outside the cabin, with the baby sleeping near her in the small hammock she had rigged up for him. Kit knelt in front of Ariel and cried; he asked her for forgiveness. She remained mute; he rose and collapsed onto her to kiss her. Her mouth was dry and hollow, a socket, no longer a well, as if she had no tongue to kiss with. His excitement meant nothing to her; she felt she was covering him with a pall of ash.

He fell back down on his knees and prayed, then, to his Jesus God, and she watched him beating his forehead on the ground, where the marks of Sycorax's rites still lay in charcoal tracks. She took up her child and clutched him to her, for his frail, warm, sleeping form seemed to put up a shield between her and the falling ashes around them.

Her position was more dangerous now; the tension between the strangers and the islanders was growing. When the settlers had shown no signs of departure at the end of the agreed six months, the islanders negotiated with them again. They pointed to the solidity and height of the buildings raised on the land—the broad and fragrant house at Belmont where Kit Everard was now living, the smaller, but equally sturdy dwelling of Tom Ingledew on the opposite bank, of James Lariot around the bay. When Tiguary indicated the gun emplacements at intervals in the Belmont stockade and asked what they were for (he had an idea), Kit waved a hand and answered, "So the chickens can pop in and out. We don't want to keep them prisoners in here, you know."

On the whole, Kit ignored their questions, sued for a little more time, talked of harvests and animals' breeding cycles.

So, faced with his reluctance and the size of the settlement, the islanders laid battle plans. Tiguary, at the north tip of the island, could muster about five hundred men; from the length of the northern shore, the headmen there could raise another four hundred; on Oualie, Dulé could promise a force nearly two hundred strong of a mixed crowd of men: a core of maroons from islands in the archipelago colonized already; some redlegs, or tallow men, renegades to their own people and the more ardent to fight for that very apostasy (some of them former prisoners and others who had been press-ganged into sailing service). Among the men who had joined Dulé on Oualie were also many who resembled him in body—square-shouldered, chestnut-colored men with good balance. They mainly lived by the sea, making the crossing to Liamuiga with catches of lambie conch and spiny lobster, parrot- and butterfly- and damsel-fish from the shady eaves of the coral reef, sea urchins and grouper and eel, to exchange against cloth and vessels and other useful goods they did not make themselves as yet.

As Dulé had never heard his mother tongue, he and his new companions could only surmise, from the similar flare of their nostrils, the high broad set of their shoulders on slender frames, and the deep oval plunge of their chins on thin, round necks, that he too came from the same part of the hinterland of West Africa, and was of the Ibo people in his origins.

Some of them had a memory of metal, of bronze heads, and shields and tools; when they came upon the hulk of a wrecked ship in one of the cays of Oualie, they found rusted nails and coopers' bands and knew that they had remembered right something the islands had never known. Others among his newly constituted group were taller, broader in build, spoke another language and came from Dahomey. These

youths had all escaped in one way or another from forced labor throughout the archipelago and the mainland colonies; there were some women
with them, but not many, and Dulé planned to bring Ariel and her
baby to live with him on Oualie. She should choose among his friends,
he decided—or rather hoped.

Under the captaincy of Tom Ingledew, the *Hopewell* had returned
late but safely the first autumn of their occupancy of Everhope, laden
with goods, with candles, skillets, nails, lace shirts, hats, hammers
and shoes (Kit was going barefoot, since his had been eaten by some
animals one night), and other necessities of civilization, as well as
several more of their countrymen willing to try their fortunes in the
Americas. Among them, tradesmen—a cabinetmaker, a cooper and a
joiner—all single men, but this first return voyage also brought Mistress
Ingledew, Tom's wife, and their three children, the first family to take
the step and turn the settlement into a whole society-in-the-making.

Tom had also stopped at a Dutch trading post on a island to the
north and purchased, in exchange for some provisions in short supply,
some twenty-five Africans. Among them were men from Dulé's people—five of this first shipment of slaves; they were all to work on the
new sugar plantation, to stake out cane fields in the rain forest.

"In the City, the talk is sugar. Sugar, only sugar," reported Tom.
"Our good patron the Lord Clovelly enjoins you, Kit, not to squander
our chances here on indigo and tobacco. The market will soon be
sated, in his opinion. Sweetness is in the air!" In London and in Plymouth, in Paris and in Toulouse, in Madrid and in Venice, the appetite
for sugar was growing, the demand greedy, he told them. The slaves
would work the cane, the Spaniards had already demonstrated how
well they tolerated the crop's conditions, and most of the slaves were
strong, young males. Tom proposed that two of these should be used
as studs, or servers; there were five women, he said, who were to be
"brood mares" for the plantation.

"A fair passage!" Kit congratulated his friend in delight. "I grew
anxious when you did not appear, but you had good reason, and I'm
glad of your foresight in this matter."

Yet there was no news from the King, no acknowledgment of Kit's
adventure, nor reward for his service. This gave him a pang of disappointment; however, in view of the providence they were enjoying
in so many other respects, he did not allow the feeling to pierce him
long.

During the first summer and autumn on the island, the English had built another sloop—thirty tons, clinker-hulled, two-masted—from felled mahogany trees they dragged down from the forest; they then fitted her with four "barbaresque" guns forged in the Italian style, transported from Europe by the *Hopewell*. Their first tobacco ripened; it was cut and hung to dry on trellises. By the time the *Hopewell* returned, the crop was ready to be baled and stowed and sent to England. The men only had to scrape the ship and careen her, recaulk her seams and overhaul her rigging in readiness for the voyage home to market.

After the Africans arrived, it was they who worked, while the Englishmen, who had previously labored, now drilled under two army sergeants who had been recruited and brought out to the settlement. Between military exercises, they rested, they smoked, they consumed the Madeira purchased en route. The Africans chopped and hauled the timber for the continuing building; it was they who stirred the stinking indigo, with Sycorax fleering from the side at their imitation of her skills. Soon it, too, was dried and cut into bricks for shipping.

All over the island and its neighbors, the indigenous islanders grew more anxious at the bustle of the settlement, at its expansion. Did the new ship mean that the strangers were planning to sail on after the harvest, as had been agreed?

Early the following year, the *Hopewell* was loaded once more with the harvests of cotton and indigo as well as its principal cargo, 9,500 pounds of tobacco, and she set sail from the harbor with her sails reefed against the season's squalls and a small crew on board. The rest of the growing colony was left behind, so the islanders accepted that the settlers had no intention of fulfilling the terms of the treaty and leaving.

Though it grated on their code of hospitality, the island hosts then decided there were to be no more gifts of food or drink, no more counseling or mapping, no more lending of labor or advice. They wanted to free Sycorax, without further delay, and Ariel too, though some doubted her allegiance and were willing to abandon her for carrying the stranger's child.

At the meetings called in different villages, some proposed a raid on the *Rebecca*, as the new sloop was called; others planned to murder the guards in the food stores behind the stockade at Belmont and set them on fire; but when Dulé and his companions sailed in from Oualie to discuss the best strategy, they suggested slow, persistent attrition:

waylaying the occasional soldier or watch, outside the compound, or in the sturdy dwellings of the English leaders, until the islanders had accumulated at least twenty guns, as well as the necessary tackle to go with them, the gunpowder kegs and pouches for shot, the ramrods to load the barrels.

Dulé added, "It's a skill, firing these weapons. I've tried, but my eyes aren't suited to the task. But we have men who have used them before." He pointed to one or two of the maroons who accompanied him. "Once we have the weapons, they'll handle them."

"There was a time," one said, with a choking laugh, "I could splinter a hazelnut tossed up in the air at five hundred yards!"

"We'll train others, too." Tiguary indicated the group of youths standing round the clearing where the council was being held. "We're not short of men."

"We should take prisoners," said Dulé. "The time has come to pay the strangers back in kind. We can exchange them, in due course." He paused, and frowned. "No killing, at this stage. We must exchange hostage for hostage. An English chief for Sycorax, an English boy for Ariel."

The islanders were successful in their first sorties; they stole some guns, and they took their first prisoner, one Harry Butt, who seemed glad to give up without a struggle. But Kit Everard would not exchange him against either of the women, and indeed, showed little interest in recovering him. Harry later—not so much later—sought to marry an island girl, and settled down. Three days afterward, a group of men from the Belmont camp, out hunting for some game fowl for their supper, strayed into an ambush. This time, the prizes were more valuable, for Philip Ingledew, Tom's fourteen-year-old son, was among the hunters. Tiguary's men recognized his value from the chased silver on his powder horn and on the barrel of his gun, and the gleaming gold gimp on his velvet breeches. They picked him and one other as their prisoners, and let the rest of the group free to spread the news.

So, by the end of February, with the *Hopewell* in mid-ocean and all his fortunes pinned on her safe arrival and a high price for her goods, Kit wasn't in good heart. The kidnapping of his friend's son, the policy of intermittent small-scale attacks, together with the persistent driving winds (no hurricane had hit, but nevertheless the late autumn gales had torn at the trees all night and blown his nerves to bits), and the impending birth of his child by the savage girl who'd taken possession of him—all this harried Kit Everard in his sleep until, more than once, he was ready to move on, find another island, preferably entirely uninhabited, yet, like his Everhope, verdant, gently sloping, not rugged, watered by many fresh streams, rich in fruits and animals good to eat. There'll never be such a place without people in it already, he groaned. His troubles also gave him a longing to escape, to try again, with Mistress Rebecca noble and pure at his side: a fresh start, without the muddles he had already made.

"It's the start of a thing that's sweet," he told James Lariot one evening, drawing on a long pipe filled with the first pluckings of their own tobacco. "Now, I don't know which is worse, the chigoes or the natives. They nip you here, bite you there, they creep in under your skin and lie curled there. Till they suddenly wake, and—nip!—another man gone, another musket. Now young Philip, too."

"But Kit," James reminded him. "Not much more than a year ago, we hardly knew that this paradise existed. And think of it, when our ship returns, we could shoe our horses with silver! If we had horses!— By the way—next voyage, let's have some shipped. We don't have to live by the sweat of our brow. Others may be obliged to. Not us. We can stand by and watch the crops ripen and grow. Sunshine by day, sweet dew by night, the soft wind. I tell you, this is the original garden God forgot to close."

"Shush, don't tempt Providence. Pray instead our ships reach harbor. And that the price of tobacco holds."

"Why don't we send for horses, truly? You know, they'd do very well here."

"To ride in these hills would indeed be pleasant." Yet Kit sounded anxious. He went on, "I worry, James, does the Almighty approve our venture? Are we true apostles in his grand design, as I hope we are? The coming struggle fills me with fear—there'll be bloodshed, there must be bloodshed. They're stealing our weapons, you don't seem to grasp that—we'll be outnumbered and we'll need more than our superior skills—we'll need the Almighty on our side."

"You've always said, my dear Kit, that we shouldn't play pirates on the high seas any longer. We're to be civilizers, settlers, landholders, indeed; men like the ancient heroes, who founded cities and gave laws and trade to the world as a gift. War's simply a necessary early stage, we'll—"

"Yes, yes," Kit butted in, "yet these natives chafe me. I want their happiness, I seek their salvation, and I see I can't convince them, and I don't care for it."

"Yet you have your amazon princess, I think! Your enemy brought to tameness to eat bread from your hand . . ." Kit's friend smiled at him.

"Oh, how it shames me! I pray day and night for escape—for her soul, as for mine."

"Some would think you a fortunate man—in this remote place . . ."

"Enough!"

"We should perhaps remind them of the dangers they run, provoking us to . . . retaliate."

"They might refuse our requests, then we'd have to declare battle— I can see no other course."

"If we treated with them, we could gain valuable time—we need to wait for the *Hopewell's* return. Then we'll be able to see what our harvest has brought from London, what we can expect from this place, and from the King."

The Englishmen did not have time to put their delaying tactics to the test, because the islanders struck, in greater numbers than ever before, and armed with muskets and other stolen firepower.

Two hours before sunrise on the ninth of March, 1620, twelve 40-foot-long pirogues slipped out of the mangroves where they had been concealed; each craft was carrying around ten men, each man an ax with a blade of sharpened rock, and a sharp stick, gouge of oyster shell in the cloth tied around his waist; three in each had quivers full of arrows and a pouch of manchineel sap, also at their waists; one man in each was armed with a gun. The fighters had conjured strength together in a dance on the eve of the attack, for striking in the darkness on the water filled many of them with foreboding.

Dulé was only lightly armed, in his boat; his task was different, for his skills at diving fitted him to a particular duty. In the bottom of each boat was a gourd of pitch, alight and smoldering, but covered with a lid to prevent the reek from escaping and alerting the watch on the *Rebecca*. He was gliding softly through the water toward the deep ultramarine stain the sloop made in the brimming blackness all around; the stars were fading, the half-moon had set; the land behind floated in the blind blackness, with nicks of silver where the leaves of certain trees shone as they moved in the breeze, as if it were an irregular and battered meteorite floating in the emptiness. In this otherworldly space of time, the surprise could be complete. Dulé was to slip into the sea, then, binding a container of burning pitch to his head with a deep cushioning of reeds in between to prevent his getting burned, he would swim to the ship, gouge holes in the hull with his knife and, taking dry tinder from a companion in a canoe alongside him, light spills from the fire and pass them through the wall of the ship, then slip back under the cover of the mangroves and lie in wait for the panic. Others would follow suit, working from canoes brought alongside. The ship would burn, or sink, or both; the crew, taken by surprise, would leap into the water, where the waiting canoeists would finish them off.

As Tiguary announced the plan to the assembled chiefs, Dulé could see the scene in his mind's eye: the fire licking up one mast, then leaping in the rigging to the other, snaking through the spars, then falling in sparks and setting the decks to smoldering while sleepy men sloshed water about with the balers, yelling orders to one another, until, when the flames had lit up all the timbers and the ship blazed in a transparent lattice of spars and ribs, her defenders would fling themselves into the sea and the warriors would swoop out of the shallows and fall on them: it would be as easy as catching fish.

Meanwhile, the greater forces would be assembled in the forest: the fire in the sloop should act as a decoy, so that the army of over five hundred warriors could fall on the settlement while its defenders were distracted, sweeping down on them, while the English flapped around the burning ship, from the rain forest where they would be concealed till then.

The day before the battle, Dulé had marked certain rocks on the beach in an attempt to warn Ariel; it was a way he had communicated with her now and then, on his sorties from Oualie. She was still occasionally allowed to leave the compound under guard, on the pretext of gathering ingredients for the settlement's pharmacopoeia. The settlement increasingly depended on her lore for the relief of its ailments.

Ariel saw the *timehri*, a chevron cut by a downward stroke, signifying great peril; then again, later, after she had told Jack Elsey that she could not find the necessary seaweed for a certain panacea on this stretch of the shore, but must go farther, she found another rock, with the same fresh cipher. So she begged Jack to let her go for a swim, as it was so hot that day, out to the reef, where she could find the weed she needed in fresh, young supply.

When she dived, she felt around in the tussock of tough brown japweed for the knubbly cigua whelks underneath, and prised some off the coral just below the waterline. They were more common than the spirals of the indigo snails that Sycorax had once used now and then, and a grave hazard the islanders understood always to avoid. After storms disturbed the sea, the fish themselves could be contaminated by secretions of the disturbed mollusks.

Ariel wasn't thinking clearly, her brain was fogged by the din around her and the rage of Sycorax, but the message in the stones summoned her to some action, something to break the silence and the stasis that held her prisoner.

She thought, Now, this was the time to kill him, the time she had been planning; the thought lit her up, she felt unaccustomed muscles in her face move again, felt her tongue seek her lips and pass over them as she considered how to do it.

On her return, she told Jack she must see his leader, so he sent one of the lads with the message, and the answer came back that Ariel could present herself to Kit. She shook her head, pointed to the baby first and then to Sycorax, as if her maternal cares in both their cases meant she could not stir a moment from their side.

"Tell him it's important. Tell him . . ." She thought awhile. "Tell him Sycorax is dying."

He came, for Ariel had never summoned him before. He sent the boy to call her out to him, alone. He could not bear to see the pale-cream child tied to her back with his small head bobbing on her shoulder, or bundled to her breast, asleep in satisfaction after food. But she disobeyed him, brought the baby out, and he had never found her so gay, so welcoming. She'd caught a rumor no doubt that Rebecca Clovelly was on her way, in the return voyage of the *Hopewell*, and like a woman, stung by a rival, wished to make him cleave to her. The child, her charms. He would not, could not; he bunched his fists and looked away from her fierce brow and curving lips and asked her brusquely what she wanted.

She held out the child to him. "He's yours," she said. "Look, see he is." She told him if he could not face her and the baby, he must let them leave this place.

He looked at her then. "You've suffered no harm. No one treats you ill." He tried to chaff her. "You're my guarantee against all manner of harm."

"Tiguary will offer you other hostages—more valuable . . ." She paused, with a sly smile. "More diverting, too?"

She put the baby in the small hammock hanging between branches in the shade by the hut and came closer, put a hand to his cheek and stroked it. At the touch of her dry, quick hand, which he remembered on his back, his neck, his thighs, his cock, the bridge of flesh at the root of his balls, he felt a shiver run through his limbs, of renewed longing again. She caught sight of it and put up her other hand, and with a finger stroked his bottom lip until he flinched and turned his head away, parting his lips as he did so, however, to bite her finger slightly, and close on it.

Even as he felt the danger of his need sweep over him, he perceived another danger beneath it: he let the pleasure of her carry him off, but within his pleasure's flow a small bitter seed remained, as if it were stuck between his teeth, offering him warning.

They sat down together facing each other, her face full of unaccustomed excitement, and then she rose to fetch him a dish to tickle his appetite, six pale gleaming mollusks like oysters, with wedges of lime around them, prettily, and a sprinkling of red pepper over them. Yet he set the dish aside, and noticed the shadow pass over her face.

"Is the Old Mother failing then?" he asked, as if thoughts of Sycorax distracted him from tasting.

From the dim interior Sycorax cursed them. Ariel heard her call, "My death would please you so, I swear I'll not do it, I'll not die. By all the powers I can command." Her voice was so dry now that sometimes Kit fancied he heard her when he could not—in the scraping of the boughs of trees, the footfalls in the dusty earth. He made a cross of hands, to ward off her evil.

Ariel paused, and tried a smile. "While there's life in her, she goes on raging."

She began again to caress him; rose to sit kittenishly in his lap, but she was as clumsy at this babying as she was grand at being leopardine, and he found it possible this time to check his lust; she bent to blow on his neck and ear, as he liked her to do, but he twisted sharply to avert his head, and struck her on the upper arm to beat her off, and then, without another word, his face blazing with the effort of his denial, he turned and left her.

He had not touched the whelks.

The return to speech and motion had cost Ariel so much that when Kit had gone, she choked and vomited from the pit of her belly until green bile came up and burned her.

Sycorax called her over. "Get me up, now, I want to get up. Why have you left me here today?"

Ariel went to her, and held her by the shoulders and raised her till her feet touched the earthen floor, then pitched her forward till she stood in her crooked hoop. She supported her and whispered,

"We are going to leave today, my mother, and you are coming with me. One step at at time, out of the gate, you, me, and my baby."

"So you've rediscovered speech, have you? What's it like, talking again?"

"No, don't, not today, don't rail. One step at a time, tonight. Or you can ride on my back, if you prefer. You'll have to promise to stop railing, because nobody must hear us, or realize what we're doing."

"You're more of a fool than I ever thought you were."

"One step at a time, my mother. Tonight."

"You believe you can do this? That you have some magic powers? You're more deluded even than a dying old fool like me."

"Now I'll get you up. You must tell me what you want to take. Later, we'll walk away. We'll wait, then we'll go, one step at a time."

Kit Everard was not a vain man, and he knew that even in the encounters that had given Ariel some pleasure (later, when he'd learned to check his premature excitement with her), she had not cared for him with her heart. He thought she might not have a heart, or tried to explain away her indifference by imagining she was made of obsidian through and through. He needed to think that he had been well-intentioned, but her consent or inclination did not figure among the considerations with which he weighed the matter. She did not believe in sin, after all, and her people knew only sensual gratification, he knew, not the higher principle of love between man and woman. So he persuaded himself, for it made his own sin less grievous, that he was not leading her into temptation too. For she and the other natives of these isles lived at a time before sin, it seemed to him, a happy time, but inferior in intelligence and humanity to the enlightened ideals of his kind.

So he was suspicious of her welcome, her sudden ardor, her new-found tongue to kiss with and to speak.

Then he understood: she wasn't inveigling him to return; she was bidding farewell.

Moreover, he understood another, deeper thing: it was not clear which of them was departing.

"They'll quench you," she had said of the whelks. "After hot work."

(It was so unlike her to tease.)

Quench you.

Yes, but she could be parting from him in a different way—stealing away, running off; he was surprised she had never done so, that she hadn't killed the old woman with a poison in the way she had perhaps schemed to kill him, that she had not held her under just a moment too long when she took her swimming, that she had not simply abandoned her in the settlement. These natives, they certainly respected the old, they had a sense of family, you had to grant it.

He sighed.

He had it then, as clear as a map of a well-charted route unfolded on the captain's table, what lay in store for him and for the settlement; though the islanders had not burned wet leaves and swelled white smoke into a pillar of cloud to issue a warning, the signal might as well have been as clear.

Kit Everard shared his suspicions with Tom Ingledew, who, though he feared terribly for his son's life, agreed that they should seize the offensive, in secret, and place all their forces on the *qui vive* that night, in readiness for battle in the morning.

There were around two hundred Englishmen, far fewer than the islands' combined forces, as they realized. They were short of footwear, but they had cannon, muskets, and pistols, as well as swords, and knew how to use them well. The slaves could come in, if need be, as support from the rear, resupplying the front line; but Kit was loath to call on them at all, and they would have to fight unarmed. Meanwhile, they were to be kept under guard. He gave the two armed men on the slaves' camp orders not to leave their posts, as he did not want more hands taking advantage of the confusion to run away and join the maroons infesting Oualie nearby. (If he won, he would clear them off Oualie—how he coveted that island's green streams and slopes!)

He moved the most experienced soldiers in two squads of twenty-five men each, and deployed them to make a wedge within the stockade, their lines defending its walls, the point of the wedge facing the valley formed by the stream below the hot springs. He reckoned his enemies would be concealed in the forest, and if they were mustering in any strength at all, would need to use the comparatively level and open banks for their attack. While the force inside the stockade could batter the attackers from behind its stout fence, another detachment of men could steal out and close in on the attackers' flank on the landward side; the *Rebecca*'s guns covered the beach below the settlement, so they would not be able to make their approach from the beach, unless they discounted major losses of life.

Ariel was saying to Sycorax, "Remember, you loved me once, it was I who ran away from you, I didn't understand, I couldn't see ahead. Tonight I'll strap Roukoubé to my front, and put you on my back, and we're going to leave, we're going to step out of this place. I shouldn't have done it, I know. But I so wanted . . . something. To give me what you'd so often described to me."

"You meant the world to me," Sycorax whispered from inside the hammock. "But it was a long time ago, before . . ."

She was calm, and did not rail in spite, that night, as they waited for the island's noises to change to the night's flutings and clicks and sighs. Then Ariel bent over the drowsing Sycorax.

"Come, let me lift you," she whispered.

She leaned in and stooped to take her under the arms; like a peach tree blighted by leaf curl, Sycorax lay tinder-dry in a narrow crescent, her body hardly filling the hammock's web.

With Sycorax on her back, Ariel dropped onto her haunches and took up her baby and tied him in a cloth to her breast; she rubbed his mouth with soursop juice to keep him dry so that he would not howl with discomfort to be changed (she packed soft moss against his bottom, just to be sure); then she took a basket of her herbs and preparations and whistled softly to Paca, the last of her caveys, to follow.

Ariel steps through the reed curtain and into the night. Though Sycorax is wasted and weighs little, Ariel can't move fast with her double burden, and her usual springy tread falls heavily on the earth. The guard posted at the entrance to their quarters is a man she does not know well; Ariel registers this discrepancy, wonders about it, thinks of Jack Elsey with a moment of affection. The absence of the customary guard is connected to the danger Dulé has warned her of, she knows. But her mind still works only dimly, and she cannot make the connection now, she must trudge forward, following the one impulse that has taken possession of her: to escape. She tells him she is taking Sycorax for a piss and the man backs away, scared, and lets them turn behind their dwelling. The moon has set (the warriors with Dulé are still gliding toward the *Rebecca*; the sloop is growing broader, taller, blacker as they approach her), but the stars are burning in the dark-blue distance, one of them sparkling emerald and ruby and sapphire, as if shaking drops of water from itself after a bath in the liquid of the sky. This star is Canopus, which Ariel and her people know by a different name.

Ariel starts across the clearing; the trees and undergrowth, the tangle of roots and flowers have been razed, she must trudge across open ground to reach the sea, which is her aim; she will walk out on the west side of the settlement's boundaries, where the stockade has not yet been driven into the beach, past the rinsing and brewing pools which have already come to look neglected, the waterline slimy with weed, the flies hatching on the surface. They circle Sycorax's saman tree, where stands the hut Kit used as a temporary headquarters before Belmont House was finished, and they turn south to pass out of the colony into the residual forest, where they can hide until it will be safe to join a village—if her people will take her in again.

She thinks of Dulé, for he beckons to her; they will cross the channel to Oualie and be with him, perhaps, as he has asked, the three of them together again, with Roukoubé as well, and Sycorax will recover. She hears the guard who is posted by the slaves' quarters to her right call "Halt!" but she doesn't stop; she keeps on, and he begins to shout, the torch at his side bobbing and smoking, he doesn't come after her (he must not leave his post), but halloos. Then she feels Sycorax struggling, and though she clamps her arms over hers, where they are clasped around her shoulders so that Roukoubé's head lies against them, Sycorax is letting go. She is whispering to Ariel, "Run, my darling, run!"

Ariel feels the old woman flapping feebly with her legs, and though she holds on, Sycorax slides off her back and onto the ground; she cries to Ariel again to run, run as hard as she can, and from the ground she begins to shriek, till the guard himself cries out, and drops on one knee to take aim in the pitch-dark. He knows it is the hostages, the old witch, her precious daughter, and her whelp, and he's scared to the marrow of his bones. He screams back at her to be still. But the hag keeps up her terrifying noise, her writhing and screaming, to pin down the youth's attention, stop him from pursuing Ariel, and she succeeds; he cannot bear the sound of her hissing and shrieking another moment. Ariel clasps Roukoubé and runs toward the sea; the shadows conceal her, she hears the shot, but then she splashes into the shoals and turns to run along the tideline to keep her bearings in the dark. The silver water shatters under her feet, the child bounces as he rides on her breast, and she no longer hears Sycorax, only the pulse of the sea as it breaks in frills on the smooth and shiny sand, the splash of her stride and the drumming of her heart as she makes for the forest to the north, her back turned to the bay where the English ship rides at anchor, where the sea battle will take place.

16

THE LIDS OVER the cannons' eyes slid open as the pirogues approached; the watch would have thought that he was only imagining the narrow prows breaking the black water, but the order had been given—Full Alert—and so the English sailor trusted his eyes and raised the alarm. When the guns exploded from the *Rebecca*'s beam, three of the boats capsized in the heave of the sea under the impact of the cannonballs; in spite of their horror of the lightless waves, some the these warriors swam on, thinking to scale the vessel. Others struck back for the beach. There was another burst of fire from the *Rebecca*; two more canoes overturned.

The salt air began to smell of rending, and the islanders in the water knew that Manjiku liked nothing better than blood in the water. (His desire to become gravid was so fierce that no menstruating woman was safe from him—he might strike even by day, if he caught the iron whiff of her menses.)

Seven surviving canoes struggled on toward the sloop, a place of safety now, as well as the target at which they aimed; they reached the port quarter of the *Rebecca*, and sought to shin halfway up her walls, hoping to be concealed by the overhang of the gunwales. Managing to grip the clinker boarding of her hull, they jammed their sharpened sticks of wood—lignum vitae, hard as metal, rustproof—

into the softer timbers of the sloop, or chopped holes in the sides. But then one of their number was cut down by musket fire, to which they could not reply, for, clinging to the side, they had no hands free. One of the attackers, an Irishman, got a handhold on a gun casement; he was a redleg from Oualie who had fled forced labor on a nearby island and determined to survive in freedom. He twisted there, shouting for one of his fellow raiders to join him and pass the tinder into the ship through the opening; but the cannon's blast came again and flung him loose, sideways into the water.

Dulé's canoe had not foundered in the first rounds of gunfire, but kept skimming on toward the *Rebecca*, with the remaining boats still around him, offering cover. They had not achieved the essential element of surprise on which he had counted, and he was filled with foreboding. If this decoy assault should fail to draw the English troops from the camp at Belmont, he knew, the islanders could not match the outsiders' firepower in open battle.

The sky was beginning to lighten to the east, streaks of day, as bright as magnesium flares at the meeting point of sea and air, set a fresh breeze stirring and whipped up a rhythm on the water's surface. The sea's turbulence increased; the noise of the cannons' fire was terrible, unknown, the men felt panic rise inside them, yet the fear lashed them into frenzy of battle—then another canoe tipped up, and another, but still not the one in which Dulé rode.

He urged them on through the waves until all at once they, too, had reached the *Rebecca*, and he decided against swimming, and came alongside as well. He was able to ram one hole, fill it with pitch, then another, and another, round the hull, beneath the overhang of the bows, in a rain of missiles, with fire sizzling around him and his fellow fighters coasting beside him, waiting for the moment when the timbers would be ablaze. He rammed in the pitch, keeping his balance in the tossing pirogue as only he could, he with his funambulist's antennae, who might have scaled the ship on a free-floating ladder if it had been a parade, a feast, a time of play and rejoicing.

But now, the men on board ship above him were screaming, and with three holes fired on each side of the vessel, he gave the signal to bear away as swiftly as they could ply their paddles.

Some eighty men took part in the attack on the sloop *Rebecca*; of those, Dulé and some of the crew of his boat survived. Among the victims from the other boats, they counted, when they made a rough reckoning on the beach, thirty-three men. The youngest was a Spanish cabin boy who had run away a few years before from his vicious captain; the oldest a maroon from Benin, who had fled a plantation on an island to the north: he had stowed away in a pirate ship that had stopped to draw water on Oualie. But they were only two of the dead and dying. Twenty of the men who fought with Dulé that early morning died in the water, maimed by the cannon shot; eleven drowned in the confusion of fire and shipwreck in the attack on the *Rebecca*.

The first survivors who reached the shore regrouped up the estuary past the bony tangles of mangrove in the forest at the arranged meeting place; they were met there by a waiting group of islanders, men and women, ready to rearm them and send them back into battle. The old men, past the age of warfare, were dressed in fronds of palm and banana, with garlands of poui flowers and hibiscus on their heads. They sang and stamped and danced on the earth and shook the petals in their hair and beards to make the warriors laugh at their travesty and forget the nearness of the dead. So they tried to revive their warlike spirits, while the women rubbed and slapped their heavy limbs and applied ointments to the survivors' burns and bruises.

It was full dawn, a silver-gray dawn of the late days of spring, and it was still cool by the water's edge. The wounded who were carried in from the attack on the *Rebecca* lay in the shade under the trees while their hurts were being dressed. By the creek, the main force of the islands' fighters was gathered for the simultaneous assault on Belmont, which was shaking the ground even at this range, like the bass drum of a ceremonial band.

When Dulé and his companions regained the beach, they were so stunned and wearied by the water and the flames, the howling and frantic clangor of their rout, that they dragged themselves and their boat to the first cover they could find, and lay face-down against the earth; they could sense it trembling as if it were an animal, alive beneath them.

The battle at the creek had begun, and they were far too undone to join it.

In the hour before dawn, when the islanders' forces knew that the raid on the *Rebecca* had started, they rose and advanced against the Belmont stockade, thinking to find only the skeleton watch Kit posted nightly and everyone else in their beds. Instead, they fell against some fifty concealed musketeers deployed behind the robust palisade of the settlement at the easiest point of access, the gate by the bridge over the stream.

The defending Englishmen were clustered in groups of three at intervals around thirty yards apart, strung out along the stockade itself and its command lookouts; in the stream that passed through the settlement and bounded the headland where Belmont's Great House now commanded the rise, they stood in a double row to bar access to the settlement by that approach; in the mangroves at the mouth of the stream two young sentries kept watch, though the prevailing easterly breeze rendered it unlikely, the English commanders decided, that the islanders' attack would come from the sea on that shore.

Kit Everard had calculated that the *Rebecca* made a sitting target; she would draw the enemy and pin down some of the fighting men on both sides. But when he surmised the attack was due that night, Tom Ingledew agreed that they would have to sacrifice some fighting capacity on that front—and even some lives—in order to gain the maximum advantage from keeping the sloop as a decoy.

In the interval between night and day, when it appears all color may have been leeched from the world in the blood wedding of sea and sky the night before, the men in Tiguary's warrior band crept softly toward the English compound, some picking their way in the sulfurous stream, others moving in single file along the banks. They aimed to pass over to the other side of the stockade through the gap between one section and the other, where the bridge spanned the stream. They considered this the most vulnerable point in the settlement's defenses, as Kit himself recognized. When they reached it, they spied two men standing at the ready, as they had expected: the passage through the palisade over the water was always manned by a guard or two. They fanned out, their feet far stealthier on the undergrowth of smooth-skinned roots and tumbled vines than the animals they were used to stalking. Yet the watch caught a glimpse of the movement, for he had been warned.

The islanders were now very near the English hideouts; the fighters drew out an arrow each, dipped it in manchineel and took aim.

The air was beginning to blush with the first reassuring glow of the mounting sun, and the breeze that had tossed Dulé and his companions in the pirogues was freshening. The morning stirred in the trees and interrupted the sleep of stem and leaf and fruit and blossom no less gently and efficiently than a mother lifting the cover from her child's bed and blowing on her face in play to wake her. When Kit, informed by his scout that the enemy was present, gave the first order to fire, the soft promise of the light burst into flame; the vanguard of the islanders fell back from the English muskets.

Soon after, from the turrets of the stockade, three cannon opened fire, blowing off the legs of several among the attackers, blasting fragments of earth and rock into the abdomen of others.

Dulé and his companions, face-down on the beach, shuddered with the thud of the cannonballs, and caught the smell of the flames, of split flesh, and heard the howls and cries of the wounded and dying.

The green men in their cloaks of leaves and branches then discovered them, and came down to the beach and circled Dulé and his companions where they lay prone, and shook their fronds and squatted on their haunches and kicked their legs and tossed their heads and slapped palm to thigh, in order to rally them and send them off again, pouring spirits and water into their faces to invigorate them, beating out a rhythm with their feet. At last, Dulé rose and forced his dragging limbs to take steps; he shouted at the fighters with him, and roused them to stand by his side. While the rhythm of the dancers speeded up in pleasure at their revival, he told them,

"Remember what you suffered in the past!

"Those of you who have known slavery, remember the life you led then!

"When the conflict is bitter, think of the time when you were not your own masters, how its bitterness can never be forgotten!

"Think of our fellowship and our lives on Oualie!

"And you, you who remember the past in far distant and happier places, think of what you have lost!

"For the tallow men smile with one face, they murder with the other."

Their helpers strapped poison gourds to the full quivers of those who preferred blowpipes or arrows for their weapon; others were given horns of dry powder, and issued with muskets and daggers and clubs made of splendid polished mahogany. Then, prodded by the older men in their topsy-turvy costumes as the quick spirits of sap and growth, they gradually unbent and felt the thirst for blood sing again in their veins.

Dulé took a path westward, following the shore, with Belmont on their right to the north and the burning ship behind them. As they drew nearer, the sounds of battle made the ground shake, and when they stood still, the percussion of the fighting vibrated through them, as if they too were strings stretched over shells and struck. When Dulé looked back he smelled the burning of the *Rebecca* on the breeze; his companions told him that the column of pitchy smoke rose in the dawn like an offering.

But the burning of the sloop in the bight was to be the only successful venture of the day on their side.

Gradually, as they stole up to the Belmont stockade, Dulé distinguished different sounds—the fierce explosions of musket fire, the shrieking of the attackers, the yells and shouts and curses and groans of fighting men, their voices thick with fury, the different languages reduced to meaninglessness by the struggles, as men grappled, stabbed, battered, poked at one another's eyes and even bit one another in the combat at close quarters; while at a distance the screams of rage and pain merged with the volleys of musket fire and the singing of the arrows.

The morning sky was smudged yellow and gray with smoke and the heat was beginning to beat down on the fighting when Dulé gave a leg-up to one of his fellow fighters to scale the stockade. From the top of the fence, the man squinnied at the settlement of Belmont. He reported scorched bushes, a blazing building, and the plantings of indigo and cotton and vegetables inside the fence trampled by the battle. He nodded encouragement to his fellows, and they shinned up after him and dropped down into the stockade.

They moved from cover to cover within the compound, advancing toward the rear of the battle, following the sounds that would lead them to their own side and to news of the day's progress. The reek grew stronger of flesh and carbon and gunpowder and smoke, and the chaos and noise more ferocious as at last Dulé came up behind the gaggle of the English defenders. They were now concentrating their fire on the bank beyond the gate; there the main force of the islanders was still dug in, sending a steady shower of arrows and the occasional round of musket fire.

In Belmont, English sailors and other men lay, some puffed by poison, others with missing limbs, still groaning.

Dulé passed them and remembered how he had only felt wonder, not this stab of pleasure, when first he saw them sleeping on the ground near Ariel's cabin that long year ago.

The line of islanders was entrenched behind burning shrubs on the bank of the stream, at the point where the stockade was indeed vulnerable, but they hadn't penetrated beyond it, though they had inflicted damage on the settlement's defenders. Failing to pass through it, or change their strategy and invest the compound from another route, over the fence, as he had done, their plan had stalled at the resistance the settlers were able to muster at that very node. Now the row of islanders, at least two men deep, confronted the stockade where four cannon had been brought to bear on them; the English forces were firing in furious waves of shot from the top of the stockade.

Dulé waved to his group of survivors: they would attack one of the cannon's crew from the rear; no fire until they were upon them.

Yet he feared they were like biting fish in a fine-mesh net, if they swam forward they would never escape; he saw them lifting their limbs with automatic motion, as crayfish with their lumbering claws knock against the basketwork of the pens in which they have been trapped.

He asked a scout to search through the turmoil and pick out Tiguary, if possible, or someone who could give him a message. The heat was intense now, it was mid-morning, nearing the zenith, and the men steamed in their huddles, as the firepower battered them, their eyes red and swollen from smoke and weariness and the horror of the mutilations and deaths among their companions. Dulé found himself longing: This carnage, this bloodshed must come to an end, we must call a truce, make a new treaty.

Yet he and his companions were creeping toward the stockade's turret, where one of the guns exploded, as they were spotted; one shot picked out the young man next to Dulé. Dulé saw him fall, and ran, swung himself up the smooth wall of the redoubt where the gunners were hard at work, and found himself at a mere arm's length from one. Before he could reach out and stab him as he planned, and then kill his companion too, and, with support from his companions, seize the cannon himself, he heard a scream of pain behind him and realized that another of his fellow fighters had fallen from the ring fence onto the ground. And in that moment, as he winced at this new casualty, he lost the advantage that the suddenness of his irruption into the gun chamber had given him.

He heard one Englishman shout at him, as he was thrown to the ground by another and pierced by the halberd on the end of his musket, like a sunfish in a rock pool.

Ariel crawled into a shelter of leaves by the sea to the west and clasped Roukoubé to her breast, where he snuffled as he nursed. She heard the sounds of the battle; she could not even croak out a song to him, for her tongue cleaved to her palate as if, while her baby drank, she were dying of thirst.

17

From *"How We Played: A Family Memoir"* by Sir "Ant" Everard

Kit Everard to the Lord Clovelly, The Worshipful Company of the Hesperides, 2, Cinnamon Alley, London. Fifteenth of March, Year of Our Lord 1620

Dear Father (as I hope you shall be ere long),
My letter to your Honour of the fifth January last being writ before the great events that are upon us now, would lead your judgement astray as to our progess in these fair Isles, for mighty Saturn threw his sinister shadow heavy upon me at that juncture and many un-toward and grievous events had combined to cloud my spirits that now are light as a summer breeze again. For I have news of great moment to report, viz. that on Friday last by a night when the moon shone but weakly we had intelligence that our neighbours in this land were embarked upon a most fiendish and treacherous Enterprise, namely to do every man among us fatal harm while we were still sleeping in our beds. A villainous raid upon the Stockade where the men do lie and even upon ourselves where we dwell at Belmont would have robbed us of all we have assured thus far by the Grace of God. Such however is the mighty Providence that guides us, we were adverted in due time withal and haply able to forestall the deadly peril to our settlement, that is still but a mewling infant scarce able

to totter on bandy-legs. After fierce and bloody struggles on sea and on land in which much noble blood was spilled, alas, we were able to declare the day ours and the Battle of Sloop's Bight a chapter in the history of God's Kingdom Come.

In these remote parts we try and work His Will and shew His Loving Mercy to many of these forsaken and heathen Souls. In the southern-most bay we engaged most valiantly with a band of savage islanders who scaled the walls of the sloop *Rebecca* and torched her timbers, but we consigned the greater part of them to the sea for pasture for the fishes that teem therein. Their captain (for so I must term him—though their forces understand no battle order and hurl themselves pell-mell on us like mere animals who must quench their parched throats with blood), a certain youth who is called Dulay to his people, with a trick of the eye that makes him seem to look at you and yet not see you (and other tricks besides—I have seen this same swart creature climb a ladder into the air as if it were a tree planted there four-square), we apprehended as he fled from our justice. By due process of law we have sentenced him to be slit in the hamstrings to be an example to those who would follow him and make him a hero to the people.

Nought but a rabble he had gathered together on the fair island that lies to the east—of buccaneers and booty-hunters and ruffianly runaways from the slave-ships that are plying these waters most usefully. These fugitives that are Negroes go by the name of Maroon, whilst the renegades to the King's laws are called by the common sailors redlegs (that being the colour our white skins take on in the heat of the sun in these regions). Our prisoners are kept safe in the bilboes you were prescient to despatch, and I would have had this Dulay hanged but that he might in death prove a beacon to this same rabble and draw them on to greater reprisals against us, and we are still but few in number. Our men fear his witchcraft.

I would entreat your Honour to muster thirty men and send them to us and put shoes on board with them, for we have committed one great error in not putting shoes on board with the last, which was occasioned by means of a dispute with the cobbler about the price. But I do not like a company of bare-footed soldiers. We still are in some necessity of joiners and coopers and any trades; for the rest, we are buying slaves from the same merchants who put in to anchor here and take on our water and our salt. The African is as strong as a plough-ox, each man can do the work in this clime of two or three of men like us. The aforesaid captain I shall endeavour to keep beside me as my bondsman; hobbled, and under my eye, he cannot do me injury. He has a mordant wit, 'tis plain, and it diverts me to teach him our language as he serves me. He has already learnt how to curse.

Some of our men call him "cannibal," seeking to undo the power of his monstrousness by naming it, like to conjuring. 'Tis to my mind a false notion, and I prefer the lisping usage of the children, Caliban.

We gave our permission that the women should gather up the dead and give them burial according to the fashion of this people—'tis said they strip the flesh and griddle it for a delicacy beforetimes, but I for one do not give this credence. I know them to be human creatures made in God's image too, the womenfolk most lovely and most temperate (for the most part), and I would not abet the evil Spaniard in his slanders. Yet some are dangerous to our cause, and we cannot brook their contumelious conspiracies against us. Hence I keep their captain before them for a show of mastery. And I shall have him flogged in their sight when I perceive dissension to our wise governance. This policy is most politick, for many leave the island daily in their rough-hewn barques for other parts and thus confirm our powers here: the world is open to them, they can wander abroad at liberty until they discover those skills of civility to settle a land and make it their own. The Good Book has taught us their image, they must be outcasts with the mark of Cain upon them, Ishmaels for whom the savage wilderness is home till they come to know the wisdom of the Lord. I wait upon your answer and the supplies inventoried on the enclosures.

Your Lordship will smile, I trust, at the progess your loving son is making for the Company; to whom we are beholden for our wherewithal and our signal progress in this land. I expect to double the yield of Tobacco this harvest, but I am sensible that you desire us to put more land under the cane, this sugar trade being the more profitable at home and the Negroes most apt to its cultivation. (It is a most irksome toil for others.)

Your devoted son,
Christopher Everard

18

WHEN THE SIGNALS to cease battle had been exchanged and there had come a respite in the noise, the islanders fell back and took stock of their situation. The dead lay in rows under fans of palm and banana; so many dead, the survivors had wept that they had been spared. The massacre was shameful, the losses piteous. The blood of the wounded trickled from the bank, spilling like one of the showers that freshened the earth each day, and flowed downstream toward the sea, which was not so far that its rich scarlet could diffuse before it met the waves.

The first touch of the setting sun that day, which usually misted the mirror of the sea with its pink breath, found the water already cloudy red. From beyond the reef the big fish swam in to lap, the monsters the islanders most feared: the white Manjiku with his frilly fins and laciniated snout, the pewter-colored smooth-bodied sharks, the huge idling skate. Many had never shown such ferocious and shameless appetites by day before, but usually feasted invisibly and secretly at night.

Their presence made it hard for the women to rescue the corpses of the drowned, and many bodies had to be abandoned to them. This inflicted great sorrow on their families, for without burial of the flesh, the victims would become phantoms and speak to the living without ever finding rest. Though the ghost army would also persecute their murderers by their chatter, their relatives would have preferred that they find quiet.

The Battle of the Belmont Stockade, or Sloop's Bight, as it came to be known, was a defeat from which Liamuiga's people would not recover: more than four hundred warriors were killed, among them Tiguary, their leader, shot through the bowels. He died slowly, in pain, in spite of the drugs his companions administered to him to relieve it.

Dulé survived, however, to be brought to trial as a ringleader, to be an example to others.

With Sycorax, the islanders were more successful in administering the proper rites, for during the treaty negotiations that followed the battle, her eldest daughter's husband, who had been wounded in the foot but survived, pleaded for the bodies of the few who had died inside the stockade. Sycorax was lying in the common pit, alongside the cadavers of islanders who had also been caught in the fighting and were awaiting return for burial under the terms of the peace.

They wound Sycorax's light dry spoil in two banana leaves, laid lengthwise and sewn together with dried strips of aloe, and then chose to dig a vertical grave at the foot of the saman tree, the designated place for which they had been granted permission. The tree was gleaming green with new foliage that had broken out from the charred branches of the first encounter between the English and the islanders. Her papoose—not much bigger than a child of ten or twelve, so insubstantial had Sycorax become—was slid into the shaft feet-first, so that Sycorax's head was nearest to the surface of the ground, slightly tilted so that she would face upward in death, her mouth near the earth and the living who walked on it. It was at Ariel's insistence that she was buried there in a cenote, the kind of grave the islanders reserved for their prophets, and Kit had yielded to her, even though it was well inside the stockade. She made an offering of flowers and fruits, spurred pennants of scarlet heliconia from the rain forest, blue-blushed rue and sorrel vines with tendrils trailing, and laid it on the pit.

Then Ariel took Roukoubé and clicked to Paca to follow, as Sycorax before had taken Dulé and Paca's predecessor, and they embarked for Oualie. The numbers of the settlers there were growing: their community was strengthened by more maroons, escaped from the colonies, from the Spaniards' silver mines, the sugar and tobacco plantations;

redlegs and pirates were joining them, some of them women. At first, Roukoubé was the only baby in their fledgling enterprise.

Ariel's offering at the foot of the saman tree was the first of many such laid there to win the intercession of the sorceress, Sycorax their mother. The fruit and flowers and occasional small animals were offered by—who could tell?—suppliants inside the stockade, as well as the islanders outside. Sometimes one or two of Oualie's inhabitants, on a raid for weapons or a mission of sabotage, slipped into the settlement in the dark and remembered Sycorax.

Another summer passed, and another harvest; the next ship from England, a large three-masted schooner, the *Destiny*, sailed with a smaller, forty-ton, four-gun pinnace, *The Tyger's Whelp*. The *Destiny* brought three score slaves and supplies; the smaller boat carried Mistress Rebecca Clovelly, a parson, a chest of tea, and a charter from the King to the representative of the Company of the Hesperides, Kit Everard.

After *The Tyger's Whelp* put in at the harbor at Liamuiga, also known as Everhope, the winter after the Battle of Sloop's Bight, the letter from the King in England to Kit was delivered to him on the veranda of the Great House at Belmont by the captain, one Rowland Grasscocke, who was plying a regular trade between England, the West Coast of Africa and the Hesperidean chain. It was a painted scroll, and there Kit read:

James, by the grace of God, King of England, Scotland, France and Ireland, Defender of the Faith, et cetera. To all to whom this epistle shall come, Greetings—Whereas we have been credibly informed by our well-beloved subject the right honourable Lord Clovelly, of Bury St. Edmunds in Suffolk, and on behalf of our well-beloved subject Christopher Everard, Gentleman, that the said Christopher Everard hath lately discovered several Islands in the Hesperidean seas towards the continent of America, the one called Saint Thomas's, alias Everhope (though this be error), or in the native tongue Liamuiga, and another, as the savages of those parts name it, Oualie; that we are further informed that these said Islands are possessed and inhabited only by the aforementioned savages and heathen people, and are not, nor at the time of the discovery were, in the possession or under the government of any Christian prince, state or potentate, and thereupon the said Christopher Everard, being set forth and supplied on our shores for that purpose, made entry into the said Islands for and on behalf of our dear Father in heaven and hath since with the consent and good liking of the natives made some beginning of a plantation and colony and likewise of an hopeful trade there and hath caused divers of our subjects of this our realm to remove themselves to the said Islands with purpose to proceed in so hopeful a work: KNOW THEREFORE that the said Lord Clovelly and Christopher Everard may be encouraged and the better enabled with the more ample maintenance and authority to effect the same. We do commmand the said Christopher Everard to be possessed of the said Islands and all our other loving subjects under him: And of our especial great and certain knowledge have given and granted unto the said Christopher Everard during our pleasure custody of the aforesaid Islands and of every creature, man, woman and child upon them, together with full power and authority for us and in our name and as our Lieutenant to govern, rule and order all.

In witness thereof we have caused these our letters to be made patent.

Witnessed ourself at Southampton the thirteenth day of October . . .

The signatures of the Archbishop and the Chancellor followed, and the great seal of England was attached.

The parchment was illuminated: an Englishman stood waist-deep in an ocean of scalloped rills, drawing a galleon of far greater tonnage than any ship Kit had ever sailed in as if it were a child's toy boat; he was pulling it toward a pair of islands, like pease puddings, smoking from their rounded summits on the pretty dish of the sea, garnished with sea creatures: one had a spiraling tusk and frilly fins, another a crocodile's saw-toothed snout. Tiny natives in their feathered headdresses and skirts besported themselves on the water's edge, far more ostentatiously than Kit knew them to do.

He was that Englishman, these were his islands. It did not matter the King had refused his name, Everhope, for the new colony and returned to Columbus's christening; he could not mind that beside this prize, the governorship itself. And the charter made a pretty picture. The perusal of it swelled his heart with joy; he found he had to read it twice, and the pleasure of its proclamation left him flushed from top to toe.

On Christmas Day 1620, Kit and Rebecca were married by the parson in the churchyard of Saint Blaise, as the church itself was still under construction. Rebecca had silk slippers on her feet, with the device that the King had granted the Everards embroidered on them;

it had amused her, during the serene days between squalls on the voyage from Plymouth, to sit on deck and stitch the image of the sea monster harnessed by the naked man, halfway up to his waist in water, while natives in feather skirts cavorted on the shore behind. Kit could not tell her how he had managed to win such a victory against the local savages. It was a unique triumph in the annals of attempted colonization in the Americas: he had been extraordinarily well-prepared for their attack.

In other parts of the Americas, settlers had been done away with, by what means, nobody later could discover, for new arrivals would find the incomers' stockade deserted, with not a sign of struggle. They had been annihilated by stealth, it was rumored, or even by sorcery. The natives were treacherous people, as everyone knew, ungodly and faithless, and their early shows of friendship were nothing but a ruse to lull the pioneers into a false feeling of security, so that they could ensnare them in their false enchantments, pounce on them unawares and kill them while they slept.

Only on Everhope had the heathen met the fate they deserved. Kit's success would make Rebecca's father rich, much richer than the family had ever been since the squandering of the fortune made in the service of the Earl of Warwick during the Hundred Years' War. Kit was a lessee of the Lord Clovelly's company, his daughter had brought him a dower of part shares in its wealth, as a reward for a feat of arms unrivaled in the territory.

One afternoon, Kit told James Lariot, as they paced the border of the new fields where the sugar cane was shooting, sturdy and green, "I was warned."

"You were warned—you mean, a spy?"

"My dear James," Kit laughed. "This may feel like home to you by now, but this isn't our fair native land where spies abound. We have none here; how could we?" He pointed to his hair and to his skin and gave a merry chuckle again. "Spies on our side could hardly pass unnoticed."

"You may laugh, Kit, but there are renegades, you know that, among the ruffians on Oualie—"

Kit interrupted. "Oualie no longer, but Little Saint Thomas's, a Christian name for a Christian place. As it will be, soon, if we have our way and God is on our side . . . I have a campaign planned. We'll invest the island; it will be a harder struggle, but with the men drilled and ready, we shall overcome that rabble—some of their force are mere chits of girls, who would do better to wear petticoats than breeches!"

James nodded, pleased. "And when do we plan to visit Little Saint Thomas's?"

"In the coming spring we'll be ready. Soon. As I say, we are like Cadmus and the field of Thebes, we'll plant dragon's teeth there and raise up Christian gentlemen."

"I hardly think the Thebans were of our faith."

"Oh, James, how nice you are!"

"But you were telling me you had been warned, the night of our God-given victory."

"No more, I leave you to imagine; in all honor, I cannot say."

"Honor comes into it?"

"Honor," repeated Kit, a smile dancing mischievously in the corner of his lips, giving him for a moment the look of a sprite, a red-gold Puck no stranger to mischief.

"Aha!" said James. "Your fair amazon!"

"Hush," said his friend. "And never where the sex is present, if you please."

19

ENFANT-BÉATE, 1700—

SYCORAX SITS HUNCHED under the earth, her head fallen sideways, face up, on to her knees which her hands clasp; her mouth—what is left of her mouth—gapes open in the direction of the ground above. She's a floury heap of bones and those bones are worm-eaten. Once a femur or a forearm would have played a pure note if you'd used one for a pipe, but the pieces would whistle harsh and off-key now from the holes bored into them by the efficient mandibles of her companions in the vertical grave, the cenote where they placed her after the battle, during the truce.

Her long death has barely begun, however, for she can still hear the prayers of those who come to bring garlands of pink and white hibiscus and poui flowers and golden allamanda and nectar-laden frangipani, as well as the gnarled soursop and the smooth-skinned mango. They push a tack into the bark of the saman tree and make a wish, they whisper their pleas to the spirit inhering in the tree, as they imagine, rightly (though Sycorax has no power, nor ever had, except in dreaming).

The sea breeze blows in Enfant-Béate and turns the tropical heat to balm of an evening, it stirs the jadelike waxy foliage above the elephantine trunk and picks up these entreaties made by islanders who come here with their offerings: the tack or nail, made of tin or brass or iron or copper, supplied by the goods store at sharp expense, one of the manufactures that are sent from the mother country in return for sugar. They drive one into the bark as they utter the wish, which has been properly formulated, with the conventional phrases of worship and respect, so that the loa deep inside the tree will not take offense and will grant what they wish. They know the formulas, they have been transmitted from generation to generation down the years. But even so, only someone with greater powers, who enjoys intimacy with the loas, can ensure the efficaciousness of their prayers.

They remember that the guardians of the tree run back through time to the one who only sang and never spoke, who used to keep vigil by the tree, where the sorceress Sycorax (but they have forgotten her name) lay deep with her grave goods. To her daughter who came sometimes to weep here silently and only opened her mouth to sing tonelessly after . . . well, after many things the details of which are best forgotten.

Beyond them they can see other mighty divinities—Jesusmaryand-allthesaints, Peterandpaul, Matthewmarklukeandjohn. They sometimes fancy they pick up the voices of the past, answering their prayers, and, after presenting their gifts of flowers and fruit, they come away filled with hope that the great loas have agreed to grant whatever they were being implored to do.

The slaves pressing their tin tacks into the tree whisper:

—their love of a man, their love of a woman

—their love of a child

—their hopes of reprieve from punishment

—their thanks for surviving punishment

—their fear of being burned alive on a barbecue like the young slave who ran away last week and was caught and tried and sentenced to death by this method

—their terror of having a foot chopped off for stealing (some of them have been stealing)

—their trust that their little boy will recover from the quartan fever.

Some women ask for:

—a fertile womb (they also ask for a barren womb sometimes)

Many pray, on the death of the master:

—that the new one may not be worse.

They imagine torments more atrocious for the bakkra (which is what the bosses are called) than they have themselves received at the order

of mistresses who wear bonnets and corsets and use the civilized manners of Liverpool or Birmingham or London.

They think of their children's warm squirming bodies and entreat
that as they grow up they will not be hurt as they have been—

They beg to be protected against partings, disease, death and sorrow—

They also ask to send the ball singing over the stockade at Flinders—

And Sycorax hears them, her teeth chatter and through her wasted
lips there comes a sigh—

Over and over she utters her lament:

—O airs and winds, you bring me stories from the living, rustle of
leaves and heave of branches, you speak to me of pain, and you,
streaming magma from the belly of Adesangé and cold rivers too
spouting from down below, you swollen sea where Manjiku glides,
and you, shining pale moon, and you, O bright sun of the zenith
and green-glittering star, HEAR ME! I once governed you (for so
she thinks) and you did as I wanted, you let me deliver Dulé, my
wonder, my child, a hero to our people, from death by water; I healed
the barren and the sick and granted the silly dreams of lovers, and
much other magic besides, so HEAR ME NOW, now that I only hear
groans and Dulé hobbles on slit ankles as he rails and Ariel is captive
again and croons over Roukoubé and does not speak. Turn back your
currents in their course, the stiff breeze and the gentle wind, pull
back the tide and send the sun, the moon, and the stars spinning in
the churn of the heavens—so that we can return to the time before
this time.

—I would know then, once back in those days before everything
changed, that my power is of little weight and not worth using. I would
abjure my art then and there, leave off cursing, leave off binding fast
and loose with spells—

But the soft messages in the air still come to her and flick around
the bones of her long-vanished ears, for she cannot set limits on her
powers, neither then nor now. Only the faithful who pray to her and
draw on her strength can do that. She cannot abjure, give up, control
the force by which she is possessed. On her own, she cannot stop the
churn from tumbling round and round.

But she overestimates herself, and she does not know better than to
blame herself. She and the island have become one; its hopes come
to her in the wind bending the palm fronds on the beach, making the

halyards sing against the masts in the bay, in the tree frogs' piping, the rattle of the fleshy leaves of the saman.

She breathes her lament into the earth filling her mouth, saying over and over, for the habit of power had made her take the past on her shoulders:

—If I could return to that time, I would no longer change men into beasts as I did, and then find myself unable to change them back again into men—

The isle is full of noises.

❧ S E R A F I N E I I ❧

20

Kensington, 1951

"CRIK!"
"CRAK!"
"TRIK!"
"TRAK!"
"CORCORICO!"

This is what Miranda remembers, how Serafine began a story, and how, at the age of nine or so, she would answer, more quietly, in chorus with Xanthe, both wanting to hear Feeny:

"Cocorico!"

This is a story that Serafine Killebree tells:

—On the leeward side of my island, the water's often calm and heavy as syrup, the breath of the wind sweet and shallow like a young girl sleeping, aïah! There, in the mouth of the stream where it meets the sea and its sweetness gets mixed up with the salt, a fisherman I used to know set his traps. Those were distant days, when the fishermen on my island had long woven baskets like loaves of bread. They'd let them sink down to the bottom and drift there with the long-haired weeds—

Serafine sways with her hands, Xanthe follows, imitates gigglingly, but Miranda is too grown-up for such play-school ways. She feels too old to be sharing a tub with Xanthe, but she is staying the night at her grandfather's, as often happens, and this is the drill—bathtime, bedtime together.

—Going now one way, now the other, says Serafine. Up and down, with the flow, on the tide.

—The fisherman had a wife then. Her name was Amadé, and it was she wove the baskets. She cut palm fronds from the palms. Tore them up into strips. Then dried them, up on the roof of their small house. Their whole house was no bigger than this bathroom—She looks around, describes the space with her hands. Xanthe's bathroom is raspberry and cream, with toile de Jouy curtains of shepherds and shepherdesses with crooks and ribbons fluttering from them, and Feeny's sitting beside them in her flowered pinafore by the tub, on the stool with matching toile de Jouy cover and frill.

—This little house they lived in was made of strips of palm too and tied together with the tough liana ropes. It was like a bigger basket. The hill people cut the palms down in the forest and brought them to the shore for fish. The islanders didn't have money then, and as they didn't have money, they didn't know what "poor" meant. No, nor "rich" neither. So they were happy as can be. Oh yes.

—The fisherman was called Amadou. He baited his baskets and set them in the water, he was so cunning! He put a little fish to swim inside, looking like it's wriggling free. But he'd made it swallow a hook beforehand—(Serafine opens her mouth and wiggles her little finger inside and both Xanthe and Miranda squirm at the sight of her soft tongue, imagining the laceration, the capture.)—And this little hook's at the end of a thread, and the thread's attached to a trapeze of sticks hanging above. It was so clever, his way of catching fish! The trapeze hangs lightly from a toggle, the toggle hangs from the end of a proper fishing line, the line passes over a springy pole to the door over the mouth of the basket where the little fish's wriggling so free. Such temptation! The big fish seeing the little one there glides into the basket to gobble him up. He goes in, he trips the toggle, the toggle jiggers the trapeze, the trapeze lets go the springy pole, it whips back, it pulls up the door to the basket . . . the big fish is the prisoner now. How did it happen? How?—(She is tickling them, pretending to be a fish; the little girls respond fiercely, their hands jab at hers, they snap open and shut trying to catch Feeny's in the water, they are laughing, they don't need to hear every word, they've heard this story before.)

—The sea round my island teems. Oh, so many creatures. Some of them fish, with fins and tails. What fish: tunny the size of small islands themselves. Flying fish. Sunfish. Swordfish. Sculpin. Flounder. Star-gazers. Eel. Hatchet fish. Grouper. Skate. Stingray. PIRANHA—(She snaps her teeth, laughs.)—Every one a monster, whiskers, jaws, fan-ning and lurking. After the fishes there come other sorts of creatures: sponges—(this is the signal for washing, the little girls reach obediently for their sponges)—and long-streamered squids—(She squeezes Xanthe's sponge, whooshes it through the water, making siphon noises, then begins to wash her back and neck.)—Seashells swim about as well. Spreading their skirts, like they were dancing and billowing. Weeds too, join in and shake their waists, wave their long arms, flicking their hands—

Sometimes Feeny will rise and sway, humming, with her arms above her head waving, remembering carnival's forbidden dancing, sashay-ing down the streets of Jamieston in the wake of the bands weaving like a single creature on a hundred legs, through the alleys and in and out of the backyards. But tonight she doesn't, she soaps Xanthe, urges Miranda to rub and rinse, then helps Xanthe up and lifts her clear of the edge of the tub, onto the mat, and wraps her in a pale-green towel and sits her on her lap, spreading her knees to fit her on, as Xanthe is getting big for this babying, but still enjoys it, as does Serafine.

—Of all the creatures in the ocean, there's none so terrible as . . . —

"Manjiku!" Miranda shouts out the name and then covers her face, giggling; Xanthe turns, buries her head in Feeny's breast.

—Manjiku's got a snout like a crocodile, Manjiku's got pointed green teeth arranged in double rows, and a mane of spikes like sea urchins, and a forked tail with razor edges he uses to slice up his food. And cut his enemies to pieces! Anything that gets in his way, slash, slash. He can work up the ocean to scuds of foam when he's cross. Manjiku's pale, pale, he can't bear the light of the sun, it burns his pale skin, his pale flesh, it leeches the life out of him in blisters and wens. You can see his bones through his warty hide, like a jellyfish, like an X ray. He's lived that long in the sea, he glows in the dark. Phos-phor-es-cence—

She almost hisses, and Xanthe and Miranda understand this word because one of Miranda's special treasures, which she keeps in her treasure drawer under lock and key, but has shown Xanthe in a moment of love, is a figure of Jesus on the cross which glows greeny-white under the bedclothes if you've shone a torch on it beforehand and saturated it with light.

—What Manjiku wants—more than food, more than drink, more that sweet life itself—is to have a child of his own. Yes! Not just to have it, like a father—no, he wants to be a mother, to bring the child out of his mouth, spit out a little Manjiku, think of that! For Manjiku is a monster, a sea dragon, he sets fear in the heart of every man. Yet he wants nothing better than to be a woman—

And Serafine laughs.

"You'll find out, children, that in this world, people burn to have things they can't have, and strange things at that."

She is patting Xanthe softly now, dreamily, and she stands her up and drops the nightdress with the rabbits over the little girl's head, and turns her to fasten the top pearl button at the back.

Miranda is lying on her tummy for she has the bath to herself, and she's pretending she's swimming, thinking of it getting dark and Manjiku rising, rising from the deep, tracking her.

Serafine slaps her bottom, softly, with a chuckle, and tells her, "Out now." She pulls out the plug, and the water drains, so Miranda cannot swim anymore, and lies there, feeling the water suck away from her.

"Come on out now, Miss Miranda," says Feeny. "The bath's no place to lie catching cold."

Later, when they are both tucked in, one at each end of Xanthe's bed, tickling toes together on purpose, they beg her:

"Story! Story!"

"What do you say, then, my little ladies?"

"Crik!"

"Crak!"

"Trik!"

"Trak!"

Feeny laughs, whispers, "Cocorico"; they whisper back and she takes up the thread where she left off back in the bathroom:

—Manjiku specially likes to eat women: juicy, dark women full of blood, the way we are when we get old enough to be mothers. Manjiku thinks he'll have a baby himself if he eats enough women, especially women with babies inside them waiting to be born—

The girls shiver in spite of the warm white cellular blankets that cover them. They curl up, hugging themselves, but their eyes shine.

To check her fright, Miranda cuts in quickly, "You had a baby once, Feeny, didn't you?" She really does wants to hear again about Feeny's daughter, whom she left in Enfant-Béate long, long ago. And she also wants to quell the excitement leaping under her ribs.

"Hush," says Feeny. "One story at a time. Listen:

—One evening, Amadou goes to check the trap and in it, what does he find? A beautiful silver starfish, with points of light all over its body, sapphire and rose-pink and silver. He picks it up, and sees that it's a tiny silver woman, with hair like spun silk and blue eyes like pieces of the sky come down to earth—

Xanthe likes this bit, she has blue eyes and fancies they're like the sky. Miranda's are button-brown, like her teddy bear's, like her father's, Kit Everard.

—Amadou has never seen a beautiful white starwoman like this, and she speaks to him in a soft low voice like the south breeze stirring in the palms, like it does just before the sun sets. She asks him, "Where am I?" She's far from home, you see, she's strayed into tropical waters. She has no business to be there, but this is the way the story goes— (And Serafine sighs.)

—Amadou doesn't take her home to show to Amadé. He keeps her a prisoner in a fish pond where he stores the catch. He shades the rock pool with a rush mat, so she doesn't overheat, for she looks delicate, as if the sun on the water'd get too much for her. He fishes for oysters and leaves them for her lunch. He doesn't want anyone to see her. He wants her for himself. He's like Manjiku, all men are, aha! He says nothing to Amadé. Amadé notices, just the same, something's taken hold of her man, eaten into his heart. She can almost see the sickness there, like a worm in a nut.

—The days pass, Amadou thinks of nothing but his glittering starfish, of pleasing her, of taking care of her. He forgets Amadé and their life together. It's a spell, you see, the mermaid has the power to cast spells. With her white hair, her eyes like bits of the sky.

—One day, Amadé follows him in stealth to his fish ponds, and she sees him—well—she sees him loving and petting his new love, and she feels her heart inside breaking. "I know about her," she tells him later. He cries salt tears, he doesn't want to hurt Amadé on purpose, no, he doesn't. But that's the way of things.

—One day Amadou returns from the shore, and Amadé sees he's crying: his care's got him nothing, the silver girl's dead. A sunstroke did for her, and he found her floating, with her hair fanning out around her, her jeweled skin still sparkling like she's alive—

Serafine tips Miranda back against the pillows in the position of sleep, and gently pulls the thumb out of her mouth, shaking her head and smiling, "No," then turns to Xanthe, smooths her hair, for she is already drifting, eyes half-closed.

—Now Amadé isn't just clever at making traps and baskets: she's a wisewoman, that too, you know, she understands plants and stones, and what they can do. And once, a little while before, she was with her brother in the forest. Hunting game for supper, when he saw the leaves flicker. Quick as a flash, he shoots an arrow, but when he runs forward, he finds nothing but a stringy tree rat. He curses then, as young men do (but not young ladies), he pulls out the arrow roughly, then leaves the creature there, where it lay down and died.

—Amadé looks on the rat's body with sorrow, she's soft-hearted, you know that, when the rat wife comes running out, eyes left and right, watching out, a red flower in her teeth, and she makes passes over the dead creature from tip of tail to tip of nose. Once, twice, three times, until, yes, it goes and opens its eyes and gets right up, right as rain—

She pauses, she is thinking of this scene; Xanthe's eyes widen. "Go on," she orders with her frown. "I don't want to go to sleep."

—Amadé knows the flower, which one it is, and now she needs it, she goes in search of it. And when she's found it, she goes to the fish pond, where Amadou's sitting, head in his hands, grieving over the silver stargirl he's lost. She's beginning to foul the air a little, she's that dead. Amadé gives her man the flower—it's called by my people the flower of Adesangé, the red god of fire and life, who lives in the volcano of the island—

The children like this part, when the mermaid comes back to life, they quiver with pleasure at the strong magic of it.

—Then Amadé says, "I understand loving, so here's your love back," She passes the flower over the floating corpse, turns away from the scene she can't bear to watch.

—That night, a perfect night for Manjiku, when he goes prowling in his hunger, under a moon that's big as the sun, Amadé slides her body into the sea and feels chilled with terror, though the water's not really cold, the sun shines on it all day. She hopes Manjiku'll come soon to eat her, and out she swims. The sea falls from her arms in

green and black and silver, the emeralds of Manjiku burst like stars in
the bubbles clustering on her limbs, and she's amazed they're so beautiful, for she's not been in the water at night before.

—When Manjiku comes, she shuts her eyes and lets herself fall
down his throat past the barbed teeth and come down to land in
the foul bilge water in his gut. He begins to shake, she's rocked
from one side to the other as she feels the tail thrash at the sea and
Manjiku rear and toss. She opens her eyes—all is white, snow-white,
she cannot see, but she puts up her hands to stop falling down; still
the roll and pitch goes on, she's thrown about and her head bursts
into stars against the whiteness, till all at once Manjiku splits open and
there's no more night blindness nor blind whiteness neither, but the
good hot yellow sun up above. She's cast up ashore and a man's standing
before her, waiting for her to open her eyes. He's a handsome man,
oh yes, brown and glossy, with a light in his eye, and a smile on his
lips and a way with him, you know—(Feeny smiles to herself)—and
he says to Amadé, "Lady, you've set me free. I'll serve you forever."

—For Manjiku was under a curse, you know—(Serafine is talking
softly, very softly.)—Only a woman who knew what real loving is
could undo its power. And Amadé it is understands real loving—

Serafine stops, pauses for the silence to settle, then whispers, "Good
night, Miss Xanthe.

"Good night, Miss Miranda."

But they're too fast asleep to reply to Feeny.

She sits for a while beside them, her arm laid alongside the night-
light on the table; the shoe of the Old Woman, with a pink bulb
inside, lifts the shadows in a comforting way. The stories of Manjiku
she had heard on the island, when she was herself a girl, had not had
happy endings: Manjiku continued to raid the inland waters for women,
his hunger was not to be appeased, his need to have babies of his own
still raged.

Sometimes in the morning, the tideline was strewn with translucent
green pearls: sea emeralds, the Béatois called them, dropped by Manjiku as a promise of more treasure to the women, the future mothers
he was trying to lure into the waters, for these jewels only appeared
overnight, and could not be fished from the sea by day. Manjiku had
taken Mr. Anthony's first wife, the island wife, the one that died by
drowning. And many others, before her, natives: Manjiku has an appetite for them especially.

But this savage story isn't seemly for the little English girls, so Serafine has adapted it, as storytellers do.

There's another story with a happy ending they know, not just from Serafine; it's traditional in their family, and in the history books in which the Everards have a mention.

How the first Kit Everard won the love of an islander and how she saved him and his brave band of pioneers.

It's come down through the years, this story. From firsthand sources, authenticated. Serafine knows it; all her family, working on the Everard lands, knew it; they passed it on:

Long ago, when the colony was flourishing and sugar was being shipped in quantities of menhir-shaped loaves to the storerooms and the kitchens and the taverns and the parlors of the capitals of Europe, a French missionary priest, one Père Labat, wrote one of the first comprehensive travel books about the new world of the islands, chronicling the natives and their customs (as far as he could) as well as the way of life the settlers had developed, with their fine mansions and wide verandas, ornamented with brattishings and cool with shutters and fringed jalousies. He reported that he had met a survivor from the heroic days, an ancient Indian hag, he said, bald as a vulture and wizened as a walnut, with one black tooth left in her head. She could not speak; indeed, it was said she had not spoken for decades, though once she had been a singer and made up songs that others learned after her and still sang. (He gave examples in an appendix, for he was a scholar of the Age of the Enlightenment and frankly admired the arts of the native peoples of the islands.) He was taken to meet her, for she was a famous character: the concubine of Kit Everard, she had redeemed the savagery of her people.

She was living then, according to the observant father, in a ramshackle but tidy palm-leaf cabin by the saman tree "which these primitive people in their ignorance still worship, studding its gnarled trunk with nails of tin or brass to register their desires. She has been the guardian of this wishing tree in the English churchyard since anyone alive can remember, though before that, the rumour was that she had lived in a wild state, before the islands were properly civilised.

> Mme. Verard, [he continued], for so they called her, in order to pay her that honour due to her staunchness and fidelity (though the union had never been blessed in God's sight), had heard among her people

that they planned to fall upon the settlers and massacre them in their beds one moonlit night. And hearing this, out of the great love she bore the founder of the island, Sir Christopher Everard, and on behalf of the love-child she had borne him, she raised the alarm.

Thus, the enemy forfeited the advantage of surprise, and they found the English heroes ready for them when they struck. Some Christian lives were lost, but after a bloody conflict, the night was theirs. One thousand savages fell in that struggle, which is called today the Battle of Sloop's Bight, after the first engagement in that cove, where a Christian ship, the *Rebecca,* was fired in a daring sortie. These great events took place in the year of Our Lord 1620, and after that time, though there were disturbances from some of the remaining natives, there was no more profound danger, and the colony could begin to flourish as it does today.

Mme. Verard was in her hundredth year or more when I was fortunate enough to take in mine the hand that proved the loyal instrument of God's will for this pagan place and its people. She was the last person living to speak the language of the native islanders, so it was a pity that she could no longer use her tongue, except now and then to rasp out a harsh fragment of a song.

Her example proves the nobility of soul the native can possess when tutored in the ways of godliness and truth. She was a lamp of truth to her people.

One of Ariel's songs which he appended went like this, and sometimes Serafine sang it, and Xanthe and Miranda both enjoyed singing it with her, calling it the "Song of Manjiku":

> The juice of the green melon is sweet,
> The yellow is sweeter, I know,
> And there's a fruit that's still riper.
> I can't tell you its name,
> I won't show you its face,
> Or I shan't ever eat it no more, no more.

PART IV

Gold/White

To Fill a Gap—
Insert the Thing that caused it—
Block it up
With Other—and 'twill yawn the more—
You cannot solder an Abyss
With Air.

—EMILY DICKINSON

21

HOWEVER MUCH THE hotel maid sprinkled her lemon scouring powder, the Salle de Bain (so designated by a chipped blue-and-white oval enamel plaque) still smelled of stagnant drains, as if it functioned as an extension of the narrow street outside, where a section of the gutter exuded a steady reek of staleness, sweetish-sour, and not entirely unpleasant to Miranda.

She had rinsed out the tub, and lowered the big tarnished metal plug into the hole. The water began to trickle down its old tearstains below the taps; she hoped there'd be enough hot to wash her hair. She pulled a strand under her nose and sniffed; the smoke from the blondes she'd sumptuously smoked the night before saturated it. Again, sweetish, not unpleasant; she was in that time of her youth when ripeness in any form spelled pleasure.

It was half an hour past noon, when the corner hotel was quiet; an hour when Marie-Angèle could let her slip into the bathroom with her pass key without telling Madame, who would otherwise charge her 400 francs (anciens) for the tubful of hot water. In return, Miranda did not mention the occasional missing pair of stockings, headband, hair-slide, and, on one occasion, she was almost sure, British Home Stores knickers she'd had since school, where they had been modestly itemized as "linings" in the list of uniform requirements and had her school number scrawled on the waistband by Astrid with a linen marker of indelible ink (the other girls had Cash's name tapes in cursive script or small capitals). Such items seemed a fair exchange for free baths.

Then, just as she was about to step into the water, Marie-Angèle's voice rose in a shrill whisper at the door.

"Madame!" she called, and Miranda quickly bundled up her clothes and streaked across the landing, as the proprietress came heaving up the curving stair, the rail quaking in her grasp.

Marie-Angèle met her, deflected her; then spoke, and Madame turned to descend again.

There was a caller for Miranda downstairs, reported Marie-Angèle. "Un monsieur." (This was why he had not been allowed up to seek out Miranda in her room—though she had managed on several occasions to sneak some of her new friends past the desk, while at night, there was no porter and she had her own key to the wrought-iron-and-glass front door.) But Madame Davenant kept a clean and respectable and quiet private hotel, which is why it had been chosen for Miranda and why she liked it, on the whole.

Miranda could tell that Madame wasn't angry that she had had to climb five floors to Miranda's chambre, la quatorze, on the level just below the mansarde, where Marie-Angèle had her quarters, for the maid looked cheerful as she nodded in the direction of the Salle de Bain and promised, "Une autre fois."

As Miranda was halfway down the dark and narrow stairwell, she realized who it was who had so disarmed Madame that she had not scolded Marie-Angèle (for not being downstairs to hand, to run the message up to Mlle. Everard), or waited to reproach Miranda herself for allowing visitors to call without appointments and cause all this trouble to her hostess in the hôtel Davenant. For it wasn't the first time this had happened; by no means. Paris—or, to be precise, the Paris made up of Montparnasse, Saint-Germain and the Mouffetard—was like a party: meeting someone on the street in that quadrant did not constitute a pickup. Miranda Everard had been raised always to avoid pickups.

She was almost certain it would be the tall man with the unseasonal yellow gloves with pearl buttons, so personable and well-spoken, who bore the name of a well-known apéritif. She had met him in the Coupole the night before when she was sitting with her friends from the atelier, and he'd known one of them and come over. They ordered calvados and played canards, dipping the sugar cubes in the tawny liquid so that the surfaces just met, the liqueur drawn up through the sugar, flushing and softening it until, at just the right moment, a split second before the sweetness might dissolve and fall into the drink and spoil it, you tipped your head back and took the lump on your tongue and either let it melt there, or gnashed the singingly sweet grit of the sugar grains. And then again, but this time on a coffee spoon, with the other half of the sugar cube. The calvados did not flow like fire if taken with sucre en morceaux like this: it just gave a funny kick in the area of her chest, and made her gurgle with the heat of it.

She was remembering how this M. Apéritif looked at her—the French, especially d'un certain âge—were such moon-calves when it came to flirting, rolling eyes and winking shamelessly; she was in consequence smiling to herself when she reached the hall. To the left, opposite the reception desk, in the parlor with the rubber plant and the lace half-curtains, where she sometimes had her breakfast (if she was up before ten, when Madame stopped serving it), she saw her grandfather, Sir Anthony Everard, erect against the window, with her young aunt, his daughter, beside him, Xanthe Everard, Miranda's nursery playmate.

"Didn't you receive my letter? I wrote, my dear—oh, a week ago."

Miranda reached to peck him back and felt the smooth skin on his chin, smelled the lotion he used on his hair (not bay rum, not like her father, but a sweeter perfume, lime water and rose). Then she turned to Xanthe, whom she could avoid kissing, to keep her unbathed body away from the young girl's groomed presence as far as she was able without coldness.

She held Xanthe at arm's length, to look at her, and revolved her, almost prancing to distract attention from herself, and exclaimed, "Everyone must say this, but you look amazing."

Her father said, "Yes, Goldie's no longer a little girl!"

"Goldie?"

"Yes. Goldie—I don't like being called Xanthe. It's my new name."

Like a child in an eighteenth-century aristocratic portrait, Xanthe, now eleven verging on twelve, was not dressed in children's clothes, but in doll-like versions of her mother's couture style: a sage-green fitted jacket with narrow lapels and a large and fancy button at the nipped-in waist, a wheel of a skirt, the hem hanging straight, over strong legs in pale seamed stockings. Even in her confusion, Miranda noticed this, the workmanship involved in hemming without a droop, the quality of Xanthe's hose.

"All right, Goldie it is, why not? Plain English." Miranda tried not to make a face.

Sir Anthony too was all bon ton: a gray flannel suit; with a striped tie in pale-green and pink, signaling membership of a desirable club; a deeper crimson in the handkerchief casually thrust into his breast pocket; and light shoes of a complementary oyster sheen. His face, too, was a paler, healthy pink, and so close-shaved that he looked, with his bladelike glance, as pristine as the shoot from a bulb in spring.

Her grandfather had written to her, she had forgotten. He was always punctilious; she did not have a diary; today must be the day she had thought so far off when he had proposed meeting Kit and Astrid in Paris and then taking all of them out for lunch. She was confused, one of her friends was picking her up at the studios that afternoon, not M. Apéritif, but a doe-eyed Persian who was—he said—training to be an engineer. He was going to walk her to her other job in the bar, across the Jardin du Luxembourg; perhaps they'd sit in the late sunshine, near the thin young naked girl who looked exposed and hence signified Truth, the inscription said.

"I haven't been well," she stuttered. "I lost track of the days. But this is fantastic. To see you here!"

"We hadn't heard."

"Oh, I didn't tell anyone. It wasn't serious. Besides, I wouldn't have wanted to worry you."

Sir Anthony asked, "Where are your parents now, by the bye?" He spoke into the air, as if inconsequentially.

Miranda faced him, and schooled her features.

"In Le Touquet, it's the championship." Her voice was firm, gay, just as she would wish. "I had a postcard yesterday. Of a miniature golf course—you have to get your ball over a lunar landscape . . ." She made a gesture of a hop and curve of a spinning ball. "They're coming back."

It was ten days ago that she'd heard from Le Touquet, and that series of games must be over by now, she knew. But she held fast under her grandfather's look, which lifted past her, reflectively, intent on the piegonholes where the room keys lay in their niches.

"Soon? I hope so."

"Oh yes, absolutely . . ." She glanced over at Madame. "Everyone here is very kind."

"Meanwhile, you've everything you need?"

"Oh, it's bliss . . ." she began, then noticed Xanthe's delicate widening of her eyes and a slight wrinkle of pale nose, like white jade, and noticed that on her fair curls she was wearing a small molded felt cap, with a slantwise spray of fluffy feathers—egret?—curving into her nape.

Miranda faltered. "I'll just get changed to go out—I was about to. Sorry." She looked around the vestibule, suddenly aware that this room where she ate a brioche and drank milky coffee as if at a feast of the gods on those mornings when she managed to get up in time was a mere dingy parlor, the curtains gray with city smuts, the tables pocked and charred by cigarettes. She began to wave to a seat, but stopped herself—she realized it must look grimy to them as well. She could see her grandfather was keeping his hands to himself, standing quiet and still, as if he wanted to make the least contact possible with the room.

Madame raised her crackling voice from the large brown desk where she presided in the hall beyond, and asked them with unusual largesse if they would like some refreshment.

"Grenadine, pour les demoiselles?"

Sir Anthony's lips slid over his small teeth in what passed for his public smile, and he accepted, without waiting for their answer.

Miranda began, again, addressing herself to the young girl, "While I'm getting ready, would you like to come up and see my room?"

Two glasses of grenadine appeared, bright carmine, with whorls of lighter tint where the thick syrup was melting into the water.

"Offerte de la part de la direction." Madame's smile showed the effort of her boon.

Sir Anthony thanked her, his lean form bending in a half-bow with discreet and final grace that did not allow further conversation. She sighed, but departed not entirely ungratified, and took her position by the keys.

Upstairs, Miranda pulled the bedclothes up to tidy the bed and patted the lumpy result, beckoning to Xanthe to sit down there; there wasn't anywhere else.

"So how's London? It must be holidays—how's your ma? And Feeny? Go on, tell. I want all the news."

Xanthe spread out the soft folds of her skirt and looked at them as Miranda quickly splashed water into her armpits, round her neck, on her face, muttering, "I wish I'd just had time to wash my hair."

"Serafine's hip's getting worse—with the winter coming, she gets stiff, you know, and it makes her lame. She's wheezy too. Otherwise everything's fine, I think. She sends you much love, of course." "Goldie" Everard sounded as if she were delivering an elocution exercise. "I don't see her much anymore. She doesn't exactly look after me anymore, you know." She added, in a different, child's voice, "Her room smells funny, like an old jar with something sticky and brown in it you can't tell what it is."

"I must write to her." Miranda had swung out the bidet now, from under the basin, used a rubber hose from the top to fill it and was rapidly dunking her feet in the water, a procedure Xanthe watched in surprise.

"Sorry to hold you up, but I feel filthy—you know I'm serving in a café . . ." She said "café," it sounded right, though it was really a bar, Le Rosebud, down a side street in Montparnasse. "I just fall into bed any old how, it's sometimes so late when I get back." Xanthe shivered slightly, as Miranda dabbed and ran on, "Will you or your ma promise to read her the letter if I write her one? You know, in the past . . ." She trailed off, she could sense that she'd better not squat on the bidet to wash between her legs in front of Miss Goldilocks.

"I'll hurry up," she said instead, and took her best dress from behind the flowered cotton curtain on the bendy wire that served as a wardrobe. It was a bit summery for the weather, but had the same small waist as Xanthe's tailored number, in a kind of light-green figured gauze over a satin underskirt, with a broad belt and wide lighter-colored lapels, with a big Perspex buckle like bottle glass. She found a pair of stockings, passed her hand through to check for runs, discovered a small one near the heel and dabbed it with the bar of soap to hold it; put on her two-tone coffee-and-cream high-heel shoes, then, looking close in the mirror, applied some eyeliner with the flick of a tail in the corner and painted pale lipstick on her mouth.

Xanthe was still talking, perseveringly, at her hands folded in her lap, "Mummy nearly came with us. But at the last minute, she had too much on."

"That's a shame," said Miranda, and gave her hair three strokes backward with her brush to make it puff.

"There, I'm ready. How do I look? Will your pa approve?"

Xanthe nodded, with a swallow. Miranda had a skewed air, her dark curls sprang up on her head so that the younger girl noticed little black hairs running down the vertebrae of her neck to the nape; there was a feral shine and speed to her too, something uncontained, and it scared the younger girl.

Xanthe had caught snatches of her parents talking in London before they left. There was trouble, always trouble stirring in the air round Kit and round Astrid.

—Miranda, who's considering Miranda?

—Us, of course. The ball always ends up in our court.

—They left her where?

—In an hotel on the Left Bank?

—She's eighteen, just turning nineteen.

—Well, if there's nothing wrong.

—But alone in Paris?

—I mean.

—I know what you mean.

The voices grew even lower, then, when money came into the question.

—I've forked out before, and I'll be forking out again, no doubt.

—You're generous to a fault.

—But I couldn't cover his marker—why should I?

—He should have learned by now. Let them look after themselves.

—You're the one who's generous, my dear. Who's understanding of my peccadilloes. Lord, what a mistake that was.

—You were a young man. Once! Besides, as you say, noblesse oblige.

—Still am, when I look at you.

—Ooh, you wolf.

"Tramp" was a word Xanthe had learned from her mother. Also "tart." And "call girl." And "courtesan." She liked the sound of these words, even delivered with her mother's genteel sneer, but Miranda didn't match any of these, they were too glamorous. Except tramp. Her room was so grubby too, with nothing but a bed in it and that bidet and that bit of rag for a curtain over the small old propped-up suitcase and some clothes. Had Kit and Astrid stayed here too, before they left her behind? It was so different from the rooms Xanthe and her father had taken in a former hôtel particulier of a family of the ancien régime, round a courtyard off the Rue Saint-Honoré, with ormolu chests of drawers, lace-trimmed bolsters and a chiming clock on the writing desk in the small, light sitting room where stood striped chintz chairs with gilded lyre backs and a matching silk-covered settee.

Xanthe's mother is saying to her father,
—She should learn a skill.
—I believe she wants to study art. She shows some talent, or so I've been told.
—That family thinks money grows on apple trees.
Her father is sighing, agreeing. Then he asks,
—What's a girl like her do these days?
—Shorthand typing, pharmacy, stablegirl, acting, oh, really, you know the kind of thing.
—She has a good head on her shoulders.
—She's no fool, I know. But she's awfully swarthy. Do you think employers would take to her? It might put off likely customers.
—Really, Gillian.
—Well, I mean.
—She's not very dark. There's many Welsh darker-eyed than her.
—She's not Welsh, Ant darling.
—What do you mean, dearest? Think of Cleary, the dear fellow and Pindi and . . . I could go on. All first-rate chaps, friends.
—They were Flinders friends, darling. Players of the game. This is different.
—You don't have to tell me, my dear. I know girls are a special case. Girls are different from chaps, I do know that. But everything's changing, all the time. My word, that's one thing that stays the same, at least. And Ant laughs good-humoredly; Xanthe's father is never cross, never ruffled, never at a loss.

"Go on, how do I look? Am I different?" Xanthe stood up in the narrow space between the bed and the door in Miranda's room, and said, "You look rather beatnik." Xanthe spoke the word carefully, caressingly, Miranda noted, as it it might snap at her if she didn't handle it well. Miranda grinned back.
"And?"
"You're thin."
"I am," she whispered close to Xanthe's cheek, and the younger girl sniffed the sweet tobacco on her breath. "I'm having a fantastic time."
Then, on the stairs, she turned to say to Xanthe, who was behind

her, going more slowly, unfamiliar with the shallowness of the treads
and their tight twist, unlike Miranda, who'd had weeks of running up
and down them, "But don't let on to your pa. He might make me come
back to London, and I couldn't bear it. Ugh."

You could take Goldie—show her the sights.
    —It'd be a good opportunity, she's old enough now to appreciate
it, the Orangerie, the Louvre, the Café de Paris.
    She'd held her breath, hoping they'd agree.
    —Why don't we go, the three of us?
    —No, my dear, I'll stay here and hold the fort. Take Goldie, go
ahead. Show her Paris. I've seen it.

"Well, shall we make our way? Are you all prepared?" Sir Anthony was
addressing Miranda, though he wasn't looking at her. His gaze was
fastened on his daughter's last careful steps down the stairs, as if he
could barely restrain himself from running forward to hold out a hand
to her. He'd always had such courtesy, could make a frump feel like
a star, so Gillian used to say a little ruefully. She quoted him: on one
occasion when the Princess had waved him away, pleading a cold, he
had breathed back at her, "It would be a privilege to catch a cold of
yours."
    Gillian snorted as she repeated her husband's gallantry, but it was
plain she took some pleasure in it too.
    "We'd better drink Madame's offering," he added, directing Miranda
to the glasses of brilliant cordial; she sipped and made a face.
    "So sweet."
    Xanthe stole a look at the reception desk, then passed behind her
father and tipped hers into the rubber plant's garish jardinière, stifled
a giggle and beckoned Miranda to do likewise.
    "You're a naughty girl," said Sir Anthony, aglow, when they were
in a taxi, heading for Le Grand Condé. He patted both Xanthe and
Miranda on the hand, chuckled, and went on, "How delightful to have
both my girls with me"—giving Miranda's a special squeeze—"I'm all
ears, my dear. I want to hear all about your life here. Every detail!"
    Through her time of growing up, Miranda had had to talk so loud
to interrupt the brawling, crying, canoodling jag that was her parents'
marriage, to entertain so insistently in order to divert them from the
partying, bickering, kiss-and-makeup affair that absorbed them totally,

that she had become as deaf to tremors and to nuances as her former games mistress shouting "Bombs Coming Over" or "Scrub the Decks" through a megaphone in the gym at the dim convent Miranda had been sent to for those three years of her childhood when the family had been in funds. When Astrid asked her daughter a question, Miranda would rush to reply, as fully and as dazzlingly as she could; her mother liked to be amused and was easily distracted by something else. When her father reached for a cigarette, Miranda intercepted his hand as it searched for his lighter, and touched the flame to the tip to make contact with him. If she learned to be self-effacing, cultivated a mysterious absence or aloofness, they might forget her altogether, or so she feared deep down, not openly, not admitting to herself this appalling possibility. So when asked by her grandfather to tell all, she plunged in, heedless of the need for caution which Xanthe, at an early age, had grasped should always be observed with parents, and especially her father. Miranda sensed her family had come to the rescue, and she was only keen to show that she was striking out boldly, freestyle, not sinking.

Once Astrid had taken her shopping (she was about four at the time) and set her down on a stool by a counter when she tried on earrings in a round mirror on a stand; a salesgirl with a promotional tray of perfumes approached her and Astrid turned and extended her wrist to sample it. Later, Miranda imagined that the salesgirl was offering a discount to customers who bought a certain range of cosmetics—for her mother had wandered off. Miranda had remained quietly on the stool looking at her fat knees, as if she were happy doing so, until one of the shopgirls in costume jewelry leaned over the counter and said, through scarlet lips, "Where's your mummy gone to then?"

At which Miranda had burst into tears, and continued sobbing, holding on to the store detective's hand as she heard the announcement: "Would Miranda's mummy please come to Lost and Found. On the first floor."

Astrid was laughing when she came running up, coat and scarf flying, shopping bags like jibsails billowing, her pretty mouth with little teeth making her seem to shine all over.

"Oh God, it's so awful of me! I forgot I'd brought you!"she exclaimed as the store detective pushed Miranda into her mother's sleek legs, only to provoke a little skipping step to the side.

"Careful! My best nylons!"

. . .

The invisibility that threatened her drove her to perform to attract attention, so she had done well at school, been picked for the hockey and the swimming teams. She had taken after her father, Astrid said, that dogginess—always going after a stick, leaping high to please the thrower, waggingly racing back with it and repeating the action as long as it pleased. She flung herself at friendship and blurted her thoughts and feelings, jokes and secrets till she had no flora in the lining of her inner spaces to help her absorb her experiences slowly, nutritiously. So she had no idea, when her antics were effective, how she was using herself up in her efforts to ward off her disappearance from the world, in her girlish desire to please.

At school, she had been considered something of a "character"—a freak by her enemies, an eccentric by those loyal to her, or touched by the high voltage of her need. Her attention-seeking bore the outward marks of sincerity, in spite of the gush—and Miranda's exclamations, declarations, confessions and other self-revealing speeches seemed filled with inadvertencies, guileless admissions and a heroic individuality of voice and response. Yet all this frankness was fundamentally an act: to fill the silence that she feared in others, to ward off the invisibility she feared in herself.

Her father laughed softly at her sometimes, throwing his head back and exhaling lazily: "What a chatterbox you are! You don't get it from me." Round him, she was talkative in order to provoke him into replying, and the attempt made her a habitual confessor, though she would have been amazed if she had been charged with talking about herself all the time.

They were driving down the Boulevard Saint-Germain toward the river; the Seine's fast-flowing current, parted hard against the piers of the bridges, seemed to Miranda's eyes to capture the pace and temperament of this city where she felt so happy, where she wanted to stay. She began, excitedly, plunging into her strategy of convincing her grandfather she was prospering, "Oh, I'm learning such a lot—it's a piece of luck. Rob—he started it all, oh, ten or more years ago— he lets me do odd jobs around the studios in return for—well— anything I want to do, it's fabulous. I can use the presses, he even lets me have paper free. I do a bit of modeling, sweeping up, errands, fetch orders of croque-monsieurs, grands crêmes . . ." She laughed, catching the shadow on Anthony's forehead. "Oh, I don't model in the nude! We do lots of different drawing exercises, drapery and still life and other stuff—and we take it in turns to pose."

He looked relieved, as if he believed her gratefully. The cab swerved into the Place de la Concorde, she felt them whirling as they joined the vortex round the obelisk as if in a fairground swing as it lifts and spins.

"Rob's a fantastic teacher—people come from all over the world to study with him. I'm really lucky, honestly. He says I'm doing well, too. I've been concentrating on my technique, so soon I could try working straight onto the plate. I'm terribly excited about it, I'm learning every day."

"And today? What were you learning today?"

Miranda tried to ignore this, and pressed on, "We have guest speakers, and we've had lectures on Pollock and Kandinski—" She turned to speak to Xanthe. "One woman talked about female beauty and art. Shaving your temples and sticking out your tummy versus binding your breasts to flatten them and pulling out your teeth . . ." She giggled. " 'Beauty is power,' that's what she said. 'If Cleopatra's nose had been a little shorter . . . ' "

". . . it would have changed the face of the world. I know." Xanthe touched her own neat nose. "I think that's stupid, actually. Cleopatra was a queen, and rich, and pretty clever too, I think, she knew what was what."

Miranda was silent for a beat. "But she was the most beautiful woman in the ancient world."

Xanthe looked out of the taxi windows at the broad plane leaves shifting and the throng swinging down the pavement, jackets still unfastened, panels loose, in these first mild days of autumn. "I think they just say she was beautiful," said this new Xanthe Miranda had not known before, this precocious, sharp-witted little girl in the chic outfit. "To explain away what she managed to do." Miranda waited to hear more. How smug she is, she thought viciously. Her father, too, smiling into his smooth, pink chin.

The taxi swerved out of the Champs Élysées, down the Avenue Georges V, and came to a sudden halt on the corner.

Anthony Everard looked at the meter with his customary care with sums, however small, and began to unfold a 10,000-franc note from a small gold clip, then hesitated, and looked again.

Xanthe stiffened by his side, when he plucked her by the sleeve and nodded to the meter. "Look at that."

The driver turned and said, worried now, "Mille neuf cents soixante francs, monsieur."

"If I'm not mistaken," said Anthony Everard, "today's the first of September, 1960—no?" He paid, and still looking thoughtful, escorted the young girls past through the mahogany-and-brass revolving doors into the burgundy-colored, upholstered, mirrored and gilded interior of Le Grand Condé, where in heaps of rosy cumulus, nymphs with come-hither looks and not a stitch on except a few blue satin ribbons frolicked between the mirrored panels on the walls and ceiling.

Ant Everard pulled a small leather-bound notepad from his breast pocket and wrote out for them, 1/9/60. "You see, the fare's the same as the date—and the date as the year—I'd already noticed that, of course. But this fare's a numerical coincidence, by God, of a rare sort. A moment more, a moment less, a foot more, a foot less, and the meter would have given a different reading. Auspicious, I'd say, without a doubt." He touched Miranda on the elbow as he steered them toward the lectern where the table-reservations ledger stood. "Do you think I should tell your father—in Le Touquet? The odds against such a thing are . . . incalculable." The head waiter came toward them, and Anthony gave another name, not his, and they were ushered to a table by the window, overlooking the *terrasse* where a few customers were sitting in the open.

The menus were presented, mauve ink in loops formed unfamiliar words, to Miranda too, for she was more accustomed to café fare, a sandwich au jambon, a croque-madame. Or, if she was feeling bingey, a feuilleté de champignons au porto, which was the single cheapest item on the Coupole's menu.

Miranda, from her advantage of a month in the city, struggled to interpret for her young aunt.

"Raped carrots, what are they?"

"Crudities!"

They began giggling.

Sir Anthony quelled them, and then rose as a plump and dark-haired man came bouncingly to join them.

"Cher Maître!" he cried in greeting.

Xanthe made a face at Miranda, and Miranda, too, was disappointed, she had indeed hoped to have her grandfather and her old childhood companion to herself. In the ladies', where they went to explore and while away the length of time a restaurant meal always took, Miranda began, "Who's that man, then?"

Xanthe answered, "Oh, one of Poppa's old friends, I expect. Mummy calls them his worshipers—he has to have at least one of them around."

Miranda, surprised, changed the subject. "You look fabulous, you know," she said, deciding to take the part of generosity over envy. It gave her a rush of feeling noble, which on balance hurt less than letting her dismay at Xanthe's poise work its sharp point into her.

"Goody," said Xanthe. They looked at the picture in the mirror of themselves side by side. Miranda taller, with her bushy hair and coloring that the Italian's whose paintings she'd been looking at in the Louvre rendered by priming the canvas with a copper-based green paint, creating a complexion that draws light in rather than gives it out; Xanthe beside her with her candy radiance of pink and gold, and rounder too, more neatly assembled, wrist to hand, neck to shoulders, ankle to foot. All these junctures in Miranda were knobblier and more angular.

Miranda thought of M. Apéritif last night, and decided she would let him go further when she next saw him, in spite of the lizard-darting of his small and oddly hard tongue in the kiss she'd allowed him at the door of the hotel. It excited her to feel a man like him shudder as he pressed himself against her, to feel his weakness underneath all that Parisian aplomb. She knew what she could do to him, things she bet porcelain Xanthe would never know.

Xanthe for her part considered her image beside the young woman she'd been brought up with, and thought how sorry she felt for her. Miranda would always look a bit cheap, just as her mother said, because she never looked altogether clean. It must be hell to be her, with her crazy parents who were always on the scrounge, though she didn't seem even to be aware of her situation. Which really made matters worse.

Yet Xanthe's tidy existence felt mussed in Miranda's company; she experienced a sudden, vivid awareness of prohibitions hedging her about, and with the awareness, a desire to break them.

They smiled at each other in the mirror, and Miranda said again, "You do look so beautiful and grown-up, it's amazing to me!"

Still, in spite of the assiduous attentions which M. Apéritif and others paid her, Miranda would have liked Xanthe to make some reassuring remark in return. Men always had a obvious motive, so their compliments didn't mean anything; a woman's was more honest, usually. But none was forthcoming from Xanthe, and the silence, like so many in

Miranda's experience, quickened her panic and her urge to make her mark.

Behind them Madame Pipi, in black dress and white bib and apron, ostentatiously returned from the cubicles they had used and flourished the cloth with which she had wiped the seats. Xanthe looked at Miranda. "Have you something to tip her?" Xanthe didn't carry money, in this respect at least she was still a child. Miranda shook her head, and Madame blew her disgust through her teeth, and sat down with a magazine with a cover picture of the future Queen Fabiola of Belgium smiling on the arm of her optician's pinup of a fiancé.

They pushed through the padded door, back toward the dining room, and Miranda confided, "When I'm really on the breadline and someone's taking me out, I sometimes tell them I haven't any change for Madame Pipi—they give me something. If I do that two or three times, I can make about half the cost of the room per day at the hotel— honestly."

"Don't they think it funny you have to go so often?"

"Maybe, but you can't ask about things like that."

Xanthe sucked each leaf of her artichoke thoroughly, leaving precise teeth marks above the fleshy pad, then laid each one down on a plate in overlapping circles until she'd formed a rosette, a second artichoke that looked almost untouched. She and Miranda talked; Xanthe was at day school in London, but riding was her passion, she was learning dressage on a black mare with a white star and three white pasterns.

"Actually, Rob says he knows you! Robert Brett-Haynes? I think it was because of you he took me on." Miranda was addressing her grandfather. "He's been in Paris donkey's years, but he's still awfully English—mad about Flinders. He saw you play, one summer when you occupied—was it a Figtree?—before the break for tea—nobody'd done that before. The ball sailed over the stockade, he said, and the crowd's sigh followed its arc the whole way. He's never forgotten it."

Sir Anthony acknowledged her, and smiled at Maître Perreyve. "Flinders is a complete mystery to the Gallic mind, n'est-ce pas?" The Frenchman was a lawyer, and Sir Anthony was on the board of the building firm which Gillian's father mostly owned; air traffic was increasing, bonanza time, and the company had appointed Anthony to be their emissary on a proposal for a joint Franco-British venture on a new terminal.

"My granddaughter, she's studying in Paris." Sir Anthony had concluded his business with the plump lawyer as far as he was able to overcome his distaste for discussing deals or mentioning money, and he was holding back the brambles for her, as it were, letting her into their company, and she butted through, a young dog again, let out for a walk. She'd had a glass or two of wine, and it had helped to float her off. She began to boast, the people she'd met, about M. Apéritif, how comic men were with their courtesies and snapping lit-up eyes.

"I learned this word, *draguer*," she said. "There's no equivalent in English. It's an entirely French idea. A way of making friends. Everyone in Paris is trying to make friends, and some of them with me."

"And where are you staying, chère mademoiselle?" Maître Perreyve asked her.

A muscle moved in Everard's cheek when Miranda replied.

"That's an excellent location," said the lawyer. "Near the lovely Jardin du Luxembourg, the loveliest park in Paris, in my view."

"Oh yes," said Miranda, "I walk across it every evening to my job . . ." She trailed off. "My other . . . well, to make ends meet."

When the bill came, Maître Perreyve paid it cheerfully, and Anthony Everard, demurring to begin with, finally capitulated with a gracious closing of the eyes in acknowledgment.

"It's not up to me to ask you what you think you're up to," her grandfather began, when they were once more alone together with Xanthe in the sitting room of their hotel suite. "Nor is it your fault, of course." He sighed. "You've no idea where they are, have you?"

Miranda began to cry.

Everard stood up, embarrassed by her lack of control; the family trait had skipped him by, but it had surfaced in Kit with a vengeance, and, of course, as he might have expected, been compounded in Kit's daughter by Astrid's capriciousness. "I think I might make inquiries, try to trace them. After all, we can't leave you living like this."

"Why not? I'm so happy. There's nothing wrong, nothing at all." She was beseeching him.

"What? You've been seeing men, men you don't even know. You're modeling in an artist's studio. And working in a bar. Living off tips." The italics in the mild voice were shrieking at her. "And quartered in that shabby place. You say nothing's wrong. Tell me, young woman, what is right about this way of life? Tell me what you get up to, on your own like this? Tell me, though I don't think I want to hear. Goldie, you'd better leave the room. Go down to the lobby and see if you can find me a copy of . . . *The Times*. It should have arrived by now."

Xanthe looked pinched, but went without a word.

"Has anyone laid a finger . . . um . . . kissed you?" He was still turned away, his back as braced as a victim at a flogging stake.

Miranda then found herself half-laughing through her tears. If he turned and looked at her, she might have to give a straight reply, but to his narrow back, which could have been the back of a much younger man, she began to tease, in the way that she had learned so many of her new friends liked, when they made similar inquiries too, like the painter who'd lain on her bed and asked her earnestly if she'd ever experienced simultaneous orgasm, or the musician who'd volunteered he'd show her a "perversion" he was sure nobody would have demonstrated to her before, and began nuzzling between her legs. How they always wanted to know what other men did. How they puffed themselves up to outstrip others in their pleasure-giving powers, how they boomed when they protested they'd avenge assaults on her innocence by others.

"No, never! Honest. What do you think?" She checked a giggle of hysteria. "One does call me his *tulipe noire*, you know."

—Blood will out, Gillian had said.

—Blood is thicker than water, he had replied.

"They say passionate things to me, but absolutely nothing more, oh no. Another says I smell of the sea, like oysters, fresh and salty." Miranda giggled. "Another told me he had a dream, there was a fountain and it had a name, clear as a bell in his dream: Jouvence. He was dipped in it by me. Oh, I'm an exotic to them—being a bit of a 'musty,' as Feeny used to call it, isn't anything to deny here in Paris. Everyone loves me for the very things that you want me to cover up! Only the Persian engineer with the sloppy eyes doesn't see me as exotic, because he's that way himself." She wasn't crying or laughing anymore; numbness was taking over.

Anthony turned to look at her; his eyes were kind, she had moved him, he'd perhaps remembered something, her grandmother, his boyhood. He brushed a hand across his forehead. "You all grow up too quickly, nowadays." He paused. "If I can't find your father and talk to him, I must ask you, my dear child—you are still a child, appearances to the contrary—to come home with us of your own accord." She went toward him, for he seemed suddenly spent, a man getting old, far out to sea, trying to swim. "I was contacted—by the consul in Monte—oh, I shouldn't tell you these things, but . . ."

He looked at her with his blue eyes that made you feel you were in the far distance and he was bringing you into focus gradually, like a ball magnetized to drop into his outstretched hand, be clasped by his fingers. "There was some trouble. You know the kind of thing, I think. My dear, I can't tell you how sorry I am."

She quivered, then his gaze traveled past her, and she was able to say with quick energy, "Daddy'll climb right up again, he always does. He's a brilliant player."

"One of the best." He paused. "It would be such fun for Goldie, too, if you came back and stayed with us. She's so attached to you. And you to her, I know."

Miranda dropped her head. She was now trying not to cry. "Mum and Dad want me to be here, I know. To wait for them."

Anthony came up to her, handed her the spruce crimson silk hand-kerchief from his breast pocket and touched her hair, awkwardly. But she felt the tentativeness in his touch, the memory of something at his fingertips.

He sighed. "Soon I'll be having to cope with Goldie too, I suppose."

Very soon, thought Miranda, looking up at him, irises bruised from all the emotion. "Oh, Goldie'll have no problems, I could swear to that." She pushed a smile into the corners of her mouth. "I don't have any, either. This is the life." She tried the cliché, then smiled at its failure.

"You could come out. Gillian and I'd be glad to help with that— Queen Charlotte's ball, you could wheel the cake, wear white samite, you know the kind of thing, a garden party at the Palace, plenty of young men. And the right sort of young men, too." He could not continue to look her in the face. "Do the season, the works. We couldn't afford a dance for you—I've Goldie's to consider, in four years' time, not so far off. If it's worth doing, it's worth doing well. So maybe another kind of gathering for you—a tea party somewhere nice, maybe even in the Assembly Rooms at the Stockade, they've been hired before now. What do you say?"

"Are women allowed in?"

"There's a special bit—for entertaining. Come, what d'you say?"

"That'd be next summer, no?" Miranda said slowly, calmer now, for she saw the clouds clearing ahead.

"Yes, I suppose so, yes."

"I could stay here till then?" There was a knock on the door, and Miranda jumped to let in Xanthe, carrying a crinkly airmail-paper version of *The Times*, and a copy of *Paris-Match* with a photograph of Bardot, which she held up for Miranda to see. Bardot appeared three-quarters view, in a pink gingham décolletage, frilled with broderie anglaise, and spike heels of white kid on the end of her round legs. The light slanted across her skin in such a way, the tiny blond hairs showed like fair fluff.

"I'm trying to persuade Miranda to come back with us to London," began her father.

Miranda pleaded, "I'm sure Mum and Dad'll be back soon. You know them. They're expecting me to stay here."

"Yes, I know them," said her grandfather, and took the paper with a fond sad smile at Xanthe and sat down. "And I think you'd better come home."

"I'm sure Miranda's looking after things really well while they're gone," said Xanthe, giving her a steady look. Her father's habitual mild-manneredness, which usually protected him from responding, became brittle and porous when he was in contact with his daughter; Miranda could see that he reacted to Xanthe's silkiness as if she weren't a clear, sparkling water, but a fiery solvent that he, for all his well-preened feathers, could not resist.

He was listening to her, as she pressed on.

"Uncle Kit and Aunty Astrid are bound to surface again. They always do. It's not a good idea to leave Miranda all on her own, so why don't we keep her company? Daddy, why don't we stay on, just until they do?"

She was her accomplice, and Miranda sat, quite still, amazed.

Ant Everard put down his paper, looked at his daughter, his face a supplication of mercy from her; he looked back again at Miranda, and his concern turned into a frown, and he came visibly to a decision.

"Goldie," he said. "You are still too young for Paris."

He flinched at the stoniness in her sky-colored eyes.

"Poppa, think! We could go to the Louvre, and I could practice my French—Miranda's French is smashing—you heard her talk to that old stick-in-the-mud at lunch, and we could visit Versailles . . . There's so much to do here. I've hardly ever left London. Honestly, please let me stay."

Miranda held her breath.

Ant Everard was smoothing the tissue *Times* with the flat of his hand. "The omens have been rather strong today," he said. "That taxi fare . . . very strange. Once in a while, the numbers fall, the abacus clicks into a pattern. Perhaps the Maître was offering an opportunity I shouldn't let pass . . . ?"

"Oh yes, Daddy, yes. You can do business and we'll . . . we'll study together."

"The question is always interpretation, however. The augur's skill didn't consist in luck with the omens, but in reading them right. That's what sorted out the sheep and the goats. My famous bump of Flinders savvy, my *sangay* tells me . . ." He was trying to joke, and Miranda's spirits dimmed.

"Oh yes, it's a lucky day for you—and for me, for us." Xanthe was still pressing him.

"I'm not sure, little lady." Miranda could see by his grip on the newspaper, the thinness of his lips, and above all how he directed his words to her, not to his daughter, how much it cost him to refuse her anything. "Besides, your mother would never agree. Would she, now?"

"Tell her, just tell her. I want to stay here. Please."

"Tonight, we'll do something special, and then . . ." He pulled the paper up to hide his face. "We shall all three take the night train out— tomorrow. I expect Miranda can be packed by then."

Xanthe's face flushed, but she did not cry, unlike Miranda, who began to beg, in a mess of tears and mucus and smeared makeup until her grandfather, two high spots of vexation coloring his cheeks, ordered her to return to her hotel and prepare for her departure.

At the door, Xanthe took her by both hands and held her so hard, Miranda felt her nails cut into the palms and her eyes met hers with a pale-blue flare, as clear as her father's and as unassailable, as she breathed out, holding Miranda by her side and keeping her from leaving and turning to face her father across the room. "I hate you," she said, "I hate you."

"Really, Goldie!" Anthony Everard tried to laugh away his daughter's fury. "We'll do something utterly delightful today, and even tomorrow: take a bâteau mouche, ride the lift to the top of the Eiffel Towel— what d'you say to that?"

"No," said Xanthe. "No."

The voice, so accustomed to obedience, continued in courtesy, but its ring of conviction was sharpening, and Miranda sensed that Anthony Everard had reached the point when, if he could not phrase a command as a request, he would assert his authority undisguised. "It's only for your good, my little ladies," he was saying. "I know the world, more's the pity."

"No," said Xanthe again. "I'm old enough for anything, and I want to stay here longer."

Anthony Everard sighed. "There will be time enough, later in your life. Plenty of chances for you when you're older. But not now, not this time, little woman. It's for the best, trust me."

22

MIRANDA WAS ALONE in the compartment and glad of it, as it was an old-fashioned commuter train, with no corridor, just a door opening straight onto the line. She wasn't scared of the company who might join her on the journey, for fright was not a condition she admitted; she only wanted to study her surroundings without discretion, and such intensity made strangers feel uneasy.

The train was passing through a part of the city she did not know; it jolted along slowly, so she could not draw. But it gave her a clear view into the houses backing onto the tracks, the private mess usually tidied out of sight, the outside lavatories with unhinged doors, the laundry racks flimsy as the skeleton of a bird's wing, with trousers and underwear like broken feathers hanging; a burst, sodden mattress. A CND sign was scrawled on a shed, with "She loves you, Yeah Yeah!" alongside; more, newer anatomies of obsolete equipment—prams, tin bathtubs, hutches—lay tipped beside coal bunkers in some back plots.

She lowered the window by the leather tab and clicked the lip into the groove of the embrasure to hold it down so she could take some photographs; several boys climbing over the fence on the railway banks hooted at the sight of her camera and posed, arms akimbo, pretense starlets.

The famous film director from France could speak no English, and so Miranda was being sent to do the interview as well as provide the paper's weekly caricature; she had the address of the location, a news-agents' in the High Street of a part of the city she had never heard mentioned before, Giblett Park, though she had lived in London most of her life; the Press office had said that he would give her ten minutes between takes, or more if she was lucky and the filming was going well and Jean-Claude Meursault was feeling mellow.

The paper's usual film reporter would write the story from Miranda's notes; he'd already attended several days' shooting of the new, as yet untitled, film, the first Meursault to be made in Britain, which was a supreme sign that the decade was making all the difference to the world's view of the country, and its relation to the avant garde.

"It's a gas," the journalist had told her. "There's this young girl in a Mao tunic and a red star on her cap—she Jean-Claude's latest—and she's sitting on a bookcase, high up, legs swinging. It's in a porn shop, so there's bums and tits hanging out all around her, and she's reading aloud from Gramsci, fantastic stuff about seizing the time, the end of oppression—power to the people! It was fabulous, seeing her sitting in that heap of consumer capitalist garbage, pure, unmoved, like a flame, burning for the cause." The film buff was a slim young man, with long hands and feet and fair hair in a thin veil to his shoulders. He worked as one of the cooperative who ran *Blot*, the alternative newspaper where Miranda often published—though *Blot* in her view was well-named, for every page was printed in several colored inks and a variety of types, and then overprinted in palimpsest. Any image, black and white or color, was always worsted in this optical smorgas-bord.

It was hard work getting paid, as well. Still, she liked one or two of the collective. Xanthe had put some money in (actually five hundred pounds, a fair whack) when Miranda had asked her to, so she felt bound to give the paper some support in kind, and the office was fun—she liked pitching in with headings, sidebars, suggested stories, and pasting up till the small hours, with the help of ciggies and carafe wine; the sex gossip was the best in town, which made up for the coffee (though they could afford dope, they couldn't rise to real coffee, and had at one time even resorted to the bitter brown syrup Camp, with the turbaned lascar on the label).

She reached the address; there was no sign of activity. The window was full of magazines, lying edge to edge and hanging in yellowed cellophane wrappers from clothes pegs; she was reminded of playing shop as a child, and lining up the tins of food and boxes of soap flakes and bags of flour, all in miniature. The models behind the sunbaked cellophane smiled with shining teeth or pushed out pouting kisses or let their dewy bottom lip drop; they arched and twisted and perched, strategic stickers interrupted the full view of their parts, spotted animal skins here and there hinted at biting beasts on the loose. She tried the door. It did not open; she found a bell, hesitated about ringing it, then did so. It tinkled, an old-world merriness. The shop fittings had not been changed since it had been a High Street draper's, or a confectioner's, perhaps? A man came to open the door; he looked, Miranda thought, as if warnings against self-abuse might be true after all: whey-faced, with a camel's twitchy nose, though he was probably not much older than she was.

"The film?" he repeated. "They messed up the shop, terrible it was. I've been picking up after them all night and all morning. There's some people in the world should be kept in the zoo." He rubbed his forehead; he was wearing a rubber thimble with rubber spikes.

"How should I know where they are?" he went on. He wasn't letting her in, she could see racks of magazines behind and a dark wooden counter, bare. Lines of eyes peeping and ogling, rows of breasts hoisted and nipples tweaked and Vaselined; reddened mouths gaped at her, naturists demonstrated star jumps, plump pink bottoms poked, arch looks pinned her down, and fingers crested with scarlet points beckoned.

Miranda began to feel curious for a closer look. At the O.K. Corral—as she preferred to call what some of its visitors termed her quim (the phrase struck her as useful after she'd seen the Western)—some men proved themselves and others came to grief, and both kinds had male competitors on their mind and wanted to outgun them. But meanwhile the O.K. Corral continued, and it was keeper of her own wild troop of horses, whom she knew how to handle, unlike some of the sharp-shooters and champions and wildmen exhibiting their prowess.

Sex in Miranda's experience wasn't a matter of spectacle, but of darkness and touch, magnified by her senses' usually exacerbated state, the extremes of the night, of smoking and drinking and hunger and tiredness, and she was a blind swimmer through walls of warm water, and knew nothing of the practice and technique of the models in the pictures crammed edge to edge in the shop. She was used to seeing men's bodies; but she had never seen a woman's strike the poses of these images.

She wondered, Do I do it wrong? I never do any of this and haven't any of the underwear either. Perhaps she wasn't a real woman, after all, with the proper innate grasp of communicating with the opposite sex. She faltered. How would such a very real woman cope with this situation? She tried a smile, showing her teeth. "You don't know where they went?" She raised her voice just enough to hint at domination.

The seller of specialist magazines grimaced when she smiled, and as he pushed the door shut to the frisky chiming of the bell, he grunted, "Try the showroom, they might know. Or the pub." A homebody's disgust with the restless owners of fast cars, a temperate man's contempt for drinkers were impacted into this begrudged advice.

When she eventually tracked down the location, Miranda was speeding on a mix of excitement and anxiety. She found the wrecker's yard down an alley just behind the station, about an hour and a half after she had first arrived there on the train.

A girl in a mackintosh and low-heeled pumps, pale stockings, and a short glossy bob was running across the dirt floor of the yard; the hulks of cars were heaped behind her, the record of fatal crashes scored legibly in their twisted drive shafts, passenger doors stove in, and disemboweled interiors where plugs and levers hung from strings like fallen teeth on the ends of nerves. Oil glinted prettily in puddles like mussel shells.

In some of the wrecks other young women were sitting. Miranda saw one naked girl in dark glasses leaning back on the banquette-style front seat of a big old Rover, thin white legs in heels just touching the cinder-strewn wasteground. She was reading aloud, a man holding a boom mike was registering her voice; she was declaiming from *Soul on Ice:*

> I hate you
> Because you're white
> Your white meat
> Is nightmare food.
> White is
> The skin of evil.
> Loving you thus
> And hating you so,
> My heart is torn in two.

The words spoke truth; they shivered up and down inside her, earthing right down to the O.K. Corral.

Later, when she watched the scene during the shooting, she'd find more girls in the pile of smashed-up cars: one putting on lipstick high in a lorry's cab, another lying on the bonnet like a mascot, face to the car's prow, giving a feline look as she too read aloud, from a French philosopher who later, in a fit of madness, pushed his wife under in the bath, and held her there till there were no more bubbles.

Their pale flesh in that wreckage made her shiver; it stirred morbid thoughts of the fragile membrane retaining blood inside the body, the tender transitions between limb and limb, the throbbing larval transparency of scientific diagrams showing the fetal development of . . . infant salmon, infant monkeys, infant anything. The woman in the mack was running, a camera on tracks was following her, a group of men clustered around it, pacing, several attached to it, one on a high seat, another underneath the lens, Jean-Claude Meursault on foot at their flank. She recognized him at once from the blunt-nosed profile and pepper-and-salt hair en brosse and the large tinted lenses of his glasses, and the way he hooked his head to one side and forward like a boxer butting. She would have no trouble catching him on paper, but she took some photographs just to make sure.

Then he lifted his arm and brought it down, hard and fast, and suddenly, from behind the cars, rose three freedom fighters in terrorist gear, black berets at an angle over their brows, black tracksuits, lace-up boots on their long shins, bandoliers slung oblique, rifles in one hand. They leapt down the car wrecks and legged it across the ground toward the girl. But too late. At another signal from Jean-Claude, the girl in the mack clutched her side and stumbled, then collapsed on the ground and, shuddering, turned over as the camera came close and moved out to hover over her face and catch her bitter smile as she died. At least, so Miranda imagined.

They cut, and the actress scrambled up and examined her knees; a woman from Wardrobe ran up and gave her a change of mack, and bent to apply panstick to her hands where they had been dirtied by the wrecker's-yard floor; she checked her hose and brushed her hair and the actress shook her head slowly from side to side so that it fluffed. The Black Panthers slapped one another and joshed with their weapons: Miranda took a few more photographs to draw from later. They were standing against the light, and their profiles overlapped at

close quarters, and haloed them; they made a vivid show of cock-of-
the-roost virility, and she chuckled to herself with pleasure.

One of the actors then noticed her camera and hailed her. She
waved back gaily; his shoulders set haughtily and he turned away.

They were directed back to their positions by the first assistant and
his megaphone, and a second take began; Miranda was now able to
make some sketches of the action as well, as she knew its shape.

When the break for lunch was called, the press girl came and fetched
her. "About ten minutes, okay?"

Miranda sat down beside Jean-Claude Meursault in a canvas chair.
She would have liked the brune he offered her, but couldn't cope with
her note-taking, the paper with the questions written out in the *Blot*
office, the unfamiliarity of speaking French after an interval, as well
as Meursault's cult reputation, all at the same time as smoking. So she
declined, then immediately regretted it, because she realized it might
have pleased him, made them complicit together.

He hardly looked at her, but kept his eyes trained on her hands, or
on his, but now and then she caught his look behind the smoked glass
of his lenses, a milky, slightly protruding glance, mild as a trout.

Later, when the interview appeared, overprinted on Miranda's
scrawly, twiddly and multicolored impressions of the shoot, it was
translated and edited to read (though it was rather hard to decrypt
from the graphics):

> BLOT: You've said, Jean-Claude, that the problem isn't making po-
> litical films but making films politically. Could you explain what you
> mean by that?
> MEURSAULT: We're living in an arsehole culture (une civilisation
> de cul). Shit rules it, and what else is shit but money? Money is
> politics—you try and make a film like this and you'll discover that—
> and money is shit—so where does that leave politics?
> BLOT: That sounds as if you think we're caught in a double bind
> from which there's no escape.
> MEURSAULT, with a gallic shrug: What is oppression? Us. What is
> liberation? Us. No, I'm not depressed. I like shit.
> BLOT: In earlier films, you've suggested that female sexuality and
> capitalist codes of production are intertwined. With this new film
> you're turning your attention to the position of blacks in our society.
> Do you think there's a similarity?
> MEURSAULT: If I made you suck my cock, this would be political.
> If I make a black man sweep up my trash, empty my dustbins, wash

the vomit from my floor and kill for me in in my imperialist wars . . . well, what do you think?

The difference is that women collude in their subjection. They think it's power. The blacks don't—they don't even have an illusion of power. (He shrugged, gestured toward the actors with the tip of his Gitane.) Except, of course, these rebels.

Miranda had missed a beat as she translated back in her head the French phrase "sucer ma queue," which M. Apéritif and others of her circle had not used—in conversation. She thought, listening to the famous film director, that she had not had an experience of oppression, of violence, at least she had not experienced her life in those terms, as she continued:

BLOT: Your interpretation of women sees them as objects of desire, images in advertisements, pinups—how are you going to express the inner thoughts of Black Panthers? Isn't the consciousness of the blacks even more closed to us than women's?
MEURSAULT: I don't think there's a way of entering inside someone's head. The interior is a hall of mirrors—a sequence of traps, lies. You know that about yourself. [She started, but kept on scribbling notes.]

No, the way to interpret the inside is by assembling the exterior with all the means you have: you will find that this aesthetic process yields the moral. Or the lack of moral. Ethics and aesthetics cannot be held apart.

At this point, Meursault looked up at her for a moment, seemed to appraise her, then back down to his hands, and commented, "With such good French, there's a man in the story." Miranda let it pass, though his assumption of a single owner rather riled her. He went on, he was now in free flow.

The great lie of the last two hundred years has been the mistaken idea that realism is a way of telling the truth. Is Shakespeare realistic? I like it very much when Othello says, "Rude am I in my speech," and then speaks like eloquence itself. That is Art. That is the essence of Art. Do you think Hamlet the Dane spoke such beautiful English? And Racine's Phèdre, organizing her sentences in such poised Alexandrines, does she talk like a woman driven mad for love?

My films never pretend to be anything but artifacts—they're unnatural, contrived, fashioned, unrealistic—on purpose. They're directed. I make dramatic tableaux. Like this one. Not vérité photographs—pretending there isn't a mind behind the camera or a finger on the button. [Meursault leaned over, and tweaking the sheet of questions from Miranda, continued]:

But this is boring as shit. People always talk to my reputation. It's a bore. I'm making this film now because . . . I couldn't get the money for the film I wanted to make. I do not know—I could not tell you or . . . *Blot* what my film means. I make a montage. You might say reality is stranger than fiction. I say, fiction is always much stranger than reality.

Meursault drew on his butt and looked down at his hands, clasped in his lap. "Now we have to shoot again," he said, and stood up.

"Great stuff, Miranda," the thin fair man would say, when she handed in the transcript. "Shame it's small pickings, though." He turned the two sheets as if hoping to find them double-sided. Miranda did not tell him why she had not had the nerve to buttonhole Meursault again, in a later break in the filming. The *Blot* editor understood, he said, giving her a spacey grin. "He was abrasive, hell, no shit. I can see he made it tough for you." He almost winked, he liked the man's up-frontness, this was the era when honesty was prized above all virtues. So she did not tell him that she was too shaky later to resume the conversation for a different reason; she did not describe to him—or to the readers of *Blot*—what ensued.

For it turned out that she felt protective toward the actor George Felix and preferred to keep their encounter private. And she had an incoherent sense that he and she together were being pushed in squares of black and white across the game board, and she didn't want to comply with the games masters by speaking aloud, let alone complaining, of the antagonisms they orchestrated.

When the interview ended, and Jean-Claude Meursault had risen, shaken her hand gravely, and then quickly joined the group around the camera at the end of the track to Miranda's right, she began sketching in her small pad and taking the occasional photograph when the noise levels permitted. The scene began again: the drone of the invective started up as one actor read,

"A cult of death,/need of the simple striking arm under/the street lamp. The cutters, from under/their rented earth. Come up, black dada/nihilismus. Rape the white girls. Rape/their fathers. Cut the mothers' throats."

The girl in the mack was scrambling again through the puddles in the dirt of the wreckers' yard, the invisible and soundless shots from out of frame felled her at a signal from Jean-Claude and the partisans rose from the auto hulks, their own guns blazing.

After the call came, "Print," Miranda stayed focused on the group of three actors. She'd work from the photographs later. One of them was chunky, the full lines of his mouth emphasized by the trim of his mustache and beard. The other two men were taller, one lanky, with slow flapping hands as he walked—Miranda guessed he had not lived in London long. The third was the youngest, square-set, and of the three, looked most like an actor dressed up in costume for a part.

She was becoming excited by what she was getting, she could develop it later into an almost sculptural grouping of their limbs and heads, when the third Panther broke from his two companions and came striding toward her. She was caught up in her work, in the looking it required, a gaze that was intense and scrutinizing without allowing any personal exchange of feeling to take place, when he was all at once bearing down on her, shouting, his right fist tight around his weapon, his left hand hitting the air and pointing at her with accusing index finger. She dropped the camera from her face as the lens filled with his anger, and he receded to a safe distance from her; but he was still bearing down, yelling, "What the fuck is going on? Who gave permission for this? I want you to know round here that if anyone's taking pictures, you better ask George Felix before." He was getting closer, and shouting still: "No jumped-up photographer comes to this set and uses my image without my saying so, you hearing me, you hearing me right?

"Some bitch exploiting me, joining in the fucking imperialist adventure, selling my image . . ." He thumped his chest with his gun. "Oh baby, you just go right ahead and grab what you can when you can."

She was waving her hands at him to deny what he was saying; the press girl was running up, but Jean-Claude, she realized later, as she reconstructed the scene in her mind, was leaning up against the cameraman's steel chair on the traveling rig and smoking, his hands cupped over his mouth as he did so, like a wise monkey hiding his speaking, his eyes half-closed behind his glasses, more lizard now than trout.

She said to George Felix, "I'm from *Blot*."

"What shit, *Blot?* Who wants to know about *Blot?*"

He reached her, he was face-to-face with her, the press girl Annabel was plucking at his clinging black roll-neck's sleeve gingerly, with her fingertips.

"George, keep cool, okay? *Blot*'s an alternative paper. They're doing a story on Jean-Claude—I should have asked you. I didn't, it's my fault. I'm sorry." He shook her off, with a toss of the head; Miranda saw all of a sudden the theatricality of the gesture, and something inside her relaxed. George Felix was surely in a rage, but he was also enjoying being angry, and that was something that never happened to her father, whose rages had made anger such a familiar monster.

If only Kit could enjoy the scenes he made, she thought, instead of being eaten alive with remorse, and she stuttered in response to the Panther's exaltation, "I'm, with you, I didn't want to do anything you wouldn't like." She made a gesture of pledging, her hand hovering over her heart. "I didn't have a moment to ask . . ."

"You hear that, the fuck you hear that, one and all?" He flung both arms out, the one with the gun aloft, and bowed in the direction of his two companions. They were idling uncomfortably behind him, neither reinforcing his fury, nor retreating from support altogether. The older man shook his head slightly, his mouth made a round shape. "Aw, come on, cut it out, man," but not loud enough to be heard. And George Felix plunged on, "Aha, whitey just didn't get a chance to ask. And isn't that just the case with everything you gone and done over the centuries of black oppression? You never had the chance to ask—the slaves, the chain gang, the artists who got burned out making entertainment for you and looking real pretty for you, taking whitey's junk, the white pigs' white junk. Oh baby, you're one hell of a fantastic heap of self-delusion, you say you're on my side. You bourgeois liberals—you're the pits. I'd rather have a racist straight up and on the rocks any day. You don't know shit." He threw out his hands again and set a grin through clenched teeth on his burning face. "Aw, shit, just take my picture! Go right ahead, don't ask me how I feel."

He hadn't hit her, or snatched her camera, but stood square to her, holding his hands up as if he knew not to, bouncing on the balls of his feet, while Jean-Claude and his group looked on, keeping very still, and Miranda wondered, for a moment, if the camera was rolling, for she felt on display under George's attack. She was trembling, hot tears sprang to her eyes, she wanted to cover her face with her hands but did not dare attempt such a defending gesture, for it would have seemed a patent provocation; besides she knew how to stand her ground in the face of anger. And at the same time the racing of her blood was only partly fear, and she could see that he knew it, that he had discovered this power and tuned it to performance pitch, that the insults were a kind of invitation, the display of force a plea turned upside down. And she also wanted, because she longed to please, to take off her clothes then and there and let him down from his prideful pose, and soothe him with her obedience to his rage. She was like a young dog, the kind her mother scorned, and she could only leap and lick after a blow such as he had fetched her.

"You might like the results, I turn them into drawings, I don't just use them as photographs." Childhood in the wings of her mother and father's raging had taught her a degree of courage; she never ran away from anger.

He snorted. She kept on, her fatuousness was her gift to him, a kind of amends, to prove him right. "You could see them beforehand— of course we wouldn't publish anything without showing you."

Her voice sounded tinkly to her ears, tinkly and absurdly well-brought-up; his own voice was vibrant, an actor's timbre, trained to come from deep in the diaphragm, while his accent slid around, hinting at American films and North London schooling and drama classes, and beneath these layers the islands' underswell rose, so that from the sound of him she grasped the archaeology of his life.

His eyes opened wide at her. "Aw, shit, you think I care?" He made a fist and shot it in the air by her cheek.

She dropped her gaze, flinched, she wanted to say, again, absurdly, "I'm with you, all the way. I'm on your side, I'll always be on your side. I can't tell you how bad it feels to be one of them; besides, I've not chosen . . . I don't want to be a member of the . . . to be bourgeois." She knew she was absurd, she heard herself clearly.

It was the end of the decade, and she was labeled with the name of the criminal class. She couldn't defend herself without rousing him to greater ferocity; she knew that in the moment of conflict, no enemy can ever protest to be a friend and be believed; she had seen the distrust Kit's sudden switches of mood inspired. Indeed, she would have liked to tell him about her father, who was called Nigger Everard at school and spurned in his own family because his mother had been Creole; she wanted to tell him about Feeny whom she loved; how she herself was a musty, couldn't he see it?

She didn't because the moment was not right; she did not yet know that she could not plead from her position of privilege that she had suffered too. "So you want to annex our wrongs as well, do you?" he might well have answered to her in just bitterness. This, Miranda did not yet understand. That day, she only realized that nobody wants a special enemy, chosen with care and attacked with force, to renounce the role and throw down weapons and instead open arms for an embrace.

Jean-Claude joined them, made a puffy sound through his smoke and laid a hand on the arm of George Felix.

"Let's make movies, huh?" he said in English, and gave Miranda a smile from the corner of his mouth as he steered the actor away.

Her knees were weak, and she sat down on a chair the press rep brought over for her; she could not have trusted her legs to walk over to it. She felt vaguely flattered, it was odd. Jean-Claude's sidelong half-smile had felt congratulatory. She took the cup of tea she was offered and did not stop Annabel from spooning sugar into it.

"Two, three?"

"That's fine, thanks." She drank it, it was consoling. Her father's bouts of fury weren't strategic, they never achieved anything but trouble for him: there were some houses, she knew, where he had played and was no longer welcome because he'd made a scene. Never about bad cards, of course, he was much too professional for that; never about the fall of the dice in backgammon; he had himself under control—just—when his bridge partner made a miscalculation and played unnecessarily into an opponent's finesse. But he could be touchpaper, and a spark from a fancied slight, a disagreement over politics, a moment of heedlessness from someone, and he would catch and soon the conflagration was at full blast, consuming everything in its path—new friendships, old friendships, new clients, his reputation, his wife's love, even that. Astrid, who had once found him such fun, was fed up with his tinder temper. She wouldn't stop at his side anymore to watch him play, though he liked her to, for she was his lucky charm, and her presence concentrated his mind wonderfully. Or so Kit said.

Annabel's briskness brought Miranda back to herself: she'd had it easy, and besides, in her case, when people noticed the caramel flavor of her looks, as they had in Paris, it worked to her advantage. She really wasn't a beautiful young woman, not like Xanthe; her features were irregular and plumpish, however thin the rest of her body became. But the touch of the exotic in her appearance improved the effect she made. She hadn't suffered injury or contempt; she had no reason to blaze, unlike George Felix. To others she merely looked a bit different, and it lent her glamour, but to him, she was as different as anyone who wasn't black.

She looked across at the scene as once again the actress ran, and fell, and the gunmen rose from the car wrecks where the nudes lay or sat reading aloud. She wanted to tell someone how it had counted for her rather than against her; how in that dimming world of the Left Bank nearly ten years before, she'd set lovers adrift on Gauguinesque and Baudelairean voyages of *luxe, calme et volupté*. Then she thought, But I should declare my allegiance now.

"You okay then?" inquired Annabel. "Don't give it a thought. He's just a bit uptight—filming's tough. We've been at it since six."

"I can't help feeling guilty, though. Classic liberal guilt—would like to do something, but can't think what."

"Not true, no way." Annabel smiled firmly. "We're changing every-thing! Look at the movies—think of Jean-Claude's movies! They're just unimaginably different from anything that's happened before and they're changing everything. There aren't any barriers, no holds barred, nothing we can't do now!

"You only have to want it and want it enough."

Then she added, giving Miranda's arm a squeeze, "Just do it, darling, like the man says, Do it!"

23

MIRANDA ARRIVED IN the cake shop before Xanthe and decided against sitting outside on the pavement, although the weather was warm. She chose instead a small round table by the till near the door, where she immediately felt in the way. However, this was not an unusual feeling, so she could put up with it well.

The baker had originally been Viennese, and his shelves were heaped with loaves scattered with poppy and caraway seeds, with glazed and resinous black bread, with tea cakes made of sweet doughs glistening with melted sugar, while in his window was spread a frothy quilt of his confectionery, feathery slices of mille-feuille pastry, strawberry rosettes shiny as satin, pastry horns spilling twists of cream, slim dark matt sachertorte and fatter, foamier gâteaux with light scrapings of chocolate sprinkled on the icing, as well as rolls and buns and croissants and *palmiers* and twists and braids.

Forms like these must have inspired the great Parisian milliners, Miranda thought, and wondered how many fashion designers had had mothers who were cooks or bakers, and then in turn how many artists' mothers had been glove makers or hatters or haberdashers or corsetières. She'd begun a series of drawings, "Heroes and Heroines of Today," like old-fashioned cigarette cards, for one of the decade's new youth mags, *Quasar;* readers could cut out a coupon and collect the series. She'd had a moderate success, and the pay kept body and soul together, plus some boutique clothes, including one or two hats she had grown very fond of. The caricatures included the answers to a quiz: Miranda asked her subjects their favorite color, music, book, food, place, stone and so forth, and concluded the list with their own choice of hero or heroine. She decided to specify sweets in the questions; people's taste in cakes and puddings could be revealing and they'd be fun to draw.

Miranda had been summoned by Xanthe to meet her here; she herself tried not to indulge her sweet tooth, though she still always accepted Feeny's golden-syrup sandwiches when she went to see her. She was wearing her new shoes for the occasion; cork clogs on platform soles three inches high. She had red tights on; the eye-catching interest of this apparel disguised, in her view, the inadequacy of her legs with their scooped thighs and prominent knees. On top, she was wearing green suede shorts with stenciled daisies and a figured blouse of sage-colored chiffon, its corners tied in the front at her waist over a pale-green undershirt. She had dabbed her skin generously with patchouli, and had recently frizzed up her hair with currycombs to give herself an Afro.

The cake shop was a meeting place for the area's chess players, and a group of them, murmuring now and then in a language Miranda could not identify, were watching the board where two of their number were contending. The spectators were sitting at a nearby table, some leaning out from chairs, one or two standing, smoking, as they followed the game. She ordered a coffee; the waitress came back with her cup and a strawberry tart. She objected, but the waitress shrugged and pointed: one of the foreigners sitting at the table was smiling in her direction, indicating her and her table with a cigarette.

"You need to eat," he said. He made expansive gestures, as if he would have liked to inflate her then and there. "I come?"

He had a pointy little beard, gray and scraggy, and his skin showed through the hairs, and a pointy little skull as well, sparsely covered, to the same effect. She shook her head, told him she was waiting for her sister. Would he like a coffee, though? He accepted, and she ordered for him. He called out to her as it was set down in front of him that he was a refugee from Prague, but felt at home because he had always listened to the World Service of the BBC. He pointed to one of the players.

"I am very good radio ham! Every night I find him, past the jammers' whistle, and listen to him and love him. Then I meet him in Bush House and I discover he is like me, drunk and absurd man who is not happy."

The subject of his remarks looked up a moment from the game— he wasn't playing, but monitoring closely—and grinned. They both had ruined mouths, Miranda noticed, an unusual sight. Postwar reforms had generally overhauled the population's teeth. How he loved England, he was saying, London especially, it was a terrific city, no one in his right mind could ever be bored in London. He walked every day, a new area, discovering corners, people: "Wonderful, I am called 'Darling'!"

He paused, added, "Only the expense is problem. Everything is so expensive—in my country books cost very little. Magazines too. But you have different books here, different magazines. They are too expensive for me."

Miranda was about to agree.

"Look at the pornography," he said. "It cost far too much."

She was laughing when Xanthe arrived, and she had not laughed for a month, not fully, not since the day of the interview with Jean-Claude Meursault. It was curious, she was thinking, as Xanthe sat down, that the Czech didn't sound offensive. Would he have got on with that frowsy sneering little man who sold special magazines? Would he have bargained with him for some choice items on sale? He was probably a part of the system Jean-Claude was attacking—or saying he was—that made wrecked cars and nude girls interchangeable.

Yet she liked talking to a stranger.

Xanthe sat down, giving her back to the group playing chess by the window, and ordered a coffee, and then, with a glance at Miranda's plate, added a cake for herself.

"Yum yum. I love this place." She lived quite near, in a first-floor flat with floor-to-ceiling French windows giving onto a small stone balcony, and she'd obviously walked, as she now swept one of the ornamental combs she was wearing through her curly fringe to set it back in place; the rest of her hair was coiled into a smooth chignon at the nape of her neck, and set off by a well-cut shirt in fine blue lawn; she had on coffee-colored satin jeans with contrast cream stitching and Cuban-heeled crimson boots.

She was like a tablet of costly, scented soap; there was no purchase on her smoothly milled and creamy surfaces. Miranda, loving her indeed like a sister, turned her sharp envy of the younger woman's cool and self-sufficient harmonies into pleasure at her success. She herself was always disheveled—outside and, more crucially, inside as well. People took off their glasses when they were talking to Miranda, and wiped them absentmindedly, not certain whether the smudginess in their image of her was on their lenses or something in her aura.

Xanthe had once said to her, "There's a kind of skinny childishness about you, Miranda. That's why you get by so well, why you don't come a cropper—in spite of all the craziness."

She had meant Astrid and Kit for parents, of course, and Miranda had winced, and felt the wick of her indignation catch. Why should Xanthe mock them, when it was their relaxed way of bringing her up (Ant and Gillian called it rather "laxity") that had made it possible for Xanthe to escape her parents sometimes, have some good times, clandestinely?

"But I have to be careful," Xanthe had gone on, "because I look as if there's nothing I don't know. And of course, that's not altogether mistaken." She'd laughed. "You're like a young animal of some sort—nobody has the heart to hurt you."

Past her head, Miranda could see her Czech trying to catch her attention. She ignored him and concentrated on Xanthe, who was saying, "I've a plan, and I want you to come in with me on it. Poppa's being really obstructive, so what's new? Bloody old Scrooge—I need you, you must help me out." At the thought of her father, her huskie-dog eyes, usually polar-blue, turned smoky with annoyance.

The Czech called out, "Beautiful sisters!"

Xanthe turned, looked at him, and a small frown of scorn puckered her smooth forehead as she asked Miranda, "A friend of yours?"

"No, I just met him."

"He'll probably give you crabs."

Between quick exact forkfuls of her chocolate gâteau—Miranda wondered at how neatly Xanthe dispatched it, while at her place there were crumbs and drips down the side of her coffee cup—Xanthe brought Miranda up-to-date.

She'd met a clever man; he was in property, hotels, catering. She didn't fancy him, he was a tub of tallow, but he didn't mind, because he liked her to be around, and she liked being with him too, he was funny, worldly, full of schemes and plans. Xanthe understood his feeling for her; she didn't reciprocate, but she wasn't a monster, and she could sense how other people could become attached, and sympathize with them.

Miranda forced herself to nod; Xanthe had never loved anyone; nobody had been allowed near her at home, and the illicit evenings in jazz clubs she had snatched with Miranda under pretext they were going to the theater, or some such respectable excuse, had given her a taste for conquest, with no repercussions, no consequences of friendship, let alone love. Her father had seen off many of Xanthe's aspiring boyfriends, one after another, when they began to haunt the Everard house (now situated in a blossom-filled street very near Doggett's Fields). Miranda remembered, and couldn't help a giggle at the memory, how once she had come into the garden to find Ant and a suitor standing on their heads on the lawn, while Xanthe watched them, holding her wristwatch and timing them.

Ant, who was of course half a century older than Xanthe and most of the boyfriends in those early days, had had to give up first, and spring upright, his normally pale face puce with the effort, his serenity ruffled, while the youth remained on his head, Xanthe still counting steadily as he wobbled until he too finally fell. Xanthe pronounced him the victor and kissed him, and her father threw him out, in spite of Gillian's mediation. For in the one matter of his daughter, Ant Everard could not keep a straight stick. He provoked her visiting friends to compete with him—physically, as in the round of headstands; or mentally, in argument—and he would then show them the door, coldly advising them to use their brains if they had any, go back to work, and stop filling their heads with arrant stuff and nonsense.

Now Xanthe had her own flat, her father could only stand guard at the end of the telephone. But something inside her had been stunned by his assiduous rivalry; she did not seem capable of passion. Astrid said, "When Xanthe falls in love, she won't know what's hit her."

And Miranda could see her mother wanted Xanthe to fall, wanted her to be punished by the longing and the pain other people felt and the mess it made of the rest of their lives. However, she feared the time Xanthe might experience such weakness; Miranda needed her to be more resilient than anyone else, to possess a spirit of such strength and purpose that sometimes she imagined she could see it, past Xanthe's eyes, turning slowly deep inside her, like the slender helical blade of pure steel that powers a turbine.

As for Xanthe herself—though others sometimes regretted on her behalf that she had not experienced, well, so much that makes up life's pleasures—she did not feel a lack. There was time, others would say, and something could happen that would turn her upside down and inside out. Behind her back, they said she had a splinter of ice in her heart from the Snow Queen's mirror, it was plain to see in her eyes, like the blue of reflected light in snow.

Her mother fretted, but her father was proud; and the smile of his Goldie could still light him up as nothing else could except a sequence of perfect bids and plays from the England team at Doggett's on a peachy summer's day.

So that was why Xanthe had been taken aback when she asked him to do something on her behalf and he first said he would, and then took it back and announced, at the last minute, as it seemed to her, that he would not come with her to Enfant-Béate for the 350th anniversary of the landing of the pioneer planter Sir Christopher Everard, their ancestor.

Miranda murmured surprise. "Why not? How odd. You'd think he'd want to go back, see it again, his old country, after all. They'd probably give him a hero's welcome too."

"He won't. I can't budge him. He's stubborn as a mule when he wants to be. You know how he is. He's turned all superstitious about it, too, talks about the day being unlucky for him. I don't know. He goes to that bloody fortune-teller, and he'll do anything she says—cancel meetings, change travel plans, what have you. It drives Mummy absolutely round the bend. But there it is. That's what *sangay* does to you in old age. Turns you into a crank. He's got much worse. He's over seventy, so it's not surprising, I suppose."

Xanthe had heard her parents discussing it; she imitated to Miranda her mother's wheedling, " 'Darling, Belmont was the scene of your triumph. A Double Sloop and Creeks galore—I've heard you mention the tour of 1921 with such pride.' But it was no good. Poppa just corrected the score.

"I'm fed up to the eyes going down memory lane with Flinders, as you know, and I was drifting off to think of other, more pleasant things, when something in Poppa's mournfulness made me pay attention." She mimicked her father's dry, level tone: " 'But you see, my dear, I was a nipper then—it was my first important game and I was lucky. In those days, I was playing for the islands—imagine it!'" So then Mummy's butting in, protesting, she's so embarrassed, you know, when Poppa says something that reminds her he's a colonial. 'Oh darling, it's so hard to remember that you could have been—on their side.' 'It wasn't their side. It was our side, our team was just one of many, representing a part of the whole nation, like a county team. Enfant-Béate was the country, and England was the town—just that little bit farther away.'

"Both Mummy and I were trying to egg him along to come, but he was stuck like a limpet. 'I don't like the way the game is going,' he said. 'It's the spirit that's changed, it's upsetting your father,' Mummy says, fussing around. 'He's a player of the old school, when it was a gentleman's game and it took days and days to play a single match.' 'Yes, Mummy,' say I, and Poppa whitters on a bit about the spirit of chivalry dying in these one-day specials."

Xanthe had waited, kept her eyes on his slim-cheeked face, the clear blue gaze and the strong transverse marks on the brow and in the corners of the eyes, from standing in the open ground of stockades all over the Flinders-playing world.

"He choked out a few words to me about how he felt," Xanthe continued. " 'There's a killer spirit in the game now. It's foreign to its core. They're not athletes anymore, they're gladiators. The crowds bay for blood. Even the committee agreed to weight the balls to make them more deadly. It's not the sport I knew, it's a prize fight.' He was angry, he pressed his lips together till they went pale—you know how he looks when he's angry. 'It's not play anymore. It's war.' "

Miranda was half-listening. In the company of other people, Xanthe concurred with the usual paeans to her father's skills, courtesy, general niceness, so she usually held forth against him in Miranda's company, where she was free to say whatever she wanted.

"He can't bear it," Xanthe concluded to Miranda. "He wants to live in the past."

Miranda thought, Poor old Ant, he's been put out to grass by the young Turks and he's sulking. The players from the islands had been victorious for a decade now, their assault impregnable as their missiles twisted in flight and skimmed suddenly upward like stones flung onto the tensile surface of calm water, soaring at ferocious, invisible speeds, their defenders a rampart of stone, their scores piling up. They lacked the craft or the judgment of an Everard in his prime, they called Houses that they could not always gain. But their prowess was matchless, and the crowds roared with delight at the heroic scale of their game. Their championship had given them influence in the international committees where decisions were handed down.

Oh, Ant Everard was just envious that he was no longer the only power to reckon with.

"He's like a little boy," Xanthe said, "who's been toppled from being King of the Castle and finds himself the dirty rascal, and then starts bawling."

Gillian Everard had made tea for her husband and her daughter, soothingly, hoping to change Ant's mind; she was curious to see the Great House where the Everards had lived, and the famed Belmont stockade where her husband had won his youthful spurs, and the beaches and coral reefs of his birthplace. She knew that the changes in the game had begun long ago, for many of their friends discussed with her privately Ant's self-destructive ostrich attitude and hoped to encourage her to sway him; there were great difficulties ahead and he, with his easy influence over the committees at Doggett's, could be useful to their successful outcome and the healthy future of The Game.

Gillian had set down the pot in front of her husband on a lace mat with a beseeching look. "I would so like to go, you know, Ant darling."

It was then that Xanthe's father had delivered his final verdict, from which wife and daughter knew there could be no retreat. "Besides, the day of the anniversary is unlucky for me; I've never achieved a house I wanted on the twenty-third of any month. And I've been warned what could happen to me and to the game they play there if I'm present with my record in this particular combination of figures." He looked mild enough as he pronounced these words, but there would be no shifting him, both Gillian and Xanthe knew it, once the fortune-teller's auguries had been invoked.

The chess group in the cake shop had gone very quiet: the players were into the stretch of the end game.

Miranda said, "If he won't change his mind for you, he's hardly going to for me."

"No, no, I don't expect you to try and move him. But I want you to come with me, instead of Poppa." She paused. "You could do some painting, some sketching—and I want you to persuade Kit to come too."

Miranda felt a funny tightening in her throat. She swallowed, but no words issued to interrupt Xanthe's fluency.

"He is the head of the family, after Poppa, the only son and all that, and he should be there to represent us."

"What?" She was too surprised to speak, and Xanthe, noticing, amplified, "There's going to be the celebration, the pageant, a special one-day game of Flinders, just what Poppa detests, fancy dress, dancing in the street, you know the sort of thing. The Governor-General looking pi beside some royal while lots of faithful members of the Commonwealth leap about in traditional war paint in front of them."

"Xanthe!"

The younger woman giggled into her paper napkin, her eyes mischievous above it. "But I want you to come, you'll love it—think of the scented nights and the sapphire sea and the conches blowing through the palms! And I'm taking you, so that's that. Both of you. You don't have to come over all bashful about it, I've got the bread to do it and I wouldn't do it if I didn't want to. So there, you've just won a holiday for two in the West Indies and you didn't have to guess how much the fridge cost or whatever it is they do on those game shows."

"But Xanthe, should we go at all? I mean . . ."

"Of course we should, it's History with a big *H*, you can't make it happen or unhappen just as you please. The Elizabethan sea dog, the dream of Eldorado, the lost Paradise, this is the past that we belong to, you can't hide from it." Xanthe suspected that her father was hiding from it, that he was only sheltering behind his astrologer and her prognoses because he was a coward.

"Hiding from it isn't the same as not wanting to celebrate . . . I feel uncomfortable, that's all."

"About what exactly?"

The look on Xanthe's face kept Miranda from replying. She would have said, The slaves, the slaves. The sugar, the Indians who were there, the Indians who were brought there afterward. Feeny and Feeny's parents and grandparents and . . . her daughter, the one she had to leave behind. The plantations. The leg irons and the floggings. Sugar. Sugar.

She was silenced as she contemplated her thoughts.

Then she stumblingly told Xanthe about George Felix and his outburst.

"He rang up, actually, later," she went on. "He said Annabel, the PR girl, had given him my number. I told him it was fine, there was no need to call. I didn't want him to apologize, I really didn't. I was frightened he was going to say he was sorry and I didn't want him to feel he ought to do that, so I kept talking at him. I'm still shaky over it. Because he was right, deep down, right. Though there was something else going on, on the set. Meursault was somehow present and active in everything, even when he wasn't actually directing, if you see what I mean. He gives out the energy that makes this kind of thing happen. It's a bit like those mass visions people have, when crowds hundreds strong see the same statue hover in the air. Currents, vibrations—I don't know. But I don't feel good about it, one way or the other." She touched her hair. She felt it might help her not be mistaken.

Xanthe nodded, she understood the Afro halo now on Miranda's head. "You're exaggerating his power, no one is that charismatic. But what a prick, that actor," she said experimentally, watching for Miranda to bristle. "First he bawls you out, then he rings you up all Mr. Nice Guy, and thinks you'll be creaming your jeans waiting for him. Anyway, how can you feel guilty about something you had nothing to do with? All that stuff about oppression . . . Miranda! It happened three and a half centuries ago . . .

"Guilt is unhealthy anyway." Xanthe was at her most brisk. "It only leads to frustration and depression, and they don't do anyone any good at all, let alone those people you want to help. Be logical. You aren't responsible for whatever you think happened. If you were, every single German should have been punished for the Nazis—but we don't say 'Chop off his head!' about every goddamn mein Herr we come across. It would be absurd. And now you believe—because of this uptight fucker Felix—that you've got the blood of ten million slaves on your hands."

Miranda was trying not to tremble. "You've got the words, Xanthe, you're much sharper than me, you can articulate things, and I can't." She felt the actor's hand in the small of her back, the other sliding fingers into her, gently, asking her softly, "Do you like that, do you?" She couldn't now tell Xanthe that she'd invited him over when he telephoned, that she had leapt at the chance with all her puppyish longing to stop the mouth of anger, to stanch the flow of hurt, and that he had slunk away in shame at the tenderness he had disclosed to her, and leaving her bed had put on his testosterone strut again and said, "So long, baby." But she didn't mind; in a way she could not quite understand, or did not want to examine, she felt the act and the pleasure it had given them had undone the earlier bout of rage and made them quits.

"Darling," Xanthe said, "you're upset and there's no need. Listen, it'll be fun. Think of it! Sun'n'sea! Rum'n'cokes! Rum'n'*tokes!* It's just your bag, darling, come on!"

She let Xanthe's hand lie on hers, she was quite glad of the comfort of contact. "Why do you want us to come with you? I mean, couldn't you be the representative? I'm sure Dad couldn't care less. And as for me . . ."

"I don't think that's true, and anyway even if it was, it's not true of the people over there. The name Everard means a lot there. I know. But not the distaff side, never that. I won't do, you won't do. Kit's the one, he'll be just perfect, the eldest, the only son, and Englishman, born on the island too. I'm not right. I'm not . . . convincing in the part." She gave a little laugh.

"You could be, I'm sure, if you put your mind to it." Xanthe kept her hand on Miranda's; it was cool and light. "The point is, I'd like you to come. And so would Sy."

"Sy?"

"Sy as in Simon—Simon Nebris, the developer I was telling you about. He'll be our host there. I'll get the tickets, that's the least I can do, but we'll stay with him. He has interests there. A small hotel, plans for another . . ."

"What about Mum?"

Xanthe smoothed a strand of her hair back over an ear. "Better not, if poss."

Miranda bit her lip, said nothing.

"How is she, by the way?"

"Up and down." She swallowed, forced her voice to issue and report. "They've started her on a new course. Lithium, it's called. It seems to be working." She couldn't ask Xanthe to include Astrid in her invitation. "But it makes her a bit dopey, and that's depressing itself, so it's a vicious circle, as always."

The waitress took their money and handed Miranda a note. "One of the regulars left it to give to you." She jerked her head toward the empty chess table. Miranda opened it; it said, "Thank you for the coffee. Please come here again. Your friend Karel." Xanthe turned to look at the empty table. Her high forehead wrinkled under her fringe of curls. "Well, well," she said. Her eyes rested on Miranda. "That mangy specimen of humanity? Have some sense, Miranda, really."

Miranda wanted to say that he'd rather amused her, and that maybe he could teach her a better game of chess. Kit had never had the patience. But Miranda's instincts gave her vague directions, like a practice wall in the gym with such shallow handholds that only the most determined limpets could feel out the bumps and crawl over it. She wished she could share Xanthe's degree of conviction about her tastes, her desires; she must learn not to feel sorry for men when they went all cow-eyed and seemed to be lowing in their longing at her. Xanthe had the right attitude, she knew.

Admiration, the attraction of opposites, self-flattery and the need for reassurance, mere fancying—though in that "mere" there was huge power impacted—these were some of the springs of love in Miranda's experience; but Xanthe made Miranda want to be like her. It was as if she had a set of keys in her keeping to a concealed chamber Miranda wanted to enter, or a magic sword or a cap or a pair of boots, invisible but rendering her invincible, and Miranda, in order to find out what the secret of her invulnerability was, had to stay close by Xanthe's side.

"By the way, I see you've gone Afro," Xanthe was saying. "It's fabulous, you look terrific. Don't change it before we go."

24

THE CONVENT OCCUPIED a gabled family house in a prosperous Victorian suburb; a steep flight of steps led up to the glass-canopied front door, and chivalric motifs of dragons and dragon-slayers were carved on the window lintels and the pilasters on both sides of the entrance; it now sheltered forty terminally ill patients and four nuns to look after them. Miranda had dreaded the complicated tube journey there, and put off a visit to her mother for weeks, no, months, until her impending departure for the islands forced her to make the effort.

The Little Order of the Compassionate Heart of Mary was a Belgian foundation; which is how Astrid had come to hear about the sisters' work. She had gone to an exhibition in the Museum of Albion on the seaside architecture of *cottages ornés* in Knokke-le-Zoute, and her ankle turned over and she snapped her heel; she was walking past three sisters in their short gray veils and matching dresses, and one of them had helped her up. The nuns' order had another hospice in Knokke, and it was featured in the show; they showed Astrid the old plate-camera photographs of it under construction, the architect's plans, and the images of old men and women lying in beds out in the open air with the sisters, the wimples which the sisters wore then blowing out around their heads like white spinnakers as they held the hands of the sick and dying and faced the camera.

Astrid had gone to the museum because the last time she remembered being truly, deeply happy was when she was digging for razor-clam shells on the beach at Knokke in the summer holidays of her seventh year. Her father had taken her to stay with her grandma in one of those cottages by the sea for the summer. Speaking Flemish again— it was like working an old lock, she needed graphite on her tongue to loosen it into the old language of youth, of lost family—she imagined she was revisiting that beach, and she saw her father's pale smooth nails like shells themselves as he dusted off the sand to hand her one of their prizes.

When Astrid asked the nuns if she could visit them, they told her there was always work to do. Something clutched at her heart at that moment: this was how she would save herself. She had always wanted to be good, she told Kit. She had just forgotten how much, in all the confusion of living and loving him; she was now returning to the path from which she had strayed. She looked so gaunt as she said this, her arms, brittle as wicker, hovered shakily in the air around her mouth and eyes as if she were blind and trying to ascertain the reality of her own face by contact with the heat rising from her; her eyes had become huge in her head like a child's in a charity ad, and her voice deep as a torch singer's, from the smoking and the gin—and the ebbing of her hormones, too, no doubt—as she gradually starved herself to death. They had tried detoxification in a clinic; but it was enough to drive anyone to drink or worse, said Astrid, being surrounded by all those young people throwing their lives away. Old people dying was different; their time had come, they needed comfort. So Kit went to see the sisters of the Little Order, who told him, in careful English, with unclouded expressions in their eyes and brows, that they were accustomed to taking in lambs that are lost and that sometimes they were able to sustain them, but not often. They needed plenty of helping hands, and if Astrid couldn't manage the work, then, well, God would find another way of helping her.

"You are sure, now?" Kit was trembling as he held Astrid by the shoulders, gently, in the parlor that smelled of ammonia and beeswax and stewed tannin. "You really do want to stay here? I can take you away now, darling. We can go home and forget all about this."

"No," said Astrid. "I feel at home here. It was fated: everything, my ankle turning, the exhibition, the nuns' being there. I'm sorry, Kit darling, to leave you on your own . . ." At this she struggled with tears. "But it's so exhausting, living with you."

He nearly flared up, to protest that he showed her more patience than any man alive. But the prioress entered and took Astrid by the elbow and nodded toward the door. "Good-bye, Mr. Everard." He left, smarting under the nun's possession of his wife to his face; as he walked away, heartburn rose hotly in his throat, salt stung his eyes at the sudden parting.

Yet he was soon able to reassure himself, with a measure of ironic amusement, that Astrid would not be able to put up with life in a house of the dying for very long. She had a short fuse; few of her chosen refuges had been able to hold her. The record was held by the Tibetans, in Dumfriesshire. She had stayed there for three months, until the absence of central heating drove her back to London and to Kit.

On this occasion, it had been about two months, and Astrid was still floating on the excitement of her newfound vocation. She was febrile, Miranda noticed; she was speaking rapidly, her features alive with expressions of disgust, humor, fury in manic succession, but she did look as if she had been eating. Miranda supposed that her mother hadn't been drinking, or perhaps not so much as usual. When she'd rung to say she was coming to visit, Astrid hadn't asked her to smuggle her in something—"Oh darling, please,"—as she had every other time she'd been to see her in the drying-out clinics and other places of refuge she had attempted. Perhaps Astrid was becoming cunning, or perhaps she was genuinely reforming.

They talked about Astrid's duties, and she dismissed Miranda's surprise at her tolerance of the tedium and, above all, the squalor.

"I'm not doing it for myself, you see. It's different when you can focus on the love of God: it alters the nature of the most boring task. I like peeling pounds and pounds of potatoes. I like strewing tea leaves about to sweep up the dust—that's the smell, by the way, the smell all through the house—the old tea leaves we use. We don't have lay nuns to do this work anymore. The sisters are highly educated. Not the superstitious peasants they used to be when I was a girl. And I like helping the old dears to the lavatory, honest. Down in the straw, that's where I like to be."

But she really wanted to talk about Kit, Miranda could feel, as soon as Miranda had managed to say that he was coping very well, considering, but of course felt a bit stranded. Couldn't they just consider

getting divorced like ordinary married people? Instead of all this blowing hot and cold, this coming and going, quarrels and reconciliations—
didn't she find it exhausting? But as she said the words, Miranda knew
how much her parents liked the tempest of their relations.

"I still love him, darling," Astrid sang out in her ropy voice. "Very,
very much. He was the man for me from the moment I first saw him."
Miranda winced.

"Don't make that face. It's not romantic gush, it's true. It's just that
we can't live together. You wait. I wish you'd find someone, by the
way. I don't know how you stand the way you live."

"I know that," said Miranda.

"When I think of it from here, I can't believe what we put ourselves
through out there in the world. It's so peaceful here, the peace that
passeth all understanding."

Miranda shivered, she found the closeness of the dying oppressive.

"No, darling, you get to love it, to envy the dead, truly, they're
going to a better place, I'm really quite jealous, where the love of
God will enfold them. Here, we can put behind us all the pettiness,
all the idiotic things that matter so much out there. When I remember
certain things! For instance, one night, your father and I"—she was
off and running, happy now, Miranda realized, and the visit was going
to be a success, her own circumstances mercifully forgotten—"rather
wanted to make a splash (and all that seems so hollow now, so un-
important), Kit was making a real effort, he had these clients, they
were helicopter-hire people and they wanted an administrator with
legal know-how, and your father has got a very good, clear, mathe-
matical brain."

She paused and gave a small smile. "Well, we know where that's got
us. So we were taking them out, and Kit had won—yes, he really
had—in a house game. In those days we played a lot in private houses,
and he'd a marker from one of the company, who turned out to own
a restaurant or two, and Kit—you can't fault him on generosity—oh
darling, have you got a ciggy?" She was looking at Miranda's bag as
if it were a goatskin of water and she a wanderer in the desert of Judaea.
"It's one of the things I don't hold with the nuns about, not smoking.
The other is sex. I tell them, 'Think of all that energy that's being lost
suppressing urges. Why not play with yourself? God gave you the
equipment. You may not want relationships, marriage, the responsi-
bilities, the social duties, the oppression of men, oh yes, I can see

that, the tyranny of being attractive, of losing your looks.' Oh, this is so good, thank you, darling. Heaven." She dragged deep and held her breath. "Oh, now I feel dizzy, how marvelous." She was purring, hunched over the fag, her eyes round and swimming in her pale wrinkled face like a small gibbon's grave countenance seen through bars beside the sign "DO NOT FEED THE ANIMALS IT IS UNKIND. They are given all they need by their keepers." Miranda felt a pang, as her mother continued, "Where was I?"

". . . helicopter people . . ."

"Yes, Kit had won a great deal off this man—and he'd let him off paying him *en liquide*, as he should have, if he'd been a regular gambling man, there's a certain code. But he was the rabbit, the easy mark of the game, and your father actually felt a little sorry for him, and so it was agreed, we could eat in his restaurant instead." She held the stub of Miranda's tipped Player's No. 6 between finger and thumb like a specimen. "You really should smoke a better brand, this rubbish is bad for you. Best not even think what's in them. The Everards are all ghastly snobs—I don't mean Kit—or you, darling—but you know what I mean. I'm a snob about fags, that's my little vice. Otherwise I hate snobs."

She picked up the statue of Saint Anthony of Padua on the side table, with a small glass vase of wilted flowers in front of him, holding the baby Jesus in his arms and contemplated him with a tender smile. Then she stubbed her cigarette out on the underside of his pedestal and handed the stub to Miranda, who dropped it into her bag.

"So Mum, what happened? In the restaurant, with the helicopter bloke?"

"He had a wife, except she wasn't his wife, it was that sort of crowd, she was about to be his second or third, you know the sort. We'd invited two other friends as well, so that it wouldn't look as if Kit was actually doing business. We'd eaten there before, to celebrate the win. I remember we had a row, inevitably, I suppose, because I didn't want to eat much—I was really on the sauce then, I can admit it now, and Kit was furious, he was hissing at me that we didn't have to come out to drink gin as there was plenty of that at home, and anyhow when he held me in his arms he thought he might accidentally snap me in two, I'd got so scrawny, and I started crying"—Astrid was chuckling now—"because he was telling me I'd lost my looks. It seems funny now, because I don't care anymore, that's one thing I've learned from

the sisters, the worthlessness of external appearance and the true nourishment of the spirit from within . . ."

"But it's not true anyway," said Miranda on cue. "You haven't lost
them. You're still ravishing, Mummy, you know you are."

Astrid smiled, waved a hand in dismissal, and went on, "Anyhow,
we returned to the restaurant because we've a certain fondness for
places where we've had one of our really good rows, we confuse
quarreling with intimacy—don't make the same mistake, darling, don't
believe for a moment anger and jealousy mean a man cares for you.

"That's another thing I've learned from the nuns. Oh, I do love them,
they're truly wise, and their tranquillity's an effect of true love, the
identifying mark of the genuine article, and nothing else. Which is
why I am 'apprenticed to tranquillity' in here. That's the phrase that
Father Sylvester used the other day when he visited the community.
Father Sylvester is a living saint—and he rides an old BSA motorbike.
It's his pride and joy. He showed me all the gears. He kicks them in
with his sandaled foot.

"So we were back in the restaurant—by the way, it's Crespi's, it was
the in place about four years ago (I'm telling you so you'll be warned
and never go near it—you'll soon see why) and Kit was ordering
champagne and we were all gorging, we'd reached the main course,
and Kit asks for the wine list to order some red, he was saying it would
go better with the dish our guests had ordered, and when the wine
waiter takes the order, for some expensive château-bottled stuff—not
Italian, French—the waiter says, just like that, 'Your credit has just run
out, signore.'

"That bastard. He was keeping the tab on Kit, after all Kit had done
to make things easy for him.

"The helicopter job would've been hell. Those bloody machines are
aptly named. It'd have meant living in the country too, near the bloody
heliport. There probably wouldn't have been a decent Catholic church
for miles, just beastly Nissen huts left over from the Free Poles in the
war. Or something equally mis. That is why Kit went back to the
tables, I want you to know that, as his only child, his grown-up
daughter: he hadn't anything else. He's a good player, as you know.
But the big boys, they like to play for very heavy stakes. Oh, in
backgammon, you can get up to huge sums quickly with some of these
lunatics, and your father doubles and redoubles because he knows he's
the better player, and then the sums start to rattle him, they're too

big, they're filling up his head, and that's when he loses it, as the Americans say. When he played championships, he was always diamond-sharp, but in the casino—don't make me look back on those days."

"We're going to Enfant-Béate," said Miranda. "Together. It's all been fixed. Dad wants to come."

She did not mention Xanthe. Astrid, even the reformed Astrid, apprenticed to tranquillity and sisterhood and the Little Order, might recoil and spit like a mother cat with her kittens at her back at the idea of Xanthe Everard inviting them, laying it on, organizing them, patronizing. But she reckoned without her mother's sharp-wittedness.

"Kit never took me to see his native land, oh no." She paused. "I'm glad I've discovered another, better world here, otherwise I think I'd be hopping. People like Xanthe—or like Ant, for that matter—she's the very spit of her darling Poppa after all—need lots of mirrors around them all the time. Mirrors to look at their munificence in, looking glasses for their bounty and their beauty. Xanthe, so gilded, so impeccable, so unruffled, she's her father's absolutely favorite mirror, of course she is. But of course she doesn't like that, it's not nearly enough for her. Baah! Beware the Greeks bearing gifts, how true. So how are we feeling about her these days? Miss Me-too? She brings that out in all of us. Disgusting, someone who's got everything and just hogs her way through life without thinking about anyone else for a single minute."

Miranda didn't intervene.

"Give me another ciggy, darling. And tell me, sweetheart, how's life treating you otherwise?"

25

THE FAT MAN traveled ahead, to prepare for their arrival. "Must see to the airing of the sheets," he hummed. "The mending of the mosquito nets, lavender bags on the hangers—can't have our visitors nibbled or nipped, you know." Kit and Miranda had met him one evening with Xanthe, and the modest success of the encounter decided Kit to accept Xanthe's invitation—and some business the fat man discussed with him in confidence helped to sway him.

Sy Nebris was a sleek and shiny figure, with a dolphinlike tapering at feet and hands, so that he did not seem gross, but rather buoyant, as if in order to keep upright and sustain the mass of his ideas and jokes and plans, he needed a body like a flotation bladder. He wore a gold signet ring on the little finger of his right hand, with a goat's head on it—"Family crest, family motto, you know: 'Tutto nel mondo è burla—Life's but a jest,' in plain English, my dears"—and he smoked through a short cigarette holder of tortoiseshell, touching flame to his and others' cigarettes with a slender gold lighter. "I love bits of gold, don't you?"

Xanthe softened in his company, seemed more her age, less seasoned by experience. His obvious fondness laid no claim on her—a eunuch-like butteriness characterized his flesh anyway, and Xanthe told Miranda she trusted him. "He's not the sort for heavy

breathing," she said. "You know how I loathe that kind of a man."
She also liked his wealth, and the carelessness with which he spent
it. She wanted money so that she need not charm others in order
to survive; she saw, in Simon Nebris, the ease of manner that
having people in your gift can bestow. But she'd never want to belong to him, she'd never want to place herself in jeopardy. His generosity toward her—and her family—would retain the character of a
business transaction, if she had her way, as she expected she would.
She'd deliver quid pro quo: to this end she had leaned on Miranda
and through her on Kit Everard, who would do something for his
daughter that he might not do directly for his half-sister. And Kit
could be very useful to Sy's plans, in which case Sy would be beholden
to her.

Xanthe was tired; Miranda had taken a large yellow sleeping pill on
the flight to New York, given to her by her father from a pillbox of
assorted nostrums in his pocket, but Xanthe had refused. She disliked
drugs in all forms; they distorted her control over herself.

In New York, they'd changed to a small airplane bound for Charlotte
Amalie in the Virgin Islands, and there they first felt the breath of the
tropical wind stroking their bared legs and necks and heard its kite-
tail movement in the trees. It stirred them, like those thoughts that
come in the half-waking state before the day, filled with hopes and
dreams.

From Charlotte Amalie, they embarked on a cargo boat to take them
on the final leg of the journey, to Enfant-Béate. The main island, Grand
Thom', had an airstrip, but no passenger services worked the route,
only freight planes and sporadic military traffic. (Sy apologized that
he had no plane himself as yet.)

The ferry's benches were painted sky-blue, and were shaded by a
leaf-green tarpaulin; in front of them, a middle-aged man with steel-
wool curls, wearing clerical gray, was reading the Bible with full concentration, in spite of the heat and confusion on board, the piling of
baskets bearing vegetables and fruit, the loading of boxes full of fish
and bright-yellow crates of soft drinks and beers, and the shaking and
roar of the engine; an old woman, like an ancient walnut dusty and
dried up in the shell, leaned fretfully against the wheelhouse wall
holding a hanky over her mouth and nose, moaning at the motion
of the boat; she had open gray sores on her legs of a kind Miranda
had never seen before. A pair of lovers, with the polish of youth

on their bare arms, sat behind her snuggling together; he cooed and she cackled and pushed him away; he repeated his message into her ear, and she exploded with delighted peals once again. A young mother near her was dandling her baby, walking him in her lap on his bendy plump dimpled legs until he smiled at her, his mouth pink and translucent and soft like a flower with light in its petals, the tiny teeth like stamens.

There was only one other party of English people on the boat; yet Miranda did not feel she was sticking out in the crowd. Their group was paid little attention. She saw that no one had frizzled hair like hers; most of the men smoothed it back with oil, the women set it in stiff helmets like Feeny's, while the children were generally braided and beribboned. She fingered her aureole of artificially assisted Afro and felt a twinge of unease.

Kit had not sat down, but stood at the rail watching the sea; it was nearly noon and the high sun's heat shone on the surface as if on hammered silver. Islands broke the surface like the crested heads of spouting sea monsters, green as wrasse, maroon as kelp, with plumes floating above them of cumulus that mimicked the arrangement of the land masses below, so that the archipelago appeared to Kit three times over, first in fluffy whiteness in the sky above, then in the marine troop of dark islands on the sea, and then again in the reflection of both cloud and island that he could see fathoms down when the boat tilted on a wave and the blinding silver hardness of the sea suddenly developed velvety depths and showed him his own face in the water. He was wrapped in the presence of the islands, and yet, recognizing them, all he could feel was the stab of loss. He could not know any longer what it meant to belong somewhere.

He lit a cigarette, turning his back to the wind and cupping his hand to do it, and Miranda and Xanthe smiled at him; they were talking together and laughing. He walked over to them, put an arm around both, and asked them why two such pretty ladies didn't either of them have a husband.

"The inadequacy of men," Xanthe lost no time replying.

"My father doesn't think anyone good enough for his Goldie, does he?" said Kit. She nodded agreement. "Miranda, on the other hand, has her own reasons, I know. About Independence and Freedom." Miranda turned to watch the sea. "A new breed, the woman of today. You don't want life easy, I know. You'd rather it was interesting." He put his arm around Miranda, and she stiffened, irritability mounting inside.

"You're not exactly an advertisement for togetherness, are you?" she responded. "You can't exactly reproach us for wanting something different."

"I don't know about that," Kit replied. "Your mother and I are still married, some would think rather an achievement. And I still . . ."

"You love Mum very much, I know." She chanted, "And she loves you too." She turned away, her throat choked with scorn.

"You're too inflexible," she caught his answer. Then Jamieston came into view, a straggle of low buildings, lemon and pink and pistachio under the blue mass of the volcano and the soft silky green of the sugar-cane fields spread on its broad slopes, and, beyond it, the sharper, darker cone of the small island, Petit Thom', nearby.

Kit said, "I don't remember it very well. I can't tell if it has changed. Perhaps it hasn't." He'd been on the offensive, chaffing to control his excitement, but it now showed plainly in his voice.

When the ferry docked, bumping against the rubber tires hanging from the wharf, and the crowd pressed forward to catch the bales and baskets thrown down by the boat hands, Xanthe spotted Sy in Panama and white linen and waved and he saw them and raised his hat.

They came ashore, one of the hands shouting to the crowd to let them pass, and Miranda had to accept their precedence, and follow Xanthe and her father. Sy kissed Xanthe, and then, joining fingertips together, made a namaste and a small bow to Kit and his daughter.

"Welcome, dear friends all, welcome to the land of your forefathers! Indeed I hope—nay, expect—that we shall be the best of friends—"

"Oh God," muttered Miranda. "Don't."

"The boat's here," said Sy, waving over a slim youth in white shirt and trousers. "This is Nelson, my . . . one of my boys . . . Nelson, see to the bags, will you." He gleamed proprietorially at the youth, who remained grave in response as he obeyed, turning to the ferry and shouting up to the crew to throw down the cases for Xanadu.

"We have to wait for one other couple who came over with me this morning, for a spot of sightseeing. Ah, there they are!" He lowered his voice. "Big in rubber; from Akron, Ohio." He smiled wickedly, and faked a yawn and rolled his eyes. "She's on a salt-free diet. Can you beat it? But a mere hôtelier like myself must put up with . . . you know."

Soon they were all settled in the hotel launch, with Nelson at the wheel, their bags stowed, introductions made, the outboard puttering and on their way across the Strait of Oualie to Petit Thom', where Xanadu lay in the hills.

"Formerly called Oualie, hence the name of this channel," shouted Sy above the engine. "Nest of pirates, buccaneers, maroons and cannibals. The island's still strewn with bones." He laughed, showing his small teeth between his full lips, and Miranda worried, I'm not going to like him, I'm really going to hate him. And felt a sudden affinity with the condemned Ohioans for their dullness. Sometimes sparkle struck her as more wearisome.

Nelson brought the launch alongside by some steps on a small pier of volcanic stone, the lava bubbles clearly visible in streams rising in the gray mass where the water slapped; Miranda felt giddy with the traveling and the tension and folded herself carefully into the black saloon to which Sy escorted them. He left Nelson behind with the luggage, saying he'd send the car back later. The Americans, seeing the numbers, agreeably proposed they should stay behind for the second shuttle to the hotel.

Kit stood meanwhile on the wharf, facing across the channel to Grand Thom'. Then he put out his cigarette and got into the car next to Miranda in the back, and said, almost to himself, "You see the pleat in the sugar cane?" He pointed. "Just there, that's the creek below Belmont, I think. The house would be up in those trees, to the right."

"You'll have all the time in the world to go à la recherche, dear chap," answered Sy. "This is the place of lost time if ever there was one. Island tempo, no hurry, nowhere to go, nothing to do."

They were driving on a tarmac road through the small port, past the customs house, identified by the British flag and a brightly painted colonial seal—that tusky sea monster and more fringe-skirted natives—on past warehouses and an empty arcaded market building. It was early afternoon and the heat of the day had suspended activity. Then the surface of the road became bleached and the car slowed on strewn shells mixed with sand. From the shade of the odd tree by the wayside, a field worker now and then stood up and looked in their direction, but the gaze would slide past them as if the car and its occupants were transparent. A few of these islanders held a tool in their hand—a hoe, a garden fork, a machete, with which to dig in the ground or cut back a bush or clump of grass. The women were dressed in faded cotton, and dust lay on their exposed limbs.

Miranda was to discover that islanders never looked an Englishman or -woman in the eye: for they had been taught over the centuries that meeting the masters' glance was dumb insolence. Later she learned too that in consequence the islanders considered exchanging looks brought bad luck.

A small animal bounded, with a lopsided gait, across the track, and stopped, paws lifted like a small kangaroo, before it disappeared into the grasses and shrubs. ("Oh, that's a cavey," Sy responded to Miranda's exclamation. "Very tame, very sweet, very greedy. A kindred spirit, you might say.") Then they passed through the stone pillars where turtles reared worn heads. ("From the old Great House, one of the few things that stood up to the hurricane of 1875") and drove under a double row of royal palms, their fronds tossing in the warm northeasterly, like girls shaking their hair over their heads to dry in the sun.

Xanadu came into view on the slope, a long two-storied plantation house with lemon-yellow louver shutters and a broad veranda all around, where creepers flowered and birds, in plumage to match, sipped and darted. Inside the gates there was a sense of order; a glimpse of a kitchen garden laid out in rows, unlike the providence of pumpkin vines, cotton bushes, self-seeded fruit trees and fallen coconuts glimpsed from the car.

Moments later they drew up under a tall tree dropping a tracery of aerial roots to the side of the main building.

"We've arrived! I'll deliver you to your rooms," Sy prattled on. "Then, as soon as you've spruced up a bit, we'll have a rum punch maison, a dish of conch fritters with Angostura, perhaps a dip in the pool, the ever-obliging sunset, and my dears, you'll put the journey behind you." He squeezed Xanthe's hand. "My darling Goldie, dearest Miranda, dear boy! You'll all feel transformed!"

"I'm much too excited now to be tired," said Xanthe in level tones, and squeezed Sy's hand back.

Miranda noticed, with surprise, that Sy Nebris had adopted Ant's pet name for Xanthe.

Sy took the two young women up the outside staircase; they had rooms in the house, side by side, on the west side, with a connecting balcony. Kit was given one of the garden cottages down the path by the swimming pool.

"Big boys can cope alone with bats and toads, hoppers and other creatures of the night," called out their host. "Such wild things sometimes pay a visit to the cottages."

Xanthe ran up to him and leaned over his great paunch on tiptoe to reach his pink cheek.

"You are lovely, Sy. It's fabulous to be here."

As he was leaving them, he called out, "Drinks on the terrace in an hour. In time for the sunset."

In her room, Miranda clenched her fists to stop herself from crying. Such words as Xanthe found easy to say would choke her; such treacly friendship would make her gag; she couldn't let a smooth bag of guts like Sy with his little feet and his mighty stomach anywhere near her. She stripped off her crumpled clothes and turned on the shower and stood under the gush of cold water wanting it to wash away all her grief and envy with it. She wouldn't ever find lasting love from anyone, anywhere, her father was right to taunt her. On the other hand, she didn't want such a love, she didn't believe in it, it was the self-deluding dream of his generation. Nor would she settle for half-measures and compromises either. Her bloody father, reminding her of her state, making it seem a mission.

Yet, in his clumsy way he'd fingered something: she did have intimations of pleasure that went far beyond what life put in her path; she understood her mother's quest for absoluteness, she understood Kit's restless discontent. They knew that there was something ardent to be experienced, and like them she wanted it too. But she also knew that the tension of hunger inside Kit and Astrid caused people to fight shy of them, that their very ardor caused recoil, as if their poles were charged too powerfully with the stuff of emotion, and those who possessed the same charge, but temperately, under control, were repelled by their incontinent and unbridled force. By being empty of longing, Xanthe was always given more than she desired, and then she seemed not to care, which only shook down more golden dresses and slippers from her wishing tree.

The water was beginning to calm Miranda, as her flesh started to tingle and flush under its cold torrent. She grasped all the lightness she could muster, thought of where she was, of the tropics as a paradise on earth, and stepped out of the shower to look appreciatively at her well-knit brown body with its hollows and wells where pleasure still lay in hiding, promising futures of plenty. And she laughed, and put on her favorite miniskirt of crushed mulberrycolored satin with appliquéd stars in silver leather and a halter-neck top which showed her pretty armpits—someone had once loved her armpits, licking the tuft of hair that grew there into a flattened curl. She had recovered from her fit. Yes, it was just one of those fits, travel fatigue, crossing of time zones, lack of food, low blood sugar, the time in the month, nothing serious, nothing that would mean anything tomorrow because of course she and love were no strangers. It was Xanthe rather who was to be pitied: she did not know highs and lows or heat or cold but only the tepid no-man's-land in between.

And Xanthe, who was opening every drawer in her room and every cupboard and examining the lining paper and unwrapping the hotel gifts of soap and shower cap and palpating the fruit that stood in a basket on the low table between two easy chairs upholstered in chintz where birds of paradise coquetted among palmettos and pomegranates; Xanthe who was noting that the painters of the window frames had used brushes a tad too big and streaked the wall here and there; Xanthe who was shaking out her dresses and pegging the skirts and trousers onto the appropriate hangers and setting some aside for pressing after their journey in the humid heat, Xanthe was exulting; she had managed to irritate her best-beloved poppa so badly by leaving him at home and coming here with Sy, and though she was sorry, of course she was, she was also brimming with the joy of power it gave her.

From the start, Ant Everard had not liked the sound of Simon Nebris one bit; he did not want Xanthe to get mixed up with business, but if she wanted a profession, and he could understand that the young women of today did take up work in a serious fashion, then she should continue with the law, go into chambers, or use her education, in insurance, or even journalism. But not catering. Not hotel-keeping. Not property development. When he had met Sy, one evening when they'd all gone to the theater to see *The Royal Hunt of the Sun*, he'd been so infuriated by the fat man's prancing and exclamations and loud jollity that the tip of his pale nose and the tips of his strong fingers turned white. Xanthe had enjoyed their combat, she liked locked horns around her, while her mother had fussed and tried to interpose distractions; but Xanthe knew they were fighting over her allegiance and it was gratifying.

Later, her father said to her, "I can't imagine why you want to spend time with that pansy," and he imitated with a vicious jerk of his hips the wiggle of Sy's walk, and fluttered his fingers.

"I like 'pansies,' Poppa," she'd replied. "I feel comfortable with them. They like me, they want to be like me, and they don't want anything from me."

"I suppose that's a blessing, at least there's no danger of foolishness."

'Foolishness' was her parents' word for sex. "We don't want you to do anything foolish" was their preamble to the excruciating lesson in restraint (and contraception) she had been given at sixteen, two years after one of the family's old friends had fumblingly felt her up whenever he could snatch the chance, and she hadn't turned a hair, for no one could get a purchase on her spirit, and make her lose control.

"But Poppa," she'd added, "Sy isn't queer, actually. He's both. Or nothing. Depending on how you look at it."

Sy had very small, albino-mouse-pink genitals; he'd shown them to her soon after they met, as a proof of his adoration of her. "You see, my darling child, I put myself in danger to take bread—or whatever you'll let me take—from your hand. I'm a hostage to your fascinating ways, and you could, if you wanted, be extremely cruel, make terrible fun of me to your friends, shame me in front of them, or behind their backs. But I know you won't, I know you'll keep my secret and be my ally." In default of virility, Sy was adept at other techniques; Xanthe let him plate her till the bed—sometimes the carpet—underneath her was soaked in his greedy mouth-watering and her thin, salty cyprine.

Poppa claimed—it was only a claim—that he wanted her to have a manly companion, not an old and flapping grotesque who did a poor imitation of Noel Coward. But the truth was that he had never wanted anyone to come near her, ever. He'd assert his possession with the most uncharacteristic violence—after all, he was famed for his courtesy and mild-manneredness on the field. But the dinner after the theater had finished with a struggle between Sy and her father. Xanthe had never seen her poppa reach for a bill with such alacrity. Sy had to grasp the piece of paper on its dish very firmly and turn his plump

shoulders to the company in order to read the total and place his credit
card upon it and, with finger and thumb firmly holding them, wave
for the waiter. Later, on the telephone to his daughter, Anthony Everard
complained, "Such vulgarity too, flashing his credit card around like
that." (It was rated gold, and in those days, such a card was still a
rarity.)

Kit, for his part, in his cottage with the reproductions of Maria
Merian studies of flora on the walls, the bushy indigo and the fluffy
cotton silk tree, opened the duty-free bottle of Scotch he'd bought
and poured until the tumbler was half full, lit a cigarette and stepped
out of the French window onto the little terrace that gave onto the
lawn sloping down to the sea. The sun was melting gold and tugging
at the edges of the high cirrus in its descent; the heavens looked as if
they were being poured into a bowl of molten glass and taking the
arched palms and the flapping banana trees with them as decoration
on the rim. It still looked far away to Kit, like a poster, like a photograph
in a calendar, and he stood there trying to feel real, trying to connect
with this place, but the more he squeezed out memories, the more he
reminded himself, "I was born here, or almost here, next door, my
mother drowned here, that sea in front of me was where she disappeared, my life is interwoven with this place, with these people," the
more numb he felt and the less he understood. Why had he come?
Why had he not followed his father's example and avoided a return to
what was irretrievably lost? Except, as he stamped on the butt and
downed the liquor, it was an opportunity, an opening perhaps, and he
needed money, and if Astrid was serious about staying in the convent,
well, he must find the money to pay for her, and he too, must seize
his chances of changing his life.

He closed his eyes under the burden of his failure and then the
island became real to him all at once through the sound of the wind,
and he remembered Serafine telling him once when he was a child
about the orphanage for the blind in Jamieston, and how they learn
to see with their hands. "They're taught to tell the darkies from the
white folks, that's something they have to know, and how's they going
to know it if they can't see the color of the skin? So the orphan teachers
teach them to feel"—she closed her eyes and ran her fingertips over
her head. "But I think that smell will do the same—more reliable, too.
You smell like a white man, Kit Everard, I'm telling you, but you feel
like a black man to me." And she cradled his head between her dry

hands and kissed him hard on the forehead. Feeny must be in her seventies now. Her tall thin frame had been slowed by a hip replacement that had half-worked and the worrisome asthma that years in London had aggravated. He should have thought of bringing her with them; but it would have been no use. He wondered, Did she have relations still on the island? Perhaps Miranda had some information; she still visited Feeny sometimes in the sheltered flat the council had placed her in when Gillian could not stand her presence any longer and had prevailed against Anthony.

"You have to train them to do the simplest things," Sy was saying to Xanthe, placed on his right at the dinner table. "Salt fish and rice in a little bowl, eaten with one hand, sitting on the dirt floor—that's their idea of breakfast, so what do you expect?" He eyed the young islander in a white uniform and pointedly switched a dessert fork and spoon from one side to the other. "They've never seen—" He waved his hands over the table where they were sitting, under a trellis of scarlet trumpet vines on the terrace overlooking the sea where the setting sun had gored itself an hour before, and Miranda followed his gesture and for a moment saw the high apparel of the dinner table with the eyes of the novice waitress—the squat glasses for water, the stem goblets, fluted for hock and belled for claret, the several particular forms of implement, the cellars for condiments and dishes for butter, and they suddenly took on the strangeness of a museum vitrine where the paraphernalia of some long-forgotten customs were displayed with explanatory notes (Romans paring the oil from their skin with strigils; Druids gathering mistletoe; Egyptians mummifying cats: "From circa 1620 to 19– the English plantocracy of the Caribbean dined with elaborate ceremony, using . . .")

   She thought she might do one of her series of cigarette cards on Good Manners—"Eight Ways to Fold Dinner Napkins," "Three Correct Methods of Holding a Knife and Fork and Five Incorrect." Her father was talking now, saying, "This is a beautiful spot, of course, but it's remote. If you want to catch the big boys, the high rollers, you want to be discreet, certainly, but nearer to hand." His eyes lifted to look across the blue-black waters drilled with the stars' reflections to the amber smudge of Jamieston's harbor lights on Grand Thom'. "You need to be over there. Your guests disembark, a courtesy car's there to meet them, the hotel's a minute's ride away, the tables beckon, and they'll soon be well away."

"My dear chap, you read my mind."

Xanthe laughed, and said, "Sy has the very spot; and it's practically in the bag."

"Agreement to a Gaming Act is gaining ground fast at home. But here, there's still resistance—at the highest level," Sy went on. "For various reasons, you'll soon discover. But the Governor tells me that we'll be wanting to let go soon; Enfant-Béate will follow all the other islands of the archipelago with independence. I ask you, I ask the Governor, I ask everyone, How will they survive? Sugar? Yes, well, sugar. With punitive tariffs against us from the United States Sugar Corporation? Demand is falling everywhere, and rightly"—he patted his heart—"it's so bad for one, the bottom should fall out of the market, for everyone's sake.

"No, the answer is tourism—and this is where I hope you'll come in, dear boy—and Goldie my darling—and—yes, Miranda, you too, darling girl, if you've a penchant for it, of course. Enfant-Béate will have to enter the fray, against stiff competition. These two islands are more beautiful than anywhere else in the archipelago, and I've known this part of the world since—I shan't say." He leaned across and whispered, looking intensely at his three guests, first at Miranda, and then back across to her father, and last, lingering on Xanthe. His eyes were different from his manner, Miranda noticed, they had stars deep in the dark-blue irises, where his energy was burning under the froth. "But they're backward. They're so backward that I put it to the Governor that he should resist handing over the reins to the locals. They'll make such a mess of it, and we're quite willing to stay on and help. I love it here, I feel at home here. I have friends here. Of course, not like you who belong here, in a special way—history, my dear Kit, is history But I do love the people, this is my spiritual home. However, if independence proceeds, and I think at this stage it must, I need a native to front my operation. That's the long and the short of it. To keep the goodwill of the new bosses!"

Her father was very quiet, almost spellbound; once or twice his face darkened while Sy spouted, but the fat man was quick, and caught Kit's displeasure and soothed him with a self-deprecatory raising of the hands or eyebrows, as if to call into question in the very act of speaking his authority to do so or his belief in what he was saying. "Tell me what you think, dear fellow, I'm all ears."

Kit began, "There are splendid individuals, of course, but on the whole . . ." He shook his head. "Chaos is the word. Chaos in the family, one woman will have children by two, three, four different men; none of them will give her any support. Chaos, I hardly have to tell you. They'll speak about it openly, they'll say . . ." And Kit slipped into a local accent—" 'Yes, I do have my girlfriend here, and another one there, that's the way we do it, that's the legacy of slavery when we was split up mother from child, man from his woman. Even the priests understand it, even they accept that's how it is.' "

"But it *is* the result of slavery!" Miranda spoke with passion.

"What's done is done, and it's not a bad way of life," Kit grinned, and Miranda found herself thinking, He's coarse, my father has become brutish and coarse. He doesn't care, he never did care, he just takes what he can, it's the way he lives now, that's what Mum can't stand, that's what's driven her into the convent.

Sy was saying, "I need you, you must see, I need your insights, your experience, your standing here. The Everards who are authentic, native sons, if I may turn a phrase . . ."

Miranda fought to keep her balance in her fury and tiredness, after drinking—rum punch before dinner, wine during it—and listening to Sy's patter, and she spoke up abruptly, saying that she hated tourists, that tourists spoiled things, that there must be other things the island could do to get by. She said, "What about Cuba, what about what Che Guevara was trying to do before the pigs got him?"

But her father shook his head. "Cuba has terrible problems."

And Sy blew a little kiss at her and cooed, "You keep your ideals, they're for the young, they're very precious."

Xanthe smiled sweetly, then added, "Miranda still believes in changing the world. She has faith in people's goodness, 'original virtue.' Which is why people like me need her so much."

Miranda felt something kindling, under her commitment to helping out her lonely, râté father and the perpetual craving to oblige and win approval, to jump for the stick when it was thrown. But she was all at once drained of strength.

Sy went on, "Other islands have tried. My dear, your sentiments are noble. But romantic, and the world isn't romantic. Earning a crust isn't romantic, not if you're a tiny pair of islands offshore from the most powerful nation in the world. In other places they've tried light industry, assembling this and that, but these people are not Chinese, with nimble fingers and an unslakable thirst for work. No. Delightful and warmhearted and handsome in face and limb they may be. Better-natured than any other race. But they are hopeless. What did that famous writer say, a few years ago, when he came back to see the land of his birth? That history's built around achievements, and that nothing was ever achieved here in the Caribbean. He lacks charity, it's a drawback in a human being. Though perhaps not in a writer.

"Nevertheless, my dears, I'm afraid he's right about this place. Nothing was achieved here, except the slave system and that's best set aside. Nothing will be, either, in the sense that you and I mean—art, music, the life of the mind, culture, society."

"Sy, darling, you mustn't talk like that to Miranda," said Xanthe. "She's become one of them, don't you see? Look at her, listen to her! She thinks being black is like a religion, you get the faith and then you become it, you adopt it and believe it and practice it, don't you? And quite right too."

Miranda looked at her, helpless, "You know I don't . . ."

Sy breezed on, "She looks lovely, if it's her hair you mean, Goldie. Full of character." Then, in an aside, he said, "You must learn not to be so catty, Goldie, or nobody will want to play with you anymore, not even me." He giggled, then straightened his features and resumed, "No, these islands will survive if they accept their limitations and let us help them. Only if they do. We must help our fellow men—and women." He placed his hand on Xanthe's. "But the ways are few and far between." He took a last draft of Burgundy from his glass. "But I'm neglecting your entertainment! Come!"

They rose and followed Sy indoors, to the hotel's main lounge, where rattan easy chairs, upholstered in a chintz of pink cabbage roses and lime-green lyrebirds, were set under the large languid blades of ceiling fans, and Nelson, in bow tie and white tuxedo, stood gravely, hands folded, behind a small bar. Miranda accepted a little brandy from him; when she tried to smile, he did not respond in kind, and she was too tired to persevere. She announced she would go to bed; but exhaustion struggled with loneliness and she dragged her feet. Her father signaled good night to her from the backgammon table where he had settled down, and Sy left the game to stand up and kiss her, and then Xanthe too, who pitched into Miranda, giggling softly, "I think you'll have to carry me up, I'm ready to drop."

"Leave me alone." Miranda refused to take Xanthe's weight.

"Oh, darling, you're not cross with me, are you?"

"I'm just exhausted."

"Goody." Xanthe made another attempt to lean on Miranda, who this time accepted her. "I'm tired too—it's been quite a day." She dropped her head on Miranda's shoulder. "I didn't mean to be horrid, you know that."

"Do you want to sleep in my room? The bed's big enough, I shan't kick you," Miranda asked Xanthe as they lolled side by side on the first-floor veranda outside their bedroom doors, in the clicks and whistles of the night animals and the bending sighs of the trees. "Do the noises scare you?"

"Of course not, silly," said Xanthe, rousing herself to enter her room. "Good night, sweetie." She put her cheek forward for Miranda to kiss. "And another," she said, changing sides and waiting again. She bit her lip for a moment. "Darling, I think I should marry Sy, don't you? He's such fun. I don't think I'd ever be bored." But she didn't wait for Miranda to answer.

Miranda would have liked Xanthe to stay with her, so she could argue with her about marrying Sy; but she could already hear her mocking Miranda's ideas of mutual love and shared freedom. "You may want to bang like a shit-house door in a thunderstorm," she'd once said, chuckling at her choice of words, "but I actually don't like shagging. Penetration, abandon, they're not my line."

Miranda slid between the sheets and shivered, not at the delicious chill of the pressed cotton on her hot, inebriated limbs but at the thought of Xanthe with the fat man for her husband. Money, that was it, no doubt, and I hate money, she told herself.

The tree frogs were hooting on the roof; in the distance a donkey brayed in what seemed an agony of yearning, and other, indecipherable noises of the island sounded in the night outside like voices speaking a language she did not know, an esoteric system like the table manners Sy was teaching his hotel staff. As she drifted in and out of wakefulness, Miranda was also visited by the muteness of Nelson and the awkward attentions of the waitresses on the terrace, and for a moment, by the soft mouth of George Felix on hers, that had once spat such fury at her as well, and she thought, I should send him a postcard, then remembered she didn't have his address. As she drifted, she saw anonymous figures heaving towers of tottering gambling chips with magnified pound signs toward her father, who was crowing at a poker table in dense blue smoke while the couple from Ohio on one side of him puzzled over their cards and Xanthe in a bride's veil presided imperturbably from her position at the shoe, dealing precisely with ivory fingers, and Sy, embarrassingly naked as people so often were in Miranda's dreams, was calling out to her, as he bore down on the table, "We must help our fellow men, my dear, and the ways are few and far between."

P A R T   V

Green/Khaki

> . . . there's no hand

> to take me home—
> no Caribbean
> island, where even
> the shark is at home.

> It must be heaven.
> There on that island
> the white sand shines
> like a birchwood fire.

> Help, saw me in two,
> put me on the shelf!
> Sometimes the little muddler
> can't stand itself.

> —ROBERT LOWELL

26

SITTING IN THE Governor's box beside Xanthe, overlooking the play in the stockade, Miranda read in the program that a harvest festival at Saint Blaise Figtree was taking place as part of the celebrations of the English landing 350 years before. There were a few other events planned for the day as well: evensong later, after the game, in the cathedral in Jamieston, while santapee bands with masquerade dancers were promised for the evening. But Flinders was to dominate the celebrations.

Miranda looked out over the shorn turf where the players in light cotton shirts and trousers of their national colors stood and faced one another in the intricate measures of the game. It was a bright prospect: flags flew from the pavilion, raised to declare the Houses which the opposing teams had bid to enter and occupy; smaller homemade ones were waved by supporters in the bleachers and in the promenade area around the edge of the stockade. At first she occupied herself drawing the scene, but soon tired in the heat. Being a girl, she had never learned to play; the commentators she sometimes caught on the radio, with their genial patter and encyclopedic knowledge of past feats and strokes and bids, sometimes conveyed to her a part of the thrill she knew the game's followers felt. They would sigh, "Ant Everard's opulent, unrivaled sweeps at the ball singed the distant green chase in stockades the world over," or would invoke, enraptured, "The sweet whir of a ball as it spins! And the thock as it makes contact with the meat of a stick wielded by a master striker!"

The Visitors were playing first; they had not aimed high with their bids for Houses, for they feared the deadly speed of the islanders' throws. The crowd was disappointed by the opening of the outsiders' challenge; then, when the Home team's captain responded without doubling, furious catcalls broke out from the supporting fans, and swelled with additional stomping and banging of beer cans and bottles when he followed this act of circumspection with a very high bid— for a Belmont—on behalf of the Islanders. For if the Islanders did manage to gain a Belmont, as their captain had declared—this involved an early gain of a Rebecca and a minimum of thirty-three different gains around the Chase—the home team's total score would only have assured them the day if he had doubled the English bid. If not, the game could end in a stalemate. Their fury that he had failed to take this gamble broke out in wave upon wave of jeering round the Stockade. But it was too late to change the call.

In the Governor's box, the muddled declarations caused an exchange of exclamations between the male spectators and aficionados of the game—Sy, Kit Everard, and the incumbent Governor, who was glad to be leaving the island and returning to his cottage in Sussex when independence came, and he would be handing over to Sir Berkeley Seacole.

Sir Berkeley was sitting on the Governor's right, and Kit next to him, on his right, as the representative in direct line of the pioneer family who had planted Enfant-Béate. Independence of the Béatois from the Motherland was imminent; Sir Berkeley Seacole was a prominent member of the coming generation of indigenous and non-white officials, hand-picked to handle transition to nationhood on account of his British education, his sturdiness and loyalty. "The game," he had said earlier to Miranda, "puts knights into the lists. Those players out on the field need you to preside, to inspire them with thoughts of virtue and, yes, love." He was a plump man in his fifties, with a neat mustache and a sprinkling of white hair in his curls and black moles in his complexion, like wild rice; a certain severity of manner overlay the soldierly directness. But he had a kind face, Miranda thought, as she remembered Sy's warnings about the hard men headed for power.

Kit had on his Panama with the Doggett's ribbon round the crown;

he had remained very quiet ever since they had arrived in the islands, as if he were holding his breath. On the second day, he'd inquired of his daughter, "Do I look as if I belong here? I feel that I do, that I never left—oh, the air, the soft air!" He'd snuffed it up voluptuously, eyes closed, face tilted to the wind. But he didn't look like the Béatois; his eyes had not become lambent like the light-colored irises of so many of the islanders, his voice no longer moved to their pitch and roll; he had become as distant and foreign as his daughter.

Sy was seated on the left of the incumbent Governor, and was wearing a blue hibiscus with a long red pistil ("Naughty flower!") in the lapel of his suit of amber tussore; Lady Seacole on his left, and Xanthe positioned behind them.

"The Captain of our team was a compromise choice, you might say," Sir Berkeley commented, turning to smile at the two young women from Britain seated behind. "Many of our people believe it would have been better to have selected a local man, a Negro. But . . ." At this he managed a quick smile that faded so fast Miranda was not sure she had seen it at all. "The international team representing all the islands now has a Negro—not from here, however—as its Captain and we confidently expect that we shall see him lead our national team to the highest pinnacle of success. This does not mean we will discriminate, however, on the grounds of race or creed or color. We should represent all our countrymen, regardless. As I'm sure you will agree."

As the players lolloped on, the crowd hooted derision or ecstasy; when the scores rose in the direction they desired, they applauded every motion of the hero defending the target area at the one end of the chase. When a stroke failed, they howled; when it succeeded, they roared; when the island team were pitching and the balls flew at the striker, whirring at velocities that rendered them invisible to an ordinary eye, the crowd fell silent with tension; then burst into an uproar of delight if the player, his stick whirling as in Japanese sword-play, failed to hit a single one. At moments of such sweet success, some let off firecrackers, others hurled their pennants into the air; throughout play, except at the very moment of strike, the spectators kept chanting to the beat of drums and the blowing of conch shells.

The tumult did not help the game to speed up, Miranda noticed, and the cacophony increased the tedium. Between outbursts there sometimes developed a long rally, and she could not help admiring the speed of reflex of the striker, the balletic assaults of the throwers as, with strike after strike, the flying bullets were parried and the runners on the chase unable to gain another point on their circuit. Then the stockade seemed suspended as the players and their audience followed the action as if they had become a single organism, breathing as one, rapt, and the tropical sky's bright clouds spooled lazily over-head. But then a missed ball, a direct hit on the body of a player, a runner run out, something—would interrupt the rhythm, and the crowd on the benches, in the stands, rammed against the inner fence of the stockade, hanging from the trees outside its boundary, would explode into frenzy once more.

The box was a gated portion of the main stand facing foursquare to the chase and the player in the target; there they were offered orange squash and Madeira cake. At moments of mounting turbulence, the Governor beckoned over his equerry, who was sitting at the back, next to Miranda and Xanthe, and they exchanged a few quiet words. During the periods of steady and concentrated play, as ball followed ball into the target and was repulsed with varying degrees of force and skill, the crowd would settle down again, and the Governor resume his attention to the game.

"Mr. Everard is an experienced hotel manager," Sy was telling Sir Berkeley, during a long moment of discussion on the turf as a set of new balls was called, refused, debated, refused again. "He has a deep knowledge of the workings of the finest establishments in Europe." Sy nodded to him, to urge him to speak on his own behalf.

"You see, Sir Berkeley," Miranda heard her father at his most plau-sible, "I'd like to return, bring something back to my birthplace, and Mr. Nebris has offered me the opportunity." Kit bared his teeth in a smile; Miranda looked away. Her father was such a con artist; she couldn't believe it wasn't as patent to everyone else as it was to her. "One of my favorite hotels," he continued, "is the Lustucru in Deauville, Sir Berkeley." (And I wonder if you're allowed back there, Dad?) "It is very discreet, it has the feel of an intimate, small-scale private hotel, though it can provide accommodation for a hundred guests in the bedrooms, nearly five times that number in the restaurants and at the tables."

"Nebris, old boy, you know as well as I do that there are at present on Enfant-Béate, that is both islands, on Grand Thom' and Petit Thom', only around ninety hotel beds all told," the incumbent Governor put in. "And twenty-five of those are yours, in that little paradise of yours, the land of milk and honey you've created, Xanadu. Could the islands tolerate an expansion of the order you're proposing? We'll have to leave it to the new, internal government to decide, once you"—he faced Sir Berkeley—"are in charge."

Sir Berkeley's eyes stayed on the chase, as he replied, "It would be"— his face crumpled as if in pain—"painful, yes. For the people here, who are unused to foreign invasions." He smiled again, so swiftly it seemed hardly to have happened.

Kit said, "It would certainly have to be handled carefully. With professional expertise."

Miranda felt she had to leave, the air had become so heavy on her head and chest; the Flinders would have been tolerable, but her father's angling . . . it shamed her.

Sir Berkeley responded, "I do not think that the matter will rest with me. We cannot count on the success of my party in the forthcoming elections, much as we might wish it. After all, Enfant-Béate is a child of British democracy, and the outcome of the people's vote cannot be foretold, even by a man who likes playing with numbers." He nodded at the pad on Kit's knee where he had been jotting the odds of his combinations.

"The opposition has its supporters, good men, some of them. And women." He turned and smiled at Xanthe and Miranda, and continued in his formal manner of address, as if English were an official language, "You may have heard of my young niece, who is one of the opposition's bright stars. She was Leader of the Union in college in England, and has made the newspapers on several occasions, I believe, in these heady days of the late sixties. Do you recall the name at all? Atala Seacole?" Some softness now glimmered under his stern manner.

"Attie Seacole!" Xanthe exclaimed. "Of course I've heard of her. She's been all over the papers. She used to lead demos, didn't she? She really gave the press a run for its money. They huffed and puffed, about how some people should go back where they came from if they didn't like it here, et cetera, et cetera."

"To which the reply is, 'We're here because you were there,' " said the future Governor. Then he smiled again, and added, "She did come back, and she's still a troublemaker. A thorn in my side. A thorn in my party's side, I should say. I sometimes understand why Saint John the Baptist had his head chopped off after preaching the abominations of Herod—you should hear dear little Attie's views on her Uncle

Berkeley if you want a taste of Caribbean politics—if you're at all curious about our paltry affairs. *You* don't believe any of that Marxist-Leninist nonsense, I know."

"I've heard it before," said Xanthe. "I've been a student too, you know."

"Of course, this is still hypothetical," said Sy, with an inconsequent air, "I'm a mere prospector! Investors will have to be found, of course. And who knows, maybe they'll not be forthcoming. Enfant-Béate's getting off to a slow start—other islands in this archipelago, they're all jumping already, if I may use a local term."

"If you want to stay friends with the Béatois," Lady Seacole interposed, "you know you mustn't compare us to the other islands—not to our disadvantage, at least!" She chuckled; but Sir Berkeley did not laugh with her.

During the mid-morning break, Miranda went to her father and told him, discreetly, that she was tired, and was going back to Belmont to rest; he made her apologies to the Governor, who sent his equerry after her to see her to a taxi. But as soon as the young officer had passed through the gate back into the stockade, she paid off the taxi and took the path away from Belmont, walking toward Saint Blaise Figtree.

Her spirits revived as soon as she left the game, the talk in the box, the cutting of the deal between the politicians and her father and Sy.

When she reached the churchyard, she found one tent marked "Native" and another, alongside, marked "Home Country"; both were showing mighty specimens of flowers and fruit and vegetables. Pretending an interest in the champions with their rosettes, she began sketching the few growers who had remained in attendance on their nurslings. They eyed her and beckoned her over, exclaiming over her scribbles—"And I used to think I was a beautiful woman now!" "I hope you intend to use some color here, where would flowers be without color in them?" Then they let her continue without further interruption. Concentration on her work rubbed her spirits as soothingly as a massage.

The saman had lost its crown in one of the hurricanes that tore across the islands at intervals, and its girth was now much thicker than its height warranted. Like a dark toad, it squatted among the tombs, and the nails stuck in its warty hide glinted as if it had been patched by a thrifty cobbler. The vicar's predecessor had confiscated the small piles of fruit and flowers, Miranda was told; he'd gathered up the couple of bananas, the single pineapple or mango or quilted sugar apple when they appeared overnight, and removed them to the Lady Chapel altar inside Saint Blaise's. But even he had not tried to prise out the nails that were pushed into the bark—though he stripped off the written petitions attached to them.

"Oh, I chose the line of least resistance," the vicar of Saint Blaise had said, indicating the offerings still laid at the foot of the giant wishing tree in the churchyard. It was no use preaching against the custom. Saint Blaise's congregation of planters and managers and factors and shipping clerks and shop owners and servants of the Empire either did not take part in the rites of the tree, or would never have owned up to doing so. The islanders attended different churches, in small square brick edifices marked simply, in handwritten script over their doorways, "Church of God" or "Tabernacle of Christ" or "The Congregation of the Love of Jesus"; these improvised buildings lost their roofs in the hurricanes, but a corrugated tin sheet could be hammered back more easily (after several years' fund-raising efforts) than the tiles and leading of Saint Blaise or other stone churches with tall spires. These were the topmost landmarks on the islands, the special targets of the winds' ferocity, and they therefore stood, gale-torn, with parts missing, like the pirate ships that used to put in to careen and refit their rigging in the hidden cays and coves of the archipelago.

Epitaphs to Everards and Everard wives and mothers and children, to Ingledews and Flitwicks and Ormonds and Barnfathers and other Englishmen and -women and their children were scattered under the long-tailed grasses and the trailing allamanda among the more recent crosses in the graveyard. They made Miranda uneasy, provoked sentimentality she did not want to feel.

Wound in trailing pumpkin vine, there was a granite slab in memory of her grandmother, Estelle Desjours, set against the low wall round the graveyard: "Gathered up in her 35th year." How odd, thought Miranda, to think of a drowned woman being gathered up, rather than going down. And, near the church door, under a fretwork canopy, lay the marble memorial to Sir Kit himself:

> First read then weep when thou art hereby taught
> That Everard lies interrèd here, one that bought
> With loss of Noble Blood Illustrious Name
> Of a Commander Great in Acts of Fame.
> Trained from his youth in Arms, his courage bold
> Attempted brave Exploits and uncontrolled

By Fortune's fiercest Frowns, he still gave forth
Large Narratives of Military worth.
Unsluice your briny floods, what! Can ye keep
Your eyes from tears and see the marble weep?
Burst out for shame: or if ye find no vent
For tears, yet stay, and see the stones relent.

In the last hurricane, the bell of Saint Blaise's had been torn from the belfry and dashed to the graveyard, where it smashed through the roof over the tomb and landed on the gravestone, cracking the sarcophagus and breaking the inscription in two and scoring certain words, so that Miranda, reading it with Xanthe when they'd been taken to visit the monument on the second day of their stay, found a different sentence, "Weep . . . blood . . . in Arms . . . uncontrolled . . . Narratives of . . . shame . . . ," and tracing the fissure with her finger, read it aloud to Xanthe, who laughed.

"As it happens, I'm going to want an ace set of postcards, Miranda, so pull your finger out and maybe I'll use your pictures," she'd said. "But watch it, I don't want nothing new-fangled or polemical; the visitors wouldn't like it. You just do me some nice trad Royal Society of Watercolor jobs . . ." Miranda had returned, but her heart wasn't in the work of making picturesque views of buildings, or constructions, or gravestones.

She wanted to draw people, but the locals on the whole were proving either too shy, standing stockstill or turning away when they saw her head bobbing and her pencil poised, or too eager, striking self-conscious, stiff attitudes; failing people, she liked animals—the trotting pewter-colored piglets, the comical caveys that looked like oversize rabbits but behaved like clever pointers and showed the wagging affection and energy of beagles, the coquettish birds that pecked from your plate at breakfast and the egrets who, unlike almost all the other creatures on the islands, did not blend in the dapple of buff, blue or emerald but moved in their conspicuous white plumage on the stately backs of silvery cattle.

The vicar's call for a harvest-festival display had been a success. Escorting Lady Seacole, who'd agreed to judge the entries, the vicar had been able to oversee a distribution of rosettes calculated not to ruffle the feelings of any of his parishioners from the plantocracy and their progeny; by good fortune, no direct contest between white and black had been offered even within the same tents. Many islanders who cultivated their patch with lettuce and christophene, tomato, sorrel and bay, who shared a mango or a star apple tree with a neighbor, had entered the "Native" competition, alongside "English" lady gardeners, who had concentrated on flowers instead and presented frilled croton bushes, variegated hibiscus in subtle shades of pearl and even blue, and barbed yuccas, sharp as cutlery. Lady Seacole was a nurse, and she judged the flowers before her with cheerful enthusiasm, as if they were new hairstyles that patients in a geriatric ward were sporting.

"There you are!" Xanthe appeared beside Miranda. "I've found you— you thought you could skive off without me, you skunk. You might have said." She gave Miranda a kind of slap, half a caress, half a punch. "You weren't really tired at all. You're just fed up with that god-awful game. Like me. But now we can choose to go where we damn well like," she went on in a whisper, though there was no need. "God, what bliss to be left to our own devices. Much as I love him, Sy's exhausting to be with."

They turned south down the road from the promontory where the church stood, and headed toward the sea. There was still almost nobody about; the island was at a standstill, everyone attending the one-day-special between the Béatois home team and the players from England. Now and then a roar went up behind them, followed by bursts of fire. Miranda was startled by the explosions; Xanthe less jarred. They passed cabins with tin roofs and wooden shutters standing on brick pillars at a little distance from the road; pumpkins and beans were planted in the unfenced areas in between, and chickens and other small creatures foraged underneath; curtains of flowery cotton—or sometimes net, as in the city suburbs of England—blew in the casements, and through an open door, they occasionally glimpsed a table painted azure blue or peppermint green and a calendar with the sacred heart of Jesus or a Beefeater at the Tower of London or Bob Marley in concert. One woman came out and shielded her face, waving the strangers away with the other. In the absence of people, and of children especially, the island seemed to have floated out of time, turning slowly in its drifting passage on the sea, with the breeze speaking in the rigging of the trees and their top-heavy masts creaking, while a phantom crew worked the sheets and manned below decks, so that Miranda struggled to piece together meanings from the scraps of sounds falling around them as they walked in the empty road, before she caught herself at such nonsense and checked her fancies.

The solitude they found themselves in was a contrast to their previous experience of Enfant-Béate. In a few days Miranda had become used to the elfin crowd of little ones running about and the transformation of the older ones into severe scholars, as they set out in the morning, and again at lunchtime and in the late afternoon, walking to and from school in blazers, the girls in neat pinafores with their hair in plaits and ribbons, the boys in gray shorts. But a public holiday had been given out to let everyone attend the game (few would have turned up at school anyway).

One or two animals were tethered at the side of the road; they paid the two young women no attention, though both felt the animals were keenly aware of their passing by and the anomaly of their presence. A sense of disquiet began to form; then they came across a small group clustered in an alley. When they drew nearer, they saw the glow of a bread oven inside and in the tiny subterranean kitchen two women baking, shiny with the heat, loading baskets with the hot round loaves; wood stood in piles to feed the fire.

"This good corn bread, miss, this the finest cornbread," said one, a line of anxiety between her brows. As if I was a medical inspector, Miranda thought, and before she could stop her, the young woman had snapped a loaf in two to show her and run her hand up to the elbow in the flour bag standing on the floor to bring up a fistful of the free-flowing browny-yellow powder. "See, pure as the dew from heaven . . ." She looked even more startled as she uttered these words; the two laboring women stood up straight to face her as if readying themselves for a challenge from the bakkra, the bosses. Miranda, looking in, wanted to soften the air between them, which was setting hard like the cocoon a certain insect spits around an enemy, paralyzing it and tying it fast.

She would so like to find a way of making an image of such women, with their opal eyes and skin lustrous as horse chestnuts, which would be neither exotic-erotic like Ingres or Matisse odalisques, nor indignant-realist like Abolitionist propaganda, neither Noble Savage nor Heroic Victim, but would connect with their history all the same. Many of Miranda's friends from her art student days had turned to photography: the lens's clean surgical objectivity could excise the corrupt legacy of racism, imperialism, Orientalism, and all the other isms that turned all Western consciousness into damaged goods. Or so they hoped.

I can't go along with this completely, thought Miranda. When I take a photograph it still comes out with my stamp on it. My limits show—if only it were so easy to escape out of oneself. The so-called authentic snapshot always pretends that the photographer didn't have to be there, isn't responsible, hadn't anything to do with it. Like a realist novel, like the comments people make about situations they're involved in as if they weren't—her father and Sy, for instance. And Xanthe too . . . She stopped herself, she would make some drawings for her own purposes of Sir Christopher's grave before it was restored, as Sy and Xanthe were planning to do.

The new hotel was to be built on the beach below the church, within walking distance for the hotel guests. And the graveyard would become "a feature" in the amenities.

"Aren't you going to watch the Flinders?" she managed to put to the baker women, who still eyed her with alarm. Her voice struggled through the cocoon their blankness had wound round her.

There came a titter; one grinned at her, all of a sudden, while she caught a soft cry behind her: "Her brother's in the team."

"Won't you be watching then?"

"Later, he's playing later, they not yet called our team into the Chase."

"But . . ."

They were becoming more animated now, Flinders had the power to dissolve the cocoon, to melt the air between them.

". . . you might miss something important. Do you have to work today?"

"We're taking bread down to the stockade—there'll be good business today," one explained.

It was punishingly hot in the doorway near the oven and Xanthe stood back, waiting, but Miranda lingered.

"He's a striker," said the woman with the brother in the game. "And a sweet sight to see when he's in the target. You have to have all your wits to even see them, them balls's moving like greased lightning. But in the stockade, out in the fields . . ." She shrugged.

Before Miranda left them, she bought two sugared buns.

"I'm not sure I paid right."

"Don't worry about it," Xanthe had answered. "You're always worrying—it's not worth it, really. You think everything you do matters so much. It doesn't. And it's a kind of arrogance to think it does."

When they reached the beach, they began to follow the shoreline.

A shallow brown run-off from the mountain spread over the sand, and mangroves rose like giant spiders on its edges; they paddled to cross it, and saw the road crossing it to their right, on arches high above the present water level, for the stream suddenly swelled in stormy weather twelve, fifteen feet above its present trickle. This confluence of fresh water from the mountain, together with the tidal rise and fall of the sea, created the right conditions for oysters.

"This is Sy's idea—one of Sy's ideas," said Xanthe. "He thinks that we might be able to cultivate a special oyster, a crescent-shaped sort that's even more delectable than the big fat scallop-shaped kind. They grow on the stems of mangroves. He thinks that if we had a dam further upstream, we could control the flow of fresh water into the tidal creek here, which oysters need to grow. I'm keen."

After the creek and the bridge came the sea frontage Sy had bought for development, with seven acres abutting the boundary fence of Saint Blaise Figtree and the wishing saman in the churchyard.

"The road will have to be diverted, taken to the north of the church property." Sy had tapped the map in the car the first time they'd visited the site; it was where the first Kit Everard and his men had made their momentous landing; the ruins of some buildings—barrack rooms, an outdoors kitchen—were built of English red brick, transported all the way from an English yard as ballast. The derelict spot was marked with a metal sign, spotted with rust, above a painted notice declaring that anyone found dumping on the beach would be prosecuted. "But how many can read the notice?" Sy had pointed out, shrugging, and the strand was indeed littered with jetsam; between the scorch marks of bonfires lay a bald tire, rusted oil drums, a burst football, sea-sanded bottles, dried palm leaves and coconut trunks spat out by the sea onto the beach, as well as hundreds of conch shells, their spurs worn by the action of the sea into smooth stubby horns.

"The pebbles and shells will have to be cleared as well as the rubbish—'If seven maids with seven mops swept it for half a year, do you suppose, the Walrus said, that they could get it clear?' Dad used to like reciting that to me," Miranda said, tossing the sand with her toes from the edge of the water.

"Oh, we'll need to sink groins and build a breaker out into the bay to keep the good fine sand on the beach," Sy was saying as he watched Xanthe pull off her clothes, step out briskly into the sea and spear her body into a wave. She was a pearly color, and an elegant swimmer (she did it for exercise regularly), smooth strokes, never flailing.

He went on, while he watched her: "The winds scoop it all up and then dump it out to sea and leave this rubbish in exchange. But we can deal with everything—even the might of the sea, of the wind. But shoosh, in case the gods hear us and get a bit cross."

On the day of the match, Xanthe, ankle-deep in the lacy foam on the sea's edge and feeling the sand stream under her toes as the waves pulled back, wanted to swim again; but Miranda persuaded her to strike out farther, up into the hills along the bank of the creek, to find the famous hot springs in the mountains and bathe there instead.

Consequently, Miranda and Xanthe were not in the stockade when the game erupted into a pitched battle and the Governor had to ask the equerry to call in his regiment, the Second Cambrian Fusiliers, to quell the riot and escort the Governor and his guests safely out of the ground. To Miranda's regret, she and Xanthe missed it all.

27

At the moment of crisis, which the Governor had failed to anticipate in the general hubbub, Xanthe and Miranda were walking, excited by their own daring, along a path that led from the huge ancient saman tree hung with dried garlands and scraps of prayers ("Lord, make me well agane," "I thank you, lady, that I live to see my child walk after the bus knock her down"). It took them up along the creek they had forded toward the volcano, Liamuiga itself; sugar cane was dipping in the wind on their left; its tall tasseled lances replaced the rain forest that had clothed the island long ago.

After walking for a while, with ever more dizzy views of the purple-black high slopes of the crater above them and the curving shore and bright sea below, they caught a whiff of something rank.

"Ugh, rotten eggs!" cried out Xanthe.

Soon the pathway took them through curls of steam, stinking of sulfur; they were becoming used to the smell, and even beginning to like it, when they came upon a series of pools in a long narrow clearing shaded by trees between the cane on the one hand and the valley hollowed by the creek on the other. The pools were scooped in dried lime, and their banks gleamed with mineral traces in pink and blue like the interior of a shell; they were connected by channels in which the water flowed hot and fast. The rubble of a low-lying house with gap-toothed windows rose shrouded in lianas, sprouting greenery like hair from an old man's ears and nostrils.

All over the island, there were overgrown remains of plantation mansions, sugar-mill towers and boiling houses concealed in the vegetation on the shallow lower slopes of the volcano, but Xanthe now recalled how Sy had mentioned, in the course of one of his prolonged rhapsodies on the possibilities of the islands, the Hôtel des Bains, once renowned for its elegance. She realized that they had stumbled upon its ruins. "It was the most fashionable watering hole of the gratin of the plantocracy," Sy had said, "where the liverish and the bilious— arthritis and rheumatism do not plague old bones in the tropics—the rickety and the scrofulous came to take the cure in a summer station, in the shelter of the trees, out of the harrying of the restless wind. They enjoyed lively little outings too, to the crater, to the waterfall, in pony traps. As well as games of piquet and cribbage. So civilized!"

"I can't believe our luck." Xanthe whipped a look around, and began to take off her dress. "And there's bound not to be a soul, what with the Flinders and everything."

"You think it's safe? I mean . . ."

"You're asking me? I thought you were the one who was never afraid, who'd done everything there is to do at the age of four and a half. Come on." Xanthe was testing the temperature of the different basins and calling out reports on the variations of heat.

"I don't know—there might be broken glass . . . worms . . . bilharzia . . . I don't know, we could catch something."

"Keep your knickers on, then, if you're afraid of something swimming up you, ha-ha!"

Kit had made a complicated bet on the outcome of this game, as one in a series of inter-island and international matches; he would only know how much he had won by the end of the season. It wasn't the size of the figure that interested him, but the different odds produced by the infinite number of variables in the succeeding games; this was as heady to contemplate as the excellent champagne Sy had presented to the Governor, judiciously in time for chilling in the sunken icehouse at Belmont. (Sy had been relieved to see it produced before luncheon; he had feared that it might have been held back in exchange for an inferior regional punch, mixed with lots of fruit juice and sugar.)

Kit knew his father had refused to return for the anniversary because

he deplored the agitation taking over the game. "I can't tolerate it—
I'm not against innovation, you know me. Reform? I've introduced
reforms by the dozen myself. It was I who redefined the rules of the
Chase, after all, so that the striker didn't have to fall half-dead from
wounds before he could retire from the Target, it was I who . . . Good
Lord, I don't have to tell you this! I really cannot imagine what possessed
the committee to allow this nationalism to creep in . . . I've pleaded
with them, I've said, 'The Game is a game, not a display of national
might. It's Flinders, the game that united all colors and creeds—when
there was an Empire worthy of the name.'

"But they wouldn't listen to me. I'm over the hill, vieux jeu, out to
grass. So we're not only condemned to rush play to meet the conditions
of these accursed outright defeats or victories, but we're forced to see
the whole thing in terms of contending nations. Both sides should
wear the same gear, goddammit, and players should feel loyal to their
fellows, not their flag. Dressing a player up in a Union Jack—or, worse,
some invented rag in orange and magenta . . ." He groaned aloud.
"It's asking for trouble too. It's turning the game into the focus of all
the discontent and hate and rivalry and bitterness that it used
to . . . massage."

Kit had said nothing, but remembered instead the long boat trip he
had made with the team the year that he dropped a winch on his foot
and broke the toe and could never run again with the agility necessary
in the game. His father had had dreams of him then as his successor;
he had never really forgiven Kit for this infant clumsiness, or believed
in its effect. Kit's failure in this respect rankled beneath all the other
resentments, against his insolvency, against his inability to stop appearing as an outsider. To his father, Kit Everard looked like a man
who has somehow managed to find his way in, but has never learned
the insider's ways.

The pools fashioned in the limestone by the springs were shaded; a
breadfruit tree, its generous leaves like large hands, stood on one side
of the clearing, and a tangle of several smaller trees, with waxy jade
leaves, grew nearby, flourishing on the rich minerals the volcano's
waters fed into the soil. The sun had not cleared the top of the
breadfruit tree when Miranda began paddling in the hot stream, ac-
customing herself to the temperature, walking toward the spate in the
center of the stream's bed, from the lukewarm pool that was farthest

from the source, to the deepest and hottest pool next to the very lips in the earth that parted to let the bluish-milky water bubble up. But as she was lying in the hottest pool, the sun climbed the sky and the shadows of the leaves like hands no longer reached to shelter her from the heat of the zenith.

She was flooded with light; it set spots dancing in her vision. They were insects, she thought at first, then realized that the sunlight was so bright that it had illuminated the motes floating inside her own eyes, until she could see the cells and, in the tissue of the cells, thread veins like little tadpoles. It was scary, and she closed her eyes and rolled them inside to clear them, as if dust had got in. But then she saw only the infra-red afterimage of the same phenomenon; so she opened her eyes again, and the bowl of light in which she floated winded her with its absolute clarity and density.

Xanthe was lying beside her; with unusual gentleness, she put out a hand to Miranda, and squeezed her arm.

"It's so brilliant of you to take us away from . . ." She spoke drowsily, in a murmur, and Miranda touched her hand in response, flooded by the pleasure it gave her to find Xanthe softening. "We'll soak here for a while, and then lie in the creek. From hot to cold, delicious." She pretended to shiver in anticipation.

Sitting in the warm talcum-like sediment of the sulfur pool, with the steam rising from the almost viscous turquoise surface of the water and her limbs scalded pink by the heat, Miranda felt a wildness clutch her, a wildness that was made up of risk and terror and despair and intense joy all at once. She thought of the bodies that had steeped themselves here before her, she luxuriated in the feeling of closeness, a kind of forbidden closeness, as if, like Goldilocks indeed, they were intruding, snuggling in someone's else's bed.

"Xanthe, are you really thinking of getting married?" Her growing stupor in the warm water emboldened Miranda.

"Oh, I just might." Xanthe had her eyes closed. Miranda squinted at her in the glare to see her expression, to take in whether she was joking. Her lashes sparkled in the sunlight like the gold fringes on a doll's eyes; Miranda used to push her dolls' eyeballs in to see behind them, to their mechanism of opening and shutting. Only then could she be certain they weren't able to see her, weren't real.

"Sy?"

"Why surprised?"

"You could go on living together. It seems drastic to marry."

"It'll certainly get Poppa's goat."

It would, of course, but Miranda was surprised that Xanthe was able to declare it; it came to her as part of the general illumination in which she was drenched, even as she was sitting soaking in the dazzled dark behind her closed eyes: Xanthe was not merely facing his fury, but actively desiring it.

Miranda announced, "I'm never going to get married. I'm never going to let anyone get so close they can tell me what to do, know what I think, have a right to me. Marriage is slavery—for women! Just another form of paid sex. And I never make men pay for sex." She ended on a high chuckle. "And I shall kill myself when I have to start."

"Phewy, listen to you, Miss Go-It-Alone. You're so bloody naive, Miranda." Her words were sharp, but she spoke languorously, as if the quality of wine or food were her subject. "Much the easiest and best way to get rid of that . . . dependency you seem to hate is to have a setup that's completely legit. To be free you've got to be able to write in your particulars on the form the way it's set out: husband's occupation, permanent address, department-store customer accounts. You've got to have all that to get round it. You may think you're free, swanning around without connections to anything." Xanthe was speaking from some hidden place inside her she had rarely shown to Miranda, and Miranda listened. "I think your kind of freedom hampers you," Xanthe went on. "I'm much less . . . contingent than you, because I accept it as part of the way things are for little girls like you and me. Ha! I just know that I have to choose rather carefully who I'm to depend on. Error in this area would be something of a nuisance—though I wouldn't mind being a young divorcée." Xanthe's voice was slowing down, growing lazy and dreamy as she lay side by side with Miranda in the pool. "This is such bliss. This water feels so soft, like rose petals . . . Sy's right about Poppa. Everybody loves him, because he seems so mild and calm, but that's just his way of keeping you in his power. All that rot about his *sangay*, it's sheer mystification, there's nothing behind it. I'm grown-up now, I'm not his little woman anymore. You know, Poppa would have liked to marry me himself if he could, that's what Sy says, and he's spot on, I'm telling you. Under lock and key, lock and key, in the tower forever."

"Oh, Xanthe," murmured Miranda, who was also getting drowsy in the warm bath as she attended to her. "You're so hard on him. Poor

Grandpa, poor old Ant. He'd be heartbroken if he could hear you."

"Let him be heartbroken. You've never been thwarted every step of the way like I have."

"He's old, the old can't help thinking of themselves. He loves you, he loves you too much. He doesn't thwart you—really! Nobody could. You're impossible to thwart . . ."

"Listen to you. You're such a softy. Think of how he's treated Kit— he's humiliated him every step of the way, and Kit still can't get away from him. Look at him now, playing at being Poppa here, when everyone knows he comes a really poor second. Go on, admit it. It's pathetic. Then just look at the way Sy opens up to everybody, lavishes everything on us. They're chalk and cheese, and I like cheese."

She's swapping one dad for another, Miranda was thinking as she grew sleepier in the pool. Aloud she said, "Most women get married as little girls, turn their husbands into little boys and end up being called Mummy by them. At least Kit and Astrid didn't do that, whatever else they did to each other. Honestly, I'm never going to get married. Think of having Sy beside you talking his head off your whole life long."

"I'll be able to get on with things, won't have to worry about finding a mate, squandering time and energy looking for love. And it'd mean an end to the endless boring conversations I'm always having with Poppa about my future. It would settle the matter once and for all. Now I've found my man, and I can get on with the job."

"What job?"

"The job of living. The getting of pleasure! 'The lineaments of gratified desire'—not love, of course, in some stupid, narrow sense."

"God, how can you be so hard-nosed in this fabulous place? Stop it, stop . . . ranting. Let go for once, come on. Relax." And she hummed, "Dream, dream, dream."

"You know something? I never realized it before I met Sy. I think I've always hated Poppa, as far back as I can remember."

"And I always thought you were a changeling. When I first saw you in that row of pink cots in the hospital just after you were born. Now I know you are. Poor old Ant."

"He's a monster, he's not poor at all."

Miranda was asleep in the sulfur pool when a mud pat landed on her shoulder. It was soft and warm. All the silt around the springs had the look and texture of ice cream, pink and pistachio and vanilla in a kind of warm cassata. Miranda opened her eyes, but with the sun high above the pool, she only managed slits, and the dazzle prevented her from making out who had thrown the mud at her. Another pat landed on her, this time on her cheek; again not hard, and the sensation wasn't unpleasant, though she felt a first twinge of alarm. Beside her, Xanthe was afloat, her head with her pale hair fanning out anchored on the edge of the cistern. She too opened her eyes as mud landed on her from the trees to her left.

Afterward, everyone was furious with them, from the incumbent Governor who would have been horribly embarrassed if anything had happened to hurt them seriously, to Sy, who almost cried and talked about rape and murder and other horrendous possibilities they'd escaped. "Why do you think I never suggested a jaunt into the hills to find the old Hotel des Bains—I know about that riffraff squatting there. He's a nasty piece of work, that fellow—what's his name? Yes, Dunn. Jimmy Dunn. Ex-policeman. There was a spot of trouble. Got mixed up in something, stripped of his badge, and took to the hills. If I'd known you were off on your own there . . ."

"We're all right," Miranda insisted.

"Just furious," said Xanthe.

At the time of the assault, it was funny, Miranda and Xanthe agreed, that neither of them had imagined rape; Miranda had been dreaming, in the moments before she was pelted with mud, that she was making love with some large, hot creature, like a steam cloud enveloping her and burrowing into every pore and access point. Miranda had always been unable to avert danger; it was a failure of imagination, or even of gender in her, the scar of her unprotected daughterhood; she exposed herself because her mother and her father had never had the energy or the will to keep her under guard, like Xanthe.

Xanthe's hackles were quicker, and she was lying in shadow, to protect her pale skin, so she was able to pick out their tormentors from the moment she woke. They were chits of children, and though on the whole she did not see the point of children, she was not afraid of them.

They both sat up in the water, and Miranda tried to adjust her eyes to the blazing light as the mud came at her at shorter intervals and she could hear little grunts as her assailants stooped and filled their fists with the stuff and sent it flying.

"Hey," she called out. "Stop, it's too much now." She wasn't angry, not yet, and now that she could see them, and as they were only about six or seven years old, and little girls at that (or so she thought at first) in white dresses and kerchiefs as if they were going to communion, she thought it was a joke.

They were grouped together, and they weren't laughing in response to her, and it was then, for the first time, that she was struck by— not fear—she was never frightened of children, whom she liked when she encountered them, but by repentance. She and Xanthe were trespassing. They shouldn't have just barged in, but sought permission. But where, and how? The mud was coming faster now, and she called out, "That's enough now, really, we're going to get out now. We're sorry." She twisted round partly to give her back to the little monsters, partly to grab her clothes and make her getaway as gracefully as possible.

Xanthe was raging, as she climbed out and looked for her clothes, and when she couldn't find them, she lunged out toward the group, running across the clearing to hit them and grab back the clothes they were now flourishing aloft—Miranda saw her Liberty print skirt like a banner above a little girl's head—no, a little boy's head, as it turned out, for all the children were wearing long white tunics and a kind of turban. But they scampered from Xanthe, breaking into high mocking yelps, like animals calling out the borders of their territory.

Miranda did not give chase, she grew severe; undignified as it was in her semi-naked state, she faced them, streaked with mud and boiled bright pink as a peeled prawn and walking toward them to demand her clothes. One of them now picked up and threw something at her that wasn't the soft mud of the sulfur baths, because they were retreating from her into the wooded part, and the ground was different, the missiles were spiny husks and nuts, pellet-hard and even hooked; laughing, they aimed at her and sometimes struck her as she tried to pounce on them.

"Now, look, this isn't a nice game anymore, give me back my clothes. That's enough now, you've had your fun, I know it's bloody funny to see a grown-up running around starkers, but I've got to get dressed now. Come on, don't be unkind, you know you're being unkind; how would you like it if someone took away your clothes and made you walk around naked in front of people?"

She had a memory then of naked children—and adults—in pictures of the slave trade; Sy, one evening, even said that the planters in the old days liked to have the house slaves serving topless. "There's nothing new under the sun," he'd said. "No pleasure that hasn't been tried already."

She stopped running after their tormentors, the ground underfoot was treacherous to her feet, unaccustomed to go without shoes; one shoulder was hurting from a larger shard one of her persecutors had hurled at her, and she stooped to pick it up to see what it might be; it looked like an ornament, perhaps for a belt, or for hair, encrusted with deposits from the sulfur baths, lunar silver and iridescent and crackled with mineral lace, like a fragment of ancient glass. She kept it in the palm of her hand, as she continued to try and cajole her persecutors. But she was having no effect: they had even stopped jeering and had never once replied. It was as if they were deaf and dumb; she was now afraid.

Behind her, sitting clasping her knees to her chest to cover her nakedness (she had not even kept on her knickers), Xanthe was shouting, "Give up, Miranda, don't waste your time on those charming little fuckers."

Later, they were able to laugh about it; about the spectacle they would have made returning to Jamieston dressed in next to nothing and covered in mud; maybe they would have stripped some banana leaves from a tree and pinned them together with thorns to avoid a complete scandal. But at the time, Miranda was too distressed to think clearly, and Xanthe so enraged she was past thinking, occasionally raising her head to scream abuse at the vanished children.

"God, if I ever see you again, I'll wring your bloody necks." A nut hit Xanthe in the face as she was shouting, and blood started to flow into her eyes, and then she huddled her limbs together and started to rock as she sobbed dry tears. Miranda hugged her, and soothed her, but she too felt choked up now, that a bunch of little kids should take her for an enemy; so she wept as well.

The pelting had stopped altogether, when a man's voice said, "Here are your clothes. Now get up and leave us."

Miranda looked up, still crouched, covering her bare body so that he could not look at her. Like the children, he too was wearing a long white tunic like a jellaba, and a headcloth also of white twisted loosely on his curls; he had a short beard around full lips. "My children are strictly brought up," he said. "We have standards for our women, and when they see others who live . . . differently . . . they do not like it."

"We have standards too," muttered Xanthe, pulling her items of clothing from the bundle on the ground between her and the man. "We don't think flinging mud at perfect strangers is good manners." She held the clothes to her body to cover herself, and went on, red in the face, with blood smeared on her cheek and running into her mouth, which she wiped away with a furious gesture. "Stoning people went out with the Dark Ages where we come from."

"Xanthe!" Miranda put out a hand to restrain her. "Come on, let's get dressed, let's get out of here."

The man turned in silence, and Xanthe, stung by his impassivity, hurled at his white back before he stepped into the tall green wands of the sugar cane: "You fucking bastard. You won't get away with this."

Miranda and Xanthe's sandals remained on the ground, neatly side by side, as if they had left them there to pray at a shrine. Miranda picked up Xanthe's and took them over to her, then dipped her skirt in the pool and wiped the wound on Xanthe's forehead and bathed her eyes. She had the missile that had hit her earlier still in her hand, and as she tended Xanthe she put it in the pocket of her skirt. She felt the full weight of the man's contempt, for no anger like Xanthe's rose to protect her against it; she felt how she had polluted him and his family. His displeasure and his scorn had scalded her, as she saw him in her mind's eye again, turning on his heel in silence and leaving them loftily to disappear into the canebrakes, following the children.

A section of the crowd supporting the Home team of the Béatois burst through the perimeter fence and overran the Stockade when the umpire dismissed their last-but-one player. He was only two strikes short of completing the contract for a Creek and ensuring an overall victory over the Visitors that day. The spectators behind them began hurling bottles and tins and flagpoles, and even whole empty oil drums onto the field, and when the stewards shouted through megaphones for order, they could not make themselves heard for the catcalling and blowing of conches and explosions of firecrackers. So the police rushed the protesters with truncheons whirling, and were met with a rain of missiles. (Later, people said some bad elements had come with riot in mind, their pockets full, convenient beer cans stashed under the benches.)

For ten loud minutes the players of both teams stood helplessly on the stockade turf. The trembling umpire tried to run away, as the protesters swelled in numbers and struggles broke out raggedly the length of the Chase, between factions of Home fans and local British patriots as well as between the troublemakers and the forces of order. But he was hauled back. Then the English captain went over to the Béatois captain and the latter signaled to another man, the last player, to take up position in the Target at the end of the Chase, but he hesitated before crossing the pitch to his post in the Target, for the crowd was baying louder and louder for the dismissed man to return, howling his name. The captains of both teams then ordered the last man to play, but in the uproar, he could not gather himself together; he lunged at the ball and missed it, even though the first pitcher was all nerves too and had thrown a soft wavy arc that a schoolboy could have returned to the edge of the Stockade.

When the crowd saw this, the din increased and more furious spectators hurled themselves onto the field, breaking through the line of police and pouring into the Creek itself; so the Cambrian Fusiliers charged, and the carefully rolled turf of the Stockade was churned by their horses' hooves, which caused many in the crowd now fleeing the place more sorrow than the blows rained on the protesters. The captains exchanged looks, and with the Stockade strewn with increasing débris of glass and tin and cardboard and stakes and poles, they made their way through to the pavilion, with as much dignity as they could, followed reluctantly by their teams. One Visitor was tackled by a screaming islander, and hit him back; this unleashed even more rage in those nearby, which grew in intensity when the loudspeakers unnecessarily announced that the match was over, leaving the Home players defeated by a hair. Seeing the frenzy, the Governor gave the command to the equerry to call in an escort of cavalry for himself and his party, including Sir Berkeley and Lady Seacole, Kit Everard and Simon Nebris.

Half an hour later, as Miranda and Xanthe were trailing back in exhaustion to Jamieston, they found the main street in an uproar, with the crowd from the Stockade—virtually the entire population of the town—running pell-mell and screaming as huge horses with gleaming harnesses, and cavalrymen in white-and-gold-braided dolmans, followed the orders to disperse them by charging into them and galloping through, some lashing out with their crops from side to side, some with sabers to boot, others merely with truncheons. "It was bloody fantastic more people weren't badly hurt," Sy said later. (There were only five casualties at the hospital in Jamieston, but this was a most unreliable indication; many wounded stayed back fearing prosecution.) Kit said, "They shouldn't be allowed drink. It's insane to souse an excitable crowd like that in barrels of rum and gallons of beer. I'm surprised Flinders ever gets a decent play in such conditions. I know what the sauce does. I know what it does to me." And to Astrid, he thought. To both of us. Yet we enjoyed our evenings, getting squiffy, then a little plastered, then, in our salad days, falling into bed or the equivalent of.

The umpire had known the risk he ran, knew how close the Home team was to victory, how high feelings were running, because their captain had led them so timorously. But their champions had managed to outplay his incompetence and almost cancel the shame of his equivocations, only to find the sweets of the day snatched from them.

"Even if the ball did graze the Target," some said, commenting on the crisis later, "after it bounced off the striker's stick—and no one is sure that he saw it do that—the umpire shouldn't have declared our man fallen."

"He didn't realize," said Sir Berkeley Seacole, "that this is a historic stage in the game, when even we, from a small, backward place like Enfant-Béate, black people, former bondsmen, protégés, pupils, are emerging as world-class players. The umpire may have been mistaken. He was sticking to the rules. But the time has come when we must change the rules sometimes. Fair play is not always fair to all sides in the question. Flinders is a great teacher—but the lessons are not always instantly understandable."

The equerry, mounted on his great chestnut mare, spotted Miranda and Xanthe in an alley between two stores where they were hiding, clinging together, from the fray.

"Hold on, girls, I'll get a guard to you in a tick."

They held on to each other, not speaking, and accepted an arm of the two policemen who shortly appeared and walked them to a car, got in with them, and drove past the now thinning skirmishers to Belmont and the Governor's mansion.

"We're fine," said Miranda, in reply to their concern. "We just went for a walk. Xanthe slipped and hit her head on the root of a tree and it bled rather a lot—head wounds do."

Xanthe gave a little gasp, and Miranda squeezed her by the arm to keep her from saying more. "It's not serious, in fact."

Two days later, Xanthe took the launch and a boy from the hotel and crossed the straits; she went into the main post office in Jamiestown, where the colonial arms of the island on a shield above the counter had been repainted in bright colors so that the feathered Indian bearer on one side was rose-red and gleaming ebony on the other, like the flesh and the pip of a watermelon. She sent a cable to her father: in those years there was no telephone link between Enfant-Béate and the home country and Sy had been informed by the Governor that Sir Anthony Everard had been in touch with the Colonial Office in some consternation after receiving notice of the riot at the Stockade.

POPPA DARLING DO NOT WORRY EVERYTHING DANDY EXCEPT STOCKADE TURF STOP SY SENDS LOVE STOP MARRIED BY TIME THIS REACHES YOU STOP SEND BLESSING STOP ALL LOVE GOLDIE

In her room, Miranda held in her hand the sharp object the children had thrown at her; beneath the encrustation of salts she found a piece of oyster shell; at a certain angle, it seemed as if it had been carved on purpose to look like a bird in flight.

Its birdlike form must be an illusion, she decided, like those shadows in snow that resemble the face of Jesus or bleached animal bones in English fields that look like Henry Moores. Unless it was of recent manufacture, made by the children themselves. It was common knowledge that the indigenous people who had lived on the islands during the time of first contacts had left nothing of themselves behind.

28

Gillian Everard to Xanthe
Kensington, 197–

Darling Goldie,
I expect you know what you're doing, you've always been one to
land on your feet. You reached your majority some time ago and
parents these days have no authority anymore—children come first,
anything they want they can have—just like that. It was different
in my day. We didn't expect you to ask our permission, though your
father would have liked you to listen to his advice. He loves you
very much—I know you know that—and with you so far away, I'm
left with the explaining to do on your behalf. I confess it defeats
me, though I married an older man myself and have been happy with
your father. But he had been married once before and widowed—
Sy's a different kettle of fish altogether. Will you have children?
What kind of a marriage is it? We try to understand, but you haven't
helped us, not a word since that cable. You've broken his heart,
that's the long and the short of it. I wouldn't have thought it possible
for a man with so much—the esteem of thousands, all the *sangay* in
the world on tap, the faithful love of friends, and, I believe, comfort
and harmony at home—to be so utterly destroyed by something like

this. His appetite's never been good, as you may remember if you cast your mind back to when we last saw you, and now—well—if air can keep him alive, air will. He won't write to you himself—but I'm not so shattered nor so proud, so I'm asking you—please, give us a sign of life. You probably know that Sy's in touch, but your father wants to hear from you. Sy tells us how thrilled he is, what a fantastic girl you are, how he's made all kinds of financial arrangements for you—and even for Miranda—just because you two are thick as thieves and he says he's grateful to her for being such a good friend to you both. He'd love to do something for us, anything, he says—he's invited us out to one of those ghastly nouveau riche hotels of his. But it doesn't wash with your father. He'll never forgive him—he was looking forward to your wedding as the proudest day of his life, and you cheated him—you just chucked yourself away, he can't get over that. In many ways it's turned him into an old man—I hardly recognize him, he's wasting away and I can't forgive you for that either, Goldie, when you have everything still before you and he has only you. Or that's how he sees it, which I find charming, as you might imagine. But then imagination was never your strong suit, was it. I was brought up to believe that life repaid in kind, "Do as you would be done by" was a kind of charm that worked. But it's not true, you've always had your way without lifting your little finger. I'd better stop now, I don't want to get angry. It's your life. Except that it isn't, it's mine and your father's too. I hope that at least it's made you happy.

With my love, truly, in spite of everything,

Mummy

29

LIAMUIGA, 1983

UNDER THE BROAD-BRIMMED Panama with the pastel-blue ribbon of his London club, Simon Nebris had gone bald. He had not lost his hair out of anxiety in the ten years since he had bought the land on the promontory and developed his new hotel; The Spice of Life, as the 180-bed establishment was called, was a success. It suffered from expected snags, of course—the island's generator could not always be counted on to produce the steady current which visitors from America desired and he had been obliged to install independent backup; Xanthe's efforts at provisioning the hotel from its own kitchen garden had been frustrated by some guests' insisting on familiar home comforts such as William pears, which rotted in the tropics. The tree rats and the caveys and some insects were troublesome too (though all the rooms had automatic screen doors and the surf of mosquito veiling foamed above each bed).

"Now I understand the real character of the Hanging Gardens of Babylon," Sy would remark, "since that would be a tremendous solution to some of the dear little pests. How they so love to gobble up all Goldie's succulent shoots and nibble through the netting to feast on her soft fruit! Really, we should all still live in baskets in the trees— like the tribespeople who were once here!"

In the slow season, Sy and Xanthe usually came back to London, and entertained from a small Chelsea hotel whose proprietors came to stay reciprocally in Enfant-Béate at a reduced, friendly rate. Sy visited his club and ordered wines, Xanthe renewed her wardrobe, sampled the latest restaurants and made notes of new fashions in taste ("Every year a new vegetable—I do wish yams or akee or something easy for me to grow would become the mange-tout of the hour.") Kit never came with them; he managed the two places in their absence. "We have to have someone responsible, absolutely," they'd explain. "Especially at the casino. You never know what might happen." But Miranda knew that Kit would not come back because he was afraid of her mother's building resentment at her abandonment: Astrid had convinced herself that Kit's acceptance of her last attempted withdrawal from their marriage amounted to profound treachery.

Sy would rattle on, the blithe voice offering Miranda his understanding of the situation: "Kit won't help himself, he wallows in his loneliness. Why doesn't he get himself a girl from the islands, forget England and Astrid and his father? I'm telling you, I do wish the old boy would finally pop off. It'd be a release for all of you. It's very hard on Goldie that he's clinging on; a second childhood, so undignified. Babbling on about his daughter." "And past scores at Flinders, as well," Xanthe put in, impatiently. Sy carried on, deflecting her. "Kit drinks enough, you'd think he'd be able to forget whatever it is that's eating him. But no, it's all present to him—his failed marriage, his failed relations with Ant—you name it, just as if he'd never left the old place. Thank God, darling, the family melancholy passed you by." So Sy was pleased that Kit had taken to the oyster fishing with silent concentration; with the two men who did the work, Kit learned the trade, sitting in the stern while they puttered out quietly at low tide in the estuary to check the beds, watching the surface of the water, the shadows of fish and other sea creatures shifting the shadows over the gleam of the mother-of-pearl matrix where the oysters grew.

"Xanthe's inherited Ant's old flair," Sy also said, in the course of another of their summer visits. "Kit, too, it must be said, has a certain way with Dame Fortune—sometimes." Xanthe tossed her head. "It's just common sense," she retorted. "It's nothing to do with *sangay*. That's all pure superstitious rubbish. But I'm lucky in one way, I don't hanker—not like some people." She laughed and looked Miranda in the eye and offered her more to drink.

Hurricane Margaret swept the island in the new hotel's fourth year—

they could hardly have hoped otherwise—but the warning reached them from the meteorological station on the mainland in time to batten down. The oyster beds were uprooted and hurled out to sea by the enraged churning of the waves, and consequently they'd had to start them again from imported Japanese seed. The hotel had suffered superficial damage otherwise; bespattered with flying earth and animals and branches and other foliage, the cottages and the main house of The Spice of Life looked devastated when Sy crept out into the gray lull after the storm was spent; but the American engineering techniques used on the foundations were developed to withstand the grinding of the earth's plates on the San Andreas Fault, and they had been further refined by architects in Japan to withstand wind speeds of over two hundred miles an hour. The hotel buildings swayed and bent to the force of the hurricane, like the cane itself, which looked threshed to the ground, but sprang up again in time, while the cabins and the tin-roofed huts of the islanders' homes, as well as other buildings—the churches, the schools—were smashed to smithereens.

Sy was still rotund, pinkish-cream all over; he never went into the sun, and kept himself covered in baggy linens from head to toe in daylight hours. In their sleeping quarters—he and Xanthe had always had separate bedrooms—he floated bare and adipose under braided jellabas he'd bought wintering in Marrakesh in the early sixties. His fatness was still densely textured, reliable rather than sickly, and Xanthe found his flesh comforting and his good humor uncrushable. "He's still my fat knight," she told Miranda.

Over the years, Xanthe's fairness had become peculiar in the climate: her skin still had a pearly sheen from the sunblocks she used to prevent freckling and the blotching of incipient skin cancer which appeared on her limbs, for, unlike Sy, she loved the sea and struck out from the shore in the early morning when the water was calm and pale as the phantom ring of the new moon. Her hair had kept the gold flossiness of a tassel of barley, but such child's hair looked incongruous framing the face of a woman in her mid-thirties, with its heat-dried paperiness, and made her look like a typhoid survivor whose hair has grown back with primordial fineness. Miranda noted consolingly to herself that she had changed less than Xanthe with the years; she now had her hair cut short so that the curls became spiky. Xanthe's vanity had never been of the kind that worried she might be fading or aging; she was thoroughly entertained by the circumstances of her life—repining, yearning, experiencing absence or loss continued to be foreign to her nature. She had reached contentment to a degree Miranda could only observe, for the older woman could not even imagine happiness consisting of a husband like Sy, a job like the hotels Xanthe ran, with their clientèle, their odd and risky accommodations with governments, financial enterprises, former empires.

The Spice of Life did not allow children as guests; the proprietress decreed they were a nuisance and reckoned that enough people in the world of winter travel would agree to fill their beds. "A gambling hotel does not need a crèche," she declared. The hotel afforded her the pleasures she wanted in all sufficiency: it was always growing, changing, acquiring a new character under the impulses of her fantasy. She wrote out each day's menu and posted it on the guests' notice board in Reception. During the Christmas season, she added an "authentic Caribbean appetizer!" for the visitors from Florida and Vancouver who had the Northerners' sweet tooth: "Oysters in Gravy Bastard—Simmered in their own juice and a dash of local beer, with a touch of ginger, saffron, and—this is the essential, magic ingredient," she would say as she beckoned over the guests on the veranda at sunset to taste—"sugar: just a sprinkling, so you don't know if it's there or not."

Sy chortled at Xanthe's penchant for vulgarity—for one summer, she bought stock from Mikimoto, and for a special Lucky Dip at Thanksgiving (November was high season), she filled the pool with Japanese pearl oysters; two young girls dived on request and brought up a shell—sometimes a black pearl, sometimes a pink one. "Never ever would I have dreamed of such a thing in the quiet old days of Xanadu," Sy remarked, but he appreciated her business sense: the pearl fishers were a huge success, especially with the companions of the gamblers who came for the casino. The markup on the pearls rose a hundred and fifty percent; nobody noticed.

Sy still held the only gambling permit on the two islands that made up the independent nation of Liamuiga (the old name reclaimed), much to the annoyance of the inhabitants of Oualie, who envied the flow of dollars the tables attracted. Mr. Nebris was a responsible citizen, all in all, in the view of the government: his hotel created jobs, earned the foreign currency they needed, and the clientèle was prevented from corrupting the locals by strict safeguards: no Béatois was allowed to stay there, or of course play in the casino. The croupiers were imported, too, to prevent creeping contamination. Kit was the exception. Kit, the manager of the casino, Béatois by birth, by ancestry and history, as the account offered to the guests made sure to inform them, lent tone historic and *mondain*, presiding every evening in a white linen tuxedo with cream satin revers. His indigenous status was overlooked with respect to the casino laws, for reasons everyone concerned was careful not to examine.

Xanthe's most cherished enterprise had been restoring the former Hôtel des Bains in the hills; after the incident at the springs during the game that first time she came to Enfant-Béate, she had renounced bringing charges against the squatters, much to Miranda's relief. Later, when Miranda had returned to London, Sy agreed with Xanthe that buying the ruins from the government, and evicting Jimmy Dunn, his family and all its extended members, would be condign punishment.

The Spice of Life now ran a shuttle service in the mornings and evenings for guests who wanted the latest in hydrotherapy. A mini-moke, fringed in ruched cotton, took them up the hill path past Saint Blaise and the old cemetery to the banks of the creek, and the complex of sulfur pools at various temperatures. The Béatois staff, men and women, dressed in nursing white, attended the baths. The site had been left wild and rocky, but fitted with sluices and pipes and jets so that the flow could be controlled, the pressure raised to massage the limbs of the bathers, the basins emptied and cleaned at will. The fine, health-giving silt with its mineral glints and specks was gathered and filtered and returned to vats for use in massage and mud therapy: the attendants painted it on the bodies of the guests with a brush and left them sunning like aboriginal warriors till it caked. Then, after the various traces of iron and magnesium and other nutritives had sunk through their epidermis in the fulfillment of "holistic somatic therapy," they were encouraged to take a dip in the plunge pool. There, the bright cold cascade of the creek fell from a shelf of rock, and then swirled in a deep bowl Xanthe'd had blasted into the rock with dynamite. It was fringed with maidenhair fern, which the sunlight turned glass-green; casuarina and tamarinds had been planted to give shade to the watering places, while on the terrace of the ruined hotel stood pots of plants, shrimp flowers dangling their articulated bodies; in season, creamy datura hung in heavy opiate bells.

Xanthe had not wholly rebuilt the old Hôtel des Bains building, but repaired it in its dilapidation to create a folly in the spirit of Beckford, with awnings of lemon-yellow slub linen and umbrellas over the tables to match. There, drinks were served, and light meals, lively salads and grilled fish; it was a forest solitude, the only sounds the cheeping of banana quits on the search for tidbits, and the creak of the trees, as if there were invisible inhabitants up above in the forest canopy who, while trying to walk without making themselves heard, now and then came into contact with a loose floorboard.

The spa had expanded employment in the hotel by two dozen jobs; photographs in travel magazines showed the long tanned limbs of models from Germany and Scandinavia naked on the edges of the pools while the medically white-tunicked islanders ministered to them with the mud, turning them into lunar specters, with panda eyes under the face mask.

In the evenings, over dinner, the guests who had been to the spa encouraged others to follow their example.

"You won't believe how well you feel! It's better than three weeks in a health farm at home. You really should try it!"

Nobody ever spoke aloud the real specialness of the pleasure: that the tingling and the shiver and the plenitude of it were all intensified by the hands and breath and labor of the islanders: whether it was a girl or a boy ("girl" or "boy" was the mot juste, as the attendants were picked for their youth, stamina and willingness), a guest was carried back to a forbidden dreamworld. As the black hands stroked on the mud, or kneaded the knotted muscles with supple fingers, sometimes grunting (yes, that excitement too) with the effort and arched over the prone bodies of their clients, patting and rubbing, smoothing and paring, applying cloths or scrubbing with loofahs, even if the contact did not go any further (but how often, the client would cry, "Yes, there, oh, yes, just there, yes, Yes, YES"), the stimulus was exquisite.

Sy and Xanthe had decided not to provide bedrooms at the Hotel des Bains, partly because, with Xanadu still open for the high season on Oualie as an old-fashioned haven, small and quiet in the Caribbean style of the past, they had their hands full, but also because they did not want to have to cope with the problem of staff and guests striking up longer intimacies than the hydrotherapeutic processes allowed. It was simple to turn a blind eye to what happened on the massage couches, or, later, on the beach; bedroom assignations would be harder to overlook without the neglect becoming clear and possibly, in the eyes of some, unsavory.

Jobs in the spa were popular. The tips were rumored on the whole to be munificent.

The photographs Xanthe showed Miranda in the hotel album filled her with dismay. After one of Xanthe's early return visits to London, they had had such bitter words about the pearl-fishing stunt that Miranda had spent the whole year fretting about the encounter. What was the point of attacking Xanthe's novelty features, the gambling license, the T-bone steaks and premier-cru clarets? Moral outrage cut no ice with her; and she was Miranda's family, at least her strongest and only connection with family of her own age.

Miranda's need not to quarrel with her ran deep, and so in consequence she learned to hold her tongue and keep the peace. But she grieved that she became a mere audience for Sy and Xanthe, incapable of revealing her true feelings, as if with them she were sent back to childhood and could not speak up in front of the grown-ups and reveal her disagreement because it would become rejection, rebellion, insubordination. She could not understand how this could be the case when she was a fully grown woman.

Yet when she was with them, she also sometimes felt the tenderness of a return to childhood and early youth; other friends, with whom she had much more in common, could not turn over this common patch of earth she shared with Xanthe, and give her back its smells, its moisture, its seedlings and fruits. Even the discomfort she felt with her younger sister-aunt was so familiar, it had become pleasant. But she kept her own life concealed from them and never introduced them to anyone she knew. If she thought of bringing a friend along to meet them, she realized she would be putting them on exhibition as monsters—her affection could not be conveyed and she did not want to betray it by making a spectacle of them. For their part, they did not probe into her own life—though once Sy revealed he had seen some of her caricatures. "You'd never know from being with you," he said to her, "what a keen eye you've got. I say, you're quite a dark horse, what!"

The week before carnival was a slack time for foreign tourism, but a period of intense activity on Liamuiga, as the islanders were preparing their costumes for the Independence Day parades. That week, in the eleventh year of The Spice of Life, four members of the Shining Purity of the One God Liberation Movement knocked over the policeman who was sitting in the doorway of Government House in Jamieston, where he was reading a copy of *The Sentinel* from the day before, and made their way down the corridor into the parliament chamber where ten of the fifteen deputies were present for the debate about the over-fishing of the coastal waters of Liamuiga. The opposition member was speaking with some heat about the fatal stripping of spawn beds in order to satisfy the appetites of day trippers to the Florida keys; he carried on through the warning rounds of fire which the first of the four Shining Purity warriors squeezed off in the antechamber, and the recorder, with a slight loss of concentration that caused her to drop about five words of the deputy's plea, returned to her task in a state of perplexity but not yet alarm. Both dismissed that first burst from the machine gun as a backfiring lorry in the street outside, or perhaps a squirt of firecrackers let off by children overexcited at the prospect of carnival the following week. Nobody anticipated the danger that materialized. The long-nosed rifles and lumpy black AK 47s with their wreaths of fodder were familiar as toys, wielded by six-year-olds whooping down alleys and ducking round corners; they were known as the fantastic insignia of the ghostly invaders whose voices scratched and sputtered from the old prints of spaghetti Westerns on certain days in the open-air cinema near the Stockade.

There were a few malcontents on Liamuiga, but they scarcely made themselves felt. Shining Purity was well-known to the police, of course—its leader, now called Iqbar Malik, had formerly been one of their number, when his name was Jimmy Dunn. He had been dismissed for misconduct. (He had beaten a drunk outside a bar somewhat over-zealously—the drunk had turned out to be an Australian botanist suffering from a hypoglycemic attack.) He'd then withdrawn into the bush, squatting with his family and later, his followers, in the ruins of the Hôtel des Bains where Xanthe and Miranda had disturbed him and his children many years ago. When they'd been evicted from their settlement to make way for Xanthe's spa, they had disappeared farther up the slope of the volcano, and had only occasionally re-emerged to fulminate against the mores of the day; people laughed at the gaggle of white-robed, turbaned youths and children who cried out abomination on them.

Now they had weapons? Nobody had ever seen the reptilian snout of a repeating rifle in the hands of a Béatois; the Cambrian Fusiliers who had garrisoned the islands in the colonial days had used sabers, truncheons and revolvers. Atala Seacole had an instant to exchange looks with her spokesman for environment and tourism, her most dependable and important minister in the shadow cabinet and her closest ally, and he equally quickly registered the panic in her eyes, and imitating her, fell into a crouch under the benches of the chamber. So the first spray of bullets that traversed the room at eye level, triggered by the first two fighters through the door, cleared the speaker's head and flew into the pew of the second row up, just behind the seat used by the Governor and representatives of the Queen, Atala's uncle Sir Berkeley, when he was presiding.

The group of four Shining Purity members wore khaki combat jackets over narrow white leggings, which looked incongruous with the heavy secondhand U.S. Army boots they were wearing; on their heads they'd coiled the checked headcloths of the Cambodian Khmer Rouge into wimples, with the end gagging their mouths and noses. They came in shooting, so these details were not the most conspicuous aspect of the irruption to the members of the Liamuigan parliament in session, mostly now lying prostrate between the benches. One of the members of the opposition fell spread-eagled on the floor where he had been standing to address his colleagues, the recorder huddled behind her inadequate desk, and the speaker behind his more substantial chair with the horned sea monster of the Béatois badge on the knobs of the armrests.

The assault was reported in brief in the papers in England, and the video film made by the automatic security cameras in the chamber was shown on the news; Miranda also pieced the story further together with her father afterward, when Kit returned to London for the first time since he had left to work for Sy and Xanthe.

He had put off and put off coming to clear up his father's affairs; it had seemed Xanthe's business. When Sir "Ant" finally died, many were surprised that he had been living till so very recently; Gillian had kept him well-protected, his turned wits concealed from the public's stare. The readers of newspapers nodded sorrowfully over the obituaries, where Ant Everard was portrayed as the pattern of a vanished breed, the sporting English gentleman, and the last vacant years passed over in silence.

One afternoon, he rang Miranda; he had two trunkfuls of clothes Gillian had given him. "I've kept all the important Flinders stuff here," she had explained. "I think I'll present it to Doggett's—but I don't want his clothes leaving the family." Kit had protested he'd never need morning dress or a midnight-blue velvet smoking jacket or any of the three-piece tailor-made suits or the collarless shirts that fastened with

studs, not buttons. But Gillian insisted. In his will, it turned out that
Ant Everard had settled an annuity on his fortune-teller; Gillian's relief
at his death was tempered with bitterness at this last infidelity of the
ancient charmer.

Miranda took in the two trunks; with her father, she began looking
through them. Kit watched her, but did not handle the clothes himself.
He suggested a drink, and sent out to the off-license, bringing back
Scotch for himself, a good bottle of chilled Pouilly-Fumé for her. Kit
now found his daughter someone to whom he could talk without
deception, for he trusted her to allow accusations—and there were
grounds to count him negligent in some hapless way—to remain un-
spoken. In this, she was different from her mother.

Between the first round and the second, the terrorists shouted aloud
to one another; Atala Seacole heard, from her position on the floor,
cries so frenzied and uncouth it could have been they who were being
threatened rather than their victims. She felt ice spread through her
as she hunched very tight, very still, in her pew; she declared later
that she didn't pray, but like people of faith in the past, she made a
solemn vow, that if she came out of this unharmed she would . . . she
could not then phrase her high hope to herself. She had absorbed
something of the cynicism and understatement of the English political
philosophers who had taught her in London twenty years before;
confronted with the ardent intelligence of a small, young black woman
with convent manners, they had not been able to stop themselves from
heaping irony and scorn on the Third World's chances. Even though
these tutors, were they able to admit it without feeling foolish, also
yearned to discover possibilities of recovery, of development, without
falling into the hands of the Americans, the Russians (this was before
glasnost) or, could it be, judging from the rebels' arsenal, the Iranians
(why?) or even the Vietnamese (was this possible?), or perhaps, at a
stretch, the Syrians.

However, even the most sophisticated trashing of Atala Seacole's
essays about self-determination had not snuffed out her dignified allegiance to her tiny country. In spite of Iqbar Malik's terrorist assault
and the outrage against parliament, she swore to herself, to the groans
of one of her colleagues: "Remember, he is not the enemy. Things
have gone too far. He's taken the wrong path, this is a calamity. But
in essence I know he has some justice on his side. We have lost our

way and we must find it again." She knew that Jimmy Dunn had formed Shining Purity in the hills on the volcano's slopes in disgust with the selling of the islands to the money-men behind the hotels and the casino and all the rest of the tricks the Westerners turned, without appearing to do anything but provide a bit of fun and a few jobs. He had adopted his Muslim name, gathered around him a group of followers, fathered children who had now grown into youths, who danced with sticks, refused meat and practiced retention of semen in sexual intercourse to increase their strength; they were also polygamous, hardly an unusual state of affairs in the islands, but rarely proclaimed as a principle. (Atala Seacole herself had two "problem" children at home she had adopted, though she wasn't married—and they were only two of the number on the two islands of Enfant-Béate who needed homes, shelter and care.)

Atala Seacole heard Malik shrieking orders at the three youths with him through the muffling of his gag, and then another burst of fire froze the ice that bound her even harder around her limbs, and she heard one man groaning, and the recorder whimpering, "My hand, my hand."

"Come on, get you up, now, all of you," he was shouting. He'd stripped the gag from his mouth, so he sounded clearer now. "Unless you all want to suffer the same fate . . . "

"Mr. Malik," she responded, forcing herself to get to her feet and face his machine gun and the jittery threesome with him with their jumping, glittering eyes above their gags. "Let's not have a confrontation. Let's avoid violence." There was a puddle of blood near the recorder's desk; she was slumped over on her chair, rocking and moaning, holding her arm.

"Be silent," said the former Jimmy Dunn to Atala as she was pulled down from her bench by one of his men at his signal and dragged to join the others in a huddle under the surveillance of the last two men with guns.

He had this preacher's way of talking. Shining purity of speech, too. He'd been at school with the Moravians as a child, it was the best education in the islands for those who did not have access to British schooling. But like many other islanders, he'd rejected Christianity as the religion of British imperialism, and converted, groping with an act of faith toward his people's origins and history. Atala shivered and was grateful for the hand of her friend reaching out and holding her arm.

"Hold on, Attie, it'll be all right. We'll hold steady, and it will be all right."

"No talking," roared Iqbar Malik, waving his gun furiously. "Now walk, slowly, where I say. And in silence."

They began trudging together, like a roped beast in a constricted arena, with the four machine guns trained on them, out of the chamber and down the corridor outside, where one or two visitors and staff were also being held at gunpoint. Then they were pushed into the men's lavatory, the cell selected by Shining Purity for the smallness of its window, the convenience of a water supply, and the defendability of its entrance.

The deputies were knocked down onto the tiles into the corner, the basins at chin level to one side of them, the latrines between them. Atala Seacole, stretching her skirt under her to provide its greatest possible extent of protection, was forced down between two members of the party in power; even in the horror of the situation, she was aware of the comedy that this was the first time she and the Prime Minister had ever bundled up together—in a gentleman's convenience, with the aroma of urine and bleach wrapping them, flies investigating their eyes and feet.

The Prime Minister was blinking with fury, muttering threats under his breath, while both she and his companion on the other side, the Minister of Tourism, restrained him.

"I'll tell you what we want now, I'll tell you what we need for ourselves and our children and these islands, yes I will!" one warrior was shouting. The prophet of Shining Purity, Iqbar Malik, wanted in the name of the Living God and his prophets to clean up the islands, scour them of corruption, drive the interlopers and the usurers from the temple. The embrace of Islam—his version of Islam—had taken place long after his speech had set in the mold of his native religion and his voice still moved in the cadences of the Bible schoolteachers who had taught him a Christian idea of justice.

(The Moravians had been the first to open churches for the slaves, Kit reminded his daughter, when none of the other Christian churches would admit them.)

"Terrorist methods will do you no good," Atala Seacole broke in softly, until one of her neighbors clapped her over the mouth.

"You'll get us all killed, woman."

"Just give me what I want." Iqbar stood at the door jerking his head back and forth as he kept watch on them and on the corridor. "Let's see the end of the foreign putrefaction in our land. Let's see the back of the gamblers and fornicators, the followers of Satan and Belial, who flaunt themselves in the abominable bikinis and pour the tainted rum punches and mint juleps down their throats of evil. Let us say to the U.S. dollar: 'We don't want your filth here.' Let us say to the great plastic card: 'No, we don't want you here.' Let us say to the Great White God Jesus Christ: 'We don't want you here.' Let us say good-bye to the little white lies. Yes, we have our own riches and they will buy us all we need, yes, they will.

"Let us say: 'Get thee behind me' to Coca-Cola and Pepsi-Cola and blue jeans, to the concession and the franchises, the deal and the dollar. Let us say to the Tempter, 'I see you for what you are. Get thee behind me!' "

The Prime Minister could not be restrained any longer: "Mr. Dunn, and how are you going to put food in the mouths of the people of the island?"

"My name is Iqbar Malik," hissed his captor. "And be quiet, if you have nothing more constructive to reply. You are the buyers and sellers in the temple. You have made over your people and your god to the prince of this world. And you have twenty-four hours before I start killing you one by one if my demands are not met."

Sy had gone to the airport to meet the flight from Miami, which was scheduled to bring the order of rib steaks and escalopes of veal and ground beef and other familiar foods his visitors would insist on ordering, and he noticed the maddened feeling in the air pressing on him like the first pent-up breath of an impending hurricane.

Unusually, three soldiers in camouflage were patrolling the airstrip. They did not show the islanders' usual relaxed disposition; he was asked for documents and when he showed the invoice, was escorted to the warehouse where he had to unpack the insulated boxes one by one under the eyes of a young officer he had never seen before and who refused to answer his questions. Sy's customary amiability was met with such jumpy refusal that even he began to be ruffled and to wonder what could have happened. They would not tell him. The two kitchen staff he'd brought with him to carry the foodstuffs were not allowed in to the inspection, so his merry humor darkened further as he was made to hump the boxes himself in the mounting humidity and temperatures of a tropical July to the van, where they were waiting under surveillance from another soldier.

When he ran into the roadblock outside Jamieston on his return journey, he learned of the coup, the capture of the Prime Minister and various members of his party and of the opposition, including the parliament's only woman, Atala Seacole. At the time, Sy reflected it might do her good, bring her down from her infuriating moral heights, to be confronted with someone who didn't just preach revolution but practiced it. She'll learn a thing or two about real life, he'd thought then, as he sweltered by the side of the road and worried about the condition of the expensive goods in the stationary van, for down on the plateau between the airport and the town, there were few trees and no shade.

July was a slow month in the hotel trade, as most of the clients who chose this part of the world for a holiday preferred the winter months. Still, they were half-full at The Spice of Life. Some of his guests would leave, Sy knew, as soon as they heard of the trouble, and take the first available flights out; others scheduled to come would cancel, even as far ahead as Christmas. It was a blight. Banana republics . . . He sighed. Then he remembered that Goldie had gone to Xanadu on Oualie that morning, and cursed. Kit had remained in charge at The Spice of Life.

Sy began to fret at the delay; then, crazy as it was, he ordered his two youths back into the van and turned around. He would make the whole tour of the island by the shore road in order to reach the promontory from the other side; the patrol on the roadblock seemed to think only Jamieston was affected.

Driving two hours to reach a destination twenty minutes away on the other side of the town at least gave him a sense of activity, which lifted his spirits a little.

In the first village he reached, Liverpool, he stopped in a bar to telephone Kit. The line was dead, and the barman shrugged and did not know when it had failed. Sy began moving faster now; as he'd got back into the driving seat, he'd noticed the column of black smoke over Jamieston behind him. There was no other garrison on the island besides the one in the capital.

Boiled scarlet and panting with worry, Sy arrived at The Spice of Life to find a general air of calm. He burst into uproarious laughter, in relief to find the bees still ducking down the throats of the hibiscus, the palms still tossing their plumes over their heads in the sea breeze, the hotel not ransacked, the buildings not put to the torch. Kit had heard the news from a boy bringing a basket of fruit for sale to the kitchen; with some presence of mind, he'd immediately taken him into the office and locked the door, so that he could not panic the staff.

Kit said, with a wink, "I gave him a small amount of money to keep him happy for a while. I wanted you to decide what to do." Sy marched off the two kitchen boys who'd witnessed the confusion at the airport with him, and meeting their yells of protest with a promise of reward, locked them up in the same room to prevent a general alarm.

Kit had apologized to the guests for the momentary electricity failure, he reported. On its own this had not alerted them; he had canceled the shuttles to the town and to the spa, and so, though there were disgruntled noises, most of the company had gone to the beach, which was just as well, as the staff would be bound to hear the news by some other channel.

"We'll have to use threats to keep them here, I'm afraid," said Kit.

"Let's not meet the devil with mourning," Sy replied.

It was easy at the hotel to overlook the events altogether. The breeze blew from the sea, lifting the steamy lid that bore down on the town farther inland in high summer; the cottages or units scattered in the garden were abloom with allamanda and hibiscus, shaded by the nodding feathers of the royal palms and the broad hands of the shimmering breadfruit trees. They belonged in the nowhere place of idyll and romance, as he had wished; history and politics were erased from the grounds much more thoroughly than at Xanadu, where the old coppers of the sugarworks now held water lilies and horned toads and the cast-iron cogs and hubs of the gear used for the crushing of the cane stood about the lawns like garden sculpture.

Xanthe had encouraged him to dream up an imaginary past at The Spice of Life. "Tradition is a lie," she had said. "It's always a selective process, whatever you do—the dominant class picks its tradition to suit. We're prisoners of that, so we might as well accept it and do exactly what we please. So let's have an arbitrary décor. It'll turn out not to be capricious or arbitrary, you'll see."

The Spice of Life avoided English country-house chintz and plantation memories. Instead, each of the most luxurious rooms was named for a filibuster, and there were frescoes with maps of their journeys, marked with the chief places of their exploits: Blackbeard's raids, the pirate exploits of Anne Bonny and Mary Read. Xanthe had had sconces made in cast iron tipped with gold for the bar showing Blackbeard's grinning face, with the candles sprouting from his dreadlocks in imitation of the rockets he would wind in his hair and then set alight to terrify his victims. "He doesn't alarm me," said Xanthe, "but I know people love a little fright now and then."

The coup did not excite the shivery pleasures of fear in the clientèle in the same way as Blackbeard, and when Sy announced the "little incident in Jamieston" to the company at a cold lunch he expeditiously put together with a bit of help from Kit, there was a tiresome commotion, which he could not altogether soothe. Depending on their age, nationality and reading habits, his guests were instantly exchanging bulletins on the Mau-Mau, Lucknow, the Boxer Rebellion, and Red Indian scalp hunters. Sy ordered rum punches on the house all around, and interrupted them, "Plenty of nutmeg and fresh lemon, to drive away care! Oh, I know you're all grown-ups and you can face the deep truths of life, you're not the sort to jib at the nitty-gritty, my dears, are you? Well, death is one of these realities. We're not facing death here, not by any means. Besides, we have some small arms in the hotel and will issue them if need be."

There were murmurs from a seersucker-jacketed figure. "Give me a twelve-bore and I can hit a coon at five hundred yards."

"Not that kind of coon!" said one voice.

"Aw, I didn't mean that . . . "

Kit heard this, and he broke in, "Let me tell you a story, my friends, about this island."

Sy was watchful, as Kit spoke; he'd noticed the flare of his temper in his eyes.

Miranda and Kit were having a cup of tea together in a greasy spoon when he was telling her this part: It was 8 o'clock, and they had been up since before sunrise, accompanying Gillian to Doggett's Fields, where together they strewed Ant's ashes on the Stockade. The crematorium had given Gillian the urn, and Kit had made the arrangement with the steward to perform the informal ceremony at dawn. The three of them had walked out to the Target—it was the first time Miranda had stepped onto the playing area of Flinders—and sown her grandfather's ashes on the turf. She almost heard the sighs rising from behind the Chase at this last discreet appearance.

Kit was visibly moved: the disaster of the coup and now, this last rite had pierced his entranced state, the accidie that had lulled him for so many years.

He had felt sudden anger, but had managed to hold it under control, while Sy stood by, alert.

"It was unfortunate," he'd told the assembled guests, "but once upon a time, the wife of an eminent lawyer—a silk from London—died in her sleep here in the hotel. The lawyer realized something was amiss and so he tried to wake someone to fetch help. I was sleeping in my cottage as usual, and I did not hear his weeping. But at last, the lawyer woke up one of the other guests in a hotel cottage near him. Now this man was an actor, RADA, the Old Vic, the whole caboodle, including—" Kit's voice now rose and boomed—"a voice of thunder. His call jolted me awake instantly, and when I heard the lawyer's fears, I called the doctor—the local chap—who came though it was the middle of the night. Unfortunately, the lady was dead. The lawyer whispered that he would like his wife's jewelry removed before her body was taken away. So I told the doctor, and the doctor unfastened her necklace, bracelet, took out her earrings—I don't remember what ornaments she was wearing, but they were very fine—and then found he could not slip off her rings. They had been married a lifetime, and her rings had grown almost one with her flesh." Kit was sweating slightly in agitation, but he had not lost his temper. "You follow me? So the doctor said, 'We'll have to soap them off.'

"Whereupon this lawyer from out of town, not from here, jumped up and howled, 'No, not that! Never. Is it really necessary?'

"It turned out that he'd heard the doctor say, 'We'll have to saw them off.'

"Perhaps the island accent of the local doctor, a native man, of course, misled him—it's soft and open. Perhaps, too, he had vivid notions of the savage, black, local people here. He might have believed it if the doctor had said, 'I'll bite them off!' Oh, my sister Goldie laughed, when I told her. But I didn't at the time, and I don't now. Though I assure you"—Sy placed a warning hand on Kit's arm, as Kit grew redder in the face—"there aren't any more cannibals here anymore, hah! There'll be no sawing off of fingers—or biting or long-pig stew or anything else!"

Xanthe was on Oualie, Kit told Miranda, when Shining Purity struck, but Xanadu's guests there did not flap; they were isolated from the trouble, and as English habitués for the most part, they enjoyed showing the old imperial imperturbability at mutinies or other ripples among the natives. Which was just as well, as those who would have preferred to leave would have discovered they were actually marooned: the shuttle planes were on the tarmac at the main island and the panicking tourists there had first call on the sixty-odd seats that would take them out of Liamuiga.

Xanadu wasn't humming either, Oualie was becalmed in the summer season, and Xanthe could have found out nothing except rumors; the telephones were dependent on the central exchange in Jamieston, and the ferry had not returned from its outward trip that morning. July was a restful time for their tourist trade, offering an opportunity to touch up paintwork and rehang louvers and check the hurricane shutters and doors; the oysters turned female in their ripeness at this stage of their cycle, and were swelling with soft strings of eggs and flairing the milt on the warm summer currents, waiting to conceive; soon the sea would be wafting thousands—no, millions—of spats on their few days of independent living toward the cultch of old shells Sy had had strewn on the seabed, extending the existing oyster beds in the estuary. There they would come to roost and anchor themselves and, in a few years or so, grow to edible dimensions, to load the best oyster bar in the Caribbean Sea for the winter and the visitors.

There was little pressure, so it was hard to see why Xanthe had reacted with such panic.

Xanthe had crossed over to Oualie to see to arranging the menus at Xanadu for the whole carnival week ahead, when the full program of pageants and dancing and feasting and processions would prevent her or anyone else from leaving The Spice of Life again, as one of them usually did at least once a week to supervise the operation of the older sister hotel. Cut off by the assault in Jamieston from reaching Liamuiga, Xanthe trained an old pair of field glasses she found in Sy's jumble in the office cupboard on the shore of Liamuiga across the Strait of Oualie, and the pillar of smoke materialized against the luminous horizon. She told the cook then that she did not know what to do, that she must reach Sy, and she beat her chest helplessly as she avowed this. He hadn't forgotten, for it was so unlike Miss Goldie to be at a loss.

Miranda imagined Xanthe's desperation: how hard she must have been struck off-balance when she of all people could suddenly no longer see with her accustomed adamant clarity; how the possibility of danger to Sy (she knew how some elements loathed the hotel, the tourists, and above all the spa—their old stamping ground) might have opened her up to feelings that were new to her; how Xanthe perhaps became all at once wide-awake to the threat of impending loss.

Xanthe had always lived in enthralled possession—of herself; of her family's love, her father's, in particular; of Feeny's devotion; of Miranda's own envious and tenacious companionship. She'd carelessly commanded the wherewithal of survival and more, while others like Miranda were struggling to make tuppence ha'penny. But it had not been like that for her. "Everything you touch turns to gold," Sy had said.

Now, she probably envisaged The Spice of Life razed, the Hotel des Bains destroyed, the bodies of housemaids and waiters and the cook mutilated and scattered as in earlier blood-soaked uprisings on other islands. And Sy, naked, white as a mushroom, round and large as the puffball variety, punctured and limp with his face running with blood and files of ants on the march to carry off the meat of his brains, his abdomen split as in the worst atrocities of the Tontons Macoute.

She'd brushed away a request from one of the guests almost rudely as she stood on the heights of the garden edge at Xanadu watching the smoke unfurl, before she rushed away, down to the harbor, following the column of smoke in the distance across the straits. There she insisted on taking the hotel launch on her own to make the crossing.

Later, one of the boys on the quay described how mad she'd been to go. She'd waved away his alarm that the petrol cans mightn't be full. And the boat was leaky, it was due for caulking before the high season; the paddle was stowed all right, all shipshape, Mr. Nebris, oh yes. But it was a spar of coconut, heavy to handle, and hard to grip, not much used, not handy for a lady like Miss Goldie. "Oh, Miss Goldie could have managed that," Sy retorted. But then, no flares; why had she not attracted attention with flares, if that was the answer, that she'd run out of petrol? Surely there had been flares, they were always kept in the boat, with the life jackets and the waterproof torches and the gear.

Kit spread his hands and stared into his cup, and wept for his sister. Miranda felt choked, more by the sight of her father in tears than her own bereavement. She could not touch him to comfort him; it was years since she had had contact with her father. Then the memory came to her of sharing a bath with Xanthe, in their childhood; how they had shouted with the thrill of fear at the coming of the monster.

He regained control of his voice and continued to tell what he knew. When news of the coup had arrived, it scared off the remaining hotel staff. He'd then gone down to the hamlet tucked along one of the narrow streams which fed the creek, where they lived in cabins raised on cinder blocks, shaded by the torn flags of banana leaves and the occasional, larger, frangipani, mango or breadfruit tree. He liked the village; he told his daughter he was thinking of taking a room there for himself, instead of the cottage he had in the hotel gardens. But he realized he spread awkwardness wherever he went, neither altogether boss nor worker, but somewhere in between, a lackey who is despised but also feared. He laughed, but angrily, and went on, not noticing Miranda's embarrassment at the leveling of their relation through his confessions.

In the village, he would buy a beer from the all-purpose-goods store which one of the cook's girlfriends had started up, and lean against the canary-colored wall by the cobalt letters of the beer's painted brand name, "Carib," and watch the small children at Flinders with a piece of palm for a stick and an old ball, or the women doing each other's hair out in the yard or drawing the washing up from the tub and drubbing it down again with soap, then back into the water, and stirring it about, and he would be emptied of the calculations and combinations and number sequences that hummed noisily in his head much of the time.

He never stayed long; he could feel that the staff, who made up the greater part of the hamlet's population, considered his presence an intrusion into that part of their lives that The Spice of Life did not own. He had made one friend, or almost friend, for he felt he had eased his mistrust: Lucius the oyster fisher, with whom he went out at low tide to check the beds. There too, the slick spinning of the ball in the wheel, the clean slide of the cards as they were slipped out of the shoe, the click of the chips in their stacks, rising or falling, and the pent-up cries and murmurs of the players faded into the deep distance, as if drowned in the eddies where the small white faces of the mother shells gleamed. He could work with Lucius; the fisherman teased him for his fidelity to the mysterious wife in England who never appeared, urged a choice oyster on him to juice him up. Kit only smiled and lapped the cool, delicate oyster in its sea fresh liquor and shook his head. "Even this, Lucius, won't do the trick. I've lost the drive, I can't even recall what I used to want so much. Or why."

The day of the coup, as Kit went from one group to another, political opinions were running high. He interrupted them, to tell them to come back to work instantly on pain of sacking and docked wages. In the yard of one cabin, he came across the village's carnival camp, where the costumes were standing on bamboo frames, waiting to be finished— a tall cocoon of shredded rags and plastic cups cut in half and colored papers stitched together for a Pitchy-Patchy, lord of misrule and wild-man of the woods. (He recognized the wrappings of imported foods, the tissue from crates of apples and pears salvaged from the hotel kitchen, and averted his eyes to concentrate on the task in hand, before they saw him noticing other filched elements and would despise him for letting the matter pass.)

It was hot in the hamlet, the sheltered site away from the beach and the wind off the sea clammed the air; even the glossiest and sappiest plants seemed to wilt. The children kept to the shade under the lee of the cabins' floors and investigated creatures who were digging into the ground to find coolness, or were lying panting in the muggy dark under there. He had heard, as he approached, the beat of a drum and the warbling of a singer stretching his tenor voice with emphasis, but once he had been seen, the village fell silent.

"Nigger" Everard, they used to call him behind his back at school back in Surrey half a century ago. But he was one of the bakkra to the villagers, all the same. Sy had given him a dressing-down when he'd lost his temper, at the height of the season last autumn, and stormed at the doorman of the casino and even hit him (oh God, he really had hit him) because he had refused entry to a black man. These were the doorman's orders, it was the law: no natives. It was lucky— or perhaps it wasn't so lucky—that Kit had happened to walk by, on his way to the main building of the hotel on some errand, when the guest was protesting, and Kit recognized him, an old bridge hand he'd partnered in Le Touquet and watched playing for his country—one of the mainland nations—at a tournament in Nice as well. And so he'd greeted him, and begun his explanations to the doorman to allow him to enter. But the Latin American was furious, he wasn't to be bought off with a pally handshake and excuses about the law excluding locals. He shouted about racism and threatened a scandal, and Kit caught the heat of his indignation, and it boiled up in him and he swore at the doorman and called him a bloody fool and much else besides. But the doorman stood his ground, aggrieved, for he was only doing as he was told. Which showed what a numbskull he truly was. And that was when Kit . . . struck him. Hit him till he bled, in fact, but he did not hit Kit back.

Sy was cross, even Sy's bubbling subsided and he gave Kit a warning. But the episode had not just sobered Kit up for a while; it had shamed him deeply. Acting as the front man for the casino, the job which had once seemed to meet his deepest desires, had turned sour for him. It was then he had begun to kick against his immurement with the foreigners in their special preserves.

In total, nine people died and twenty-three were treated for wounds and shock in the incidents of that July 198—. On the fourth day of his attempt, Jimmy Dunn shot the Prime Minister in the lavatory where he was still holding him hostage with his other prisoners, and then ran out of the building, shaking his weapon as if he were wrestling with it to fight it off, bursting out of the main door out into the street and into the fire of the Béatois police, who were being given backing by some soldiers of a friendly neighboring island. They had not been given the order to shoot to kill Iqbar Malik, but rather the opposite, as the government of Liamuiga as well as other states in the archipelago were proud of their democratic procedures and judicial fairness and sincerely wished to bring him and his fellow conspirators to trial. But he was zigzagging and ducking and bobbing so in his desperate rush that the low shot hit him in the head instead of the thigh and blew away half his skull.

The other six casualties included one of his henchmen who was trampled in the mêlée that followed the killing of the leader, and a family of three who had joined the small crowd outside Government House who had been awaiting developments. Two others included in the toll were a policeman from a village at the northern tip of the island and an outside recruit who had been excited to see action for the first time in his life. Thirty-six Shining Purity fighters were rounded up and jailed pending trial. (After carnival they would be charged with treason and first-degree murder, for which the penalty was hanging: the provision for capital punishment had not been reviewed, as there was practically no crime in Liamuiga besides the odd Saturday-night drunken brawl and petty thieving.) There were only five cells in the police station, which itself had also been occupied by the attempted coup; two were already filled with some petty criminals who wailed their objections to keeping company with terrorists. They were moved out to the Ministry of Tourism instead, where they were able to talk freely to the passersby through the windows on the street and concoct fantastical tales about the deeds of Shining Purity—from the moment they had appeared and taken over the police station to their surrender, after they heard through a megaphone that their leader was dead.

Within five days, the coup was over, and carnival still took place, as arranged, though the atmosphere was less uproarious than it would otherwise have been. Independence Day on August 1, the same date as the traditional Emancipation Day commemorating the end of slavery, was celebrated without further bloodshed; calypsos were composed, and the steel pans rang out. But the route had to make a circuit through Jamieston, avoiding the main street, where the Shining Purity section who had seized the post office had burned it down and unleashed a bout of frenzied window-smashing, battering and looting.

Through the Carnival days that followed, Atala Seacole worked on the terms she would lay out to the various authorities who were telephoning, telexing, and even appearing in person to take charge of the volatile situation in the islands. The dead man's former deputy had become acting Prime Minister, but the failure of his party to foresee and forestall the coup gave the opposition access to a very sympathetic hearing from the World Bank and other paymasters. Liamuiga was a speck in the world's eye, until something like the Shining Purity coup disrupted the placid and sunny Caribbean climate; then the specter of secession reared its ferocious head, and rosy bankers felt the nightmare pounce on them, with its train of attendant succubi: rights of aliens to the airstrip (and an extension of its length and capacity?), electronic espionage, strategic drug and arms smuggling, destabilization; anarchy rippling outward through the world from this small spot in the ocean.

Even a small place like Liamuiga, Atala Seacole had grasped early on, could act like a rogue virus in the immune system of world politics. "Just like sugar," she declared, "when it flowed from these islands and poisoned the age of the Enlightenment with its attendant trades and plagues! In a chain of greed, sugar linked the merchants in Biafra and the Gold Coast to the Yorkshire coal digger who was sipping his cup of sweet hot tea in the chimney nook in order to ease his lungs. Corruption here now can do the same, it can inflict such wounds on the First World that it can never recover. We have the vaccine you need against the disease you bring on yourselves!"

The financiers and statesmen in America were glad of the corpse of Iqbar Malik, but his survival, in shame and failure, would have been cleverer politics. So they urged a speedy burial, before the funeral could become a pretext for more trouble.

Under guard, a forensic expert from Miami worked beside one of the island's doctors, and together they signed the death certificate, giving head wounds as the cause of death; under heavier guard, Iqbar Malik/Jimmy Dunn was interred in an unmarked grave behind the police station (he could be moved later). This was all accomplished so fast, the lawyers hardly had time to wake from the shock of the coup and wring their hands over the waiving of many formalities. More importantly, the remaining sympathizers with Shining Purity could not learn of the event and try to provoke the general uprising their leader had hoped would follow his capture of the Prime Minister and other members of parliament, his party's seizure of the broadcasting center, the post office and the police station. He had followers, but on the whole, the Béatois found his ideas weird: stick dancing was one thing, but much of the rest was not to their taste, and some of it unholy (his ideas about sex, all that business about not climaxing). But Atala Seacole thanked him from the bottom of her being: he had cleared the way for her and her ideas. Among which were plans for The Spice of Life.

The calypso writer Blue Fishing Rod, known to all as De Rod, was soon busy writing a song for carnival:

> De man had a jug of milk
> He didna wan' to spill
> Aah No, he didna wan' to lend
> But keep it for him all alone
> He gone and said
> Keep it in, you gotta keep it in.
> Now he's keepin' it in for ever more
> Dat's what comes of stinginess
> I say, dat's what comes of stinginess.
>
> If I had a big round cow
> I like to squeeze every drop
> And pass de bowl aroun', oh man
> Pass de bowl aroun', oh man
> So sweet and good, de milk of my cow!
> No good'll come of stinginess,
> I say, No good come of stinginess.

The ninth fatality, Xanthe Everard, was counted in the official toll, though she could only be said to be an indirect victim of the coup. She'd not been seen again since she paid two boys on the quay at Oualie to drag the hotel's private launch down to the water from the boat yard where it was laid up for careening that summer. She'd never reached the coast of the big island, at least not that anyone ever discovered. Neither of the boys would go with her, they were too frightened, they reported later. She'd countered that she would swim across if they didn't help her get the boat into the water, and she looked as if she might throw herself in then and there. So they had obeyed her, and hauled it down the strand, and she'd set out on her own across the strait.

30

THE CRY BATTERED against her eardrums until she shifted, trying to set her back to it. But the grave-passage was narrow and traversed by the thick roots of the tree, which impeded her; the cry was carried on the wind, raveled up with other sounds, a chorus of voices, and she had to draw herself together to listen and part them. There was so much longing in the first piercing voice that had roused her, it recalled to her sharply for a moment something long ago. O my daughter, Sycorax whispered, and turned on her side in the trench.

Longing swelled the other cries which she began to comb out of the sleaves of sounds that shook down the tree and made her vibrate beneath the earth like a small hollow instrument, like the banged taut skin of a drum. She would have liked to return in torpor to the accomplishment of her death; it seemed at last almost to hand, her consciousness had become so fitful, her hearing so woolly with all the decades of earth and entreaties crumbling into her, stopping her holes.

But she could not escape the first cry, and once she had allowed it to reach her, more voices joined in the clamor and pressed themselves on her attention: the island's noises would not let her be.

Xanthe was swearing when she maneuvered the launch away from the jetty at Oualie, twisting hard on the grip of the outboard in her grief and her rage, letting the bows smack each wave as she took the sea wantonly. The boat was an old bucket, with a cabin in the bows in case of showers, not built to slash the swell of the sea at right angles, but Xanthe, in the stern at the tiller, exulted in the spray that splashed up from the smooth blue-purple walls of the waves and hit her in the face and seemed to help cool her fury. She swung the prow round to point straight across the strait to the harbor of Jamieston by the usual route. The plume of dingy smoke above the town streamed sideways in the stiffening wind out toward the promontory where the hotel stood.

Then the thought came to her: Rather than land in the harbor—who knows what might be going on there? That's the first place those punks would seize, isn't it, the harbor buildings and the radio station? No, she'd head beyond, round the peninsula and up the creek itself, land directly on the beach at The Spice of Life—make straight for Sy—no messing with getting a ride of some kind at the harbor—after all, that might be risky, if there was none to be had in the first place. The thought of kidnapping entered her mind—of Sy captured—the ransom she would pay—huge, extravagant, yes, to show she did care for him, madly. "Darling, I do, I do." So yes, she would bring the boat in immediately below the hotel on its own beach, killing the engine while still out at sea, let the surf carry her in, maybe to the Historic Landing Place, where the first Kit Everard set foot himself—nobody would see her, with luck it would be dusk by then, unless they were guarding every foot of the shore, and that wasn't possible, she knew there weren't that many of them and they certainly wouldn't be that together either.

But the passage to the creek made a longer crossing for the old Xanadu launch than the Strait of Oualie, and Xanthe, usually so matchlessly organized, had not checked the supplies on board.

She left the sugared-almond huddle of the Jamieston waterfront to her left as the sun was beginning to spill its gold onto the piling clouds packed on the horizon and set the waves flickering with red; she was making many promises to herself and to others, but mostly to Sy, and her words joined the traffic of messages on the wind: she would try to show him love, she swore it. Maybe they could even have a child, maybe even more than one, they could adopt. She almost laughed out loud, sitting in the stern savaging the throttle to get the launch to set her by his side—she was beginning to glow in the wake of the declining sun. How her father had hated Sy, thought him a pansy, raised all his old-school hackles, so it was a pity she hadn't presented him with a clutch of grandchildren. She'd make amends now, prove how Sy was really on the level as a son-in-law. But all too late. Why had she never wanted anything like this before? It stood to reason, nobody with any common sense would have children. Besides, what a rush it had given her to annoy Poppa, to make him suffer.

It was part of her yearning to take Sy's part, the fool's part, save him now from the arsonists and the terrorists who threatened him because they were filled with hate and envy of the money they made. What else would the island do without entrepreneurs, people like her and Sy? They were prepared to invest and work, which was more than the natives were . . . She roared for a moment into the breeze as it quickened with the coming of the night, and shook her head to free herself from strands of her blond hair flattening themselves against her eyes, "God, I swear I'll never be mean again to Sy or anyone else."

Another voice rose and joined in the babble on the air, not addressing Sycorax directly as a suppliant, but vaulting past her, to speak to someone else, to a public audience beyond, of financiers, of bankers, of international loan brokers, of politicians. Yes, the old woman would have sat up if she weren't cabined and cribbed so tight under the tree, in order to hear Atala Seacole, speaking up, calling out: "At a rough reckoning, eighty percent of the food served in the tourist industry in the two islands that make up this country is imported—and this is God's own garden where anything and everything will grow, if you just drop the seed onto the ground—

"And sixty-five percent of this food is thrown away by the hotels and restaurants that import it—oh yes, I know some of it is recycled at the kitchen door—

"But you explain to me how that is nourishing our people, our children who are our future—"

The resolve of Xanthe Everard was heard by the old woman, but it wasn't that cry that entered and rattled the old woman's bones; a New Year's resolution, routine false promises—she'd heard far too many of those over the centuries to wake up at the sound of another. The cry that shook her into consciousness came later, when Xanthe was drowning in the pearl beds which she matched with her barley hair and her nacreous skin and her thin flesh all the way through to her springy, tensile skeleton. (She had disappeared into the mouth, the maw, deep into the innards of Manjiku, the islanders claimed. It was an old story, they'd known it beforehand, before it took place, in fact.) The Princess's spell was wearing off. The godmother had made her wish in good faith thirty-five years before, at the christening, to undo the family curse of angry, avid restlessness. She'd granted that the baby should grow up impervious, because she herself had suffered so and remained so long unfulfilled, and she imagined that inspiring wild emotion and feeling almost nothing in return might lead to a happy life. In this she was not altogether wrong, as it turned out. Only at the very last minute, when so much was coming apart around Xanthe, did that fairy decree of long ago stop working and Xanthe Everard become vulnerable to love.

"My predecessors in government in this country agreed to a loan of twelve million dollars to build a two-lane highway twenty miles long from Jamieston to the salt ponds of the southern peninsula—they believe it will attract hotels, self-catering apartment blocks, wealth—

"But there is only one four-wheeled vehicle for every two hundred inhabitants of these islands—to walk or bicycle to work does not need a two-lane highway—and they will be working in these establishments, I suppose? Or will the visitors from abroad staff the hotels and use the road to drive to work in the mornings and back to the casino or whatever other pleasure they might wish to command in the back streets of Jamieston? In cars they import from the United States with petrol we must buy to fuel them?"

When Sycorax deciphers Xanthe's cry, she shakes her head softly; the wise stay empty of longing, they tip out all their desires, only the incomplete come to hope and regret and always see more that they could have. This voice had once been full and strong and solid before it cracked open with new desire pushing out like a flower stem, like a furled blade of scarlet heliconia in the forest . . .

And Sycorax thinks, I would have loved her better, o my daughter, if I had not wanted more and more from her, if I had not pushed my blade into her. Oh, to have loved her without longing to own her, to rule her, to keep her cloven to my will! To have loved her no matter what, in spite of the red child she bore . . .

The drowning voice she hears was making that same mistake; she feels the want now that drives love away, that makes loving a mirror in which you only see everything you want for yourself. Sycorax remembers, "I was blinded to Ariel's needs, her different love, so that I could not bear it when she diverged from me . . . Will my end never come?" she cried. "Will I never be delivered?"

One voice from under the sea, hers from under the earth: where would silence take hold and lift them out and upward and bring them peace?

"Every year hundreds of our men and our women leave Enfant-Béate to find work elsewhere—to cut cane in Florida for the American Sugar Corporation, to New York to drive cabs, to London to do the jobs that other people won't do in the National Health Service, in British Rail, in other public services. And how are they thanked for this? With contempt there and with broken homes here . . . "

I like the fierceness in this one, in her demands, it makes up for the weakness she has to show, exposing her wounds, asking for remedies. For years people have come to pray here for things which I can never give them—however much they entreat at the foot of my tree—how could I have such power, lying here forever dying, nothing but sere and floury bones and the dry click of leaf on leaf, the creak of branches? Oh, the heavens are so full and they are void—with stars like holes in the indigo, in the black, some of them white holes, some of them flues lit with malachite fires (like that star, like Canopus glittering in the winter night) . . .

"Where the chips fall the fix follows, I know the law of the casino and the way of the drug barons. If we are to survive we must replace the gambling dollar with another source of revenue, one which will do good to our people. We have to find something else—and you must support us, not undermine and break us . . ."

She hadn't cared, she'd never known how to love well, that golden girl—and she was rewarded because the world fears love and hates need and she was never needy as she is now. But now at least, now that she's dying, she has a glimmer of how much more she could want if she could have her life over. And she wants it, as I did and still do . . .

. . .

"No, no more," the strong, high voice continued. "The time has come for a change, my friends:

"There will be no more gambling licenses granted for the territory of Enfant-Béate. The present one is rescinded from this moment on . . .

"Work permits for two foreign nationals only will be granted for each company that has established interests here . . .

"The buildings known as The Spice of Life will become a training school . . .

"The Béatois there will learn other skills beside catering and tourism . . .

"We will not go on ravaging our beautiful land, our beautiful sea. We honor the coral reef, we treasure the rain forest where the hot springs rise to give us health . . .

"Our children must not become a class of servants once again to the bakkra, the white bakkra." And in an undertone, Atala goes on, "Like my grandmother, who went to England as a servant, following that family where her grandmother before her and others before that had all been slaves.

"No, no more of this." (And they nicknamed us Seacole to mock us, but we wear our blackness as a badge of pride.)

Xanthe's voice cut through, under Atala's, crying out from the coral palaces in the reef her pain at what she had lost and never cared for, the loving she had been given and never noticed except to scoff or scratch it in the face. The jewels and metals and other objects of permanence she had had such a taste for were heaped about her in the circle of eternity to which she had been assigned. In the soft, walled chamber of her marine host, she was mantled in pearl, layer upon layer spun about her foreign body until, mummified at the mineral heart of a pale rainbow, she became forever smooth and sheeny and hard.

Sea changes never come to stillness for some among the dead; they can speak and move in the water, and make themselves heard, like the voices that pass through Sycorax, like Dulé who stirs fathoms down, and swims as if his legs had never been crippled, as a child who is handicapped becomes lithe in a swimming pool. But for Xanthe Everard this was the final transformation: a pearl of rare size and beauty, she had become incapable of further motion in mind or body; she had given her first and last cry for the love that most people crave all their livelong days.

Then Sycorax hears Atala crying out, in a higher voice that comes through like interference on the waves, her pure and hard call of leadership is breaking into pieces and she is praying too, now:

"What shall we do if we are trapped, again? If we fail?"

Sycorax would have liked to call back, "You must not fail! You will not fail!" But there is earth in her throat. After you, she is thinking, everything that began all those years ago will be accomplished, and the noises of the isle will be still and I—I shall at last come to silence.

PART VI

Maroon/Black

When it comes, will it come without warning
Just as I'm picking my nose,
Will it knock on the door in the morning,
Or tread in the bus on my toes,
Will it come like a change in the weather,
Will its greeting be courteous or bluff,
Will it alter my life altogether?
O tell me the truth about love.
— W. H. AUDEN

31

Kit Everard to Miranda
PO Box 23, Liamuiga, 198–

Miranda dear,
When I don't write, it doesn't mean you aren't in my thoughts. As I'm becoming older, I find I think of you and your mother more and more often—I must admit that you both rise up in front of my mind's eye as you were rather a while ago and not as I expect you look now. We are keeping as well as can be expected here—the climate is kind to stiff knees and cramped spines, and I can pole a dugout over the oyster beds with surprising ease for a man who's been hunched over a cardtable the livelong day and the livelong night for most of his earthly span, what ho. At dawn these hot summer days— I'm writing this as everyone is napping but I don't seem to need so much Egyptian PT, as we used to call it in the war. I'm making the best of what time's left to me, that's what I say—I go out on the water every morning and evening, armed with pruning knife and billhook to make sure nobody's preying on my beauties as they swell up to spawn—we've nets spread to stop the egrets and the ducks and the heron feeding, so snails are the chief worry, they can bore right through the shell and suck out the flesh inside, nasty little

monsters. The Liamuiga Bluetip is making quite a name for itself—
we're flying them out by the barrel in great shipments all over the
area, of course, and further too, to New Orleans and Miami. Our
lord and master—now she's not Top Dog any more, she calls herself
the Minister for Economic blablabla—Miss NowLookHere, Miss
Atala Seacole, you will recall—is actually chuffed.

"The distinctive delicate Liamuiga Bluetip derives its name from
the tinges of indigo on the edges of its small frilled shell; the flavor
is as fresh as an early morning dip off the coral reefs of the sea where
the oyster roots and ripens . . . " that's the kind of rhubarb we're
hearing all the time. But it makes the tills ring for the island, so
Madam is pleased. And we're employing lots of people, for I'm not
alone looking after the beds of course, they're quite a job—and there
are lots of chaps and chap-esses in the office too, as well as packers
and loaders and whathaveyou—it's Business. We're preparing new
beds for the next crop of yearlings. The water's a bit warm from the
springs in my opinion but these new beds will get flushed out by the
tide when the moon's full. At least that's the current thinking. I laid
the cultch myself on the bottom, for the little spats to take root in
when they've had enough swimming around waggling their tails
(when their roving days are over!). The Japs use white tiles, but we
prefer to throw the old mother shells back in—eerie, the whiteness
winking back from the riverbed.

Sy's in good shape, not the man he was, of course, he's shrunk
so much—since, well, Goldie died. Some people's hair turns white,
he's dwindled away to nothing. His photo was in the paper at a
competition from all over the Caribbean between chefs—he won
the oyster-opening contest, a dab hand, a champion, his knife never
slips, one oyster's no sooner open than he's got the other nestled in
the palm of his hand against the ball of his thumb, the knife point
between the valves at the hinge, hey, presto, another shining succulent bluetip to be swallowed live with just a dash of Tabasco and
a squeeze of lemon to make the creature squirm. And he can still
talk the hind legs off a donkey at the same time. They—our lords
and masters—want him to go to New York and take part in another
competition there, win spurs for the Liamuiga Bluetip's renaissance,
but he's reluctant—if I'm an old man, he's an antique. (I can hear
him snoring in the hammock from here.)

We've all had to move out of the old hotel, and the training school.
Everyone. So now we're set up in a cabin by the creek—shady,
banana trees, a mite small for two, but it suits Sy and me. It turned
out the hotel foundations had been eaten through—nothing lasts in
this climate, appearances to the contrary. A royal palm can look

supple and vigorous as a young girl, then you find a termite's nest in the roots and a whisper of breeze'll knock it down. At the hotel, it was a plague of caveys boring through—concrete, brick and mortar, nothing stops them. They'd gnaw their way through granite, it's my belief. So the old Spice of Life is all boarded up now. At night, I hear the wind sighing in the cracks. The next big breeze, and . . . oh well. It was an inconvenient building for the school anyway— quite useless, really. Thanks to Miss NowLookHere, "Funds have been allocated for a new Technical College where hotel skills will still be on the syllabus, alongside training in other trades as well." As we servants to Dame Nature know, growth follows the knife.

I still play once in a while, one or two gamesters from Jamieston come over, and Sy makes up a four for bridge if I can't find anyone else.

When Goldie died, I couldn't find the right words to talk to you. I know how upset you were—how inadequate words are, you see— but you shouldn't feel remorse. You don't need to, though it's the feeling that sticks, I find. One wants to make amends, but it's not possible. And, in your case where Goldie's concerned, there's absolutely no need. She had a full life, on her own terms. It's one of those paradoxes (I know you know this, but I'm your father, after all, so I'm allowed to dish out the old paternal wisdom now and then)—people who feel less are happier—but their lot's not to be envied, all the same. Anyway, I'm glad that you've now got some money. It's a curse, never to have any money, as I know. (This isn't a begging letter, believe you me.) You owe it to Sy, you know that, he wrote your name in as the beneficiary when he took out the policy. It was his idea too that Goldie left you her little lot, never thinking of course that he wouldn't go first. But he doesn't begrudge you, not at all, and neither do I, though little did any of us dream then what would happen and she made a bundle, she was clever with money. No, he's genuinely pleased some good came of her death and he knows how close you were, even though in the circs. you were far apart.

The money's yours, of course, but don't fritter it away. I know I'm hardly one to talk (your mother and I were experts at splashing it around)! Buy property—that's my hunch. London's a sound place to invest in. Find some run-down area on the way up. And have some fun too—though I'd avoid entertainment or tourism if I were you. Such an uncertain business. But then you're a chip off an old gambling block, so who knows? Anyhow, with present-day interest rates, a lump sum like that should last: if you don't blow it all on one venture, you should be able to keep the capital topped up.

Do you ever see your mother? You can give her the love she needs where an old sod like me has failed.

You've been lucky, in some ways, and luck is a mad dog who usually bites. All in all, you're wise not have got hooked up.

Sy joins me in sending you his love,

Your loving father,

Kit

P.S. I enclose a photo from a recent Tourist Board brochure. You will notice that the local color includes yours truly and old-timer Nebris looking suitably picturesque and unspoiled—Sy thinks we make splendidly authentic natives—he forgets that's what I've been all along. As far as anyone can be said to be native at all. Cheers, old girl. (And have a whirl thinking of me.)

32

T-SHIRTS PROVIDED *Velvet*, an illustrators' agency, with a lot of business; Miranda was one of the artists the studio called on, especially for Christmas mail-order catalogs and the charities. She now drew with deliberately childlike spareness, and colored in crookedly too, though her observation was more jaundiced than it had been when she first started work as a cartoonist. In her *Blot* days, she'd doodled portraits out of multicolored curlicues and tendrils; Botticelli faces of wistful charm communicated messages of loving kindness and collective endeavor. Now she preferred stick figures and her wit was dry. She'd draw short strips showing her standard female, with the broad girth and the wire-rimmed glasses, doing humdrum things like shopping for "A Happy Husband's Little Luxuries": a miniature travel iron, personalized key rings that come when you call, a tool kit for golf, a mahogany trouser press in Chippendale style.

Her "survival" T-shirt also seemed to meet the decade's appetite for irony, and went into several editions. It featured: a white-sound conditioner, to lull the unconscious "with a variety of rain- and waterfall sounds"; a matte ionizer for sufferers from passive smoking; an inflatable neck pillow for frequent air travelers; kelp capsules against radiation in the water; one bottle of essence of calendula, or marigolds, against acid rain's effects on the skin; green mothballs, much more effective than white (the bleach adds to pollution anyway); a "spider catcher" for scooping up the creatures from the plughole or behind the curtains to help maintain the ecological balance by putting them safely outside. There was a time when people squashed insects. No longer. The cupboards in her flat were filling up with contemporary prophylactics; although her squiggly drawings looked as if she had never seen one of her subjects in the flesh, as it were, she needed to hold in her hand anything she drew.

She'd been to the new Design Museum in the City of the Future on the river and found a vitrine of objects from the twenties: cigarette boxes and ashtrays and gooseneck lamps in the shape of fuselages arranged next to a display of household goods—an electric kettle, a vacuum cleaner, an ironing board, a Kenwood mixer, a hair dryer and hair curlers of Bakelite with rubber bands attached, a nested set of pastry cutters, a fly-swatter like a gridiron. These objects had acquired the authentic look of art, so grandiloquently sculptural were their lumpy bold shapes, so great a distance seemed to yawn between their baroquely inventive appearance and their ordinary function. The label identified the cache of domestic archaeology as "The gift (in lieu of duties) of the Princess Alicia (b. 1867), in daily use at her Grace and Favour apartments in the Palace from circa 1922 to her death." So she really was that old, thought Miranda, and thrifty, too, not replacing anything. For a moment, she remembered her grandfather making the old woman laugh, his blue eyes filled with light like the translucent lip to a wave, when they were all at the christening and everything lay before Xanthe.

The owner of the studio was a fellow Blotter from the old days. "Go for it!" was his favorite phrase, and he practiced what he . . . or, as he preferred to say, "I puts my money where my mouth is"; so when the charity side of ACTion asked *Velvet* if they could help with their Christmas catalog that year, he told Miranda about the request, and added, "Go for it!" "What's your contribution, then?" she said. She no longer obliged him or anyone else as unthinkingly as she had those many years ago. She had learned to refuse; but ACTion had a program for famine relief and health education and skill development in South Africa that she believed in and cared about. "I'll throw in the printing costs, if you make the images. Then we'll find some celebs to wear the T-shirts. God! Nelson Mandela, how did you do this to me?" Miranda replied dryly, "He has that effect on people. Come on, now, doesn't it feel good! Or does it really hurt?" "Aw, shut up, Miranda, just shut the fuck up." He shook his head and dropped his eyes. "No one's as tough as they pretend to be—not me, not you, not even today's new woman." He stuck out his shoulders to imitate power-dressed pads and dropped his lower lip sulkily. "Don't start being winsome with me, I've known you too long," she said, laughing, and picked up the telephone number of their contact at ACTion.

One or two of the charity's supporters were actors, athletes, media people, the office told her, and gave her some names; she looked the performers up in *Spotlight*, and left messages with their agents. Gradually, over the spring that year, names of willing sponsors trickled through; when the designs were ready, they agreed to pick one and wear it for a photo in the campaign's catalog. Sometime she could catch a worried note in an actor's voice, or an agent's, even when they were saying yes. The violence in the townships confused everyone, and it wasn't the only thing.

An actor called Shaka Ifetabe had agreed to model; he'd a minor following from a TV series in which he'd played a veteran plainclothes officer. Miranda had heard of it, but never caught it on the box. His agent gave Miranda a date, sooner than Velvet had hoped, and rather than lose him, the studio pressed forward with the printing of Miranda's designs, and it fell to her to run round with the first batch straight off the revolving silk-screen drum to the church of Christ the King in Hackney, where he was in rehearsal. "Use the north door, it's the only one, you'll see when you get there. The building looks derelict, but it isn't. Just deconsecrated. They moved all the bones to another cemetery when the company took it over—spooky. Shaka's expecting you, so just wait for a moment when he's not needed." The agent paused. "He says he knows you, by the way. You've taken his picture before—no, I mean you've done a portrait, cartoon, something."

There was a problem on the tube and she was running late for the appointment. When she emerged from the station she was looking for the street signs to orientate herself, moving with the crowd on the pavement. It was a high street, thronged with shoppers, and she was encumbered: her camera bag was slung on one shoulder, her handbag over the other, and the canvas holdall with the T-shirts was in her hand. Because she wasn't negotiating a passage through the passersby but looking up to read the street's name, she caught the holdall in someone's legs and had to let go of it or otherwise bring him down.

The man almost fell sprawling on top of the bag, and as he did so, before he regained his balance just in time, he was apologizing to her profusely. Which surprised her, as last time she'd stumbled into someone on a city pavement, she'd been told to go and fuck herself, and when she rode her bicycle—on days when she had less baggage—she was used to drivers cursing her for refusing to be run off the road. But this man was handing her back the holdall, asking her if she was all right instead of blaming her for tripping him, and she saw that he was young and black and wearing a suit and carrying a briefcase, and she knew that he was anticipating that she—and others around them on the pavement—would think that he had tried to trip her instead in order to snatch her bag. She saw a kind of relief pass across his face when she said that no, she was sorry and was he okay? But he did not want to be engaged in any further talk, now that the danger to him was past, and he stepped out into the traffic and crossed to the other side. A kind of irritation fueled him, which Miranda saw in the angle of his spine and the speed of his pace, that he had been caught in such a false position at all.

Miranda found the church which the company used for rehearsals and stopped outside for a moment to adjust her clothes and tuck in her shirt; over a studless dress shirt that had belonged to her grandfather, she was wearing a short rose-and-violet couture jacket of Gillian's, in a knubbly silk weave with braided edges. She hitched her bags back on her shoulders and let herself in quietly. The portrait photograph she'd glanced at in *Spotlight* showed the actor she was meeting with hair dressed in gleaming oiled cane rows, so she did not immediately recognize him when she walked into the nave and saw a man lying in a twisted shape on the dais in the chancel, where the altar would have been. Or rather, she did not exactly identify him, for he looked very different. He now had longish hair swept back and it was threaded with gray; he was wearing glasses too. It was rather his voice she knew.

He was calling out,

> "and here you sty me
> In this hard rock, whiles you do keep from me
> The rest o' th' island."

The old vehemence vibrated in it, and reached her even from where he lay, prostrate on the stage, at the feet of the tall, beak-nosed actor

she recognized immediately from a whiskey ad, who had his arm around
the shoulder of a young febrile blond actress with quick hands whom
she also knew by sight.

And Prospero replied, poking at the prone and creeping figure beneath him,

> "Thou most lying slave,
> Whom stripes may move, not kindness! I have us'd thee,
> Filth as thou art, with human care; and lodg'd thee
> In mine own cell, till thou didst seek to violate
> The honour of my child."

At this Miranda noticed that Caliban could not move because he had
his ankles tied together; she then saw him thrash out with his tethered
limbs and lumber, like a stranded sea creature, toward the actress,
maneuvering on powerful shoulders, using his elbows like paws, from
behind the body of the old man her father. The actress bent down to
Caliban's eye level, presenting her breasts to his face, and spat at him:

> "Abhorred slave,
> Which any print of goodness wilt not take,
> Being capable of all ill!"

The young woman was ranting the speech, she was taunting him with
smiles, with seductive looks which then turned to scorn, and she was
wiping tears from her eyes in horror at the memory of the ingratitude
he'd shown her care for him. While Miranda, watching, listening,
shivered.

> "You taught me language . . . "

he answered her, softly now,

> "And my profit on't
> Is, I know how to curse. The red plague rid you
> For learning me your language!"

Miranda remained quietly at the back of the church, by a pillar on
which the numbers of the hymns were still slotted into a wooden
board, and she felt the edges of her body flare as if she were against
the light and outlined in the sun's fire. She remembered things she
had forgotten, the way the timbre of a voice could make a quiver or
the glance of an eye pass through her to her core and turn her molten.

And now she remembered George Felix, though she had not thought of him for years—he had simply become one of the score or more bodies with whom she'd dug up so much pleasure in those days when it cost her nothing to find it, curled up inside her waiting to unwind. She was thinking, as she watched him in the scene on stage rehearsing again, Oh God, how I'd like to learn me a new language. Beyond cursing, beyond ranting.

She would be walking with him, it would be a summer's day, perhaps, and the grass would be long enough to hide them, she would bend with love over his neat, strong body and cradle his head and push her fingers in the tight curlicues of his hair; she would . . . But no, again, she must check these imaginings, she was no longer the "me-too" girl, hurling herself at anyone and anything in the pursuit of affection. She despised the years when she had lapped troughs of experience and left not a trace of a thought behind. How we all wanted Jimi H., how we wanted him to scream and spew and burn and tumesce and die for us up there on the stage in the spurt of flame from his Zippo lighter like the spurt of stuff from his jerking hips and the spurt of howling and crying and cooing and voluble caresses from his big mouth—Be primitive for us, black man! Put us in touch with our inner selves! How could you fall for this, again and again? So Miranda turned in fury on herself. You're trapped in the fantasy, that someone like him could melt you and take you down to the thing you've lost touch with—the longed-for, missing Primitive. Light my fire! Show me paradise! Blow me away! Be an animal, show me the beast inside!

I am such a fucking racist, she was thinking, as the actor wagged a hand to his fellow actors and headed for the door. I can't get away from it, even though I of all people shouldn't be. Self-hating, denying my links. But it felt like a fraud when I used to pretend to pass for black in those days. It wasn't any kind of answer. Xanthe was right, really.

Besides, Miranda also told herself, she was an idiot too, to think he might be interested in her, after all this time. When she was no spring chicken anymore, by God. Perhaps they could be friends, though, get past the marking of the differences between them. But why want to get past the differences, any more than that between man and woman? Not for a long while, not since . . . well, she couldn't think when she'd last felt such intense longing to seize hold of a man again and make long, sweet love to him. She'd become—not merely abstinent, not merely chaste or non-sexual—but post-sexual. It had been a year, two years, that she had been telling herself how glad she was that desire and fucking and all that went with them were behind her now, how lucky she was she'd managed to come through without a brat or AIDS (she thanked the stars she'd had her wild life before that plague really got going).

Then she reminded herself: he could be married or otherwise hitched up. And she certainly wasn't going to step right on that land like a new colonist—oh my God, not that again. He could have children, he could have come out, he could be gay. Or just plain not interested.

He was making his way toward her now, pulling a hooded sweatshirt over his head, and rubbing his ankles where he'd tied them for the role. He pointed a finger at her, with a slightly prancing movement, and threw his head to one side and held out his hand.

"Been a long time." He was smiling, inviting her in to share in no-regrets for all the folly of their common youth.

"Yes," she said, shaking his hand manfully in response. "Do you have time to pick a T-shirt? And a quick photograph? For the catalog?"

"Yeees, I do. Show me the stuff." He eyed the bag where she'd stowed them. "I've only got to be back within the hour. Right?" He raised his voice, projecting it toward one of the members of the group, who were clustering around the coffee and tea urns set up in an aisle.

"Oh, it'll only take five minutes."

"Five minutes? After—mmm, let's see—nearly twenty years? You're pretty stingy, I see." He put an arm around her, to lead her to the door, not touching her, but encircling her in the air. "You're looking well, Miranda, yes, you really are. So, where do you want to do it?"

She shivered. "Do it?" She choked back a giggle. "Well, yes. I was thinking of somewhere outside." His attentiveness reassured her; perhaps because she sensed it was forced, and that he too wasn't entirely calm. She answered that she thought the patch of green nearby would do; some plane trees would scatter the light in an attractive way. Her breath was tight, but she managed, distantly, like an interviewing journalist, a stranger: "Is Caliban hard? I mean, hard to play?"

He gave her a sidelong smile, and took her arm to cross the road. "Naw," he said. "It's a great part, one of the best. And it's a relief, I'm telling you, to get away from telly work." They reached the wedge of grass near the entrance to the tube and he pulled the T-shirt he had selected over his head—it was one with a gleaming meteorite, like a lump of coal, all aglow round its edges, with the caption, in Miranda's crabbed hand: "New beginnings are in the offing."

He took up a position against a tree trunk with practiced willingness and removed his specs. "Let me take them off, for vanity's sake." He laughed. "The odd role helps keep the hand in, and pay the mortgage, too, in between times. Though the theater's in a terrible state. As you know." He rubbed his eyes and faced her camera.

"Did you ever see the movie?" he asked.

"The Meursault?"

"Yes, À Fleur de Peau—Skin-Deep." His eyebrows twitched, and he spread his hands. "Subtle, very subtle." He had a rumpled face, with inquiry lines above his eyebrows even in repose.

"Oh God, I did." She laughed, embarrassed.

"So you saw yourself?"

"A glimpse—a toffee-nosed English girl with a Sloane accent, making flapping gestures—at you." She imitated herself. "Excruciating."

"Don't say that, sweetheart—the English feel embarrassed much too readily," he said, and chuckled. "But I'll admit I'll join you there this time." He turned profile. "I wanted to see you again. Didn't know how to go about it. And you know, I was married then, and . . . well. Enough?" He shifted, to face her experimentally.

"Good. Very good. I'm not the world's greatest with this machine—crayons are more my line, but ACTion has to make do with what it can get." It was absurd, this rush to the head of romance; if she were a character in a novel, she might find that someone like George or Shaka or whatever it was he was called now was available, free, no longer married, a real widower even. But this could hardly happen in her life. She wasn't living inside one of Shakespeare's sweet-tempered comedies, nor in one of his late plays with their magical reconciliations, their truces and appeasements and surcease of pain. No garland of marriages at the fall of the curtain would draw her into its charmed circle. In her world, which was the real world of the end of the century, breakage and disconnection were the only possible outcome. She had accustomed herself to singleness: like her father on his own in Liamuiga; like Sy after Xanthe's death; like Astrid on her own now, in and out of one remedy or another, clinic to ashram to convent and back again; like loyal Gillian, still living as the forgotten great man's widow. Miranda had achieved comfortable solitariness, however, without ever being tied to anyone very long, let alone locked and wed.

Though she had not exactly been joined or possessed, she had experienced severance again and again: she had grieved for Xanthe's death, filled with remorse that she had always been so jealous of her, she had somehow wished her to death. For months afterward she dreamed she was searching for her body, searching valleys and mountains, the sea's depths and the sky's height. The dreams never came to an end, because Xanthe's body always lay beyond the fogged vista, behind the reef, under the cliff.

At sixes and sevens inside, and single outside, this was indeed the post-modern condition, she'd decided, half-joking, with friends one night, as they compared their different types of solitude, their inner confusion. Someone had said, "You know those experiments they've done, with people who've had an accident to their brains? When the left and right sides have separated? The same person does exactly contradictory things all the time—well, I think it's happened to me. At least, one part of me thinks it has." Listening, they'd all laughed, and someone else had added, " 'What God hath joined together, let no man put asunder,'—I'd like to start with my own head."

So this surge of wholehearted yearning was ridiculous; nothing could be so uncomplicated, certainly not lust. She didn't want anyone's manly arms suddenly encircling her, his sweet hot breath in her face, she didn't want her thermal vest ripped or her juices flowing, or deep kissing exchanged between their lips and eyes and whatnot, she liked her bed tucked in, clean cool sheets, all alone in it except for the cat at the foot.

"The theater's so uncertain, I had to find another trade, you know. And after the series I had a bit of money, so now I've got into the restaurant business, too. Though it's not much more reliable." He tilted his head down for the camera as he mentioned a run-down part of the city. "It isn't really hairy, not when you're a resident. Strangers build up the legend. Course there are muggings and break-ins and the kids hang out with fuck-all to do, but the media have an investment to paint it black, where black comes into it." He plucked at the meteorite on his T-shirt. "I see you're still a hippie idealist, Miranda. Not even covert, either!" He laughed. "Anyhow, my place's almost brand new, it's called Lyons Corner Shop (there was one on the site) and we serve, ah, Creole food, peas and beans and pepperpot just the way my grandmother used to make it—of course!—good music, and three hundred and ten varieties of rum. No, I'm serious. When I'm not working, and you never can tell when that will be, this profession being what it is, I like the restaurant trade. You should come by." His eyelids were slightly bruised-looking, with small swollen veins crossing from the jut of his brow to the start of his lashes, giving the lie to his cheer. She recognized rue, the rue she'd always seen marked on Serafine's forehead too.

She wanted him to mean it. She had a flash, I could go in with him, I've even got the legacy to fit the part, and I could give it to him—or some of it.

"How about it then? You'll come?"

"I guess so. I usually do what I'm told." She felt rusty, flirting, it annoyed her that she was behaving like this.

"Do you?" He was chaffing her.

"Girls usually do. That is, if they're properly brought up." But her voice dried in her throat from the clumsiness of her coquetry.

"And you're a properly brought-up girl . . . ?"

"Well," she said. "In one sense, I am, I'm afraid." To herself she said, We both know of course that I'm not a girl. Not anymore. I'm shaggy and saggy in places, last time I bothered to look. The O.K. Corral's gone to scrub, couch grass has got to it and covered it; the horses have been bridled and ridden away. In the lumpy and formless place called this world, people didn't meet before the drop of the curtain and begin a happy ending together. Besides, it was a cowardly old world, the one she beheld, the people in it ungoodly altogether.

Though in some people's lives, she had heard, there was still a low, uncertain but nevertheless existent incidence of achieved mating, like the contact of endangered species in captivity. But it was hardly reproduction she had in mind.

"You're going to be embarrassed next and say sorry again."

"Sorry!"

"Take it back."

"No."

"Ah, good, at least you didn't do what you were told."

"You want to banter, to trade lines," she said, finding a track through on her own at last. She wasn't going to comply, to take his cue so docilely. "But I'll try saying this straight: yes, I'd like to come to your Lyons Corner Shop. And not just because you told me to."

"It's just an act, the banter. A cover, you know," he said slowly. "Okay. You'll come and see this *Tempest* first. Then we'll go on down there—a little music, a little rum, a little food in your belly, make you feel good? You finished with the pictures, now?" He put his glasses back on. "Bring a friend, have some good crack—no, not the white powder, I see your eyes widen, the streets are full of dope dealers, drug fiends, wild black boys, but no, it's not like that. Your eyes I have not forgotten, Miranda. What a beautiful name, and it suits you. I changed mine in the high times, when Africa and roots were the answer—finding the lost Fatherland—and George was whitey's name for us—'Happy George,' always a-laughin' and a-smilin', God's li'l chillun. So now . . . I've ended up with no name. I am the Unnameable, ha-ha, which is why I know how to play Caliban, of course. You can feel you're marooned—have you felt that? We're maroons together now, so many of us, and we know our own, we know who we can run away with"—he tapped his temples—"mentally, that is. Oh, don't get embarrassed again—I'm not going to get heavy with you, I promise. I know better than that, now."

She looked at him; all of a sudden, she saw in her mind's eye the set of nine horses she'd loved as a child; he was going on, "No, not evil crack, but wise crack, the Oirish kind, our kind, crik-crak, I mean, a good time, talk, fellowship. Forget ACTion."—He plucked again at the T-shirt. "Forget the Middle East, forget AIDS, forget famine, the war, the hole in the ozone, torture, death, rape and murder, forget Save the Children and the disappeared, forget, forget. Forget South Africa, even, forget the mean-spirited eighties—I'm starting to forget right now, from this minute, even as I wear this. Because I'm so tired, as the poet said, of your fucking guilt and our fucking envy.

"Miranda! I'm forgetting hard as I can. And are you? How about you? You getting the drift now, you learning to forget?"

"No," she said, the beat inside her getting louder, so she wondered would he hear it. "And I don't think that's what you'd like either."

They had begun play. Their openings were well-tried, unadventurous. But these same familiar moves would take them in deep: face-to-face and piece by piece they would engage with each other so raptly that for a time they would never even notice anyone else outside looking in on the work they were absorbed in, crossing the lines, crossing the squares, far out on the board in the other's sea.

❧ S E R A F I N E III ❧

33

AT THIS ANOTHER voice, rumbly and old, like something wisely fermented, cut in above the chorus, above the heroic battle cries of Atala, the whispered discoveries of Miranda and George. It was a voice with an English mien, in spite of the viola timbre of an island origin still vibrating through it:

"Now, Miss Astrid, a cup of tea'll help you, ease the knot . . . " Serafine Killebree is soothing Astrid; Astrid is in hospital for a spell after a bad attack of DTs and expulsion from yet another place of refuge—the Carmelites in East Anglia. "Hot and wet; with plenty of brown sugar stirred in."

"I feel so god-awful, I don't think I could swallow a thing."

"Never mind now," she is telling her. "We all come a cropper now and then."

"But I do it rather often," says Astrid with a weak grin. "Oh, shit, forgive me. I know you understand, Feeny. Never again. God, I must look a sight." She clicks open a compact from the hospital drawer and groans loud and desperately, till Serafine takes it from her hand, with her fingers that are now curved and powdery-gray in the wrinkles like a hen's claws, and says, "Let's tidy you so, get you bathed and dressed, and you'll feel that much better soon, you'll see." She calls a nurse, pulls the curtains round the bed.

"Oh Feeny," Astrid calls softly. "You really shouldn't." The nurse comes, Serafine tells her she can help Mrs. Everard tidy herself in private, Astrid nods her consent, the nurse murmurs anxiety, for it's against the regulations for anyone but staff . . . but she is relieved, and Serafine, well, for all her harsh wheeze and the stiff hip joint that makes her limp, she looks like a very old, very retired SRN, a sister of experience, really, with gray woolly curls at her temples. So she lets them get on with it, she's short-handed after all, and Serafine fetches a basin of hot water and as she starts gently stroking, with a warm soapy flannel, the withered stick figure in the bed that is Astrid Everard, she says, "I heard a story these days going round about love that would break your heart, Miss Astrid."

Astrid shakes her head, looks meekly into Serafine Killebree's eyes, which have gone glassy, bluish and milky with old age, and murmurs, "Mine's all in pieces already. Nothing could be sadder than . . . "

"It's about a way you can catch a tigress. Have you never heard it then?"

"No, never, not that I know. My heart's broken already, you go ahead. You couldn't do it more damage than's done already."

"Well, then." Serafine is patting Astrid with a small hard hospital towel, which she rumples to get the stiffness out, and Astrid is beginning to entreat, "You've seen them, haven't you? You're allowed to, while some of the rest of us . . . " Serafine restrains her with a twitch of her eyebrows and Astrid closes her eyes and breathes out, "You're right, mustn't . . . Not their problem. Mine."

"I have heard, yes, I have. I've seen them. Mother and baby doing well. They're busy, very busy now. And Miranda's happy, and seeing as how she's not the happy kind, I think it's a kind of miracle."

"I never got to see them. She's forgotten about me. But just let her wait and see how she feels. Now she's a mother she'll soon learn."

Serafine says nothing. Her bottom lip pushes out, for she cannot help but be amused at the way Astrid is playing mother to Miranda, after all this time. She has seen Miranda's baby, but Astrid has been in hospital since she was born and her parents are seriously anxious about infections, like all first-time parents of a certain age: "Where's the best place to catch a disease? Hospital, of course," says the baby's father. He won't hear of Miranda or Serafine—for so they have named their daughter—going to see Astrid in her present circumstances.

Serafine begins her story: "This happened now a long time ago, before the days of guns, you know, when every human creature on the earth was a savage . . . " (She croaks a laugh.) "And who's to say much has changed?"

"Some hunters were out after big creatures one day, and they soon picked up the tracks of a beauty of a tigress . . . Oh, springy and wide her step, glossy and deep her fur! They had ways of catching big animals, nets that fell from the trees, pits covered with greenery. But for a tigress they'd a different trap: a simple, ordinary thing. A mirror, a round mirror something like that little one . . . " She points to the drawer where Astrid put her compact. "But larger, and round like the world."

"A crystal ball," says Astrid helpfully, meekly.

"Now, it is like a crystal ball, yes, but it's made of black silver to reflect like a glass. And the huntsmen ride on ahead down the path they hope the creature will take, they toss it in the tigress's path and then hide themselves downwind . . .

"She comes sauntering along, you know, and finds the round glass and sees herself in it. In little, now, this kind of mirror has a trick of shrinking things it sees. And the tigress thinks she sees a cub in it, maybe even her own cub, but it don't have any smell or fur, and she's all puzzled; she pats the ball with her paw and it pats her back, still in little, she pounces on it, playfully, and it pounces back . . . she gets involved, she doesn't hear the net rustle in the branches above her.

"Then the hunters let that net drop on her and take her prisoner."

Astrid gasps, is silent, then full of reproach: "Oh, you know that's not the way it's done!"

"That's as may be. But it's no lie neither, Miss Astrid." Serafine is drawing back the green-striped curtains round the bed, letting in the ward, returning Astrid to the group of variously ill women in with her: the seventeen-year-old with modern wasting sickness, the grandmother who's been unaccountably fainting, the heavily built young mother with toxic shock from tampons, and the old one in the corner with the cough. "It's no good always wanting the same, the same as yourself in someone else. To look for yourself in little, it's dangerous." She laughs. "It always leads to heartbreak, you know, to the disappointment that cuts."

"Why do you tell me that?" Astrid is angry now, color back in her chalk face. "Blood isn't thicker than water, not in our family. Nobody

bloody cares for anyone anymore. Nobody cares about me. I'm forgotten . . . I might as well be bloody dead . . . "

"Hush now, hush, Miss Astrid—That's not true."

She fishes in her bag and brings out a photo, puts it into Astrid's
hand where it lies on the sheet.

"I'll come by again, if they decide to keep you in."

Astrid looks at the snapshot and says, "Newborns are always ugly
as sin."

"I don't know about that, now," replies Serafine, and takes the photograph back; she fancies she hears the child's cry and smiles to herself.

There are many noises in her head these befuddled days of her old
age; they whisper news to her of this island and that, of people scattered
here and there, from the past and from the present. Some are on the
run still; but some have settled, they have ceased wandering, their
maroon state is changing sound and shape. She's often too tired nowadays to unscramble the noises, but she's happy hearing them, to change
into stories another time.

ABOUT THE AUTHOR

Marina Warner's previous novel, *The Lost Father*, was a Regional Winner of the Commonwealth Writers' Prize, Winner of the Macmillan Silver Pen Award, and short-listed for the Booker Prize. She is a writer, critic and historian, author of two other novels, as well as three studies of mythology, *Alone of All Her Sex: The Myth and Cult of the Virgin Mary;* *Joan of Arc: The Image of Female Heroism;* and *Monuments and Maidens: The Allegory of the Female Form* (Winner of the Fawcett Prize). She is currently working on a study of fairy tales, and has just finished the libretto for a children's opera, *The Queen of Sheba's Legs*, for the English National Opera.

Marina Warner lives in London with her husband, the painter John Dewe Mathews, and one son.